W9-AXI-611

THOMAS CRANE
PUBLIC LIBRARY
QUINCY, MASS.

CITY APPROPRIATION

THE COMPLETE TALES OF HENRY JAMES
VOLUME ELEVEN: 1900–1903

THE COMPLETE TALES OF

HENRY JAMES

EDITED WITH AN

INTRODUCTION BY

LEON EDEL

11

1900–1903

J. B. LIPPINCOTT COMPANY

PHILADELPHIA AND NEW YORK

695

V. 11

Copyright © 1964 by Leon Edel

PRINTED IN THE UNITED STATES OF AMERICA
LIBRARY OF CONGRESS CATALOG CARD NUMBER 62–11335

CONTENTS

INTRODUCTION: 1900–1903

THE late tales of Henry James—those written in this century—contain a more open treatment of the human passions than is to be found in the stories of the 1880's and 1890's. They are, for all their prolixity, fairly blunt and direct, at times even harsh in their appraisal and judgment of human conduct. And they express the novelist's disenchantment. Life has become difficult in middle age and the world is rather a "sell." It is filled with deception. Civilisation seems to be tissued out of lies. All this, expressed in the high art of his maturity, in *The Wings of the Dove* and *The Golden Bowl*, is reflected in the tales, in little dramas of a society James hitherto had treated with lightness and amusement. He is however no longer amused.

The prose of his final manner has been found by some to be an obstacle to the reading of these tales: the long rolling sentences gather momentum like large heaving waves that finally break—with an infinity of leisure—into irony and insistent satire. But his manner of statement is a part of his story: and the tales he collected in the three volumes of the new century, *The Soft Side* of 1900, *The Better Sort* of 1903 and *The Finer Grain* of 1910, remain among the most important fiction written during America's gilded age and England's Edwardian era.

The brilliance and sublety of these tales may be seen in the group which treats of jealousy and revenge. The theme in this form is new in James; in his earlier writings, revenge was often renounced; characters turned the other cheek, or simply backed away from the hatred and aggression required for an act of vengeance. The narrator still shrinks from the display of these passions, but this only dramatises Mrs Grantham's

7

ferocity in "The Two Faces." She has reason to hate; she is a woman scorned. Insult, moreover, has been added to injury when his lordship, having jilted her, asks her to dress and introduce into society his inexperienced child-bride. The opportunity is too much for Mrs Grantham. She overdresses the bride—"overloaded like a monkey in a show"—and by contrast she attires herself with *éclat*. We are left with the narrator's horrified vision of two faces: May Grantham's glorious triumphant face and that of her victim, "feverish, frightened," filled with "unimaginable pathos."

In "The Beldonald Holbein" we are also asked to look upon two faces: the beautiful and the proud Lady Beldonald who is always accompanied, for contrast, by a plain-faced companion. Her new companion, however, captures the centre of the stage. Artists see her as a perfect "Holbein." To Lady Beldonald's cruelty is now added a strong jealousy. Her motivation is her vanity, her "narcissism." These are stories of "small, smothered intensely private things," as the narrator observes, but James turns them into miniature dramas of the passions—a glance, the glimpse of a countenance, a perception of the cruelty of woman to woman. James is writing of beasts in the social jungle—and most of his beasts are tiger-cats.

There is hatred and jealousy in "The Tone of Time"; and cruelty and egotism in "The Special Type." And in these tales we have several examples of the worship of icons of the mind—say of the young man in "Maud-Evelyn" who enters into the make-believe of a dead girl's parents to the point of fancying himself engaged and finally married to the girl. Or of the lady in "The Story in It," avowing a secret love for a man who has no way of knowing her feelings for him. Her "romance" is intensely private. It is wholly of the mind.

The late tales are built out of old materials; but Henry James uses them in a fresh way. There are stories in this volume which belong to earlier phases; Miss Gunton is descended from Daisy Miller and Pandora Day; the pride in private accomplishment, as against the hollowness of public fame, in the tale of the Northmores, belongs with James's tales of the literary life; and "Flickerbridge" and "The Third Person" add new subtleties to the "sense of the past." But the loneliness and isolation which James experienced during these years, his disillusionment and despair, emerge in his story of "The Beast in the Jungle," perhaps his most popular tale, certainly the most frequently reprinted in recent times. In it James had his prevision of twentieth-century "existential man"—dissociated, ridden by anxiety, fashioning out of his malaise a peculiar and almost pathological dream of special privilege.

"The Beast in the Jungle" belongs to a group of tales which depict the isolation of the individual in great cities, and his inability to understand or even reach out for love. They are usually tales of two persons; they sit on their "bench of desolation" or walk in a park against some vague, murmuring urban backdrop; self-absorbed and self-deceived, they are individuals of thwarted and blunted feelings, silhouettes made unreal by self-delusion. The only reality they seem to know is fear; and this leads them to a distortion of their existence. In some thirty pages, in "The Beast in the Jungle," James makes us feel the passage of a whole lifetime; and by the use of names and symbols—Marcher and May, and Weatherend, the country house—he places in our consciousness a sense of changing seasons and "the tone of time." The surface of the story is deceptive; it moves with a slow languorous hypnotic rhythm, giving the effect of long, wasted, futile years, within which some beast is crouched, waiting to spring. Marcher's spiritual adventure in his time-jungle leads him to a final glimpse of truth; he is like Joseph K. in *The Trial*, who, led off to his execution, sees in the distance a window suddenly thrown

open and a shadowy human figure, stretching out its arms.
Marcher is to discover the meaning of his egotism.

The tale has its autobiographical side. James had known a
woman and taken her friendship, and never allowed himself to
know her feelings. She was kind and interested—and he had
never imagined an interest beyond friendship. In the end she
had taken her life, one winter's morning in Venice, in great
loneliness and melancholy. All this had happened a decade
earlier,* and out of these sombre memories James seems to
have distilled the essence of "The Beast in the Jungle." It is
a story of an unlived life; and of a man who loses the love he
might have had, through selfishness. At the last, however,
John Marcher is able to have a glimmer of feeling. He clings
to his pain and his tears—"that at least, belated and bitter,
had something of the taste of life."

Max Beerbohm, observing his new-found friend during the
period of these tales, noted that James "never smiles—rather
appalled by life." This was true of the James of "The Beast in
the Jungle." The James of "The Birthplace" preserved his
old ironic laughter, and the tale is his contribution to the issue
of bardolatry. On the question of Shakespeare, James was
always crystal clear. He found it "*almost* as impossible to
conceive that Bacon wrote the plays as to conceive that the
man from Stratford, as we know the man from Stratford, did."
He had heard an anecdote of a minor poet, Joseph Skipsey, a
friend of Rossetti's, who became custodian of the birthplace,
only to discover himself at odds with the "inquisitive tormentors"—the hordes of tourists who came to him with silly
questions. Out of this real-life material James shaped his
comedy-fable. The custodian turns on his tormentors: if the
world wants to be deceived, he will make a work of art out
of the deception. The altar of the dead may be desecrated,

* See the third volume of my life of Henry James, *The Middle
Years*, 1962.

but it will be done with imagination. As for the world, it will never know the difference. James seems to imply that it is quite prepared to pay handsomely not to hear the truth.

LEON EDEL

Gay Head, 1964

THE GREAT GOOD PLACE

I

GEORGE DANE had waked up to a bright new day, the face
of nature well washed by last night's downpour and shining
as with high spirits, good resolutions, lively intentions—the
great glare of recommencement, in short, fixed in his patch of
sky. He had sat up late to finish work—arrears overwhelming;
then at last had gone to bed with the pile but little reduced.
He was now to return to it after the pause of the night; but
he could only look at it, for the time, over the bristling hedge
of letters planted by the early postman an hour before and
already, on the customary table by the chimney-piece, for-
mally rounded and squared by his systematic servant. It was
something too merciless, the domestic perfection of Brown.
There were newspapers on another table, ranged with the
same rigour of custom, newspapers too many—what could
any creature want of so much news?—and each with its hand
on the neck of the other, so that the row of their bodiless
heads was like a series of decapitations. Other journals, other
periodicals of every sort, folded and in wrappers, made a
huddled mound that had been growing for several days and of
which he had been wearily, helplessly aware. There were new
books, also in wrappers as well as disenveloped and dropped
again—books from publishers, books from authors, books
from friends, books from enemies, books from his own book-
seller, who took, it sometimes struck him, inconceivable
things for granted. He touched nothing, approached nothing,
only turned a heavy eye over the work, as it were, of the
night—the fact, in his high, wide-windowed room, where the

13

hard light of duty could penetrate every corner, of the un-
ashamed admonition of the day. It was the old rising tide, and
it rose and rose even under a minute's watching. It had been
up to his shoulders last night—it was up to his chin now.

Nothing had passed while he slept—everything had stayed;
nothing, that he could yet feel, had died—many things had
been born. To let them alone, these things, the new things,
let them utterly alone and see if that, by chance, wouldn't
somehow prove the best way to deal with them: this fancy
brushed his face for a moment as a possible solution, just
giving it, as many a time before, a cool wave of air. Then he
knew again as well as ever that leaving was difficult, leaving
impossible—that the only remedy, the true, soft, effacing
sponge, would be to *be* left, to be forgotten. There was no
footing on which a man who had ever liked life—liked it,
at any rate, as *he* had—could now escape from it. He must
reap as he had sown. It was a thing of meshes; he had
simply gone to sleep under the net and had simply waked up
there. The net was too fine; the cords crossed each other at
spots so near together, making at each a little tight, hard knot
that tired fingers, this morning, were too limp and too tender
to touch. Our poor friend's touched nothing—only stole
significantly into his pockets as he wandered over to the
window and faintly gasped at the energy of nature. What was
most overwhelming was that she herself was so ready. She
had soothed him rather, the night before, in the small hours
by the lamp. From behind the drawn curtain of his study the
rain had been audible and in a manner merciful; washing
the window in a steady flood, it had seemed the right thing,
the retarding, interrupting thing, the thing that, if it would
only last, might clear the ground by floating out to a boundless
sea the innumerable objects among which his feet stumbled
and strayed. He had positively laid down his pen as on a sense
of friendly pressure from it. The kind, full swash had been
on the glass when he turned out his lamp; he had left his

phrase unfinished and his papers lying quite as if for the flood to bear them away on its bosom. But there still, on the table, were the bare bones of the sentence—and not all of those; the single thing borne away and that he could never recover was the missing half that might have paired with it and begotten a figure.

Yet he could at last only turn back from the window; the world was everywhere, without and within, and, with the great staring egotism of its health and strength, was not to be trusted for tact or delicacy. He faced about precisely to meet his servant and the absurd solemnity of two telegrams on a tray. Brown ought to have kicked them into the room—then he himself might have kicked them out.

"And you told me to remind you, sir——"

George Dane was at last angry. "Remind me of nothing!"

"But you insisted, sir, that I was to insist!"

He turned away in despair, speaking with a pathetic quaver at absurd variance with his words: "If you insist, Brown, I'll kill you!" He found himself anew at the window, whence, looking down from his fourth floor, he could see the vast neighbourhood, under the trumpet-blare of the sky, beginning to rush about. There was a silence, but he knew Brown had not left him—knew exactly how straight and serious and stupid and faithful he stood there. After a minute he heard him again.

"It's only because, sir, you know, sir, you can't remember——"

At this Dane did flash round; it was more than at such a moment he could bear. "Can't remember, Brown? I can't forget. That's what's the matter with me."

Brown looked at him with the advantage of eighteen years of consistency. "I'm afraid you're not well, sir."

Brown's master thought. "It's a shocking thing to say, but I wish to heaven I weren't! It would be perhaps an excuse."

Brown's blankness spread like the desert. "To put them off?"

"Ah!" The sound was a groan; the plural pronoun, *any* pronoun, so mistimed. "Who is it?"

"Those ladies you spoke of—to lunch."

"Oh!" The poor man dropped into the nearest chair and stared a while at the carpet. It was very complicated.

"How many will there be, sir?" Brown asked.

"Fifty!"

"Fifty, sir?"

Our friend, from his chair, looked vaguely about; under his hand were the telegrams, still unopened, one of which he now tore asunder. "'Do hope you sweetly won't mind, to-day, 1.30, my bringing poor dear Lady Mullet, who is so awfully bent,'" he read to his companion.

His companion weighed it. "How many does *she* make, sir?"

"Poor dear Lady Mullet? I haven't the least idea."

"Is she—a—deformed, sir?" Brown inquired, as if in this case she might make more.

His master wondered, then saw he figured some personal curvature. "No; she's only bent on coming!" Dane opened the other telegram and again read out: "'So sorry it's at eleventh hour impossible, and count on you here, as very greatest favour, at two sharp instead.'"

"How many does *that* make?" Brown imperturbably continued.

Dane crumpled up the two missives and walked with them to the waste-paper basket, into which he thoughtfully dropped them. "I can't say. You must do it all yourself. I shan't be there."

It was only on this that Brown showed an expression. "You'll go instead——"

"I'll go instead!" Dane raved.

Brown, however, had had occasion to show before that *he*

would never desert their post. "Isn't that rather sacrificing the three?" Between respect and reproach he paused.

"*Are* there three?"

"I lay for four in all."

His master had, at any rate, caught his thought. "Sacrificing the three to the one, you mean? Oh, I'm not going to *her*!"

Brown's famous "thoroughness"—his great virtue—had never been so dreadful. "Then where *are* you going?"

Dane sat down to his table and stared at his ragged phrase. "'There is a happy land—far, far away!'" He chanted it like a sick child and knew that for a minute Brown never moved. During this minute he felt between his shoulders the gimlet of criticism.

"Are you quite sure you're all right?"

"It's my certainty that overwhelms me, Brown. Look about you and judge. Could anything be more 'right,' in the view of the envious world, than everything that surrounds us here; that immense array of letters, notes, circulars; that pile of printers' proofs, magazines and books; these perpetual telegrams, these impending guests; this retarded, unfinished and interminable work? What could a man want more?"

"Do you mean there's too much, sir?"—Brown had sometimes these flashes.

"There's too much. There's too much. But *you* can't help it, Brown."

"No, sir," Brown assented. "Can't *you?*"

"I'm thinking—I must see. There are hours——!" Yes, there were hours, and this was one of them: he jerked himself up for another turn in his labyrinth, but still not touching, not even again meeting, his interlocutor's eye. If he was a genius for any one he was a genius for Brown; but it was terrible what that meant, being a genius for Brown. There had been times when he had done full justice to the way it kept him up; now, however, it was almost the worst of the avalanche.

"Don't trouble about me," he went on insincerely and looking askance through his window again at the bright and beautiful world. "Perhaps it will rain—that *may* not be over. I do love the rain," he weakly pursued. "Perhaps, better still, it will snow."

Brown now had indeed a perceptible expression, and the expression was fear. "Snow, sir—the end of May?" Without pressing this point he looked at his watch. "You'll feel better when you've had breakfast."

"I dare say," said Dane, whom breakfast struck in fact as a pleasant alternative to opening letters. "I'll come in immediately."

"But without waiting——?"

"Waiting for what?"

Brown had at last, under his apprehension, his first lapse from logic, which he betrayed by hesitating in the evident hope that his companion would, by a flash of remembrance, relieve him of an invidious duty. But the only flashes now were the good man's own. "You say you can't forget, sir; but you do forget——"

"Is it anything very horrible?" Dane broke in.

Brown hung fire. "Only the gentleman you told me you had asked——"

Dane again took him up; horrible or not, it came back—indeed its mere coming back classed it. "To breakfast to-day? It *was* to-day; I see." It came back, yes, came back; the appointment with the young man—he supposed him young—and whose letter, the letter about—what was it?—had struck him. "Yes, yes; wait, wait."

"Perhaps he'll do you good, sir," Brown suggested.

"Sure to—sure to. All right!" Whatever he might do, he would at least prevent some other doing: that was present to our friend as, on the vibration of the electric bell at the door of the flat, Brown moved away. Two things, in the short interval that followed, were present to Dane: his having utterly forgotten the connection, the whence, whither and why of his guest; and his continued disposition not to touch —no, not with the finger. Ah, if he might *never* again touch! All the unbroken seals and neglected appeals lay there while, for a pause that he couldn't measure, he stood before the chimney-piece with his hands still in his pockets. He heard a brief exchange of words in the hall, but never afterward recovered the time taken by Brown to reappear, to precede and announce another person—a person whose name, somehow, failed to reach Dane's ear. Brown went off again to serve breakfast, leaving host and guest confronted. The duration of this first stage also, later on, defied measurement; but that little mattered, for in the train of what happened came promptly the second, the third, the fourth, the rich succession of the others. Yet what happened was but that Dane took his hand from his pocket, held it straight out and felt it taken. Thus indeed, if he had wanted never again to touch, it was already done.

II

H E might have been a week in the place—the scene of his new consciousness—before he spoke at all. The occasion of it then was that one of the quiet figures he had been idly watching drew at last nearer and showed him a face that was the highest expression—to his pleased but as yet slightly confused perception—of the general charm. What *was* the general charm? He couldn't, for that matter, easily have phrased it; it was such an abyss of negatives, such an absence of everything. The oddity was that, after a minute, he was struck as by the reflection of his own very image in this first interlocutor seated with him, on the easy bench, under the high, clear portico and above the wide, far-reaching garden, where the things that most showed in the greenness were the surface of still water and the white note of old statues. The absence of everything was, in the aspect of the Brother who had thus informally joined him—a man of his own age, tired, distinguished, modest, kind—really, as he could soon see, but the absence of what he didn't want. He didn't want, for the time, anything but just to *be* there, to stay in the bath. He was in the bath yet, the broad, deep bath of stillness. They sat in it together now, with the water up to their chins. He had not had to talk, he had not had to think, he had scarce even had to feel. He had been sunk that way before, sunk—when and where?—in another flood; only a flood of rushing waters, in which bumping and gasping were all. This was a current so slow and so tepid that one floated practically without motion and without chill. The break of silence was not immediate, though Dane seemed indeed to feel it begin before a sound passed. It could pass quite sufficiently without words that he and his mate were Brothers, and what that meant.

Dane wondered, but with no want of ease—for want of ease was impossible—if his friend found in *him* the same likeness, the proof of peace, the gage of what the place could do. The long afternoon crept to its end; the shadows fell further and the sky glowed deeper; but nothing changed—nothing *could* change—in the element itself. It was a conscious security. It was wonderful! Dane had lived into it, but he was still immensely aware. He would have been sorry to lose that, for just this fact, as yet, the blessed fact of consciousness, seemed the greatest thing of all. Its only fault was that, being in itself such an occupation, so fine an unrest in the heart of gratitude, the life of the day all went to it. But what even then was the harm? He had come only to come, to take what he found. This was the part where the great cloister, inclosed externally on three sides and probably the largest, lightest, fairest effect, to his charmed sense, that human hands could ever have expressed in dimensions of length and breadth, opened to the south its splendid fourth quarter, turned to the great view an outer gallery that combined with the rest of the portico to form a high, dry loggia, such as he a little pretended to himself he had, in Italy, in old days, seen in old cities, old convents, old villas. This recall of the disposition of some great abode of an Order, some mild Monte Cassino, some Grande Chartreuse more accessible, was his main term of comparison; but he knew he had really never anywhere beheld anything at once so calculated and so generous.

Three impressions in particular had been with him all the week, and he could only recognise in silence their happy effect on his nerves. How it was all managed he couldn't have told —he had been content moreover till now with his ignorance of cause and pretext; but whenever he chose to listen with a certain intentness he made out, as from a distance, the sound of slow, sweet bells. How could they be so far and yet so audible? How could they be so near and yet so faint? How, above all, could they, in such an arrest of life, be, to *time* things, so frequent? The very essence of the bliss of Dane's whole change had been precisely that there was nothing now to time. It was the same with the slow footsteps that always, within earshot, to the vague attention, marked the space and the leisure, seemed, in long, cool arcades, lightly to fall and perpetually to recede. This was the second impression, and it melted into the third, as, for that matter, every form of softness, in the great good place, was but a further turn, without jerk or gap, of the endless roll of serenity. The quiet footsteps were quiet figures; the quiet figures that, to the eye, kept the picture human and brought its perfection within reach. This perfection, he felt on the bench by his friend, was now more in reach that ever. His friend at last turned to him a look different from the looks of friends in London clubs.

"The thing was to find it out!"

It was extraordinary how this remark fitted into his thought. "Ah, wasn't it? And when I think," said Dane, "of all the people who haven't and who never will!" He sighed over these unfortunates with a tenderness that, in its degree, was practically new to him, feeling, too, how well his companion would know the people he meant. He only meant some, but they were all who would want it; though of these, no doubt—well, for reasons, for things that, in the world, he had observed—there would never be too many. Not all perhaps who wanted would really find; but none at least would find who didn't really want. And then what the need would have to have been first! What it at first had to be for himself! He felt afresh, in the light of his companion's face, what it might still be even when deeply satisfied, as well as what communication was established by the mere mutual knowledge of it.

"Every man must arrive by himself and on his own feet—isn't that so? We're brothers here for the time, as in a great monastery, and we immediately think of each other and recognise each other as such; but we must have first got here as we can, and we meet after long journeys by complicated ways. Moreover we meet—don't we?—with closed eyes."

"Ah, don't speak as if we were dead!" Dane laughed.

"I shan't mind death if it's like this," his friend replied.

It was too obvious, as Dane gazed before him, that one wouldn't; but after a moment he asked, with the first articulation, as yet, of his most elementary wonder: "Where is it?"

"I shouldn't be surprised if it were much nearer than one ever suspected."

"Nearer town, do you mean?"

"Nearer everything—nearer every one."

George Dane thought. "Somewhere, for instance, down in Surrey?"

His Brother met him on this with a shade of reluctance. "Why should we call it names? It must have a climate, you see."

"Yes," Dane happily mused; "without that——!" All it so securely did have overwhelmed him again, and he couldn't help breaking out: "*What* is it?"

"Oh, it's positively a part of our ease and our rest and our change, I think, that we don't at all know and that we may really call it, for that matter, anything in the world we like— the thing, for instance, we love it most for being."

"I know what *I* call it," said Dane after a moment. Then as his friend listened with interest: "Just simply 'The Great Good Place.' "

"I see—what can you say more? I've put it to myself perhaps a little differently." They sat there as innocently as small boys confiding to each other the names of toy animals. "The Great Want Met."

"Ah, yes, that's it!"

"Isn't it enough for us that it's a place carried on, for our benefit, so admirably that we strain our ears in vain for a creak of the machinery? Isn't it enough for us that it's simply a thorough hit?"

"Ah, a hit!" Dane benignantly murmured.

"It does for us what it pretends to do," his companion went on; "the mystery isn't deeper than that. The thing is probably simple enough in fact, and on a thoroughly practical basis; only it has had its origin in a splendid thought, in a real stroke of genius."

"Yes," Dane exclaimed, "in a sense—on somebody or other's part—so exquisitely personal!"

"Precisely—it rests, like all good things, on experience. The 'great want' comes home—that's the great thing it does! On the day it came home to the right mind this dear place was constituted. It always, moreover, in the long run, *has* been met— it always must be. How can it not require to be, more and more, as pressure of every sort grows?"

Dane, with his hands folded in his lap, took in these words of wisdom. "Pressure of every sort *is* growing!" he placidly observed.

"I see well enough what that fact has done to *you*," his Brother returned.

Dane smiled. "I couldn't have borne it longer. I don't know what would have become of me."

"I know what would have become of *me*."

"Well, it's the same thing."

"Yes," said Dane's companion, "it's doubtless the same thing." On which they sat in silence a little, seeming pleasantly to follow, in the view of the green garden, the vague movements of the monster—madness, surrender, collapse—they had escaped. Their bench was like a box at the opera. "And I may perfectly, you know," the Brother pursued, "have seen you before. I may even have known you well. We don't know."

They looked at each other again serenely enough, and at last Dane said: "No, we don't know."

"That's what I meant by our coming with our eyes closed. Yes—there's something out. There's a gap—a link missing, the great hiatus!" the Brother laughed. "It's as simple a story as the old, old rupture—the break that lucky Catholics have always been able to make, that they are still, with their innumerable religious houses, able to make, by going into 'retreat.' I don't speak of the pious exercises; I speak only of the material simplification. I don't speak of the putting off of one's self; I speak only—if one has a self worth sixpence—of the getting it back. The place, the time, the way were, for those of the old persuasion, always there—are indeed practically there for them as much as ever. They can always get off—the blessed houses receive. So it was high time that we—we of the great Protestant peoples, still more, if possible, in the sensitive individual case, overscored and overwhelmed, still more congested with mere quantity and prostituted, through our 'enterprise,' to mere profanity—should learn how to get off, should find somewhere *our* retreat and remedy. There was such a huge chance for it!"

Dane laid his hand on his companion's arm. "It's charming, how, when we speak for ourselves, we speak for each other. That was exactly what I said!" He had fallen to recalling from over the gulf the last occasion.

The Brother, as if it would do them both good, only desired to draw him out. "What you said——?"

"To *him*—that morning." Dane caught a far bell again and heard a slow footstep. A quiet figure passed somewhere—neither of them turned to look. What was, little by little, more present to him was the perfect taste. It was supreme—it was everywhere. "I just dropped my burden—and he received it."

"And was it very great?"

"Oh, such a load!" Dane laughed.

"Trouble, sorrow, doubt?"

"Oh, no; worse than that!"

"Worse?"

"'Success'—the vulgarest kind!" And Dane laughed again.

"Ah, I know that, too! No one in future, as things are going, will be able to face success."

"Without something of this sort—never. The better it is the worse—the greater the deadlier. But my one pain here," Dane continued, "is in thinking of my poor friend."

"The person to whom you've already alluded?"

"My substitute in the world. Such an unutterable benefactor. He turned up that morning when everything had somehow got on my nerves, when the whole great globe indeed, nerves, or no nerves, seemed to have squeezed itself into my study. It wasn't a question of nerves, it was a mere question of the displacement of everything—of submersion by our eternal too much. I didn't know *où donner de la tête*—I couldn't have gone a step further."

The intelligence with which the Brother listened kept them as children feeding from the same bowl. "And then you got the tip?"

"I got the tip!" Dane happily sighed.

"Well, we all get it. But I dare say differently."

"Then how did *you*——?"

The Brother hesitated, smiling. "You tell me first."

III

"Well," said George Dane, "it was a young man I had never seen—a man, at any rate, much younger than myself—who had written to me and sent me some article, some book. I read the stuff, was much struck with it, told him so and thanked him—on which, of course, I heard from him again. He asked me things—his questions were interesting; but to save time and writing I said to him: 'Come to see me—we can talk a little; but all I can give you is half an hour at breakfast.' He turned up at the hour on a day when, more than ever in my life before, I seemed, as it happened, in the endless press and stress, to have lost possession of my soul and to be surrounded only with the affairs of other people and the irrelevant, destructive, brutalising sides of life. It made me literally ill—made me feel as I had never felt that if I should once really, for an hour, lose hold of the thing itself, the thing I was trying for, I should never recover it again. The wild waters would close over me, and I should drop straight to the bottom where the vanquished dead lie."

"I follow you every step of your way," said the friendly Brother. "The wild waters, you mean, of our horrible time."

"Of our horrible time—precisely. Not, of course—as we sometimes dream—of any other."

"Yes, any other is only a dream. We really know none but our own."

"No, thank God—that's enough," Dane said. "Well, my young man turned up, and I hadn't been a minute in his presence before making out that practically it would be in him somehow or other to help me. He came to me with envy, envy extravagant—really passionate. I was, heaven save us, the great 'success' for him; he himself was broken and beaten. How can I say what passed between us?—it was so strange, so swift, so much a matter, from one to the other, of instant perception and agreement. He was so clever and haggard and hungry!"

"Hungry?" the Brother asked.

"I don't mean for bread, though he had none too much, I think, even of that. I mean for—well, what *I* had and what I was a monument of to him as I stood there up to my neck in preposterous evidence. He, poor chap, had been for ten years serenading closed windows and had never yet caused a shutter to show that it stirred. My dim blind was the first to be raised an inch; my reading of his book, my impression of it, my note and my invitation, formed literally the only response ever dropped into his dark street. He saw in my littered room, my shattered day, my bored face and spoiled temper—it's embarrassing, but I must tell you—the very blaze of my glory. And he saw in the blaze of my glory—deluded innocent!—what he had yearned for in vain."

"What he had yearned for was to *be* you," said the Brother. Then he added: "I see where you're coming out."

"At my saying to him by the end of five minutes: 'My dear fellow, I wish you'd just try it—wish you'd, for a while, just *be* me!' You go straight to the mark, and that was exactly what occurred—extraordinary though it was that we should both have understood. I saw what he could give, and he did too. He saw moreover what I could take; in fact what he saw was wonderful."

"He must be very remarkable!" the Brother laughed.

"There's no doubt of it whatever—far more remarkable than I. That's just the reason why what I put to him in joke —with a fantastic, desperate irony—became, on his hands, with his vision of his chance, the blessed guarantee of my sitting on this spot in your company. 'Oh, if I could just shift it all—make it straight over for an hour to other shoulders! If there only *were* a pair!'—that's the way I put it to him. And then at something in his face, 'Would *you*, by a miracle, undertake it?' I asked. I let him know all it meant—how it meant that he should at that very moment step in. It meant that he should finish my work and open my letters and keep my engagements and be subject, for better or worse, to my contacts and complications. It meant that he should live with my life, and think with my brain, and write with my hand, and speak with my voice. It meant, above all, that I should get off. He accepted with magnificence—rose to it like a hero. Only he said: 'What will become of *you*?' "

"There was the hitch!" the Brother admitted.

"Ah, but only for a minute. He came to my help again," Dane pursued, "when he saw I couldn't quite meet that, could at least only say that I wanted to think, wanted to cease, wanted to do the thing itself—the thing I was trying for, miserable me, and that thing only—and therefore wanted first of all really to *see* it again, planted out, crowded out, frozen out as it now so long had been. 'I know what you want,' he after a moment quietly remarked to me. 'Ah, what I want doesn't exist!' 'I know what you want,' he repeated. At that I began to believe him."

"Had you any idea yourself?" the Brother asked.

"Oh, yes," said Dane, "and it was just my idea that made me despair. There it was as sharp as possible in my imagination and my longing—there it was so utterly *not* in fact. We were sitting together on my sofa as we waited for breakfast. He presently laid his hand on my knee—showed me a face that the sudden great light in it had made, for me, indescribably beautiful. 'It exists—it exists,' he at last said. And so, I remember, we sat a while and looked at each other, with the final effect of my finding that I absolutely believed him. I remember we weren't at all solemn—we smiled with the joy of discoverers. He was as glad as I—he was tremendously glad. That came out in the whole manner of his reply to the appeal that broke from me: 'Where is it, then, in God's name? Tell me without delay where it is!' "

The Brother had attended with a sympathy! "He gave you the address?"

"He was thinking it out—feeling for it, catching it. He has a wonderful head of his own and must be making of the whole thing, while we sit here gossiping, something much better than ever *I* did. The mere sight of his face, the sense of his hand on my knee, made me, after a little, feel that he not only knew what I wanted, but was getting nearer to it than I could have got in ten years. He suddenly sprang up and went over to my study-table—sat straight down there as if to write me my passport. Then it was—at the mere sight of his back, which was turned to me—that I felt the spell work. I simply sat and watched him with the queerest, deepest, sweetest sense in the world—the sense of an ache that had stopped. All life was lifted; I myself at least was somehow off the ground. He was already where I had been."

"And where were you?" the Brother amusedly inquired.

"Just on the sofa always, leaning back on the cushion and feeling a delicious ease. He was already me."

"And who were you?" the Brother continued.

"Nobody. That was the fun."

"That *is* the fun," said the Brother, with a sigh like soft music.

Dane echoed the sigh, and, as nobody talking with nobody, they sat there together still and watched the sweet wide picture darken into tepid night.

IV

A T the end of three weeks—so far as time was distinct—Dane began to feel there was something he had recovered. It was the thing they never named—partly for want of the need and partly for lack of the word; for what indeed was the description that would cover it all? The only real need was to know it, to see it, in silence. Dane had a private, practical sign for it, which, however, he had appropriated by theft—"the vision and the faculty divine." That, doubtless, was a flattering phrase for his idea of his genius; the genius, at all events, was what he had been in danger of losing and had at last held by a thread that might at any moment have broken. The change was that, little by little, his hold had grown firmer, so that he drew in the line—more and more each day—with a pull that he was delighted to find it would bear. The mere dream-sweetness of the place was superseded; it was more and more a world of reason and order, of sensible, visible arrangement. It ceased to be strange—it was high, triumphant clearness. He cultivated, however, but vaguely, the question of where he was, finding it near enough the mark to be almost sure that if he was not in Kent he was probably in Hampshire. He paid for everything but that—that wasn't one of the items. Payment, he had soon learned, was definite; it consisted of sovereigns and shillings—just like those of the world he had left, only parted with more ecstatically—that he put, in his room, in a designated place and that were taken away in his absence by one of the unobtrusive, effaced agents—shadows projected on the hours like the noiseless march of the sundial —that were always at work. The institution had sides that had their recalls, and a pleased, resigned perception of these things was at once the effect and the cause of its grace.

Dane picked out of his dim past a dozen halting similes. The sacred, silent convent was one; another was the bright country-house. He did the place no outrage to liken it to an hotel; he permitted himself on occasion to trace its resemblance to a club. Such images, however, but flickered and went out —they lasted only long enough to light up the difference. An hotel without noise, a club without newspapers—when he turned his face to what it was "without" the view opened wide. The only approach to a real analogy was in himself and his companions. They were brothers, guests, members; they were even, if one liked—and they didn't in the least mind what they were called—"regular boarders." It was not they who made the conditions, it was the conditions that made them. These conditions found themselves accepted, clearly, with an appreciation, with a rapture, it was rather to be called, that had to do—as the very air that pervaded them and the force that sustained—with their quiet and noble assurance. They combined to form the large, simple idea of a general refuge—an image of embracing arms, of liberal accommodation. What was the effect, really, but the poetisation by perfect taste of a type common enough? There was no daily miracle; the perfect taste, with the aid of space, did the trick. What underlay and overhung it all, better yet, Dane mused, was some original inspiration, but confirmed, unquenched, some happy thought of an individual breast. It had been born somehow and somewhere—it had had to insist on being— the blessed conception. The author might remain in the obscure, for that was part of the perfection: personal service so hushed and regulated that you scarce caught it in the act and only knew it by its results. Yet the wise mind was every- where—the whole thing, infallibly, centred, at the core, in a consciousness. And what a consciousness it had been, Dane thought, a consciousness how like his own! The wise mind had felt, the wise mind had suffered; then, for all the worried company of minds, the wise mind had seen a chance. Of the creation thus arrived at you could none the less never have said if it were the last echo of the old or the sharpest note of the modern.

Dane again and again, among the far bells and the soft footfalls, in cool cloister and warm garden, found himself wanting not to know more and yet liking not to know less. It was part of the general beauty that there was no personal publicity, much less any personal success. Those things were in the world—in what he had left; there was no vulgarity here of credit or claim or fame. The real exquisite was to be without the complication of an identity, and the greatest boon of all, doubtless, the solid security, the clear confidence one could feel in the keeping of the contract. That was what had been most in the wise mind—the importance of the absolute sense, on the part of its beneficiaries, that what was offered was guaranteed. They had no concern but to pay—the wise mind knew what they paid for. It was present to Dane each hour that he could never be overcharged. Oh, the deep, deep bath, the soft, cool plash in the stillness!—this, time after time, as if under regular treatment, a sublimated German "cure," was the vivid name for his luxury. The inner life woke up again, and it was the inner life, for people of his generation, victims of the modern madness, mere maniacal extension and motion, that was returning health. He had talked of independence and written of it, but what a cold, flat word it had been! This was the wordless fact itself— the uncontested possession of the long, sweet, stupid day. The fragrance of flowers just wandered through the void, and the quiet recurrence of delicate, plain fare in a high, clean refectory where the soundless, simple service was the triumph of art. That, as he analysed, remained the constant explanation: all the sweetness and serenity were created, calculated things. He analysed, however, but in a desultory way and with a positive delight in the residuum of mystery that made for the great artist in the background the innermost shrine of the idol of a temple; there were odd moments for it, mild meditations when, in the broad cloister of peace or some garden-nook where the air was light, a special glimpse of beauty or reminder of felicity seemed, in passing, to hover and linger. In the mere ecstasy of change that had at first possessed him he had not discriminated—had only let himself sink, as I have mentioned, down to hushed depths. Then had come the slow, soft stages of intelligence and notation, more marked and more fruitful perhaps after that long talk with his mild mate in the twilight, and seeming to wind up the process by putting the key into his hand. This key, pure gold, was simply the cancelled list. Slowly and blissfully he read into the general wealth of his comfort all the particular absences of which it was composed. One by one he touched, as it were, all the things it was such rapture to be without.

It was the paradise of his own room that was most indebted to them—a great square, fair chamber, all beautified with omissions, from which, high up, he looked over a long valley to a far horizon, and in which he was vaguely and pleasantly reminded of some old Italian picture, some Carpaccio or some early Tuscan, the representation of a world without newspapers and letters, without telegrams and photographs, without the dreadful, fatal too much. There, for a blessing, he *could* read and write; there, above all, he could do nothing— he could live. And there were all sorts of freedoms—always, for the occasion, the particular right one. He could bring a book from the library—he could bring two, he could bring three. An effect produced by the charming place was that, for some reason, he never wanted to bring more. The library was a benediction—high and clear and plain, like everything else, but with something, in all its arched amplitude, unconfused and brave and gay. He should never forget, he knew, the throb of immediate perception with which he first stood there, a single glance round sufficing so to show him that it would give him what for years he had desired. He had not had detachment, but there was detachment here—the sense of a great silver bowl from which he could ladle up the melted hours. He strolled about from wall to wall, too pleasantly in tune on that occasion to sit down punctually or to choose; only recognising from shelf to shelf every dear old book that he had had to put off or never returned to; every deep, distinct voice of another time that, in the hubbub of the world, he had had to take for lost and unheard. He came back, of course, soon, came back every day; enjoyed there, of all the rare, strange moments, those that were at once most quickened and most caught—moments in which every apprehension counted double and every act of the mind was a lover's embrace. It was the quarter he perhaps, as the days went on, liked best; though indeed it only shared with the rest of the place, with every aspect to which his face happened to be turned, the power to remind him of the masterly general control.

There were times when he looked up from his book to lose himself in the mere tone of the picture that never failed at any moment or at any angle. The picture was always there, yet was made up of things common enough. It was in the way an open window in a broad recess let in the pleasant morning; in the way the dry air pricked into faint freshness the gilt of old bindings; in the way an empty chair beside a table un- littered showed a volume just laid down; in the way a happy Brother—as detached as oneself and with his innocent back presented—lingered before a shelf with the slow sound of turned pages. It was a part of the whole impression that, by some extraordinary law, one's vision seemed less from the facts than the facts from one's vision; that the elements were determined at the moment by the moment's need or the moment's sympathy. What most prompted this reflection was the degree in which, after a while, Dane had a consciousness of company. After that talk with the good Brother on the bench there were other good Brothers in other places—always in cloister or garden some figure that stopped if he himself stopped and with which a greeting became, in the easiest way in the world, a sign of the diffused amenity. Always, always, however, in all contacts, was the balm of a happy ignorance. What he had felt the first time recurred: the friend was always new and yet at the same time—it was amusing, not disturbing —suggested the possibility that he might be but an old one altered. That was only delightful—as positively delightful in the particular, the actual conditions as it might have been the reverse in the conditions abolished. These others, the abolished, came back to Dane at last so easily that he could exactly measure each difference, but with what he had finally been hustled on to hate in them robbed of its terror in consequence of something that had happened. What had happened was that in tranquil walks and talks the deep spell had worked and he had got his soul again. He had drawn in by this time, with his lightened hand, the whole of the long line, and that fact just dangled at the end. He could put his other hand on it, he could unhook it, he was once more in possession. This, as it befell, was exactly what he supposed he must have said to a comrade beside whom, one afternoon in the cloister, he found himself measuring steps.

"Oh, it comes—comes of itself, doesn't it, thank goodness? —just by the simple fact of finding room and time!"

The comrade was possibly a novice or in a different stage from his own; there was at any rate a vague envy in the recognition that shone out of the fatigued, yet freshened face. "It has come to *you* then?—you've got what you wanted?" That was the gossip and interchange that could pass to and fro. Dane, years before, had gone in for three months of hydropathy, and there was a droll echo, in this scene, of the old questions of the water-cure, the questions asked in the periodical pursuit of the "reaction"—the ailment, the progress of each, the action of the skin and the state of the appetite. Such memories worked in now—all familiar reference, all easy play of mind; and among them our friends, round and round, fraternised ever so softly, until, suddenly stopping short, Dane, with a hand on his companion's arm, broke into the happiest laugh he had yet sounded.

V

"WHY, it's raining!" And he stood and looked at the splash of the shower and the shine of the wet leaves. It was one of the summer sprinkles that bring out sweet smells.

"Yes—but why not?" his mate demanded.

"Well—because it's so charming. It's so exactly right."

"But everything *is*. Isn't that just why we're here?"

"Just exactly," Dane said; "only I've been living in the beguiled supposition that we've somehow or other a climate."

"So have I; so, I dare say, has every one. Isn't that the blessed moral?—that we live in beguiled suppositions. They come so easily here, and nothing contradicts them." The good Brother looked placidly forth—Dane could identify his phase. "A climate doesn't consist in its never raining, does it?"

"No, I dare say not. But somehow the good I've got has been half the great, easy absence of all that friction of which the question of weather mostly forms a part—has been indeed largely the great, easy, perpetual air-bath."

"Ah, yes—that's not a delusion; but perhaps the sense comes a little from our breathing an emptier medium. There are fewer things *in* it! Leave people alone, at all events, and the air is what they take to. Into the closed and the stuffy they have to be driven. I've had, too—I think we must all have—a fond sense of the south."

"But imagine it," said Dane, laughing, "in the beloved British islands and so near as we are to Bradford!"

His friend was ready enough to imagine. "To Bradford?" he asked, quite unperturbed. "How near?"

Dane's gaiety grew. "Oh, it doesn't matter!"

His friend, quite unmystified, accepted it. "There are things to puzzle out—otherwise it would be dull. It seems to me one can puzzle them."

"It's because we're so well disposed," Dane said.

"Precisely—we find good in everything."

"In everything," Dane went on. "The conditions settle that—they determine us."

They resumed their stroll, which evidently represented on the good Brother's part infinite agreement. "Aren't they probably in fact very simple?" he presently inquired. "Isn't simplification the secret?"

"Yes, but applied with a tact!"

"There it is. The thing's so perfect that it's open to as many interpretations as any other great work—a poem of Goethe, a dialogue of Plato, a symphony of Beethoven."

"It simply stands quiet, you mean," said Dane, "and lets us call it names?"

"Yes, but all such loving ones. We're 'staying' with some one—some delicious host or hostess who never shows."

"It's liberty-hall—absolutely," Dane assented.

"Yes—or a convalescent home."

To this, however, Dane demurred. "Ah, that, it seems to me, scarcely puts it. You weren't _ill_—were you? I'm very sure _I_ really wasn't. I was only, as the world goes, too 'beastly well'!"

The good Brother wondered. "But if we couldn't keep it up——?"

"We couldn't keep it _down_—that was all the matter!"

"I see—I see." The good Brother sighed contentedly; after which he brought out again with kindly humour: "It's a sort of kindergarten!"

"The next thing you'll be saying that we're babes at the breast!"

"Of some great mild, invisible mother who stretches away into space and whose lap is the whole valley——?"

"And her bosom"—Dane completed the figure—"the noble eminence of our hill? That will do; anything will do that covers the essential fact."

"And what do you call the essential fact?"

"Why, that—as in old days on Swiss lake-sides—we're *en pension.*"

The good Brother took this gently up. "I remember—I remember: seven francs a day without wine! But, alas, it's more than seven francs here."

"Yes, it's considerably more," Dane had to confess. "Perhaps it isn't particularly cheap."

"Yet should you call it particularly dear?" his friend after a moment inquired.

George Dane had to think. "How do I know, after all? What practice has one ever had in estimating the inestimable? Particular cheapness certainly isn't the note that we feel struck all round; but don't we fall naturally into the view that there *must* be a price to anything so awfully sane?"

The good Brother in his turn reflected. "We fall into the view that it must pay—that it does pay."

"Oh, yes; it does pay!" Dane eagerly echoed. "If it didn't it wouldn't last. It has *got* to last, of course!" he declared.

"So that we can come back?"

"Yes—think of knowing that we shall be able to!"

They pulled up again at this and, facing each other, thought of it, or at any rate pretended to; for what was really in their eyes was the dread of a loss of the clue. "Oh, when we want it again we shall find it," said the good Brother. "If the place really pays, it will keep on."

"Yes, that's the beauty; that it isn't, thank heaven, carried on only for love."

"No doubt, no doubt; and yet, thank heaven, there's love in it too." They had lingered as if, in the mild, moist air, they were charmed with the patter of the rain and the way the garden drank it. After a little, however, it did look rather as if they were trying to talk each other out of a faint, small fear. They saw the increasing rage of life and the recurrent need, and they wondered proportionately whether to return to the front when their hour should sharply strike would be the end of the dream. Was this a threshold perhaps, after all, that could only be crossed one way? They must return to the front sooner or later—that was certain: for each his hour would strike. The flower would have been gathered and the trick played—the sands, in short, would have run.

There, in its place, *was* life—with all its rage; the vague unrest of the need for action knew it again, the stir of the faculty that had been refreshed and reconsecrated. They seemed each, thus confronted, to close their eyes a moment for dizziness; then they were again at peace, and the Brother's confidence rang out. "Oh, we shall meet!"

"Here, do you mean?"

"Yes—and I dare say in the world too."

"But we shan't recognise or know," said Dane.

"In the world, do you mean?"

"Neither in the world nor here."

"Not a bit—not the least little bit, you think?"

Dane turned it over. "Well, so it is that it seems to me all best to hang together. But we shall see."

His friend happily concurred. "We shall see." And at this, for farewell, the Brother held out his hand.

"You're going?" Dane asked.

"No, but I thought *you* were."

It was odd, but at this Dane's hour seemed to strike—his consciousness to crystallise. "Well, I am. I've got it. You stay?" he went on.

"A little longer."

Dane hesitated. "You haven't yet got it?"

"Not altogether—but I think it's coming."

"Good!" Dane kept his hand, giving it a final shake, and at that moment the sun glimmered again through the shower, but with the rain still falling on the hither side of it and seeming to patter even more in the brightness. "Hallo—how charming!"

The Brother looked a moment from under the high arch—then again turned his face to our friend. He gave this time his longest, happiest sigh. "Oh, it's all right!"

But why was it, Dane after a moment found himself wondering, that in the act of separation his own hand was so long retained? Why but through a queer phenomenon of change, on the spot, in his companion's face—change that gave it another, but an increasing and above all a much more familiar identity, an identity not beautiful, but more and more distinct, an identity with that of his servant, with the most conspicuous, the physiognomic seat of the public propriety of Brown? To this anomaly his eyes slowly opened; it was not his good Brother, it was verily Brown who possessed his hand. If his eyes had to open, it was because they had been closed and because Brown appeared to think he had better wake up. So much as this Dane took in, but the effect of his taking it was a relapse into darkness, a recontraction of the lids just prolonged enough to give Brown time, on a second thought, to withdraw his touch and move softly away. Dane's next consciousness was that of the desire to make sure he *was* away, and this desire had somehow the result of dissipating the obscurity. The obscurity was completely gone by the time he had made out that the back of a person writing at his study-table was presented to him. He recognised a portion of a figure that he had somewhere described to somebody—the intent shoulders of the unsuccessful young man who had come that bad morning to breakfast. It was strange, he at last reflected, but the young man was still there. How long had he stayed—days, weeks, months? He was exactly in the position in which Dane had last seen him. Everything—stranger still

—was exactly in that position; everything, at least, but the light of the window, which came in from another quarter and showed a different hour. It wasn't after breakfast now; it was after—well, what? He suppressed a gasp—it was after everything. And yet—quite literally—there were but two other differences. One of these was that if he was still on the sofa he was now lying down; the other was the patter on the glass that showed him how the rain—the great rain of the night—had come back. It was the rain of the night, yet when had he last heard it? But two minutes before? Then how many were there before the young man at the table, who seemed intensely occupied, found a moment to look round at him and, on meeting his open eyes, get up and draw near?

"You've slept all day," said the young man.

"All day?"

The young man looked at his watch. "From ten to six. You were extraordinarily tired. I just, after a bit, let you alone, and you were soon off." Yes, that was it; he had been "off"—off, off, off. He began to fit it together; while he had been off the young man had been on. But there were still some few confusions; Dane lay looking up. "Everything's done," the young man continued.

"Everything?"

"Everything."

Dane tried to take it all in, but was embarrassed and could only say weakly and quite apart from the matter: "I've been so happy!"

"So have I," said the young man. He positively looked so; seeing which George Dane wondered afresh, and then, in his wonder, read it indeed quite as another face, quite, in a puzzling way, as another person's. Every one was a little some one else. While he asked himself who else then the young man was, this benefactor, struck by his appealing stare, broke again into perfect cheer. "It's all right!" That answered Dane's question; the face was the face turned to him by the good Brother there in the portico while they listened together to the rustle of the shower. It was all queer, but all pleasant and all distinct, so distinct that the last words in his ear—the same from both quarters—appeared the effect of a single voice. Dane rose and looked about his room, which seemed disencumbered, different, twice as large. It *was* all right.

MAUD-EVELYN

On some allusion to a lady who, though unknown to myself, was known to two or three of the company, it was asked by one of these if we had heard the odd circumstance of what she had just "come in for"—the piece of luck suddenly overtaking, in the grey afternoon of her career, so obscure and lonely a personage. We were at first, in our ignorance, mainly reduced to crude envy; but old Lady Emma, who for a while had said nothing, scarcely even appearing to listen and letting the chatter, which was indeed plainly beside the mark, subside of itself, came back from a mental absence to observe that if what had happened to Lavinia was wonderful, certainly, what had for years gone before it, led up to it, had likewise not been without some singular features. From this we perceived that Lady Emma had a story—a story moreover out of the ken even of those of her listeners acquainted with the quiet person who was the subject of it. Almost the oddest thing—as came out afterwards—was that such a situation should, for the world, have remained so in the background of this person's life. By "afterwards" I mean simply before we separated; for what came out came on the spot, under encouragement and pressure, our common, eager solicitation. Lady Emma, who always reminded me of a fine old instrument that has first to be tuned, agreed, after a few of our scrapings and fingerings, that, having said so much, she couldn't, without wantonly tormenting us, forbear to say all. She had known Lavinia, whom she mentioned throughout only by that name, from far away, and she had also known—— But what she had

43

known I must give as nearly as possible as she herself gave it. She talked to us from her corner of the sofa, and the flicker of the firelight in her face was like the glow of memory, the play of fancy, from within.

I

"THEN why on earth don't you take him?" I asked. I think that was the way that, one day when she was about twenty—before some of you perhaps were born—the affair, for me, must have begun. I put the question because I knew she had had a chance, though I didn't know how great a mistake her failure to embrace it was to prove. I took an interest because I liked them both—you see how I like young people still—and because, as they had originally met at my house, I had in a manner to answer to each for the other. I'm afraid I'm thrown baldly back on the fact that if the girl was the daughter of my earliest, almost my only governess, to whom I had remained much attached and who, after leaving me, had married—for a governess—"well," Marmaduke (it isn't *his* real name!) was the son of one of the clever men who had—I was charming then, I assure you I was—wanted, years before, and this one as a widower, to marry me. I hadn't cared, somehow, for widowers, but even after I had taken somebody else I was conscious of a pleasant link with the boy whose stepmother it had been open to me to become and to whom it was perhaps a little a matter of vanity with me to show that I should have been for him one of the kindest. This was what the woman his father eventually did marry was not, and that threw him upon me the more.

Lavinia was one of nine, and her brothers and sisters, who have never done anything for her, help, actually, in different countries and on something, I believe, of that same scale, to people the globe. There were mixed in her then, in a puzzling way, two qualities that mostly exclude each other—an extreme timidity and, as the smallest fault that could qualify a harmless creature for a world of wickedness, a self-complacency hard in tiny, unexpected spots, for which I used sometimes to take her up, but which, I subsequently saw, would have done something for the flatness of her life had they not evaporated with everything else. She was at any rate one of those persons as to whom you don't know whether they might have been attractive if they had been happy, or might have been happy if they had been attractive. If I was a trifle vexed at her not jumping at Marmaduke, it was probably rather less because I expected wonders of him than because I thought she took her own prospect too much for granted. She had made a mistake and, before long, admitted it; yet I remember that when she expressed to me a conviction that he would ask her again, I also thought this highly probable, for in the meantime I had spoken to him. "She does care for you," I declared; and I can see at this moment, long ago though it be, his handsome empty young face look, on the words, as if, in spite of itself for a little, it really thought. I didn't press the matter, for he had, after all, no great things to offer; yet my conscience was easier, later on, for having not said less. He had three hundred and fifty a year from his mother, and one of his uncles had promised him something—I don't mean an allowance, but a place, if I recollect, in a business. He assured me that he loved as a man loves—a man of twenty-two!—but once. He said it, at all events, as a man says it but once.

"Well, then," I replied, "your course is clear."

"To speak to her again, you mean?"

"Yes—try it."

He seemed to try it a moment in imagination; after which, a little to my surprise, he asked: "Would it be very awful if she should speak to *me?*"

I stared. "Do you mean pursue you—overtake you? Ah, if you're running away——"

"I'm not running away!"—he was positive as to that. "But when a fellow has gone so far——" `

"He can't go any further? Perhaps," I replied dryly. "But in that case he shouldn't talk of 'caring.'"

"Oh, but I do, I do."

I shook my head. "Not if you're too proud!" On which I turned away, looking round at him again, however, after he had surprised me by a silence that seemed to accept my judgment. Then I saw he had not accepted it; I perceived it indeed to be essentially absurd. He expressed more, on this, than I had yet seen him do—had the queerest, frankest, and, for a young man of his conditions, saddest smile.

"I'm *not* proud. It isn't *in* me. If you're not, you're not, you know. I don't think I'm proud enough."

It came over me that this was, after all, probable; yet somehow I didn't at the moment like him the less for it, though I spoke with some sharpness. "Then what's the matter with you?"

He took a turn or two about the room, as if what he had just said had made him a little happier. "Well, how can a man say more?" Then, just as I was on the point of assuring him that I didn't know what he had said, he went on: "I swore to her that I would never marry. Oughtn't that to be enough?"

"To make her come after you?"

"No—I suppose scarcely that; but to make her feel sure of me—to make her wait."

"Wait for what?"

"Well, till I come back."

"Back from where?"

"From Switzerland—haven't I told you? I go there next month with my aunt and my cousin."

He was quite right about not being proud—this was an alternative distinctly humble.

II

AND yet see what it brought forth—the beginning of which was something that, early in the autumn, I learned from poor Lavinia. He had written to her, they were still such friends; and thus it was that she knew his aunt and his cousin to have come back without him. He had stayed on—stayed much longer and travelled much further: he had been to the Italian lakes and to Venice; he was now in Paris. At this I vaguely wondered, knowing that he was always short of funds and that he must, by his uncle's beneficence, have started on the journey on a basis of expenses paid. "Then whom has he picked up?" I asked; but feeling sorry, as soon as I had spoken, to have made Lavinia blush. It was almost as if he had picked up some improper lady, though in this case he wouldn't have told her, and it wouldn't have saved him money.

"Oh, he makes acquaintance so quickly, knows people in two minutes," the girl said. "And every one always wants to be nice to him."

This was perfectly true, and I saw what she saw in it. "Ah, my dear, he will have an immense circle ready for you!"

"Well," she replied, "if they do run after us I'm not likely to suppose it will ever be for me. It will be for *him*, and they may do to me what they like. My pleasure will be—but you'll see." I already saw—saw at least what she supposed she herself saw: her drawing-room crowded with female fashion and her attitude angelic. "Do you know what he said to me again before he went?" she continued.

I wondered; he *had* then spoken to her. "That he will never, never marry——"

"Any one but *me!*" She ingenuously took me up. "Then you knew?"

It might be. "I guessed."

"And don't you believe it?"

Again I hesitated. "Yes." Yet all this didn't tell me why she had changed colour. "Is it a secret—whom he's with?"

"Oh no, they seem so nice. I was only struck with the way you know him—your seeing immediately that it must be a new friendship that has kept him over. It's the devotion of the Dedricks," Lavinia said. "He's travelling with them."

Once more I wondered. "Do you mean they're taking him about?"

"Yes—they've invited him."

No, indeed, I reflected—he wasn't proud. But what I said was: "Who in the world are the Dedricks?"

"Kind, good people whom, last month, he accidentally met. He was walking some Swiss pass—a long, rather stupid one, I believe, without his aunt and his cousin, who had gone round some other way and were to meet him somewhere. It came on to rain in torrents, and while he was huddling under a shelter he was overtaken by some people in a carriage, who kindly made him get in. They drove him, I gather, for several hours; it began an intimacy, and they've continued to be charming to him."

I thought a moment. "Are they ladies?"

Her own imagination meanwhile had also strayed a little. "I think about forty."

"Forty ladies?"

She quickly came back. "Oh no; I mean Mrs Dedrick is."

"About forty? Then Miss Dedrick——"

"There isn't any Miss Dedrick."

"No daughter?"

"Not with them, at any rate. No one but the husband."

I thought again. "And how old is *he?*"

Lavinia followed my example. "Well, about forty, too."

"About forty-two?" We laughed, but "That's all right!" I said; and so, for the time, it seemed.

He continued absent, none the less, and I saw Lavinia repeatedly, and we always talked of him, though this represented a greater concern with his affairs than I had really supposed myself committed to. I had never sought the acquaintance of his father's people, nor seen either his aunt or his cousin, so that the account given by these relatives of the circumstances of their separation reached me at last only through the girl, to whom, also—for she knew them as little—it had circuitously come. They considered, it appeared, the poor ladies he had started with, that he had treated them ill and thrown them over, sacrificing them selfishly to company picked up on the road—a reproach deeply resented by Lavinia, though about the company too I could see she was not much more at her ease. "How can he help it if he's so taking?" she asked; and to be properly indignant in one quarter she had to pretend to be delighted in the other. Marmaduke *was* "taking"; yet it also came out between us at last that the Dedricks must certainly be extraordinary. We had scant added evidence, for his letters stopped, and that naturally was one of our signs. I had meanwhile leisure to reflect—it was a sort of study of the human scene I always liked—on what to be taking consisted of. The upshot of my meditations, which experience has only confirmed, was that it consisted simply of itself. It was a quality implying no others. Marmaduke *had* no others. What indeed was his need of any?

III

HE at last, however, turned up; but then it happened that if, on his coming to see me, his immediate picture of his charming new friends quickened even more than I had expected my sense of the variety of the human species, my curiosity about them failed to make me respond when he suggested I should

go to see them. It's a difficult thing to explain, and I don't
pretend to put it successfully, but doesn't it often happen that
one may think well enough of a person without being inflamed
with the desire to meet—on the ground of any such sentiment
—other persons who think still better? Somehow—little harm
as there was in Marmaduke—it was but half a recommendation
of the Dedricks that they were crazy about him. I didn't say
this—I was careful to say little; which didn't prevent his
presently asking if he mightn't then bring them to *me*. "If
not, why not?" he laughed. He laughed about everything.

"Why not? Because it strikes me that your surrender doesn't
require any backing. Since you've done it you must take care
of yourself."

"Oh, but they're as safe," he returned, "as the Bank of
England. They're wonderful—for respectability and goodness."

"Those are precisely qualities to which my poor intercourse can contribute nothing." He hadn't, I observed, gone
so far as to tell me they would be "fun," and he *had*, on the
other hand, promptly mentioned that they lived in Westbourne Terrace. They were not forty—they were forty-five;
but Mr Dedrick had already, on considerable gains, retired
from some primitive profession. They were the simplest,
kindest, yet most original and unusual people, and nothing
could exceed, frankly, the fancy they had taken to him. Marmaduke spoke of it with a placidity of resignation that was
almost irritating. I suppose I should have despised him if,
after benefits accepted, he had said they bored him; yet their
not boring him vexed me even more than it puzzled. "Whom
do they know?"

"No one but me. There are people in London like that."

"Who know no one but you?"

"No—I mean no one at all. There are extraordinary people
in London, and awfully nice. You haven't an idea. You people
don't know every one. They lead their lives—they go their

way. One finds—what do you call it?—refinement, books, cleverness, don't you know, and music, and pictures, and religion, and an excellent table—all sorts of pleasant things. You only come across them by chance; but it's all perpetually going on."

I assented to this: the world was very wonderful, and one must certainly see what one could. In my own quarter too I found wonders enough. "But are you," I asked, "as fond of them——"

"As they are of *me*?" He took me up promptly, and his eyes were quite unclouded. "I'm quite sure I shall become so."

"Then are you taking Lavinia——?"

"Not to see them—no." I saw, myself, the next minute, of course, that I had made a mistake. "On what footing *can* I?"

I bethought myself. "I keep forgetting you're not engaged."

"Well," he said after a moment, "I shall never marry another."

It somehow, repeated again, gave on my nerves. "Ah, but what good will that do her, or me either, if you don't marry *her*?"

He made no answer to this—only turned away to look at something in the room; after which, when he next faced me, he had a heightened colour. "She ought to have taken me that day," he said gravely and gently; fixing me also as if he wished to say more.

I remember that his very mildness irritated me; some show of resentment would have been a promise that the case might still be righted. But I dropped it, the silly case, without letting him say more, and, coming back to Mr and Mrs Dedrick, asked him how in the world, without either occupation or society, they passed so much of their time. My question appeared for a moment to leave him at a loss, but he presently found light; which, at the same time, I saw on my side, really suited him better than further talk about Lavinia. "Oh, they live for Maud-Evelyn."

"And who's Maud-Evelyn?"

"Why, their daughter."

"Their daughter?" I had supposed them childless.

He partly explained. "Unfortunately they've lost her."

"Lost her?" I required more.

He hesitated again. "I mean that a great many people would take it that way. But *they* don't—they won't."

I speculated. "Do you mean other people would have given her up?"

"Yes—perhaps even tried to forget her. But the Dedricks can't."

I wondered what she had done: had it been anything very bad? However, it was none of my business, and I only said: "They communicate with her?"

"Oh, all the while."

"Then why isn't she with them?"

Marmaduke thought. "She *is*—now."

" 'Now'? Since when?"

"Well, this last year."

"Then why do you say they've lost her?"

"Ah," he said, smiling sadly, "*I* should call it that. I, at any rate," he went on, "don't see her."

Still more I wondered. "They keep her apart?"

He thought again. "No, it's not that. As I say, they live for her."

"But they don't want *you* to—is that it?"

At this he looked at me for the first time, as I thought, a little strangely. "How *can* I?"

He put it to me as if it were bad of him, somehow, that he shouldn't; but I made, to the best of my ability, a quick end of that. "You can't. Why in the world *should* you? Live for *my* girl. Live for Lavinia."

IV

I HAD unfortunately run the risk of boring him again with that idea, and, though he had not repudiated it at the time, I felt in my having returned to it the reason why he never reappeared for weeks. I saw "my girl," as I had called her, in the interval, but we avoided with much intensity the subject of Marmaduke. It was just this that gave me my perspective for finding her constantly full of him. It determined me, in all the circumstances, not to rectify her mistake about the child-lessness of the Dedricks. But whatever I left unsaid, her naming the young man was only a question of time, for at the end of a month she told me he had been twice to her mother's and that she had seen him on each of these occasions.

"Well then?"

"Well then, he's very happy."

"And still taken up——"

"As much as ever, yes, with those people. He didn't tell me so, but I could see it."

I could too, and her own view of it. "What, in that case, did he tell you?"

"Nothing—but I think there's something he wants to. Only not what *you* think," she added.

I wondered then if it were what I had had from him the last time. "Well, what prevents him?" I asked.

"From bringing it out? I don't know."

It was in the tone of this that she struck, to my ear, the first note of an acceptance so deep and a patience so strange that they gave me, at the end, even more food for wonderment than the rest of the business. "If he can't speak, why does he come?"

She almost smiled. "Well, I think I *shall* know."

I looked at her; I remember that I kissed her. "You're admirable; but it's very ugly."

"Ah," she replied, "he only wants to be·kind!"

"To *them?* Then he should let others alone. But what I call ugly is his being content to be so 'beholden'——"

"To Mr and Mrs Dedrick?" She considered as if there might be many sides to it. "But mayn't he do them some good?"

The idea failed to appeal to me. "What good can Marmaduke do? There's one thing," I went on, "in case he should want you to know them. Will you promise me to refuse?"

She only looked helpless and blank. "Making their acquaintance?"

"Seeing them, going near them—ever, ever."

Again she brooded. "Do you mean *you* won't?"

"Never, never."

"Well, then, I don't think I want to."

"Ah, but that's not a promise." I kept her up to it. "I want your word."

She demurred a little. "But why?"

"So that at least he shan't make use of you," I said with energy.

My energy overbore her, though I saw how she would really have given herself. "I promise, but it's only because it's something I know he will never ask."

I differed from her at the time, believing the proposal in question to have been exactly the subject she had supposed him to be wishing to broach; but on our very next meeting I heard from her of quite another matter, upon which, as soon as she came in, I saw her to be much excited.

"You know then about the daughter without having told me? He called again yesterday," she explained as she met my stare at her unconnected plunge, "and now I know that he *has* wanted to speak to me. He at last brought it out."

I continued to stare. "Brought what?"

"Why, everything." She looked surprised at my face. "Didn't he tell you about Maud-Evelyn?"

I perfectly recollected, but I momentarily wondered. "He spoke of there being a daughter, but only to say that there's something the matter with her. What is it?"

The girl echoed my words. "What 'is' it?—you dear, strange thing! The matter with her is simply that she's dead."

"Dead?" I was naturally mystified. "When then did she die?"

"Why, years and years ago—fifteen, I believe. As a little girl. Didn't you understand it so?"

"How *should* I?—when he spoke of her as 'with' them and said that they lived for her!"

"Well," my young friend explained, "that's just what he meant—they live for her memory. She *is* with them in the sense that they think of nothing else."

I found matter for surprise in this correction, but also, at first, matter for relief. At the same time it left, as I turned it over, a fresh ambiguity. "If they think of nothing else, how can they think so much of Marmaduke?"

The difficulty struck her, though she gave me even then a dim impression of being already, as it were, rather on Marmaduke's side, or, at any rate—almost as against herself—in sympathy with the Dedricks. But her answer was prompt: "Why, that's just their reason—that they can talk to him so much about her."

"I see." Yet still I wondered. "But what's *his* interest——?"

"In being drawn into it?" Again Lavinia met her difficulty. "Well, that she was so interesting! It appears she was lovely."

I doubtless fairly gaped. "A little girl in a pinafore?"

"She was out of pinafores; she was, I believe, when she died, about fourteen. Unless it was sixteen! She was at all events wonderful for beauty."

"That's the rule. But what good does it do him if he has never seen her?"

She thought a moment, but this time she had no answer. "Well, you must ask him!"

I determined without delay to do so; but I had before me meanwhile other contradictions. "Hadn't I better ask him on the same occasion what he means by their 'communicating'?"

Oh, this was simple. "They go in for 'mediums,' don't you know, and raps, and sittings. They began a year or two ago."

"Ah, the idiots!" I remember, at this, narrow-mindedly exclaiming. "Do they want to drag *him* in——?"

"Not in the least; they don't desire it, and he has nothing to do with it."

"Then where does his fun come in?"

Lavinia turned away; again she seemed at a loss. At last she brought out: "Make him show you her little photograph."

But I remained unenlightened. "Is her little photograph his fun?"

Once more she coloured for him. "Well, it represents a young loveliness!"

"That he goes about showing?"

She hesitated. "I think he has only shown it to *me*."

"Ah, you're just the last one!" I permitted myself to observe.

"Why so, if I'm also struck?"

There was something about her that began to escape me, and I must have looked at her hard. "It's very good of you to be struck!"

"I don't only mean by the beauty of the face," she went on; "I mean by the whole thing—by that also of the attitude of the parents, their extraordinary fidelity and the way that, as he says, they have made of her memory a real religion. That was what, above all, he came to tell me about."

I turned away from her now, and she soon afterwards left me; but I couldn't help its dropping from me before we parted that I had never supposed him to be *that* sort of fool.

V

IF I were really the perfect cynic you probably think me I should frankly say that the main interest of the rest of this matter lay for me in fixing the sort of fool I *did* suppose him. But I'm afraid, after all, that my anecdote amounts mainly to a presentation of my own folly. I shouldn't be so in possession of the whole spectacle had I not ended by accepting it, and I shouldn't have accepted it had it not, for my imagination, been saved somehow from grotesqueness. Let me say at once, however, that grotesqueness, and even indeed something worse, did at first appear to me strongly to season it. After that talk with Lavinia I immediately addressed to our friend a request that he would come to see me; when I took the liberty of challenging him outright on everything she had told me. There was one point in particular that I desired to clear up and that seemed to me much more important even than the colour of Maud-Evelyn's hair or the length of her pinafores: the question, I of course mean, of my young man's good faith. Was he altogether silly or was he only altogether mercenary? I felt my choice restricted for the moment to these alternatives.

After he had said to me "It's as ridiculous as you please, but they've simply adopted me" I had it out with him, on the spot, on the issue of common honesty, the question of what he was conscious, so that his self-respect should be saved, of being able to give such benefactors in return for such bounty. I'm obliged to say that to a person so inclined at the start to quarrel with him his amiability could yet prove persuasive. His contention was that the equivalent he represented was something for his friends alone to measure. He didn't for a moment pretend to sound deeper than the fancy they had

taken to him. He had not, from the first, made up to them in
any way: it was all their own doing, their own insistence, their
own eccentricity, no doubt, and even, if I liked, their own
insanity. Wasn't it enough that he was ready to declare to me,
looking me straight in the eye, that he was "really and truly"
fond of them and that they didn't bore him a mite? I had
evidently—didn't I see?—an ideal for him that he wasn't at
all, if I didn't mind, the fellow to live up to. It was he himself who put it so, and it drew from me the pronouncement
that there *was* something irresistible in the refinement of his
impudence. "I don't go near Mrs Jex," he said—Mrs Jex was
their favourite medium: "I do find *her* ugly and vulgar and
tiresome, and I hate that part of the business. Besides," he
added in words that I afterwards remembered, "I don't require
it: I do beautifully without it. But my friends themselves," he
pursued, "though they're of a type you've never come within
miles of, are not ugly, are not vulgar, are not in any degree
whatever any sort of a 'dose.' They're, on the contrary, in
their own unconventional way, the very best company.
They're endlessly amusing. They're delightfully queer and
quaint and kind—they're like people in some old story or of
some old time. It's at any rate our own affair—mine and
theirs—and I beg you to believe that I should make short
work of a remonstrance on the subject from any one but
you."

I remember saying to him three months later: "You've
never yet told me what they really want of you"; but I'm
afraid this was a form of criticism that occurred to me precisely
because I had already begun to guess. By that time indeed I
had had great initiations, and poor Lavinia had had them as
well—hers in fact throughout went further than mine—and
we had shared them together, and I had settled down to a
tolerably exact sense of what I was to see. It was what Lavinia
added to it that really made the picture. The portrait of the
little dead girl had evoked something attractive, though one

had not lived so long in the world without hearing of plenty of little dead girls; and the day came when I felt as if I had actually sat with Marmaduke in each of the rooms converted by her parents—with the aid not only of the few small, cherished relics, but that of the fondest figments and fictions, ingenious imaginary mementoes and tokens, the unexposed make-believes of the sorrow that broods and the passion that clings—into a temple of grief and worship. The child, incontestably beautiful, had evidently been passionately loved, and in the absence from their lives—I suppose originally a mere accident—of such other elements, either new pleasures or new pains, as abound for most people, their feeling had drawn to itself their whole consciousness: it had become mildly maniacal. The idea was fixed, and it kept others out. The world, for the most part, allows no leisure for such a ritual, but the world had consistently neglected this plain, shy couple, who were sensitive to the wrong things and whose sincerity and fidelity, as well as their tameness and twaddle, were of a rigid, antique pattern.

I must not represent that either of these objects of interest, or my care for their concerns, took up all my leisure; for I had many claims to meet and many complications to handle, a hundred preoccupations and much deeper anxieties. My young woman, on her side, had other contacts and contingencies— other troubles too, poor girl; and there were stretches of time in which I neither saw Marmaduke nor heard a word of the Dedricks. Once, only once, abroad, in Germany at a railway-station, I met him in their company. They were colourless, commonplace, elderly Britons, of the kind you identify by the livery of their footman or the labels of their luggage, and the mere sight of them justified me to my conscience in having avoided, from the first, the stiff problem of conversation with them. Marmaduke saw me on the spot and came over to me. There was no doubt whatever of *his* vivid bloom. He had grown fat—or almost, but not with grossness—and might perfectly have passed for the handsome, happy, full-blown son of doting parents who couldn't let him out of view and to whom he was a model of respect and solicitude. They followed him with placid, pleased eyes when he joined me, but asking nothing at all for themselves and quite fitting into his own manner of saying nothing about them. It had its charm, I confess, the way he could be natural and easy, and yet intensely conscious too, on such a basis. What he was conscious of was that there were things I by this time knew; just as, while we stood there and good-humouredly sounded each other's faces—for, having accepted everything at last, I was only a little curious—I knew that he measured my insight. When he returned again to his doting parents I had to admit that, doting as they were, I felt him not to have been spoiled. It was incongruous in such a career, but he was rather more of a man. There came back to me with a shade of regret after I had got on this occasion into my train, which was not theirs, a memory of some words that, a couple of years before, I had uttered to poor Lavinia. She had said to me, speaking in reference to what was then our frequent topic and on some fresh evidence that I have forgotten: "He feels now, you know, about Maud-Evelyn quite as the old people themselves do."

"Well," I had replied, "it's only a pity he's paid for it!"

"Paid?" She had looked very blank.

"By all the luxuries and conveniences," I had explained, "that he comes in for through living with them. For that's what he practically does."

At present I saw how wrong I had been. He was paid, but paid differently, and the mastered wonder of that was really what had been between us in the waiting-room of the station. Step by step, after this, I followed.

VI

I can see Lavinia for instance in her ugly new mourning immediately after her mother's death. There had been long anxieties connected with this event, and she was already faded, already almost old. But Marmaduke, on her bereavement, had been to her, and she came straightway to me.

"Do you know what he thinks now?" she soon began. "He thinks he knew her."

"Knew the child?" It came to me as if I had half expected it.

"He speaks of her now as if she hadn't been a child." My visitor gave me the strangest fixed smile. "It appears that she wasn't so young—it appears she had grown up."

I stared. "How can it 'appear'? They *know*, at least! There were the facts."

"Yes," said Lavinia, "but they seem to have come to take a different view of them. He talked to me a long time, and all about *her*. He told me things."

"What kind of things? Not trumpery stuff, I hope, about 'communicating'—about his seeing or hearing her?"

"Oh no, he doesn't go in for that; he leaves it to the old couple, who, I believe, cling to their mediums, keep up their sittings and their rappings and find in it all a comfort, an amusement, that he doesn't grudge them and that he regards as harmless. I mean anecdotes—memories of his own. I mean things she said to him and that they did together—places they went to. His mind is full of them."

I turned it over. "Do you think he's decidedly mad?"

She shook her head with her bleached patience. "Oh no, it's too beautiful!"

"Then are *you* taking it up? I mean the preposterous theory——"

"It *is* a theory," she broke in, "but it isn't necessarily preposterous. Any theory has to suppose something," she sagely pursued, "and it depends at any rate on what it's a theory *of.* It's wonderful to see this one work."

"Wonderful always to see the growth of a legend!" I laughed. "This is a rare chance to watch one in formation. They're all three in good faith building it up. Isn't that what you made out from him?"

Her tired face fairly lighted. "Yes—you understand it; and you put it better than I. It's the gradual effect of brooding over the past; the past, that way, grows and grows. They make it and make it. They've persuaded each other—the parents—of so many things that they've at last also persuaded *him.* It has been contagious."

"It's you who put it well," I returned. "It's the oddest thing I ever heard of, but it is, in its way, a reality. Only we mustn't speak of it to others."

She quite accepted that precaution. "No—to nobody. *He* doesn't. He keeps it only for me."

"Conferring on you thus," I again laughed, "such a precious privilege!"

She was silent a moment, looking away from me. "Well, he has kept his vow."

"You mean of not marrying? Are you very sure?" I asked. "Didn't he perhaps——?" But I faltered at the boldness of my joke.

The next moment I saw I needn't. "He *was* in love with her," Lavinia brought out.

I broke now into a peal which, however provoked, struck even my own ear at the moment as rude almost to profanity. "He literally tells you outright that he's making believe?"

She met me effectively enough. "I don't think he *knows* he is. He's just completely in the current."

"The current of the old people's twaddle?"

Again my companion hesitated; but she knew what she thought. "Well, whatever we call it, I like it. It isn't so common, as the world goes, for any one—let alone for two or three—to feel and to care for the dead as much as that. It's self-deception, no doubt, but it comes from something that— well," she faltered again, "is beautiful when one does hear of it. They make her out older, so as to imagine they had her longer; and they make out that certain things really happened to her, so that she shall have had more life. They've invented a whole experience for her, and Marmaduke has become a part of it. There's one thing, above all, they want her to have had." My young friend's face, as she analysed the mystery, fairly grew bright with her vision. It came to me with a faint dawn of awe that the attitude of the Dedricks *was* contagious. "And she did have it!" Lavinia declared.

I positively admired her, and if I could yet perfectly be rational without being ridiculous, it was really, more than anything else, to draw from her the whole image. "She had the bliss of knowing Marmaduke? Let us agree to it, then, since she's not here to contradict us. But what I don't get over is the scant material for *him!*" It may easily be conceived how little, for the moment, I could get over it. It was the last time my impatience was to be too much for me, but I remember how it broke out. "A man who might have had *you!*"

For an instant I feared I had upset her—thought I saw in her face the tremor of a wild wail. But poor Lavinia was magnificent. "It wasn't that he might have had 'me'—that's nothing: it was, at the most, that I might have had *him.* Well, isn't that just what has happened? He's mine from the moment no one else has him. I give up the past, but don't you see what it does for the rest of life? I'm surer than ever that he won't marry."

"Of course, he won't—to quarrel, with those people!"

For a minute she answered nothing; then, "Well, for

whatever reason!" she simply said. Now, however, I had gouged out of her a couple of still tears, and I pushed away the whole obscure comedy.

VII

I MIGHT push it away, but I couldn't really get rid of it; nor, on the whole, doubtless, did I want to, for to have in one's life, year after year, a particular question or two that one couldn't comfortably and imposingly make up one's mind about was just the sort of thing to keep one from turning stupid. There had been little need of my enjoining reserve upon Lavinia: she obeyed, in respect to impenetrable silence save with myself, an instinct, an interest of her own. We never therefore gave poor Marmaduke, as you call it, "away;" we were much too tender, let alone that she was also too proud; and, for himself, evidently, there was not, to the end, in London, another person in his confidence. No echo of the queer part he played ever came back to us; and I can't tell you how this fact, just by itself, brought home to me little by little a sense of the charm he was under. I met him "out" at long intervals—met him usually at dinner. He had grown like a person with a position and a history. Rosy and rich-looking, fat, moreover, distinctly fat at last, there was almost in him something of the bland—yet not too bland—young head of an hereditary business. If the Dedricks had been bankers he might have constituted the future of the house. There was none the less a long middle stretch during which, though we were all so much in London, he dropped out of my talks with Lavinia. We were conscious, she and I, of his absence from them; but we clearly felt in each quarter that there are things after all unspeakable, and the fact, in any case, had nothing to do with her seeing or not seeing our friend.

I was sure, as it happened, that she did see him. But there were moments that for myself still stand out.

One of these was a certain Sunday afternoon when it was so dismally wet that, taking for granted I should have no visitors, I had drawn up to the fire with a book—a successful novel of the day—that I promised myself comfortably to finish. Suddenly, in my absorption, I heard a firm rat-tat-tat; on which I remember giving a groan of inhospitality. But my visitor proved in due course Marmaduke, and Marmaduke proved—in a manner even less, at the point we had reached, to have been counted on—still more attaching than my novel. I think it was only an accident that he became so; it would have been the turn of a hair either way. He hadn't come to speak—he had only come to talk, to show once more that we could continue good old friends without his speaking. But somehow there were the circumstances: the insidious fireside, the things in the room, with their reminders of his younger time; perhaps even too the open face of my book, looking at him from where I had laid it down for him and giving him a chance to feel that he could supersede Wilkie Collins. There was at all events a promise of intimacy, of opportunity for him in the cold lash of the windows by the storm. We should be alone; it was cosy; it was safe.

The action of these impressions was the more marked that what was touched by them, I afterwards saw, was not at all a desire for an effect—was just simply a spirit of happiness that needed to overflow. It had finally become too much for him. His past, rolling up year after year, had grown too interesting. But he was, all the same, directly stupefying. I forget what turn of our preliminary gossip brought it out, but it came, in explanation of something or other, as it had not yet come: "When a man has had for a few months what *I* had, you know!" The moral appeared to be that nothing in the way of human experience of the exquisite could again particularly matter. He saw, however, that I failed immediately to fit his reflection to a definite case, and he went on with the frankest smile: "You look as bewildered as if you suspected me of alluding to some sort of thing that isn't usually spoken of; but I assure you I mean nothing more reprehensible than our blessed engagement itself."

"Your blessed engagement?" I couldn't help the tone in which I took him up; but the way he disposed of that was something of which I feel to this hour the influence. It was only a look, but it put an end to my tone for ever. It made me, on my side, after an instant, look at the fire—look hard and even turn a little red. During this moment I saw my alternatives and I chose; so that when I met his eyes again I was fairly ready. "You still feel," I asked with sympathy, "how much it did for you?"

I had no sooner spoken than I saw that that would be from that moment the right way. It instantly made all the difference. The main question would be whether I could keep it up. I remember that only a few minutes later, for instance, this question gave a flare. His reply had been abundant and imperturbable—had included some glance at the way death brings into relief even the faintest things that have preceded it; on which I felt myself suddenly as restless as if I had grown afraid of him. I got up to ring for tea; he went on talking—talking about Maud-Evelyn and what she had been for him; and when the servant had come up I prolonged, nervously, on purpose, the order I had wished to give. It made time, and I could speak to the footman sufficiently without thinking: what I thought of really was the risk of turning right round with a little outbreak. The temptation was strong; the same influences that had worked for my companion just worked, in their way, during that minute or two, for me. *Should* I, taking him unaware, flash at him a plain "I say, just settle it for me once for all. *Are* you the boldest and basest of fortune-hunters, or have you only, more innocently and perhaps more pleasantly, suffered your brain slightly to soften?" But I missed the chance—which I didn't in fact afterwards regret. My servant went out, and I faced again to my visitor, who continued to converse. I met his eyes once more, and their effect was repeated. If anything had happened to his brain this effect was perhaps the domination of the madman's stare. Well, he was the easiest and gentlest of madmen. By the time the footman came back with tea I was in for it; I was in for everything. By "everything" I mean my whole subsequent treatment of the case. It *was*—the case was —really beautiful. So, like all the rest, the hour comes back to me: the sound of the wind and the rain; the look of the empty, ugly, cabless square and of the stormy spring light; the way that, uninterrupted and absorbed, we had tea together by my fire. So it was that he found me receptive and that I found myself able to look merely grave and kind when he said, for example: "Her father and mother, you know, really, that first day—the day they picked me up on the Splügen—recognised me as the proper one."

"The proper one?"

"To make their son-in-law. They wanted her so," he went on, "to have had, don't you know, just everything."

"Well, if she did have it"—I tried to be cheerful—"isn't the whole thing then all right?"

"Oh, it's all right *now*," he replied—"now that we've got it all there before us. You see, they couldn't like me so much" —he wished me thoroughly to understand—"without wanting me to have been the man."

"I see—that was natural."

"Well," said Marmaduke, "it prevented the possibility of any one else."

"Ah, that would never have done!" I laughed.

His own pleasure at it was impenetrable, splendid. "You see, they couldn't do much, the old people—and they can do still less now—with the future; so they had to do what they could with the past."

"And they seem to have done," I concurred, "remarkably much."

"Everything, simply. Everything," he repeated. Then he had an idea, though without insistence or importunity—I noticed it just flicker in his face. "If you *were* to come to Westbourne Terrace——"

"Oh, don't speak of that!" I broke in. "It wouldn't be decent now. I should have come, if at all, ten years ago."

But he saw, with his good humour, further than this. "I see what you mean. But there's much more in the place now than then."

"I dare say. People get new things. All the same——!" I was at bottom but resisting my curiosity.

Marmaduke didn't press me, but he wanted me to know. "There are our rooms—the whole set; and I don't believe you ever saw anything more charming, for *her* taste was extraordinary. I'm afraid too that I myself have had much to say to them." Then as he made out that I was again a little at sea, "I'm talking," he went on, "of the suite prepared for her marriage." He "talked" like a crown prince. "They were ready, to the last touch—there was nothing more to be done. And they're just as they were—not an object moved, not an arrangement altered, not a person but ourselves coming in: they're only exquisitely kept. All our presents are there—I should have liked you to see them."

It had become a torment by this time—I saw that I had made a mistake. But I carried it off. "Oh, I couldn't have borne it!"

"They're not sad," he smiled—"they're too lovely to be sad. They're happy. And the things——!" He seemed, in the excitement of our talk, to have them before him.

"They're so very wonderful?"

"Oh, selected with a patience that makes them almost priceless. It's really a museum. There was nothing they thought too good for her."

I had lost the museum, but I reflected that it could contain no object so rare as my visitor. "Well, you've helped them— you could do *that*."

He quite eagerly assented. "I could do that, thank God— I could do that! I felt it from the first, and it's what I *have* done." Then as if the connection were direct: "All *my* things are there."

I thought a moment. "Your presents?"

"Those I made her. She loved each one, and I remember about each the particular thing she said. Though I do say it," he continued, "none of the others, as a matter of fact, come near mine. I look at them every day, and I assure you I'm not ashamed." Evidently, in short, he had spared nothing, and he talked on and on. He really quite swaggered.

VIII

IN relation to times and intervals I can only recall that if this visit of his to me had been in the early spring it was one day in the late autumn—a day, which couldn't have been in the same year, with the difference of hazy, drowsy sunshine and brown and yellow leaves—that, taking a short cut across Kensington Gardens, I came, among the untrodden ways, upon a couple occupying chairs under a tree, who immediately rose at the sight of me. I had been behind them at recognition, the fact that Marmaduke was in deep mourning having perhaps, so far as I had observed it, misled me. In my desire both not to look flustered at meeting them and to spare their own confusion I bade them again be seated and asked leave, as a third chair was at hand, to share a little their rest. Thus it befell that after a minute Lavinia and I had sat down, while our friend, who had looked at his watch, stood before us among the fallen foliage and remarked that he was sorry to have to leave us. Lavinia said nothing, but I expressed regret; I couldn't, however, as it struck me, without a false or a vulgar note speak as if I had interrupted a tender passage or separated a pair of lovers. But I could look him up and down, take in his deep mourning. He had not made, for going off, any other pretext than that his time was up and that he was due at home. "Home," with him now, had but one meaning: I knew him to be completely quartered in Westbourne Terrace. "I hope nothing has happened," I said—"that you've lost no one whom *I* know."

Marmaduke looked at my companion, and she looked at Marmaduke. "He has lost his wife," she then observed.

Oh, this time, I fear, I had a small quaver of brutality; but it was at him I directed it. "Your wife? I didn't know you had *had* a wife!"

"Well," he replied, positively gay in his black suit, his black gloves, his high hatband, "the more we live in the past, the more things we find in it. That's a literal fact. You would see the truth of it if your life had taken such a turn."

"*I* live in the past," Lavinia put in gently and as if to help us both.

"But with the result, my dear," I returned, "of not making, I hope, such extraordinary discoveries!" It seemed absurd to be afraid to be light.

"May none of her discoveries be more fatal than mine!" Marmaduke wasn't uproarious, but his treatment of the matter had the good taste of simplicity. "They've wanted it so for her," he continued to me wonderfully, "that we've at last seen our way to it—I mean to what Lavinia has mentioned." He hesitated but three seconds—he brought it brightly out. "Maud-Evelyn had *all* her young happiness."

I stared, but Lavinia was, in her peculiar manner, as brilliant. "The marriage *did* take place," she quietly, stupendously explained to me.

Well, I was determined not to be left. "So you're a widower," I gravely asked, "and these are the signs?"

"Yes; I shall wear them always now."

"But isn't it late to have begun?"

My question had been stupid, I felt the next instant; but it didn't matter—he was quite equal to the occasion. "Oh, I had to wait, you know, till all the facts about my marriage had given me the right." And he looked at his watch again. "Excuse me—I *am* due. Good-bye, good-bye." He shook hands with each of us, and as we sat there together watching him walk away I was struck with his admirable manner of looking the character. I felt indeed as our eyes followed him that we were at one on this, and I said nothing till he was out of sight. Then by the same impulse we turned to each other.

"I thought he was never to marry!" I exclaimed to my friend.

Her fine wasted face met me gravely. "He isn't—ever. He'll be still more faithful."

"Faithful this time to whom?"

"Why, to Maud-Evelyn." I said nothing—I only checked an ejaculation; but I put out a hand and took one of hers, and for a minute we kept silence. "Of course it's only an idea," she began again at last, "but it seems to me a beautiful one." Then she continued resignedly and remarkably: "And now *they* can die."

"Mr and Mrs Dedrick?" I pricked up my ears. "Are they dying?"

"Not quite, but the old lady, it appears, is failing, steadily weakening; less, as I understand it, from any definite ailment than because she just feels her work done and her little sum of passion, as Marmaduke calls it, spent. Fancy, with her convictions, all her reasons for wanting to die! And if she goes, he says, Mr Dedrick won't long linger. It will be quite 'John Anderson my jo.'"

"Keeping her company down the hill, to lie beside her at the foot?"

"Yes, having settled all things."

I turned these things over as we walked away, and how they had settled them—for Maud-Evelyn's dignity and Marmaduke's high advantage; and before we parted that afternoon —we had taken a cab in the Bayswater Road and she had come home with me—I remember saying to her: "Well then, when they die won't he be free?"

She seemed scarce to understand. "Free?"

"To do what he likes."

She wondered. "But he does what he likes now."

"Well then, what *you* like!"

"Oh, you know what *I* like——!"

Ah, I closed her mouth! "You like to tell horrid fibs— yes, I know it!"

What she had then put before me, however, came in time to pass: I heard in the course of the next year of Mrs Dedrick's extinction, and some months later, without, during the interval, having seen a sign of Marmaduke, wholly taken up with his bereaved patron, learned that her husband had touchingly followed her. I was out of England at the time; we had had to put into practice great economies and let our little place; so that, spending three winters successively in Italy, I devoted the periods between, at home, altogether to visits among people, mainly relatives, to whom these friends of mine were not known. Lavinia of course wrote to me— wrote, among many things, that Marmaduke was ill and had not seemed at all himself since the loss of his "family," and this in spite of the circumstance, which she had already promptly communicated, that they had left him, by will, "almost everything." I knew before I came back to remain that she now saw him often and, to the extent of the change that had overtaken his strength and his spirits, greatly ministered to him. As soon as we at last met I asked for news of

him; to which she replied: "He's gradually going." Then on
my surprise: "He has had his life."

"You mean that, as he said of Mrs Dedrick, his sum of
passion is spent?"

At this she turned away. "You've never understood."

I *had*, I conceived; and when I went subsequently to see
him I was moreover sure. But I only said to Lavinia on this
first occasion that I would immediately go; which was precisely what brought out the climax, as I feel it to be, of my
story. "He's not now, you know," she turned round to
admonish me, "in Westbourne Terrace. He has taken a little
old house in Kensington."

"Then he hasn't kept the things?"

"He has kept everything." She looked at me still more as
if I had never understood.

"You mean he has moved them?"

She was patient with me. "He has moved nothing. Everything is as it was, and kept with the same perfection."

I wondered. "But if he doesn't live there?"

"It's just what he does."

"Then how can he be in Kensington?"

She hesitated, but she had still more than her old grasp of it.
"He's in Kensington—without living."

"You mean that at the other place——?"

"Yes, he spends most of his time. He's driven over there
every day—he remains there for hours. He keeps it for that."

"I see—it's still the museum."

"It's still the temple!" Lavinia replied with positive austerity.

"Then why did he move?"

"Because, you see, there"—she faltered again—"I could
come to him. And he wants me," she said with admirable
simplicity.

Little by little I took it in. "After the death of the parents,
even, you never went?"

"Never."

"So you haven't seen anything?"

"Anything of hers? Nothing."

I understood, oh perfectly; but I won't deny that I was disappointed: I had hoped for an account of his wonders and I immediately felt that it wouldn't be for me to take a step that she had declined. When, a short time later, I saw them together in Kensington Square—there were certain hours of the day that she regularly spent with him—I observed that everything about him was new, handsome and simple. They were, in their strange, final union—if union it could be called —very natural and very touching; but he was visibly stricken —he had his ailment in his eyes. She moved about him like a sister of charity—at all events like a sister. He was neither robust nor rosy now, nor was his attention visibly very present, and I privately and fancifully asked myself where it wandered and waited. But poor Marmaduke was a gentleman to the end—he wasted away with an excellent manner. He died twelve days ago; the will was opened; and last week, having meanwhile heard from her of its contents, I saw Lavinia. He leaves her everything that he himself had inherited. But she spoke of it all in a way that caused me to say in surprise: "You haven't yet been to the house?"

"Not yet. I've only seen the solicitors, who tell me there will be no complications."

There was something in her tone that made me ask more. "Then you're not curious to see what's there?"

She looked at me with a troubled—almost a pleading— sense, which I understood; and presently she said: "Will you go with me?"

"Some day, with pleasure—but not the first time. You must go alone then. The 'relics' that you'll find there," I added—for I had read her look—"you must think of now not as hers——"

"But as his?"

"Isn't that what his death—with his so close relation to them—has made them for you?"

Her face lighted—I saw it was a view she could thank me for putting into words. "I see—I see. They *are* his. I'll go."

She went, and three days ago she came to me. They're really marvels, it appears, treasures extraordinary, and she has them all. Next week I go with her—I shall see them at last. Tell *you* about them, you say? My dear man, everything.

MISS GUNTON OF POUGHKEEPSIE

"It's astonishing what you take for granted!" Lady Champer had exclaimed to her young friend at an early stage; and this might have served as a sign that even then the little plot had begun to thicken. The reflection was uttered at the time the outlook of the charming American girl in whom she found herself so interested was still much in the rough. They had often met, with pleasure to each, during a winter spent in Rome; and Lily had come to her in London towards the end of May with further news of a situation the dawn of which, in March and April, by the Tiber, the Arno and the Seine, had considerably engaged her attention. The Prince had followed Miss Gunton to Florence and then with almost equal promptitude to Paris, where it was both clear and comical for Lady Champer that the rigour of his uncertainty as to parental commands and remittances now detained him. This shrewd woman promised herself not a little amusement from her view of the possibilities of the case. Lily was on the whole showing a wonder; therefore the drama would lose nothing from her character, her temper, her tone. She was waiting—this was the truth she had imparted to her clever protectress—to see if her Roman captive would find himself drawn to London. Should he really turn up there she would the next thing start for America, putting him to the test of that wider range and declining to place her confidence till he should have arrived in New York at her heels. If he remained in Paris or returned to Rome she would stay in London and, as she phrased it, have a good time by herself. Did he expect her to go back to

Paris for him? Why not in that case just as well go back to Rome at once? The first thing for her, Lily intimated to her London adviser, was to show what, in her position, *she* expected.

Her position meanwhile was one that Lady Champer, try as she would, had as yet succeeded neither in understanding nor in resigning herself not to understand. It was that of being extraordinarily pretty, amazingly free and perplexingly good, and of presenting these advantages in a positively golden light. How was one to estimate a girl whose nearest approach to a drawback—that is to an encumbrance—appeared to be a grandfather carrying on a business in an American city her ladyship had never otherwise heard of, with whom communication was all by cable and on the subject of "drawing"? Expression was on the old man's part moreover as concise as it was expensive, consisting as it inveterately did of but the single word "Draw." Lily drew, on every occasion in life, and it at least could not be said of the pair—when the "family idea," as embodied in America, was exposed to criticism—that they were not in touch. Mr Gunton had given her further Mrs Brine, to come out with her, and with this provision and the perpetual pecuniary he plainly figured—to Lily's own mind—as solicitous to the point of anxiety. Mrs Brine's scheme of relations seemed in truth to be simpler still. There was a transatlantic "Mr Brine," of whom she often spoke—and never in any other way; but she wrote for newspapers; she prowled in catacombs, visiting more than once even those of Paris; she haunted hotels; she picked up compatriots; she spoke above all a language that often baffled comprehension. She mattered, however, but little; she was mainly so occupied in having what Lily had likewise independently glanced at—a good time by herself. It was difficult enough indeed to Lady Champer to see the wonderful girl reduced to that, yet she was a little person who kept one somehow in presence of the incalculable. Old measures and

familiar rules were of no use at all with her—she had so broken
the moulds and so mixed the marks. What was confounding
was her disparities—the juxtaposition in her of beautiful sun-
flushed heights and deep dark holes. She had none of the
things that the other things implied. She dangled in the air in
a manner that made one dizzy; though one took comfort, at
the worst, in feeling that one was there to catch her if she fell.
Falling, at the same time, appeared scarce one of her pro-
perties, and it was positive for Lady Champer at moments
that if one held out one's arms one might be, after all, much
more likely to be pulled up. That was really a part of the
excitement of the acquaintance.

"Well," said this friend and critic on one of the first of the
London days, "say he does, on your return to your own
country, go after you: how do you read, on that occurrence,
the course of events?"

"Why, if he comes after me I'll have him."

"And do you think it so easy to 'have' him?"

Lily appeared, lovely and candid—and it was an air and a
way she often had—to wonder what she thought. "I don't
know that I think it any easier than he seems to think it to
have *me*. I know moreover that, though he wants awfully to
see the country, he wouldn't just now come to America
unless to marry me; and if I take him at all," she pursued,
"I want first to be able to show him to the girls."

"Why 'first'?" Lady Champer asked. "Wouldn't it do as
well last?"

"Oh, I should want them to see me in Rome too," said
Lily. "But, dear me, I'm afraid I want a good many things!
What I most want of course is that he should show me unmistakably what *he* wants. Unless he wants me more than anything else in the world I don't want him. Besides, I hope he
doesn't think I'm going to be married anywhere but in my
own place."

"I see," said Lady Champer. "It's for your wedding

you want the girls. And it's for the girls you want the
Prince."

"Well, we're all bound by that promise. And of course
you'll come!"

"Ah, my dear child——!" Lady Champer gasped.

"You can come with the old Princess. You'll be just the
right company for her."

The elder friend considered afresh, with depth, the younger's beauty and serenity. "You *are*, love, beyond everything!"

The beauty and serenity took on for a moment a graver
cast. "Why do you so often say that to me?"

"Because you so often make it the only thing to say. But
you'll some day find out why," Lady Champer added with an
intention of encouragement.

Lily Gunton, however, was a young person to whom encouragement looked queer; she had grown up without need
of it, and it seemed indeed scarce required in her situation.
"Do you mean you believe his mother won't come?"

"Over mountains and seas to see you married?—and to
be seen also of the girls? If she does, *I* will. But we had
perhaps better," Lady Champer wound up, "not count our
chickens before they're hatched." To which, with one of the
easy returns of gaiety that were irresistible in her, Lily made
answer that neither of the ladies in question struck her quite as
chickens.

The Prince at all events presented himself in London with
a promptitude that contributed to make the warning gratui-
tous. Nothing could have exceeded, by this time, Lady
Champer's appreciation of her young friend, whose merits
"town" at the beginning of June threw into renewed relief;
but she had the imagination of greatness and, though she
believed she tactfully kept it to herself, she thought what the
young man had thus done a great deal for a Roman prince to
do. Take him as he was, with the circumstances—and they

were certainly peculiar, and he was charming—it was a far cry for him from Piazza Colonna to Clarges Street. If Lady Champer had the imagination of greatness, which the Prince in all sorts of ways gratified, Miss Gunton of Poughkeepsie— it was vain to pretend the contrary—was not great in any particular save one. She was great when she "drew." It was true that at the beginning of June she did draw with unprecedented energy and in a manner that, though Mrs Brine's remarkable nerve apparently could stand it, fairly made a poor baronet's widow, little as it was her business, hold her breath. It was none of her business at all, yet she talked of it even with the Prince himself—to whom it was indeed a favourite subject and whose greatness, oddly enough, never appeared to shrink in the effect it produced upon him. The line they took together was that of wondering if the scale of Lily's drafts made really most for the presumption that the capital at her disposal was rapidly dwindling, or for that of its being practically infinite. "Many a fellow," the young man smiled, "would marry her to pull her up." He was in any case of the opinion that it was an occasion for deciding—one way or the other—quickly. Well, he did decide—so quickly that within the week Lily communicated to her friend that he had offered her his hand, his heart, his fortune and all his titles, grandeurs and appurtenances. She had given him his answer, and he was in bliss; though nothing, as yet, was settled but that.

Tall, fair, active, educated, amiable, simple, carrying so naturally his great name and pronouncing so kindly Lily's small one, the happy youth, if he was one of the most ancient of princes, was one of the most modern of Romans. This second character it was his special aim and pride to cultivate. He would have been pained at feeling himself an hour behind his age; and he had a way—both touching and amusing to some observers—of constantly comparing his watch with the dial of the day's news. It was in fact easy to see that in deciding to ally himself with a young alien of vague origin, whose striking beauty was reinforced only by her presumptive money, he had even put forward a little the fine hands of his timepiece. No one else, however—not even Lady Champer, and least of all Lily herself—had quite taken the measure, in this connection, of his merit. The quick decision he had spoken of was really a flying leap. He desired incontestably to rescue Miss Gunton's remainder; but to rescue it he had to take it for granted, and taking it for granted was nothing less than—at whatever angle considered—a risk. He never, naturally, used the word to her, but he distinctly faced a peril. The sense of what he had staked on a vague return gave him, at the height of the London season, bad nights, or rather bad mornings—for he danced with his intended, as a usual thing, conspicuously, till dawn—besides obliging him to take, in the form of long explanatory, argumentative and persuasive letters to his mother and sisters, his uncles, aunts, cousins and preferred confidants, large measures of justification at home. The family sense was strong in his huge old house, just as the family array was numerous; he was dutifully conscious of the trust reposed in him, and moved from morning till night, he perfectly knew, as the observed of a phalanx of observers; whereby he the more admired himself for his passion, precipitation and courage. He had only a probability to go upon, but he was—and by the romantic tradition of his race—so in love that he should surely not be taken in.

His private agitation of course deepened when, to do honour to her engagement and as if she would have been ashamed to do less, Lily "drew" again most gloriously; but he managed to smile beautifully on her asking him if he didn't want her to be splendid, and at his worst hours he went no further than to wish that he might be married on the morrow. Unless it were the next day, or at most the next month, it really at moments seemed best that it should never be at all. On the most favourable view—with the solidity of the residuum fully assumed—there were still minor questions and dangers. A vast America, arching over his nuptials, bristling with expectant bridesmaids and underlaying their feet with expensive flowers, stared him in the face and prompted him to the reflection that if she dipped so deep into the mere remote overflow her dive into the fount itself would verily be a header. If she drew at such a rate in London how wouldn't she draw at Poughkeepsie? he asked himself, and practically asked Lady Champer; yet bore the strain of the question, without an answer, so nobly that when, with small delay, Poughkeepsie seemed simply to heave with reassurances, he regarded the ground as firm and his tact as rewarded. "And now at last, dearest," he said, "since everything's so satisfactory, you *will* write?" He put it appealingly, endearingly, yet as if he could scarce doubt.

"Write, love? Why," she replied, "I've done nothing *but* write! I've written ninety letters."

"But not to mamma," he smiled.

"Mamma?"—she stared. "My dear boy, I've not at this time of day to remind you that I've the misfortune to have no mother. I lost mamma, you know, as you lost your father, in childhood. You may be sure," said Lily Gunton, "that I wouldn't otherwise have waited for you to prompt me."

There came into his face a kind of amiable convulsion. "Of course, darling, I remember—your beautiful mother (she *must* have been beautiful!) whom I should have been so glad to know. I was thinking of *my* mamma—who'll be so delighted to hear from you." The Prince spoke English in perfection—had lived in it from the cradle and appeared, particularly when alluding to his home and family, to matters familiar and of fact, or to those of dress and sport, of general recreation, to draw such a comfort from it as made the girl think of him as scarce more a foreigner than a pleasant, auburn, slightly awkward, slightly slangy and extremely well-tailored young Briton would have been. He sounded "mamma" like a rosy English schoolboy; yet just then, for the first time, the things with which he was connected struck her as in a manner strange and far-off. Everything in him, none the less—face and voice and tact, above all his deep desire—laboured to bring them near and make them natural. This was intensely the case as he went on: "Such a little letter as you *might* send would really be awfully jolly."

"My dear child," Lily replied on quick reflection, "I'll write to her with joy the minute I hear from her. Won't she write to *me?*"

The Prince just visibly flushed. "In a moment if you'll only——"

"Write to her first?"

"Just pay her a little—no matter how little—your respects."

His attenuation of the degree showed perhaps a sense of a weakness of position; yet it was no perception of this that made the girl immediately say: "Oh, *caro*, I don't think I can begin. If you feel that *she* won't—as you evidently do—is it because you've asked her and she has refused?" The next moment, "I see you *have!*" she exclaimed. His rejoinder to this was to catch her in his arms, to press his cheek to hers, to murmur a flood of tender words in which contradiction, confession, supplication and remonstrance were oddly confounded; but after he had sufficiently disengaged her to allow her to speak again his effusion was checked by what came. "Do you really mean you can't induce her?" It renewed itself on the first return of ease; or it, more correctly perhaps, in order to renew itself, took this return—a trifle too soon—for granted. Singular, for the hour, was the quickness with which ease could leave them—so blissfully at one as they were; and, to be brief, it had not come back even when Lily spoke of the matter to Lady Champer. It is true that she waited but little to do so. She then went straight to the point. "What would you do if his mother doesn't write?"

"The old Princess—to *you?*" Her ladyship had not had time to mount guard in advance over the tone of this, which was doubtless (as she instantly, for that matter, herself became aware) a little too much that of "Have you really expected she would?" What Lily had expected found itself therefore not unassisted to come out—and came out indeed to such a tune that with all kindness, but with a melancholy deeper than any she had ever yet in the general connection used, Lady Champer was moved to remark that the situation might have been found more possible had a little more historic sense been brought to it. "You're the dearest thing in the world, and I can't imagine a girl's carrying herself in any way, in a difficult position, better than you do; only I'm bound to say I think you ought to remember that you're entering a very great house, of tremendous antiquity, fairly groaning under the weight of ancient honours, the heads of which—through the tradition of the great part they've played in the world—are accustomed to a great deal of deference. The old Princess, my dear, you see"—her ladyship gathered confidence a little as she went—"is a most prodigious personage."

"Why, Lady Champer, of course she is, and that's just what I like her for!" said Lily Gunton.

"She has never in her whole life made an advance, any more than any one has ever dreamed of expecting it of her. It's a pity that while you were there you didn't see her, for I think it would have helped you to understand. However, as you did see his sisters, the two Duchesses and dear little Donna Claudia, you know how charming they all *can* be. They only want to be nice, I know, and I dare say that on the smallest opportunity you'll hear from the Duchesses."

The plural had a sound of splendour, but Lily quite kept her head. "What do you call an opportunity? Am I not giving them, by accepting their son and brother, the best—and in fact the only—opportunity they could desire?"

"I like the way, darling," Lady Champer smiled, "you talk about 'accepting'!"

Lily thought of this—she thought of everything. "Well,

say it would have been a better one still for them if I had refused him."

Her friend caught her up. "But you haven't."

"Then they must make the most of the occasion as it is." Lily was very sweet, but very lucid. "The Duchesses may write or not, as they like; but I'm afraid the Princess simply *must.*" She hesitated, but after a moment went on: "He oughtn't to be willing moreover that I shouldn't expect to be welcomed."

"He isn't!" Lady Champer blurted out.

Lily jumped at it. "Then he has told you? It's her attitude?"

She had spoken without passion, but her friend was scarce the less frightened. "My poor child, what can he do?"

Lily saw perfectly. "He can make her."

Lady Champer turned it over, but her fears were what was clearest. "And if he doesn't?"

"If he 'doesn't'?" The girl ambiguously echoed it.

"I mean if he can't."

Well, Lily, more cheerfully, declined, for the hour, to consider this. He would certainly do for her what was right; so that after all, though she had herself put the question, she disclaimed the idea that an answer was urgent. There was time, she conveyed—which Lady Champer only desired to believe; a faith moreover somewhat shaken in the latter when the Prince entered her room the next day with the information that there was none—none at least to leave everything in the air. Lady Champer had not yet made up her mind as to which of these young persons she liked most to draw into confidence, nor as to whether she most inclined to take the Roman side with the American or the American side with the Roman. But now in truth she was settled; she gave proof of it in the increased lucidity with which she spoke for Lily.

"Wouldn't the Princess depart—a—from her usual attitude for such a great occasion?"

The difficulty was a little that the young man so well

understood his mother. "The devil of it is, you see, that it's for Lily herself, so much more, she thinks the occasion great."

Lady Champer mused. "If you hadn't her consent I could understand it. But from the moment she thinks the girl good enough for you to marry——"

"Ah, she doesn't!" the Prince gloomily interposed. "However," he explained, "she accepts her because there are reasons —my own feeling, now so my very life, don't you see? But it isn't quite open arms. All the same, as I tell Lily, the arms *would* open."

"If she'd make the first step? Hum!" said Lady Champer, not without the note of grimness. "She'll be obstinate."

The young man, with a melancholy eye, quite coincided. "She'll be obstinate."

"So that I strongly recommend you to manage it," his friend went on after a pause. "It strikes me that if the Princess can't do it for Lily she might at least do it for you. Any girl you marry becomes thereby somebody."

"Of course—doesn't she? She certainly ought to do it for *me*. I'm after all the head of the house."

"Well then, make her!" said Lady Champer a little impatiently.

"I will. Mamma adores me, and I adore *her*."

"And you adore Lily, and Lily adores you—therefore everybody adores everybody, especially as I adore you both. With so much adoration all round, therefore, things ought to march."

"They shall!" the young man declared with spirit. "I adore you too—you don't mention that; for you help me immensely. But what do you suppose she'll do if she doesn't?"

The agitation already visible in him ministered a little to vagueness; but his friend after an instant disembroiled it. "What do I suppose Lily will do if your mother remains stiff?" Lady Champer faltered, but she let him have it. "She'll break."

His wondering eyes became strange. "Just for that?"

"You may certainly say it isn't much—when people love as you do."

"Ah, I'm afraid then Lily doesn't!"—and he turned away in his trouble.

She watched him while he moved, not speaking for a minute. "My dear young man, are you afraid of your mamma?"

He faced short about again. "I'm afraid of this—that if she does do it she won't forgive her. She *will* do it—yes. But Lily will be for her, in consequence, ever after, the person who has made her submit herself. She'll hate her for that—and then she'll hate me for being concerned in it." The Prince presented it all with clearness—almost with charm. "What do you say to that?"

His friend had to think. "Well, only, I fear, that we belong, Lily and I, to a race unaccustomed to counting with such passions. Let her hate!" she, however, a trifle inconsistently wound up.

"But I love her so!"

"Which?" Lady Champer asked it almost ungraciously; in such a tone at any rate that, seated on the sofa with his elbows on his knees, his much-ringed hands nervously locked together and his eyes of distress wide open, he met her with visible surprise. What she met *him* with is perhaps best noted by the fact that after a minute of it his hands covered his bent face and she became aware she had drawn tears. This produced such regret in her that before they parted she did what she could to attenuate and explain—making a great point, at all events, of her rule, with Lily, of putting only his own side of the case. "I insist awfully, you know, on your greatness!"

He jumped up, wincing. "Oh, that's horrid."

"I don't know. Whose fault is it then, at any rate, if trying to help you may have that side?" This was a question that, with the tangle he had already to unwind, only added a twist;

yet she went on as if positively to add another. "Why on earth don't you, all of you, leave them alone?"

"Leave them——?"

"All your Americans."

"Don't you like them then—the women?"

She hesitated. "No. Yes. They're an interest. But they're a nuisance. It's a question, very certainly, if they're worth the trouble they give."

This at least it seemed he could take in. "You mean that one should be quite sure first what they *are* worth?"

He made her laugh now. "It would appear that you never *can* be. But also really that you can't keep your hands off."

He fixed the social scene an instant with his heavy eye. "Yes. Doesn't it?"

"However," she pursued as if he again a little irritated her, "Lily's position is quite simple."

"Quite. She just loves me."

"I mean simple for herself. She really makes no differences. It's only we—you and I—who make them all."

The Prince wondered. "But she tells me she delights in us; has, that is, such a sense of what we are supposed to 'represent.'"

"Oh, she *thinks* she has. Americans think they have all sorts of things; but they haven't. That's just *it*"—Lady Champer was philosophic. "Nothing but their Americanism. If you marry anything you marry that; and if your mother accepts anything that's what she accepts." Then, though the young man followed the demonstration with an apprehension almost pathetic, she gave him without mercy the whole of it. "Lily's rigidly logical. A girl—as *she* knows girls—is 'welcomed,' on her engagement, before anything else can happen, by the family of her young man; and the motherless girl, alone in the world, more punctually than any other. His mother—if she's a 'lady'—takes it upon herself. Then the girl goes and stays with them. But she does nothing before. *Tirez-vous de là.*"

The young man sought on the spot to obey this last injunction, and his effort presently produced a flash. "Oh, if she'll come and *stay* with us"—all would, easily, be well! The flash went out, however, when Lady Champer returned: "Then let the Princess invite her."

Lily a fortnight later simply said to her, from one hour to the other, "I'm going home," and took her breath away by sailing on the morrow with the Bransbys. The tense cord had somehow snapped; the proof was in the fact that the Prince, dashing off to his good friend at this crisis an obscure, an ambiguous note, started the same night for Rome. Lady Champer, for the time, sat in darkness, but during the summer many things occurred; and one day in the autumn, quite unheralded and with the signs of some of them in his face, the Prince appeared again before her. He was not long in telling her his story, which was simply that he had come to her, all the way from Rome, for news of Lily and to talk of Lily. She was prepared, as it happened, to meet his impatience; yet her preparation was but little older than his arrival and was deficient moreover in an important particular. She was not prepared to knock him down, and she made him talk to gain time. She had however, to understand, put a primary question: "She never wrote then?"

"Mamma? Oh yes—when she at last got frightened at Miss Gunton's having become so silent. She wrote in August; but Lily's own decisive letter—letter to me, I mean—crossed with it. It was too late—that put an end."

"A *real* end?"

Everything in the young man showed how real. "On the ground of her being willing no longer to keep up, by the stand she had taken, such a relation between mamma and *me*. But her rupture," he wailed, "keeps it up more than anything else."

"And is it very bad?"

"Awful, I assure you. I've become for my mother a person

who has made her make, all for nothing, an unprecedented advance, a humble submission; and she's so disgusted, all round, that it's no longer the same old charming thing for us to be together. It makes it worse for her that I'm still madly in love."

"Well," said Lady Champer after a moment, "if you're still madly in love I can only be sorry for you."

"You can *do* nothing for me?—don't advise me to go over?"

She had to take a longer pause. "You don't at all know then what has happened?—that old Mr Gunton has died and left her everything?"

All his vacancy and curiosity came out in a wild echo. "'Everything'?"

"She writes me that it's a great deal of money."

"You've just heard from her then?"

"This morning. I seem to make out," said Lady Champer, "an extraordinary number of dollars."

"Oh, I was sure it was!" the young man moaned.

"And she's engaged," his friend went on, "to Mr Bransby."

He bounded, rising before her. "Mr Bransby?"

"'Adam P.'—the gentleman with whose mother and sisters she went home. *They*, she writes, have beautifully welcomed her."

"*Dio mio!*" The Prince stared; he had flushed with the blow, and the tears had come into his eyes. "And I believed she loved me!"

"*I* didn't!" said Lady Champer with some curtness.

He gazed about; he almost rocked; and, unconscious of her words, he appealed, inarticulate and stricken. At last, however, he found his voice. "What on earth then shall I do? I can less than ever go back to mamma!"

She got up for him, she thought for him, pushing a better chair into her circle. "Stay here with me, and I'll ring for tea. Sit there nearer the fire—you're cold."

"Awfully!" he confessed as he sank. "And I believed she loved me!" he repeated as he stared at the fire.

"*I* didn't!" Lady Champer once more declared. This time, visibly, he heard her, and she immediately met his wonder. "No—it was all the rest; your great historic position, the glamour of your name and your past. Otherwise what she stood out for wouldn't be excusable. But she has the sense of such things, and *they* were what she loved." So, by the fire, his hostess explained it, while he wondered the more.

"I thought that last summer you told me just the contrary."

It seemed, to do her justice, to strike her. "Did I? Oh, well, how does one know? With Americans one is lost!"

THE TREE OF KNOWLEDGE

I

It was one of the secret opinions, such as we all have, of Peter Brench that his main success in life would have consisted in his never having committed himself about the work, as it was called, of his friend, Morgan Mallow. This was a subject on which it was, to the best of his belief, impossible, with veracity, to quote him, and it was nowhere on record that he had, in the connection, on any occasion and in any embarrassment, either lied or spoken the truth. Such a triumph had its honour even for a man of other triumphs—a man who had reached fifty, who had escaped marriage, who had lived within his means, who had been in love with Mrs Mallow for years without breathing it, and who, last not least, had judged himself once for all. He had so judged himself in fact that he felt an extreme and general humility to be his proper portion; yet there was nothing that made him think so well of his parts as the course he had steered so often through the shallows just mentioned. It became thus a real wonder that the friends in whom he had most confidence were just those with whom he had most reserves. He couldn't tell Mrs Mallow—or at least he supposed, excellent man, he couldn't—that she was the one beautiful reason he had never married; any more than he could tell her husband that the sight of the multiplied marbles in that gentleman's studio was an affliction of which even time had never blunted the edge. His victory, however, as I have intimated, in regard to these productions, was not simply in his not having let it out that he deplored them; it was, remarkably, in his not having kept it in by anything else.

The whole situation, among these good people, was verily a marvel, and there was probably not such another for a long way from the spot that engages us—the point at which the soft declivity of Hampstead began at that time to confess in broken accents to St John's Wood. He despised Mallow's statues and adored Mallow's wife, and yet was distinctly fond of Mallow, to whom, in turn, he was equally dear. Mrs Mallow rejoiced in the statues—though she preferred, when pressed, the busts; and if she was visibly attached to Peter Brench it was because of his affection for Morgan. Each loved the other, moreover, for the love borne in each case to Lancelot, whom the Mallows respectively cherished as their only child and whom the friend of their fireside identified as the third—but decidedly the handsomest—of his godsons. Already in the old years it had come to that—that no one, for such a relation, could possibly have occurred to any of them, even to the baby itself, but Peter. There was luckily a certain independence, of the pecuniary sort, all round: the Master could never otherwise have spent his solemn *Wanderjahre* in Florence and Rome and continued, by the Thames as well as by the Arno and the Tiber, to add unpurchased group to group and model, for what was too apt to prove in the event mere love, fancy-heads of celebrities either too busy or too buried—too much of the age or too little of it—to sit. Neither could Peter, lounging in almost daily, have found time to keep the whole complicated tradition so alive by his presence. He was massive, but mild, the depositary of these mysteries—large and loose and ruddy and curly, with deep tones, deep eyes, deep pockets, to say nothing of the habit of long pipes, soft hats and brownish, greyish, weather-faded clothes, apparently always the same.

He had "written," it was known, but had never spoken— never spoken, in particular, of that; and he had the air (since, as was believed, he continued to write) of keeping it up in order to have something more—as if he had not, at the worst, enough—to be silent about. Whatever his air, at any rate, Peter's occasional unmentioned prose and verse were quite truly the result of an impulse to maintain the purity of his taste by establishing still more firmly the right relation of fame to feebleness. The little green door of his domain was in a garden-wall on which the stucco was cracked and stained, and in the small detached villa behind it everything was old, the furniture, the servants, the books, the prints, the habits and the new improvements. The Mallows, at Carrara Lodge, were within ten minutes, and the studio there was on their little land, to which they had added, in their happy faith, to build it. This was the good fortune, if it was not the ill, of her having brought him, in marriage, a portion that put them in a manner at their ease and enabled them thus, on their side, to keep it up. And they did keep it up—they always had—the infatuated sculptor and his wife, for whom nature had refined on the impossible by relieving them of the sense of the difficult. Morgan had, at all events, everything of the sculptor but the spirit of Phidias—the brown velvet, the becoming *beretto*, the "plastic" presence, the fine fingers, the beautiful accent in Italian and the old Italian factotum. He seemed to make up for everything when he addressed Egidio with the "tu" and waved him to turn one of the rotary pedestals of which the place was full. They were tremendous Italians at Carrara Lodge, and the secret of the part played by this fact in Peter's life was, in a large degree, that it gave him, sturdy Briton that he was, just the amount of "going abroad" he could bear. The Mallows were all his Italy, but it was in a measure for Italy he liked them. His one worry was that Lance—to which they had shortened his godson—was, in spite of a public school, perhaps a shade too Italian. Morgan, meanwhile, looked like somebody's flattering idea of somebody's own person as expressed in the great room provided at the Uffizi museum for Portraits of Artists by Themselves. The Master's sole regret that he had not been born rather to the brush than to the chisel sprang from his wish that he might have contributed to that collection.

It appeared, with time, at any rate, to be to the brush that Lance had been born; for Mrs Mallow, one day when the boy was turning twenty, broke it to their friend, who shared, to the last delicate morsel, their problems and pains, that it seemed as if nothing would really do but that he should embrace the career. It had been impossible longer to remain blind to the fact that he gained no glory at Cambridge, where Brench's own college had, for a year, tempered its tone to him as for Brench's own sake. Therefore why renew the vain form of preparing him for the impossible? The impossible— it had become clear—was that he should be anything but an artist.

"Oh dear, dear!" said poor Peter.

"Don't you believe in it?" asked Mrs Mallow, who still, at more than forty, had her violet velvet eyes, her creamy satin skin and her silken chestnut hair.

"Believe in what?"

"Why, in Lance's passion."

"I don't know what you mean by 'believing in it.' I've never been unaware, certainly, of his disposition, from his earliest time, to daub and draw; but I confess I've hoped it would burn out."

"But why should it," she sweetly smiled, "with his wonderful heredity? Passion is passion—though of course, indeed, you, dear Peter, know nothing of that. Has the Master's ever burned out?"

Peter looked off a little and, in his familiar, formless way, kept up for a moment a sound between a smothered whistle and a subdued hum. "Do you think he's going to be another Master?"

She seemed scarce prepared to go that length, yet she had,

on the whole, a most marvellous trust. "I know what you mean by that. Will it be a career to incur the jealousies and provoke the machinations that have been at times almost too much for his father? Well—say it may be, since nothing but clap-trap, in these dreadful days, *can*, it would seem, make its way, and since, with the curse of refinement and distinction, one may easily find one's self begging one's bread. Put it at the worst—say he *has* the misfortune to wing his flight further than the vulgar taste of his stupid countrymen can follow. Think, all the same, of the happiness—the same that the Master has had. He'll *know*."

Peter looked rueful. "Ah, but *what* will he know?"

"Quiet joy!" cried Mrs Mallow, quite impatient and turning away.

II

HE had of course, before long, to meet the boy himself on it and to hear that, practically, everything was settled. Lance was not to go up again, but to go instead to Paris where, since the die was cast, he would find the best advantages. Peter had always felt that he must be taken as he was, but had never perhaps found him so much as he was as on this occasion. "You chuck Cambridge then altogether? Doesn't that seem rather a pity?"

Lance would have been like his father, to his friend's sense, had he had less humour, and like his mother had he had more beauty. Yet it was a good middle way, for Peter, that, in the modern manner, he was, to the eye, rather the young stock-broker than the young artist. The youth reasoned that it was a question of time—there was such a mill to go through, such an awful lot to learn. He had talked with fellows and had judged. "One has got, to-day," he said, "don't you see? to know."

His interlocutor, at this, gave a groan. "Oh, hang it, *don't* know!"

Lance wondered. " 'Don't'? Then what's the use——?"

"The use of what?"

"Why, of anything. Don't you think I've talent?"

Peter smoked away, for a little, in silence; then went on: "It isn't knowledge, it's ignorance that—as we've been beautifully told—is bliss."

"Don't you think I've talent?" Lance repeated.

Peter, with his trick of queer, kind demonstrations, passed his arm round his godson and held him a moment. "How do I know?"

"Oh," said the boy, "if it's your own ignorance you're defending——!"

Again, for a pause, on the sofa, his godfather smoked. "It isn't. I've the misfortune to be omniscient."

"Oh, well," Lance laughed again, "if you know *too* much——!"

"That's what I do, and why I'm so wretched."

Lance's gaiety grew. "Wretched? Come, I say!"

"But I forgot," his companion went on—"you're not to know about that. It would indeed, for you too, make the too much. Only I'll tell you what I'll do." And Peter got up from the sofa. "If you'll go up again, I'll pay your way at Cambridge."

Lance stared, a little rueful in spite of being still more amused. "Oh, Peter! You disapprove so of Paris?"

"Well, I'm afraid of it."

"Ah, I see."

"No, you don't see—yet. But you will—that is you would. And you mustn't."

The young man thought more gravely. "But one's innocence, already——"

"Is considerably damaged? Ah, that won't matter," Peter persisted—"we'll patch it up here."

"Here? Then you want me to stay at home?"

Peter almost confessed to it. "Well, we're so right—we four together—just as we are. We're so safe. Come, don't spoil it."

The boy, who had turned to gravity, turned from this, on the real pressure in his friend's tone, to consternation. "Then what's a fellow to be?"

"My particular care. Come, old man"—and Peter now fairly pleaded—"*I'll* look out for you."

Lance, who had remained on the sofa with his legs out and his hands in his pockets, watched him with eyes that showed suspicion. Then he got up. "You think there's something the matter with me—that I can't make a success."

"Well, what do you call a success?"

Lance thought again. "Why, the best sort, I suppose, is to please one's self. Isn't that the sort that, in spite of cabals and things, is—in his own peculiar line—the Master's?"

There were so much too many things in this question to be answered at once that they practically checked the discussion, which became particularly difficult in the light of such renewed proof that, though the young man's innocence might, in the course of his studies, as he contended, somewhat have shrunken, the finer essence of it still remained. That was indeed exactly what Peter had assumed and what, above all, he desired; yet, perversely enough, it gave him a chill. The boy believed in the cabals and things, believed in the peculiar line, believed, in short, in the Master. What happened a month or two later was not that he went up again at the expense of his godfather, but that a fortnight after he had got settled in Paris, this personage sent him fifty pounds.

He had meanwhile, at home, this personage, made up his mind to the worst; and what it might be had never yet grown quite so vivid to him as when, on his presenting himself one Sunday night, as he never failed to do, for supper, the mistress of Carrara Lodge met him with an appeal as to—of all

things in the world—the wealth of the Canadians. She was
earnest, she was even excited. "Are many of them *really*
rich?"

He had to confess that he knew nothing about them, but
he often thought afterwards of that evening. The room in
which they sat was adorned with sundry specimens of the
Master's genius, which had the merit of being, as Mrs Mallow
herself frequently suggested, of an unusually convenient size.
They were indeed of dimensions not customary in the pro-
ducts of the chisel and had the singularity that, if the objects
and features intended to be small looked too large, the objects
and features intended to be large looked too small. The
Master's intention, whether in respect to this matter or to any
other, had, in almost any case, even after years, remained
undiscoverable to Peter Brench. The creations that so failed
to reveal it stood about on pedestals and brackets, on tables
and shelves, a little staring white population, heroic, idyllic,
allegoric, mythic, symbolic, in which "scale" had so strayed
and lost itself that the public square and the chimney-piece
seemed to have changed places, the monumental being all
diminutive and the diminutive all monumental; branches, at
any rate, markedly, of a family in which stature was rather
oddly irrespective of function, age and sex. They formed, like
the Mallows themselves, poor Brench's own family—having
at least, to such a degree, the note of familiarity. The occasion
was one of those he had long ago learnt to know and to name
—short flickers of the faint flame, soft gusts of a kinder air.
Twice a year, regularly, the Master believed in his fortune, in
addition to believing all the year round in his genius. This
time it was to be made by a bereaved couple from Toronto,
who had given him the handsomest order for a tomb to three
lost children, each of whom they desired to be, in the composition, emblematically and characteristically represented.

Such was naturally the moral of Mrs Mallow's question:
if their wealth was to be assumed, it was clear, from the nature

of their admiration, as well as from mysterious hints thrown out (they were a little odd!) as to other possibilities of the same mortuary sort, that their further patronage might be; and not less evident that, should the Master become at all known in those climes, nothing would be more inevitable than a run of Canadian custom. Peter had been present before at runs of custom, colonial and domestic—present at each of those of which the aggregation had left so few gaps in the marble company round him; but it was his habit never, at these junctures, to prick the bubble in advance. The fond illusion, while it lasted, eased the wound of elections never won, the long ache of medals and diplomas carried off, on every chance, by every one but the Master; it lighted the lamp, moreover, that would glimmer through the next eclipse. They lived, however, after all—as it was always beautiful to see—at a height scarce susceptible of ups and downs. They strained a point, at times, charmingly, to admit that the public was, here and there, not too bad to buy; but they would have been nowhere without their attitude that the Master was always too good to sell. They were, at all events, deliciously formed, Peter often said to himself, for their fate; the Master had a vanity, his wife had a loyalty, of which success, depriving these things of innocence, would have diminished the merit and the grace. Any one could be charming under a charm, and, as he looked about him at a world of prosperity more void of proportion even than the Master's museum, he wondered if he knew another pair that so completely escaped vulgarity.

"What a pity Lance isn't with us to rejoice!" Mrs Mallow on this occasion sighed at supper.

"We'll drink to the health of the absent," her husband replied, filling his friend's glass and his own and giving a drop to their companion; "but we must hope that he's preparing himself for a happiness much less like this of ours this evening—excusable as I grant it to be!—than like the comfort we have always—whatever has happened or has not happened

—been able to trust ourselves to enjoy. The comfort," the
Master explained, leaning back in the pleasant lamplight and
firelight, holding up his glass and looking round at his marble
family, quartered more or less, a monstrous brood, in every
room—"the comfort of art in itself!"

Peter looked a little shyly at his wine. "Well—I don't care
what you may call it when a fellow doesn't—but Lance must
learn to *sell*, you know. I drink to his acquisition of the secret
of a base popularity!"

"Oh yes, *he* must sell," the boy's mother, who was still
more, however, this seemed to give out, the Master's wife,
rather artlessly conceded.

"Oh," the sculptor, after a moment, confidently pronounced, "Lance *will*. Don't be afraid. He will have learnt."

"Which is exactly what Peter," Mrs Mallow gaily returned
—"why in the world were you so perverse, Peter?—
wouldn't, when he told him, hear of."

Peter, when this lady looked at him with accusatory affection—a grace, on her part, not infrequent—could never find
a word; but the Master, who was always all amenity and tact,
helped him out now as he had often helped him before.
"That's his old idea, you know—on which we've so often
differed: his theory that the artist should be all impulse and
instinct. *I* go in, of course, for a certain amount of school.
Not too much—but a due proportion. There's where his
protest came in," he continued to explain to his wife, "as
against what *might*, don't you see? be in question for Lance."

"Ah, well"—and Mrs Mallow turned the violet eyes across
the table at the subject of this discourse—"he's sure to have
meant, of course, nothing but good; but that wouldn't have
prevented him, if Lance *had* taken his advice, from being, in
effect, horribly cruel."

They had a sociable way of talking of him to his face as if
he had been in the clay or—at most—in the plaster, and the
Master was unfailingly generous. He might have been waving

Egidio to make him revolve. "Ah, but poor Peter was not so wrong as to what it may, after all, come to that he *will* learn."

"Oh, but nothing artistically bad," she urged—still, for poor Peter, arch and dewy.

"Why, just the little French tricks," said the Master: on which their friend had to pretend to admit, when pressed by Mrs Mallow, that these æsthetic vices had been the objects of his dread.

III

"I KNOW now," Lance said to him the next year, "why you were so much against it." He had come back, supposedly for a mere interval, and was looking about him at Carrara Lodge, where indeed he had already, on two or three occasions, since his expatriation, briefly appeared. This had the air of a longer holiday. "Something rather awful has happened to me. It *isn't* so very good to know."

"I'm bound to say high spirits don't show in your face," Peter was rather ruefully forced to confess. "Still, are you very sure you do know?"

"Well, I at least know about as much as I can bear." These remarks were exchanged in Peter's den, and the young man, smoking cigarettes, stood before the fire with his back against the mantel. Something of his bloom seemed really to have left him.

Poor Peter wondered. "You're clear then as to what in particular I wanted you not to go for?"

"In particular?" Lance thought. "It seems to me that, in particular, there can have been but one thing."

They stood for a little sounding each other. "Are you quite sure?"

"Quite sure I'm a beastly duffer? Quite—by this time."

"Oh!"—and Peter turned away as if almost with relief.

"It's *that* that isn't pleasant to find out."

"Oh, I don't care for 'that,' " said Peter, presently coming round again. "I mean I personally don't."

"Yet I hope you can understand a little that I myself should!"

"Well, what do you mean by it?" Peter sceptically asked.

And on this Lance had to explain—how the upshot of his studies in Paris had inexorably proved a mere deep doubt of his means. These studies had waked him up, and a new light was in his eyes; but what the new light did was really to show him too much. "Do you know what's the matter with me? I'm too horribly intelligent. Paris was really the last place for me. I've learnt what I can't do."

Poor Peter stared—it was a staggerer; but even after they had had, on the subject, a longish talk in which the boy brought out to the full the hard truth of his lesson, his friend betrayed less pleasure than usually breaks into a face to the happy tune of "I told you so!" Poor Peter himself made now indeed so little a point of having told him so that Lance broke ground in a different place a day or two after. "What was it then that—before I went—you were afraid I should find out?" This, however, Peter refused to tell him—on the ground that if he hadn't yet guessed perhaps he never would, and that nothing at all, for either of them, in any case, was to be gained by giving the thing a name. Lance eyed him, on this, an instant, with the bold curiosity of youth—with the air indeed of having in his mind two or three names, of which one or other would be right. Peter, nevertheless, turning his back again, offered no encouragement, and when they parted afresh it was with some show of impatience on the side of the boy. Accordingly, at their next encounter, Peter saw at a glance that he had now, in the interval, divined and that, to sound his note, he was only waiting till they should find themselves alone. This he had soon arranged, and he then broke straight out. "Do you know your conundrum has been keeping me awake? But in the watches of the night the answer came over me—so that, upon my honour, I quite laughed out. Had you been supposing I had to go to Paris to learn *that?*" Even now, to see him still so sublimely on his guard, Peter's young friend had to laugh afresh. "You won't give a sign till you're sure? Beautiful old Peter!" But Lance at last produced it. "Why, hang it, the truth about the Master."

It made between them, for some minutes, a lively passage, full of wonder, for each, at the wonder of the other. "Then how long have you understood——"

"The true value of his work? I understood it," Lance recalled, "as soon as I began to understand anything. But I didn't begin fully to do that, I admit, till I got *là-bas.*"

"Dear, dear!"—Peter gasped with retrospective dread.

"But for what have you taken me? I'm a hopeless muff—that I *had* to have rubbed in. But I'm not such a muff as the Master!" Lance declared.

"Then why did you never tell me——?"

"That I hadn't, after all"—the boy took him up—"remained such an idiot? Just because I never dreamed *you* knew. But I beg your pardon. I only wanted to spare you. And what I don't now understand is how the deuce then, for so long, you've managed to keep bottled."

Peter produced his explanation, but only after some delay and with a gravity not void of embarrassment. "It was for your mother."

"Oh!" said Lance.

"And that's the great thing now—since the murder *is* out. I want a promise from you. I mean"—and Peter almost feverishly followed it up—"a vow from you, solemn and such as you owe me, here on the spot, that you'll sacrifice anything rather than let her ever guess——"

"That *I've* guessed?"—Lance took it in. "I see." He evidently, after a moment, had taken in much. "But what is it you have in mind that I may have a chance to sacrifice?"

"Oh, one has always something."

Lance looked at him hard. "Do you mean that *you've* had——?" The look he received back, however, so put the question by that he found soon enough another. "Are you really sure my mother doesn't know?"

Peter, after renewed reflection, was really sure. "If she does, she's too wonderful."

"But aren't we all too wonderful?"

"Yes," Peter granted—"but in different ways. The thing's so desperately important because your father's little public consists only, as you know then," Peter developed—"well, of how many?"

"First of all," the Master's son risked, "of himself. And last of all too. I don't quite see of whom else."

Peter had an approach to impatience. "Of your mother, I say—*always.*"

Lance cast it all up. "You absolutely feel that?"

"Absolutely."

"Well then, with yourself, that makes three."

"Oh, *me*!"—and Peter, with a wag of his kind old head, modestly excused himself. "The number is, at any rate, small enough for any individual dropping out to be too dreadfully missed. Therefore, to put it in a nutshell, take care, my boy— that's all—that *you're* not!"

"I've got to keep on humbugging?" Lance sighed.

"It's just to warn you of the danger of your failing of that that I've seized this opportunity."

"And what do you regard in particular," the young man asked, "as the danger?"

"Why, this certainty: that the moment your mother, who feels so strongly, should suspect your secret—well," said Peter desperately, "the fat would be on the fire."

Lance, for a moment, seemed to stare at the blaze. "She'd throw me over?"

"She'd throw *him* over."

"And come round to us?"

Peter, before he answered, turned away. "Come round to *you*." But he had said enough to indicate—and, as he evidently trusted, to avert—the horrid contingency.

IV

WITHIN six months again, however, his fear was, on more occasions than one, all before him. Lance had returned to Paris, to another trial; then had reappeared at home and had had, with his father, for the first time in his life, one of the scenes that strike sparks. He described it with much expression to Peter, as to whom—since they had never done so before—it was a sign of a new reserve on the part of the pair at Carrara Lodge that they at present failed, on a matter of intimate interest, to open themselves—if not in joy, then in sorrow—to their good friend. This produced perhaps, practically, between the parties, a shade of alienation and a slight intermission of commerce—marked mainly indeed by the fact that, to talk at his ease with his old playmate, Lance had, in general, to come to see him. The closest, if not quite the gayest relation they had yet known together was thus ushered in. The difficulty for poor Lance was a tension at home, begotten by the fact that his father wished him to be, at least, the sort of success he himself had been. He hadn't "chucked" Paris—though nothing appeared more vivid to him than that Paris had chucked him; he would go back again because of the fascination in trying, in seeing, in sounding the depths—in learning one's lesson, in fine, even if the lesson were simply that of one's impotence in the presence of one's larger vision. But what did the Master, all aloft in his senseless fluency, know of impotence, and what vision—to be called such—

had he, in all his blind life, ever had? Lance, heated and indignant, frankly appealed to his godparent on this score.

His father, it appeared, had come down on him for having,
after so long, nothing to show, and hoped that, on his next
return, this deficiency would be repaired. *The* thing, the
Master complacently set forth was—for any artist, however
inferior to himself—at least to "do" something. "What can
you do? That's all I ask!" *He* had certainly done enough,
and there was no mistake about what he had to show. Lance
had tears in his eyes when it came thus to letting his old friend
know how great the strain might be on the "sacrifice" asked
of him. It wasn't so easy to continue humbugging—as from
son to parent—after feeling one's self despised for not grovel-
ling in mediocrity. Yet a noble duplicity was what, as they
intimately faced the situation, Peter went on requiring; and it
was still, for a time, what his young friend, bitter and sore,
managed loyally to comfort him with. Fifty pounds, more
than once again, it was true, rewarded, both in London and in
Paris, the young friend's loyalty; none the less sensibly,
doubtless, at the moment, that the money was a direct advance
on a decent sum for which Peter had long since privately
prearranged an ultimate function. Whether by these arts or
others, at all events, Lance's just resentment was kept for a
season—but only for a season—at bay. The day arrived when
he warned his companion that he could hold out—or hold in
—no longer. Carrara Lodge had had to listen to another
lecture delivered from a great height—an infliction really
heavier, at last, than, without striking back or in some way
letting the Master have the truth, flesh and blood could bear.

"And what I don't see is," Lance observed with a certain
irritated eye for what was, after all, if it came to that, due to
himself too—"What I don't see is, upon my honour, how
you, as things are going, can keep the game up."

"Oh, the game for me is only to hold my tongue," said
placid Peter. "And I have my reason."

"Still my mother?"

Peter showed, as he had often shown it before—that is by turning it straight away—a queer face. "What will you have? I haven't ceased to like her."

"She's beautiful—she's a dear, of course," Lance granted; "but what is she to you, after all, and what is it to you that, as to anything whatever, she should or she shouldn't?"

Peter, who had turned red, hung fire a little. "Well—it's all, simply, what I make of it."

There was now, however, in his young friend, a strange, an adopted, insistence. "What are you, after all, to *her*?"

"Oh, nothing. But that's another matter."

"She cares only for my father," said Lance the Parisian.

"Naturally—and that's just why."

"Why you've wished to spare her?"

"Because she cares so tremendously much."

Lance took a turn about the room, but with his eyes still on his host. "How awfully—always—you must have liked her!"

"Awfully. Always," said Peter Brench.

The young man continued for a moment to muse—then stopped again in front of him. "Do you know how much she cares?" Their eyes met on it, but Peter, as if his own found something new in Lance's, appeared to hesitate, for the first time for so long, to say he did know. "*I've* only just found out," said Lance. "She came to my room last night, after being present, in silence and only with her eyes on me, at what I had had to take from him; she came—and she was with me an extraordinary hour."

He had paused again, and they had again for a while sounded each other. Then something—and it made him suddenly turn pale—came to Peter. "She *does* know?"

"She does know. She let it all out to me—so as to demand of me no more than that, as she said, of which she herself had been capable. She has always, always known," said Lance without pity.

Peter was silent a long time; during which his companion might have heard him gently breathe and, on touching him, might have felt within him the vibration of a long, low sound suppressed. By the time he spoke, at last, he had taken everything in. "Then I do see how tremendously much."

"Isn't it wonderful?" Lance asked.

"Wonderful," Peter mused.

"So that if your original effort to keep me from Paris was to keep me from knowledge——!" Lance exclaimed as if with a sufficient indication of this futility.

It might have been at the futility that Peter appeared for a little to gaze. "I think it must have been—without my quite at the time knowing it—to keep *me*!" he replied at last as he turned away.

THE ABASEMENT OF THE
NORTHMORES

I

WHEN Lord Northmore died public reference to the event took for the most part rather a ponderous and embarrassed form. A great political figure had passed away. A great light of our time had been quenched in mid-career. A great usefulness had somewhat anticipated its term, though a great part, none the less, had been signally played. The note of greatness, all along the line, kept sounding, in short, by a force of its own, and the image of the departed evidently lent itself with ease to figures and flourishes, the poetry of the daily press. The newspapers and their purchasers equally did their duty by it —arranged it neatly and impressively, though perhaps with a hand a little violently expeditious, upon the funeral car, saw the conveyance properly down the avenue, and then, finding the subject suddenly quite exhausted, proceeded to the next item on their list. His lordship had been a person, in fact, in connection with whom there was almost nothing but the fine monotony of his success to mention. This success had been his profession, his means as well as his end; so that his career admitted of no other description and demanded, indeed suffered, no further analysis. He had made politics, he had made literature, he had made land, he had made a bad manner and a great many mistakes, he had made a gaunt, foolish wife, two extravagant sons and four awkward daughters—he had made everything, as he *could* have made almost anything, thoroughly pay. There had been something deep down in him that did it, and his old friend Warren Hope, the person knowing him earliest and probably, on the whole, best, had never, even to the last, for curiosity, quite made out what it was. The secret was one that this distinctly distanced competitor had in fact mastered as little for intellectual relief as for emulous use; and there was quite a kind of tribute to it in the way that, the night before the obsequies and addressing himself to his wife, he said after some silent thought: "Hang it, you know, I must see the old boy through. I must go to the grave."

Mrs Hope looked at her husband at first in anxious silence. "I've no patience with you. You're much more ill than _he_ ever was."

"Ah, but if that qualifies me but for the funerals of others——!"

"It qualifies you to break my heart by your exaggerated chivalry, your renewed refusal to consider your interests. You sacrificed them to him, for thirty years, again and again, and from this supreme sacrifice—possibly that of your life—you might, in your condition, I think, be absolved." She indeed lost patience. "To the grave—in this weather—after his treatment of you!"

"My dear girl," Hope replied, "his treatment of me is a figment of your ingenious mind—your too-passionate, your beautiful loyalty. Loyalty, I mean, to _me_."

"I certainly leave it to you," she declared, "to have any to _him_!"

"Well, he was, after all, one's oldest, one's earliest friend. I'm not in such bad case—I do go out; and I want to do the decent thing. The fact remains that we never broke—we always kept together."

"Yes indeed," she laughed in her bitterness, "he always took care of that! He never recognised you, but he never let you go. You kept him up, and he kept you down. He used you, to the last drop he could squeeze, and left you the only one to wonder, in your incredible idealism and your incorrigible modesty, how on earth such an idiot made his way. He

made his way on your back. You put it candidly to others—
'What in the world was his gift?' And others are such gaping
idiots that they too haven't the least idea. *You* were his gift!'"

"And you're mine, my dear!" her husband, pressing her to
him, more resignedly laughed. He went down the next day
by "special" to the interment, which took place on the great
man's own property, in the great man's own church. But he
went alone—that is in a numerous and distinguished party,
the flower of the unanimous, gregarious demonstration; his
wife had no wish to accompany him, though she was anxious
while he was absent. She passed the time uneasily, watching
the weather and fearing the cold; she roamed from room to
room, pausing vaguely at dull windows, and before he came
back she had thought of many things. It was as if, while he
saw the great man buried, she also, by herself, in the contracted home of their later years, stood before an open grave.
She lowered into it, with her weak hands, the heavy past and
all their common dead dreams and accumulated ashes. The
pomp surrounding Lord Northmore's extinction made her
feel more than ever that it was not Warren who had made
anything pay. He had been always what he was still, the
cleverest man and the hardest worker she knew; but what was
there, at fifty-seven, as the vulgar said, to "show" for it all
but his wasted genius, his ruined health and his paltry pension? It was the term of comparison conveniently given her
by his happy rival's now foreshortened splendour that fixed
these things in her eye. It was as happy rivals to their own
flat union that she always had thought of the Northmore pair;
the two men, at least, having started together, after the
University, shoulder to shoulder and with—superficially
speaking—much the same outfit of preparation, ambition and
opportunity. They had begun at the same point and wanting
the same things—only wanting them in such different ways.
Well, the dead man had wanted them in the way that got
them; had got too, in his peerage, for instance, those Warren

had never wanted: there was nothing else to be said. There was nothing else, and yet, in her sombre, her strangely apprehensive solitude at this hour, she said much more than I can tell. It all came to this—that there had been, somewhere and somehow, a wrong. Warren was the one who should have succeeded. But she was the one person who knew it now, the single other person having descended, with *his* knowledge, to the tomb.

She sat there, she roamed there, in the waiting greyness of her small London house, with a deepened sense of the several odd knowledges that had flourished in their company of three. Warren had always known everything and, with his easy power—in nothing so high as for indifference—had never cared. John Northmore had known, for he had, years and years before, told her so; and thus had had a reason the more—in addition to not believing her stupid—for guessing at her view. She lived back; she lived it over; she had it all there in her hand. John Northmore had known her first, and how he had wanted to marry her the fat little bundle of his love-letters still survived to tell. He had introduced Warren Hope to her—quite by accident and because, at the time they had chambers together, he couldn't help it: that was the one thing he *had* done for them. Thinking of it now, she perhaps saw how much he might conscientiously have considered that it disburdened him of more. Six months later she had accepted Warren, and for just the reason the absence of which had determined her treatment of his friend. She had believed in his future. She held that John Northmore had never afterwards remitted the effort to ascertain the degree in which she felt herself "sold." But, thank God, she had never shown him.

Her husband came home with a chill, and she put him straight to bed. For a week, as she hovered near him, they only looked deep things at each other; the point was too quickly passed at which she could bearably have said "I told you so!" That his late patron should never have had difficulty in making *him* pay was certainly no marvel. But it was indeed a little too much, after all, that he should have made him pay with his life. This was what it had come to— she was sure, now, from the first. Congestion of the lungs, that night, declared itself, and on the morrow, sickeningly, she was face to face with pneumonia. It was more than—with all that had gone before—they could meet. Warren Hope ten days later succumbed. Tenderly, divinely as he loved her, she felt his surrender, through all the anguish, as an unspeakable part of the sublimity of indifference into which his hapless history had finally flowered. "His easy power, his easy power!"—her passion had never yet found such relief in that simple, secret phrase for him. He was so proud, so fine and so flexible, that to fail a little had been as bad for him as to fail much; therefore he had opened the flood-gates wide— had thrown, as the saying was, the helve after the hatchet. He had amused himself with seeing what the devouring world would take. Well, it had taken all.

II

BUT it was after he had gone that his name showed as written in water. What had he left? He had only left *her* and her grey desolation, her lonely piety and her sore, unresting rebellion. Sometimes, when a man died, it did something for him that life had not done; people, after a little, on one side or the other, discovered and named him, annexing him to their flag. But the sense of having lost Warren Hope appeared not in the least to have quickened the world's wit; the sharper pang for his widow indeed sprang just from the commonplace way in which he was spoken of as known. She received letters enough, when it came to that, for of course, personally, he had been liked; the newspapers were fairly copious and perfectly stupid; the three or four societies, "learned" and other, to which he had belonged, passed resolutions of regret and condolence, and the three or four colleagues about whom he himself used to be most amusing stammered eulogies; but almost anything, really, would have been better for her than the general understanding that the occasion had been met. Two or three solemn noodles in "administrative circles" wrote her that she must have been gratified at the unanimity of regret, the implication being clearly that she was ridiculous if she were not. Meanwhile what she felt was that she could have borne well enough his not being noticed at all; what she couldn't bear was this treatment of him as a minor celebrity. He was, in economics, in the higher politics, in philosophic history, a splendid unestimated genius, or he was nothing. He wasn't, at any rate—heaven forbid!—a "notable figure." The waters, none the less, closed over him as over Lord Northmore; which was precisely, as time went on, the fact she found it hardest to accept. That personage, the week after his death, without an hour of reprieve, the place swept as clean of him as a hall, lent for a charity, of the tables and booths of a three-days' bazaar—that personage had gone straight to the bottom, dropped like a crumpled circular into the wastebasket. Where then was the difference?—if the end *was* the end for each alike? For Warren it should have been properly the beginning.

During the first six months she wondered what she could herself do, and had much of the time the sense of walking by some swift stream on which an object dear to her was floating out to sea. All her instinct was to keep up with it, not to lose sight of it, to hurry along the bank and reach in advance some point from which she could stretch forth and catch and save it. Alas, it only floated and floated; she held it in sight, for the stream was long, but no convenient projection offered itself to the rescue. She ran, she watched, she lived with her great fear; and all the while, as the distance to the sea diminished, the current visibly increased. At the last, to do anything, she must hurry. She went into his papers, she ransacked his drawers; something of that sort, at least, she might do. But there were difficulties, the case was special; she lost herself in the labyrinth, and her competence was questioned; two or three friends to whose judgment she appealed struck her as tepid, even as cold, and publishers, when sounded—most of all in fact the house through which his three or four important volumes had been given to the world—showed an absence of eagerness for a collection of literary remains. It was only now that she fully understood how remarkably little the three or four important volumes had "done." He had successfully kept that from her, as he had kept other things she might have ached at: to handle his notes and memoranda was to come at every turn, in the wilderness, the wide desert, upon the footsteps of his scrupulous soul. But she had at last to accept the truth that it was only for herself, her own relief, she must follow him. His work, unencouraged and interrupted, failed of a final form: there would have been nothing to offer but fragments of fragments. She felt, all the same, in recognising this, that she abandoned him; he died for her at that hour over again.

The hour moreover happened to coincide with another hour, so that the two mingled their bitterness. She received a note from Lady Northmore, announcing a desire to gather in and publish his late lordship's letters, so numerous and so interesting, and inviting Mrs Hope, as a more than probable depositary, to be so good as to contribute to the project those addressed to her husband. This gave her a start of more kinds than one. The long comedy of his late lordship's greatness was *not* then over? The monument was to be built to him that she had but now schooled herself to regard as impossible for his defeated friend? Everything was to break out afresh, the comparisons, the contrasts, the conclusions so invidiously in his favour?—the business all cleverly managed to place him in the light and keep every one else in the shade? Letters?—had John Northmore indited three lines that could, at that time of day, be of the smallest consequence? Whose idea was such a publication, and what infatuated editorial patronage could the family have secured? She of course didn't know, but she should be surprised if there were material. Then it came to her, on reflection, that editors and publishers must of course have flocked—his star would still rule. Why shouldn't he make his letters pay in death as he had made them pay in life? Such as they were they *had* paid. They would be a tremendous success. She thought again of her husband's rich, confused relics— thought of the loose blocks of marble that could only lie now where they had fallen; after which, with one of her deep and frequent sighs, she took up anew Lady Northmore's communication.

His letters to Warren, kept or not kept, had never so much as occurred to her. Those to herself were buried and safe— she knew where her hand would find them; but those to herself her correspondent had carefully not asked for and was probably unaware of the existence of. They belonged more- over to that phase of the great man's career that was dis- tinctly—as it could only be called—previous: previous to the greatness, to the proper subject of the volume, and, in especial, to Lady Northmore. The faded fat packet lurked still where it had lurked for years; but she could no more to-day have said why she had kept it than why—though he knew of the early episode—she had never mentioned her preservation of it to Warren. This last circumstance certainly absolved her from mentioning it to Lady Northmore, who, no doubt, knew of the episode too. The odd part of the matter was, at any rate, that her retention of these documents had not been an accident. She had obeyed a dim instinct or a vague calcula- tion. A calculation of what? She couldn't have told: it had operated, at the back of her head, simply as a sense that, not destroyed, the complete little collection made for safety. But for whose, just heaven? Perhaps she should still see; though nothing, she trusted, would occur requiring her to touch the things or to read them over. She wouldn't have touched them or read them over for the world.

She had not as yet, at all events, overhauled those receptacles in which the letters Warren kept would have accumulated; and she had her doubts of their containing any of Lord Northmore's. Why should he have kept any? Even she herself had had more reasons. Was his lordship's later epistolary manner supposed to be good, or of the kind that, on any grounds, prohibited the waste-basket or the fire? Warren had lived in a deluge of documents, but these perhaps he might have regarded as contributions to contemporary history. None the less, surely, he wouldn't have stored up many. She began to look, in cupboards, boxes, drawers yet unvisited, and she had her surprises both as to what he had kept and as to what he hadn't. Every word of her own was there—every note that, in occasional absence, he had ever had from her. Well, that matched happily enough her knowing just where to put her finger on every note that, on such occasions, she herself had received. *Their* correspondence at least was complete. But so, in fine, on one side, it gradually appeared, was Lord Northmore's. The superabundance of these missives had not been sacrificed by her husband, evidently, to any passing convenience; she judged more and more that he had preserved every scrap; and she was unable to conceal from herself that she was—she scarce knew why—a trifle disappointed. She had not quite unhopefully, even though vaguely, seen herself writing to Lady Northmore that, to her great regret and after an exhausting search, she could find nothing at all.

She found, alas, in fact, everything. She was conscientious and she hunted to the end, by which time one of the tables quite groaned with the fruits of her quest. The letters appeared moreover to have been cared for and roughly classified—she should be able to consign them to the family in excellent order. She made sure, at the last, that she had overlooked nothing, and then, fatigued and distinctly irritated, she prepared to answer in a sense so different from the answer she had, as might have been said, planned. Face to face with her note, however, she found she couldn't write it; and, not to be alone longer with the pile on the table, she presently went out of the room. Late in the evening—just before going to bed—she came back, almost as if she hoped there might have been since the afternoon some pleasant intervention in the interest of her distaste. Mightn't it have magically happened that her discovery was a mistake?—that the letters were either not there or were, after all, somebody's else? Ah, they *were* there, and as she raised her lighted candle in the dusk the pile on the table squared itself with insolence. On this, poor lady, she had for an hour her temptation.

It was obscure, it was absurd; all that could be said of it was that it was, for the moment, extreme. She saw herself, as she circled round the table, writing with perfect impunity: "Dear Lady Northmore, I have hunted high and low and have found nothing whatever. My husband evidently, before his death, destroyed everything. I'm *so* sorry—I should have liked so much to help you. Yours most truly." She should have only, on the morrow, privately and resolutely to annihilate the heap, and those words would remain an account of the matter that nobody was in a position to challenge. What good it would do her?—was *that* the question? It would do her the good that it would make poor Warren seem to have been just a little less used and duped. This, in her mood, would ease her off. Well, the temptation was real; but so, she after a while felt, were other things. She sat down at midnight to her note. "Dear Lady Northmore, I am happy to say I have found a great deal—my husband appears to have been so careful to keep everything. I have a mass at your disposition if you can conveniently send. So glad to be able to help your work.

Yours most truly." She stepped out as she was and dropped the letter into the nearest pillar-box. By noon the next day the table had, to her relief, been cleared. Her ladyship sent a responsible servant—her butler, in a four-wheeler, with a large japanned box.

III

AFTER this, for a twelvemonth, there were frequent announcements and allusions. They came to her from every side, and there were hours at which the air, to her imagination, contained almost nothing else. There had been, at an early stage, immediately after Lady Northmore's communication to her, an official appeal, a circular *urbi et orbi*, reproduced, applauded, commented in every newspaper, desiring all possessors of letters to remit them without delay to the family. The family, to do it justice, rewarded the sacrifice freely—so far as it was a reward to keep the world informed of the rapid progress of the work. Material had shown itself more copious than was to have been conceived. Interesting as the imminent volumes had naturally been expected to prove, those who had been favoured with a glimpse of their contents already felt warranted in promising the public an unprecedented treat. They would throw upon certain sides of the writer's mind and career lights hitherto unsuspected. Lady Northmore, deeply indebted for favours received, begged to renew her solicitation; gratifying as the response had been, it was believed that, particularly in connection with several dates, which were given, a residuum of buried treasure might still be looked for.

Mrs Hope saw, she felt, as time went on, fewer and fewer people; yet her circle was even now not too narrow for her to hear it blown about that Thompson and Johnson had "been asked." Conversation in the London world struck her for a time as almost confined to such questions and such answers. "Have *you* been asked?" "Oh yes—rather. Months ago. And you?" The whole place was under contribution, and the striking thing was that being asked had been clearly accompanied, in every case, with the ability to respond. The spring had but to be touched—millions of letters flew out. Ten volumes, at such a rate, Mrs Hope mused, would not exhaust the supply. She mused a great deal—did nothing but muse; and, strange as this may at first appear, it was inevitable that one of the final results of her musing should be a principle of doubt. It could only seem possible, in view of such unanimity, that she should, after all, have been mistaken. It *was* then, to the general sense, the great departed's, a reputation sound and safe. It wasn't he who had been at fault—it was her silly self, still burdened with the fallibility of Being. He had been a giant then, and the letters would triumphantly show it. She had looked only at the envelopes of those she had surrendered, but she was prepared for anything. There was the fact, not to be blinked, of Warren's own marked testimony. The attitude of others was but *his* attitude; and she sighed as she perceived him in this case, for the only time in his life, on the side of the chattering crowd.

She was perfectly aware that her obsession had run away with her, but as Lady Northmore's publication really loomed into view—it was now definitely announced for March, and they were in January—her pulses quickened so that she found herself, in the long nights, mostly lying awake. It was in one of these vigils that, suddenly, in the cold darkness, she felt the brush of almost the only thought that, for many a month, had not made her wince; the effect of which was that she bounded out of bed with a new felicity. Her impatience flashed, on the spot, up to its maximum—she could scarce wait for day to give herself to action. Her idea was neither more nor less than immediately to collect and put forth the letters of *her* hero.

She would publish her husband's own—glory be to God!—
and she even wasted none of her time in wondering why she
had waited. She *had* waited—all too long; yet it was perhaps
no more than natural that, for eyes sealed with tears and a
heart heavy with injustice, there should not have been an
instant vision of where her remedy lay. She thought of it
already as her remedy—though she would probably have
found an awkwardness in giving a name, publicly, to her
wrong. It was a wrong to feel, but not, doubtless, to talk
about. And lo, straightway, the balm had begun to drop: the
balance would so soon be even. She spent all that day in
reading over her own old letters, too intimate and too sacred
—oh, unluckily!—to figure in her project, but pouring wind,
nevertheless, into its sails and adding magnificence to her
presumption. She had of course, with separation, all their
years, never frequent and never prolonged, known her husband as a correspondent much less than others; still, these
relics constituted a property—she was surprised at their
number—and testified hugely to his inimitable gift.

He was a letter-writer if you liked—natural, witty, various,
vivid, playing, with the idlest, lightest hand, up and down the
whole scale. His easy power—his easy power: everything that
brought him back brought back that. The most numerous
were of course the earlier, and the series of those during their
engagement, witnesses of their long probation, which were
rich and unbroken; so full indeed and so wonderful that she
fairly groaned at having to defer to the common measure of
married modesty. There was discretion, there was usage, there
was taste; but she would fain have flown in their face. If
there were pages too intimate to publish, there were too many
others too rare to suppress. Perhaps after her death——! It
not only pulled her up, the happy thought of that liberation
alike for herself and for her treasure, making her promise
herself straightway to arrange: it quickened extremely her impatience for the term of her mortality, which would leave a

free field to the justice she invoked. Her great resource, however, clearly, would be the friends, the colleagues, the private admirers to whom he had written for years, to whom she had known him to write, and many of whose own letters, by no means remarkable, she had come upon in her recent sortings and siftings. She drew up a list of these persons and immediately wrote to them or, in cases in which they had passed away, to their widows, children, representatives; reminding herself in the process not disagreeably, in fact quite inspiringly, of Lady Northmore. It had struck her that Lady Northmore took, somehow, a good deal for granted; but this idea failed, oddly enough, to occur to her in regard to Mrs Hope. It was indeed with her ladyship she began, addressing her exactly in the terms of this personage's own appeal, every word of which she remembered.

Then she waited, but she had not, in connection with that quarter, to wait long. "Dear Mrs Hope, I have hunted high and low and have found nothing whatever. My husband evidently, before his death, destroyed everything. I'm so sorry —I should have liked so much to help you. Yours most truly." This was all Lady Northmore wrote, without the grace of an allusion to the assistance she herself had received; though even in the first flush of amazement and resentment our friend recognised the odd identity of form between her note and another that had never been written. She was answered as she had, in the like case, in her one evil hour, dreamed of answering. But the answer was not over with this—it had still to flow in, day after day, from every other source reached by her question. And day after day, while amazement and resentment deepened, it consisted simply of three lines of regret. Everybody had looked, and everybody had looked in vain. Everybody would have been so glad, but everybody was reduced to being, like Lady Northmore, so sorry. Nobody could find anything, and nothing, it was therefore to be gathered, had been kept. Some of these informants were more prompt than others, but all replied in time, and the business went on for a month, at the end of which the poor woman, stricken, chilled to the heart, accepted perforce her situation and turned her face to the wall. In this position, as it were, she remained for days, taking heed of nothing and only feeling and nursing her wound. It was a wound the more cruel for having found her so unguarded. From the moment her remedy had been whispered to her, she had not had an hour of doubt, and the beautiful side of it had seemed that it was, above all, so easy. The strangeness of the issue was even greater than the pain. Truly it was a world *pour rire*, the world in which John Northmore's letters were classed and labelled for posterity and Warren Hope's kindled fires. All sense, all measure of anything, could only leave one—leave one indifferent and dumb. There was nothing to be done—the show was upside-down. John Northmore was immortal and Warren Hope was damned. And for herself, she was finished. She was beaten. She leaned thus, motionless, muffled, for a time of which, as I say, she took no account; then at last she was reached by a great sound that made her turn her veiled head. It was the report of the appearance of Lady Northmore's volumes.

IV

THIS was a great noise indeed, and all the papers, that day, were particularly loud with it. It met the reader on the threshold, and the work was everywhere the subject of a "leader" as well as of a review. The reviews moreover, she saw at a glance, overflowed with quotation; it was enough to look at two or three sheets to judge of the enthusiasm. Mrs Hope looked at the two or three that, for confirmation of the single one she habitually received, she caused, while at breakfast, to be purchased; but her attention failed to penetrate further; she couldn't, she found, face the contrast between the pride of the Northmores on such a morning and her own humiliation. The papers brought it too sharply home; she pushed them away and, to get rid of them, not to feel their presence, left the house early. She found pretexts for remaining out; it was as if there had been a cup prescribed for her to drain, yet she could put off the hour of the ordeal. She filled the time as she might; bought things, in shops, for which she had no use, and called on friends for whom she had no taste. Most of her friends, at present, were reduced to that category, and she had to choose, for visits, the houses guiltless, as she might have said, of her husband's blood. She couldn't speak to the people who had answered in such dreadful terms her late circular; on the other hand the people out of its range were such as would also be stolidly unconscious of Lady Northmore's publication and from whom the sop of sympathy could be but circuitously extracted. As she had lunched at a pastrycook's, so she stopped out to tea, and the March dusk had fallen when she got home. The first thing she then saw in her lighted hall was a large neat package on the table; whereupon she knew before approaching it that Lady Northmore had sent her the book. It had arrived, she learned, just after her going out; so that, had she not done this, she might have spent the day with it. She now quite understood her prompt instinct of flight. Well, flight had helped her, and the touch of the great indifferent general life. She would at last face the music.

She faced it, after dinner, in her little closed drawing-room, unwrapping the two volumes—*The Public and Private Correspondence of the Right Honourable &c., &c.*—and looking well, first, at the great escutcheon on the purple cover and at the various portraits within, so numerous that wherever she opened she came on one. It had not been present to her before that he was so perpetually "sitting," but he figured in every phase and in every style, and the gallery was enriched with views of his successive residences, each one a little grander than the last. She had ever, in general, found that, in portraits, whether of the known or the unknown, the eyes seemed to seek and to meet her own; but John Northmore everywhere looked straight away from her, quite as if he had been in the room and were unconscious of acquaintance. The effect of this was, oddly enough, so sharp that at the end of ten minutes she found herself sinking into his text as if she had been a stranger and beholden, vulgarly and accidentally, to one of the libraries. She had been afraid to plunge, but from the moment she got in she was—to do every one, all round, justice—thoroughly held. She sat there late, and she made so many reflections and discoveries that as the only way to put it—she passed from mystification to stupefaction. Her own contribution had been almost exhaustively used; she had counted Warren's letters before sending them and perceived now that scarce a dozen were not all there—a circumstance explaining to her Lady Northmore's present. It was to these pages she had turned first, and it was as she hung over them that her stupefaction dawned. It took, in truth, at the outset, a particular form—the form of a sharpened wonder at Warren's unnatural piety. Her original surprise had been keen—when she had tried to take reasons for granted; but her original surprise was as nothing to her actual bewilderment. The letters to Warren had been practically, she judged, for the family, the great card; yet if the great card made only that figure, what on earth was one to think of the rest of the pack?

She pressed on, at random, with a sense of rising fever; she trembled, almost panting, not to be sure too soon; but wherever she turned she found the prodigy spread. The letters to Warren were an abyss of inanity; the others followed suit as they could; the book was surely then a sandy desert, the publication a theme for mirth. She so lost herself, as her perception of the scale of the mistake deepened, in uplifting visions, that when her parlour-maid, at eleven o'clock, opened the door she almost gave the start of guilt surprised. The girl, withdrawing for the night, had come but to say so, and her mistress, supremely wide-awake and with remembrance kindled, appealed to her, after a blank stare, with intensity. "What have you done with the papers?"

"The papers, ma'am?"

"All those of this morning—don't tell me you've destroyed them! Quick, quick—bring them back." The young woman, by a rare chance, had not destroyed them; she presently reappeared with them, neatly folded; and Mrs Hope, dismissing her with benedictions, had at last, in a few minutes, taken the time of day. She saw her impression portentously reflected in the public prints. It was not then the illusion of her jealousy— it was the triumph, unhoped for, of her justice. The reviewers observed a decorum, but, frankly, when one came to look, their stupefaction matched her own. What she had taken in the morning for enthusiasm proved mere perfunctory attention, unwarned in advance and seeking an issue for its mystification. The question was, if one liked, asked civilly, but it was asked, none the less, all round: "What *could* have made Lord Northmore's family take him for a letter-writer?" Pompous and ponderous, yet loose and obscure, he managed, by a trick of his own, to be both slipshod and stiff. Who, in such a case, had been primarily responsible, and under what strangely belated advice had a group of persons destitute of wit themselves been thus deplorably led thus astray? With fewer accomplices in the preparation, it might almost have been assumed that they had been dealt with by practical jokers.

They had at all events committed an error of which the most merciful thing to say was that, as founded on loyalty, it was touching. These things, in the welcome offered, lay perhaps not quite on the face, but they peeped between the lines and would force their way through on the morrow. The long quotations given were quotations marked Why?—"Why," in other words, as interpreted by Mrs Hope, "drag to light such helplessness of expression? why give the text of his dulness and the proof of his fatuity?" The victim of the error had certainly been, in his way and day, a useful and remarkable person, but almost any other evidence of the fact might more happily have been adduced. It rolled over her, as she paced her room in the small hours, that the wheel had come full circle. There was after all a rough justice. The monument that had over-darkened her was reared, but it would be within a week the opportunity of every humourist, the derision of intelligent London. Her husband's strange share in it continued, that night, between dreams and vigils, to puzzle her, but light broke with her final waking, which was comfortably late. She opened her eyes to it, and, as it stared straight into them, she greeted it with the first laugh that had for a long time passed her lips. How could she, idiotically, not have guessed? Warren, playing insidiously the part of a guardian, had done what he had done on purpose! He had acted to an end long foretasted, and the end—the full taste—had come.

V

It was after this, none the less—after the other organs of criticism, including the smoking-rooms of the clubs, the lobbies of the House and the dinner-tables of everywhere, had duly embodied their reserves and vented their irreverence, and the unfortunate two volumes had ranged themselves, beyond appeal, as a novelty insufficiently curious and prematurely stale—it was when this had come to pass that Mrs Hope really felt how beautiful her own chance would now have been and how sweet her revenge. The success of *her* volumes, for the inevitability of which nobody had had an instinct, would have been as great as the failure of Lady Northmore's, for the inevitability of which everybody had had one. She read over and over her letters and asked herself afresh if the confidence that had preserved *them* might not, at such a crisis, in spite of everything, justify itself. Did not the discredit to English wit, as it were, proceeding from the uncorrected attribution to an established public character of such mediocrity of thought and form, really demand, for that matter, some such redemptive stroke as the appearance of a collection of masterpieces gathered from a similar walk? To have such a collection under one's hand and yet sit and see one's self not use it was a torment through which she might well have feared to break down.

But there was another thing she might do, not redemptive indeed, but perhaps, after all, as matters were going, apposite. She fished out of their nook, after long years, the packet of John Northmore's epistles to herself, and, reading them over in the light of his later style, judged them to contain to the full the promise of that inimitability; felt that they would deepen the impression and that, in the way of the *inédit*, they constituted her supreme treasure. There was accordingly a terrible week for her in which she itched to put them forth. She composed mentally the preface, brief, sweet, ironic, representing her as prompted by an anxious sense of duty to a great reputation and acting upon the sight of laurels so lately gathered. There would naturally be difficulties; the documents were her own, but the family, bewildered, scared, suspicious, figured to her fancy as a dog with a dust-pan tied to its tail and ready for any dash to cover at the sound of the clatter of tin. They would have, she surmised, to be consulted, or, if not consulted, would put in an injunction; yet of the two courses, that of scandal braved for the man she had rejected drew her on, while the charm of this vision worked, still further than that of delicacy over-ridden for the man she had married.

The vision closed round her and she lingered on the idea— fed, as she handled again her faded fat packet, by re-perusals more richly convinced. She even took opinions as to the interference open to her old friend's relatives; took, in fact, from this time on, many opinions; went out anew, picked up old threads, repaired old ruptures, resumed, as it was called, her place in society. She had not been for years so seen of men as during the few weeks that followed the abasement of the Northmores. She called, in particular, on every one she had cast out after the failure of her appeal. Many of these persons figured as Lady Northmore's contributors, the unwitting agents of the unprecedented exposure; they having, it was sufficiently clear, acted in dense good faith. Warren, foreseeing and calculating, might have the benefit of such subtlety, but it was not for any one else. With every one else—for they did, on facing her, as she said to herself, look like fools—she made inordinately free; putting right and left the question of what, in the past years, they, or their progenitors, could have been thinking of. "What on earth had you in mind, and where, among you, were the rudiments of intelligence, when you burnt up my husband's priceless letters and clung as if for salvation to Lord Northmore's? You see how you have been saved!" The weak explanations, the imbecility, as she judged it, of the reasons given, were so much balm to her wound. The great balm, however, she kept to the last: she would go to see Lady Northmore only when she had exhausted all other comfort. That resource would be as supreme as the treasure of the fat packet. She finally went and, by a happy chance, if chance could ever be happy in such a house, was received. She remained half an hour—there were other persons present, and, on rising to go, felt that she was satisfied. She had taken in what she desired, had sounded what she saw; only, unexpectedly, something had overtaken her more absolute than the hard need she had obeyed or the vindictive advantage she had cherished. She had counted on herself for almost anything but for pity of these people, yet it was in pity that, at the end of ten minutes, she felt everything else dissolve.

They were suddenly, on the spot, transformed for her by the depth of their misfortune, and she saw them, the great Northmores, as—of all things—consciously weak and flat.

She neither made nor encountered an allusion to volumes published or frustrated; and so let her arranged inquiry die away that when, on separation, she kissed her wan sister in widowhood, it was not with the kiss of Judas. She had meant to ask lightly if she mightn't have *her* turn at editing; but the renunciation with which she re-entered her house had formed itself before she left the room. When she got home indeed she at first only wept—wept for the commonness of failure and the strangeness of life. Her tears perhaps brought her a sense of philosophy; it was all as broad as it was long. When they were spent, at all events, she took out for the last time the faded fat packet. Sitting down by a receptacle daily emptied for the benefit of the dustman, she destroyed, one by one, the gems of the collection in which each piece had been a gem. She tore up, to the last scrap, Lord Northmore's letters. It would never be known now, as regards this series, either that they had been hoarded or that they had been sacrificed. And she was content so to let it rest. On the following day she began another task. She took out her husband's and attacked the business of transcription. She copied them piously, tenderly, and, for the purpose to which she now found herself settled, judged almost no omissions imperative. By the time they should be published——! She shook her head, both knowingly and resignedly, as to criticism so remote. When her transcript was finished she sent it to a printer to set up, and then, after receiving and correcting proof, and with every precaution for secrecy, had a single copy struck off and the type, under her eyes, dispersed. Her last act but one—or rather perhaps but two—was to put these sheets, which, she was pleased to find, would form a volume of three hundred pages, carefully away. Her next was to add to her testamentary instrument a definite provision for the issue, after her death, of such a volume. Her last was to hope that death would come in time.

THE THIRD PERSON

I

WHEN, a few years since, two good ladies, previously not intimate nor indeed more than slightly acquainted, found themselves domiciled together in the small but ancient town of Marr, it was as a result, naturally, of special considerations. They bore the same name and were second cousins; but their paths had not hitherto crossed; there had not been coincidence of age to draw them together; and Miss Frush, the more mature, had spent much of her life abroad. She was a bland, shy, sketching person, whom fate had condemned to a monotony—triumphing over variety—of Swiss and Italian *pensions*; in any one of which, with her well-fastened hat, her gauntlets and her stout boots, her camp-stool, her sketch-book, her Tauchnitz novel, she would have served with peculiar propriety as a frontispiece to the natural history of the English old maid. She would have struck you indeed, poor Miss Frush, as so happy an instance of the type that you would perhaps scarce have been able to equip her with the dignity of the individual. This was what she enjoyed, however, for those brought nearer—a very insistent identity, once even of prettiness, but which now, blanched and bony, timid and inordinately queer, with its utterance all vague interjection and its aspect all eyeglass and teeth, might be acknowledged without inconvenience and deplored without reserve. Miss Amy, her kinswoman, who, ten years her junior, showed a different figure—such as, oddly enough, though formed almost wholly in English air, might have appeared much more to betray a foreign influence—Miss Amy was brown, brisk and expressive: when really young she had even been pronounced showy. She had an innocent vanity on the subject of her foot, a member which she somehow regarded as a guarantee of her wit, or at least of her good taste. Even had it not been pretty she flattered herself it would have been shod: she would never—no, never, like Susan—have given it up. Her bright brown eye was comparatively bold, and she had accepted Susan once for all as a frump. She even thought her, and silently deplored her as, a goose. But she was none the less herself a lamb.

They had benefited, this innocuous pair, under the will of an old aunt, a prodigiously ancient gentlewoman, of whom, in her later time, it had been given them, mainly by the office of others, to see almost nothing; so that the little property they came in for had the happy effect of a windfall. Each, at least, pretended to the other that she had never dreamed—as in truth there had been small encouragement for dreams in the sad character of what they now spoke of as the late lady's "dreadful *entourage*." Terrorised and deceived, as they considered, by her own people, Mrs Frush was scantily enough to have been counted on for an act of almost inspired justice. The good luck of her husband's nieces was that she had really outlived, for the most part, their ill-wishers and so, at the very last, had died without the blame of diverting fine Frush property from fine Frush use. Property quite of her own she had done as she liked with; but she had pitied poor expatriated Susan and had remembered poor unhusbanded Amy, though lumping them together perhaps a little roughly in her final provision. Her will directed that, should no other arrangement be more convenient to her executors, the old house at Marr might be sold for their joint advantage. What befell, however, in the event, was that the two legatees, advised in due course, took an early occasion—and quite without concert—to judge their prospects on the spot. They arrived at Marr, each on her own side, and they were so pleased with

Marr that they remained. So it was that they met: Miss Amy, accompanied by the office-boy of the local solicitor, presented herself at the door of the house to ask admittance of the caretaker. But when the door opened it offered to sight not the caretaker, but an unexpected, unexpecting lady in a very old waterproof, who held a long-handled eyeglass very much as a child holds a rattle. Miss Susan, already in the field, roaming, prying, meditating in the absence on an errand of the woman in charge, offered herself in this manner as in settled possession; and it was on that idea that, through the eyeglass, the cousins viewed each other with some penetration even before Amy came in. Then at last when Amy did come in it was not, any more than Susan, to go out again.

It would take us too far to imagine what might have happened had Mrs Frush made it a condition of her benevolence that the subjects of it should inhabit, should live at peace together, under the roof she left them; but certain it is that as they stood there they had at the same moment the same unprompted thought. Each became aware on the spot that the dear old house itself was exactly what she, and exactly what the other, wanted; it met in perfection their longing for a quiet harbour and an assured future; each, in short, was willing to take the other in order to get the house. It was therefore not sold; it was made, instead, their own, as it stood, with the dead lady's extremely "good" old appurtenances not only undisturbed and undivided, but piously reconstructed and infinitely admired, the agents of her testamentary purpose rejoicing meanwhile to see the business so simplified. They might have had their private doubts—or their wives might have; might cynically have predicted the sharpest of quarrels, before three months were out, between the deluded yoke-fellows, and the dissolution of the partnership with every circumstance of recrimination. All that need be said is that such prophets would have prophesied vulgarly. The Misses Frush were not vulgar; they had drunk deep of the cup of singleness and found it prevailingly bitter; they were not unacquainted with solitude and sadness, and they recognised with due humility the supreme opportunity of their lives. By the end of three months, moreover, each knew the worst about the other. Miss Amy took her evening nap before dinner, an hour at which Miss Susan could never sleep—it was so odd; whereby Miss Susan took hers after that meal, just at the hour when Miss Amy was keenest for talk. Miss Susan, erect and unsupported, had feelings as to the way in which, in almost any posture that could pass for a seated one, Miss Amy managed to find a place in the small of her back for two out of the three sofa-cushions—a smaller place, obviously, than they had ever been intended to fit.

But when this was said all was said; they continued to have, on either side, the pleasant consciousness of a personal soil, not devoid of fragmentary ruins, to dig in. They had a theory that their lives had been immensely different, and each appeared now to the other to have conducted her career so perversely only that she should have an unfamiliar range of anecdote for her companion's ear. Miss Susan, at foreign *pensions*, had met the Russian, the Polish, the Danish, and even an occasional flower of the English, nobility, as well as many of the most extraordinary Americans, who, as she said, had made everything of her and with whom she had remained, often, in correspondence; while Miss Amy, after all less conventional, at the end of long years of London, abounded in reminiscences of literary, artistic and even—Miss Susan heard it with bated breath—theatrical society, under the influence of which she had written—there, it came out!—a novel that had been anonymously published and a play that had been strikingly type-copied. Not the least charm, clearly, of this picturesque outlook at Marr would be the support that might be drawn from it for getting back, as she hinted, with "general society" bravely sacrificed, to "real work." She had in her head hundreds of plots—with which the future, accordingly, seemed to bristle for Miss Susan. The latter, on her side, was only waiting for the wind to go down to take up again her sketching. The wind at Marr was often high, as was natural in a little old huddled, red-roofed, historic south-coast town which had once been in a manner mistress, as the cousins reminded each other, of the "Channel," and from which, high and dry on its hilltop though it might be, the sea had not so far receded as not to give, constantly, a taste of temper. Miss Susan came back to English scenery with a small sigh of fondness to which the consciousness of Alps and Apennines only gave more of a quaver; she had picked out her subjects and, with her head on one side and a sense that they were easier abroad, sat sucking her water-colour brush and nervously—perhaps even a little inconsistently—waiting and hesitating. What had happened was that they had, each for herself, re-discovered the country; only Miss Amy, emergent from Bloomsbury lodgings, spoke of it as primroses and sunsets, and Miss Susan, rebounding from the Arno and the Reuss, called it, with a shy, synthetic pride, simply England.

The country was at any rate in the house with them as well as in the little green girdle and in the big blue belt. It was in the objects and relics that they handled together and wondered over, finding in them a ground for much inferred importance and invoked romance, stuffing large stories into very small openings and pulling every faded bell-rope that might jingle rustily into the past. They were still here in the presence, at all events, of their common ancestors, as to whom, more than ever before, they took only the best for granted. Was not the best, for that matter—the best, that is, of little melancholy, middling, disinherited Marr—seated in every stiff chair of the decent old house and stitched into the patchwork of every quaint old counterpane? Two hundred years of it squared themselves in the brown, panelled parlour, creaked patiently on the wide staircase and bloomed herbaceously in the red-walled garden. There was nothing any one had ever done or been at Marr that a Frush hadn't done it or been it. Yet they wanted more of a picture and talked themselves into the fancy of it; there were portraits—half a dozen, comparatively recent (they called 1800 comparatively recent,) and something of a trial to a descendant who had copied Titian at the Pitti; but they were curious of detail and would have liked to people a little more thickly their backward space, to set it up behind their chairs as a screen embossed with figures. They threw off theories and small imaginations, and almost conceived themselves engaged in researches; all of which made for pomp and circumstance. Their desire was to discover something, and, emboldened by the broader sweep of wing of her companion, Miss Susan herself was not afraid of discovering something bad. Miss Amy it was who had first remarked, as a warning, that this was what it might all lead to. It was she, moreover, to whom they owed the formula that, had anything *very* bad ever happened at Marr, they should be sorry if a Frush hadn't been in it. This was the moment at which Miss Susan's spirit had reached its highest point: she had declared, with her odd, breathless laugh, a prolonged, an alarmed or alarming gasp, that she should really be quite ashamed. And so they rested a while; not saying quite how far they were prepared to go in crime—not giving the matter a name. But there would have been little doubt for an observer that each supposed the other to mean that she not only didn't draw the line at murder, but stretched it so as to take in— well, gay deception. If Miss Susan could conceivably have asked whether Don Juan had ever touched at that port, Miss Amy would, to a certainty, have wanted to know by way of answer at what port he had *not* touched. It was only unfortunately true that no one of the portraits of gentlemen looked at all like him and no one of those of ladies suggested one of his victims.

At last, none the less, the cousins had a find, came upon a box of old odds and ends, mainly documentary; partly

printed matter, newspapers and pamphlets yellow and grey
with time, and, for the rest, epistolary—several packets of
letters, faded, scarce decipherable, but clearly sorted for preservation and tied, with sprigged ribbon of a far-away fashion,
into little groups. Marr, below ground, is solidly founded—
underlaid with great straddling cellars, sound and dry, that
are like the groined crypts of churches and that present themselves to the meagre modern conception as the treasure-
chambers of stout merchants and bankers in the old bustling
days. A recess in the thickness of one of the walls had yielded
up, on resolute investigation—that of the local youth em-
ployed for odd jobs and who had happened to explore in this
direction on his own account—a collection of rusty super-
fluities among which the small chest in question had been
dragged to light. It produced of course an instant impression
and figured as a discovery; though indeed as rather a deceptive one on its having, when forced open, nothing better to
show, at the best, than a quantity of rather illegible correspondence. The good ladies had naturally had for the moment
a fluttered hope of old golden guineas—a miser's hoard;
perhaps even of a hatful of those foreign coins of old-fashioned
romance, ducats, doubloons, pieces of eight, as are sometimes
found to have come to hiding, from over seas, in ancient
ports. But they had to accept their disappointment—which
they sought to do by making the best of the papers, by agree-
ing, in other words, to regard them as wonderful. Well, they
were, doubtless, wonderful; which didn't prevent them, however, from appearing to be, on superficial inspection, also
rather a weary labyrinth. Baffling, at any rate, to Miss Susan's
unpractised eyes, the little pale-ribboned packets were, for
several evenings, round the fire, while she luxuriously dozed,
taken in hand by Miss Amy; with the result that on a certain
occasion when, toward nine o'clock, Miss Susan woke up,
she found her fellow-labourer fast asleep. A slightly irritated
confession of ignorance of the Gothic character was the

further consequence, and the upshot of this, in turn, was the idea of appeal to Mr Patten. Mr Patten was the vicar and was known to interest himself, as such, in the ancient annals of Marr; in addition to which—and to its being even held a little that his sense of the affairs of the hour was sometimes sacrificed to such inquiries—he was a gentleman with a humour of his own, a flushed face, a bushy eyebrow and a black wide-awake worn sociably askew. "He will tell us," said Amy Frush, "if there's anything in them."

"Yet if it should be," Susan suggested, "anything we mayn't like?"

"Well, that's just what I'm thinking of," returned Miss Amy in her offhand way. "If it's anything we shouldn't know——"

"We've only to tell him not to tell us? Oh, certainly," said mild Miss Susan. She took upon herself even to give him that warning when, on the invitation of our friends, Mr Patten came to tea and to talk things over; Miss Amy sitting by and raising no protest, but distinctly promising herself that, whatever there might be to be known, and however objectionable, she would privately get it out of their initiator. She found herself already hoping that it *would* be something too bad for her cousin—too bad for any one else at all—to know, and that it most properly might remain between them. Mr Patten, at sight of the papers, exclaimed, perhaps a trifle ambiguously, and by no means clerically, "My eye, what a lark!" and retired, after three cups of tea, in an overcoat bulging with his spoil.

II

AT ten o'clock that evening the pair separated, as usual, on the upper landing, outside their respective doors, for the night; but Miss Amy had hardly set down her candle on her dressing-table before she was startled by an extraordinary sound, which appeared to proceed not only from her companion's room, but from her companion's throat. It was something she would have described, had she ever described it, as between a gurgle and a shriek, and it brought Amy Frush, after an interval of stricken stillness that gave her just time to say to herself "Some one under her bed!" breathlessly and bravely back to the landing. She had not reached it, however, before her neighbour, bursting in, met her and stayed her.

"There's some one in my room!"

They held each other. "But who?"

"A man."

"Under the bed?"

"No—just standing there."

They continued to hold each other, but they rocked. "Standing? Where? How?"

"Why, right in the middle—before my dressing-glass."

Amy's blanched face by this time matched her mate's, but its terror was enhanced by speculation. "To look at himself?"

"No—with his back to it. To look at *me*," poor Susan just audibly breathed. "To keep me off," she quavered. "In strange clothes—of another age; with his head on one side."

Amy wondered. "On one side?"

"Awfully!" the refugee declared while, clinging together, they sounded each other.

This, somehow, for Miss Amy, was the convincing touch; and on it, after a moment, she was capable of the effort of darting back to close her own door. "You'll remain then with me."

"Oh!" Miss Susan wailed with deep assent; quite, as if, had she been a slangy person, she would have ejaculated "Rather!" So they spent the night together; with the assumption thus marked, from the first, both that it would have been vain to confront their visitor as they didn't even pretend to each other that they would have confronted a house-breaker; and that by leaving the place at his mercy nothing worse could happen than had already happened. It was Miss Amy's approaching the door again as with intent ear and after a hush that had represented between them a deep and extraordinary interchange—it was this that put them promptly face to face with the real character of the occurrence. "Ah," Miss Susan, still under her breath, portentously exclaimed, "it isn't any one——!"

"No"—her partner was already able magnificently to take her up. "It isn't any one——"

"Who can really hurt us"—Miss Susan completed her thought. And Miss Amy, as it proved, had been so indescribably prepared that this thought, before morning, had, in the strangest, finest way, made for itself an admirable place with them. The person the elder of our pair had seen in her room was not—well, just simply was not any one in from outside. He was a different thing altogether. Miss Amy had felt it as soon as she heard her friend's cry and become aware of her commotion; as soon, at all events, as she saw Miss Susan's face. That was all—and there it was. There had been something hitherto wanting, they felt, to their small state and importance; it was present now, and they were as handsomely conscious of it as if they had previously missed it. The element in question, then, was a third person in their association, a hovering presence for the dark hours, a figure that with its head very much—too much—on one side, could be trusted to look at them out of unnatural places; yet only, it doubtless might be assumed, to look at them. They had it at last—had what was to be had in an old house where many, too many, things had happened, where the very walls they touched and floors they trod could have told secrets and named names, where every surface was a blurred mirror of life and death, of the endured, the remembered, the forgotten. Yes; the place was h—— but they stopped at sounding the word. And by

morning, wonderful to say, they were used to it—had quite
lived into it.

Not only this indeed, but they had their prompt theory.
There was a connection between the finding of the box in the
vault and the appearance in Miss Susan's room. The heavy
air of the past had been stirred by the bringing to light of
what had so long been hidden. The communication of the
papers to Mr Patten had had its effect. They faced each other
in the morning at breakfast over the certainty that their queer
roused inmate was the sign of the violated secret of these
relics. No matter; for the sake of the secret they would put
up with his attention; and—this, in them, was most beautiful
of all—they must, though he was such an addition to their
grandeur, keep him quite to themselves. Other people might
hear of what was in the letters, but they should never hear of
him. They were not afraid that either of the maids should see
him—he was not a matter for maids. The question indeed was
whether—should he keep it up long—they themselves would
find that they could really live with him. Yet perhaps his
keeping it up would be just what would make them indifferent.
They turned these things over, but spent the next nights together; and on the third day, in the course of their afternoon
walk, descried at a distance the vicar, who, as soon as he saw
them, waved his arms violently—either as a warning or as a
joke—and came more than half-way to meet them. It was in
the middle—or what passed for such—of the big, bleak,
blank, melancholy square of Marr; a public place, as it were,
of such an absurd capacity for a crowd; with the great ivy-
mantled choir and stopped transept of the nobly-planned
church telling of how many centuries ago it had, for its part,
given up growing.

"Why, my dear ladies," cried Mr Patten as he approached,
"do you know what, of all things in the world, I seem to make
out for you from your funny old letters?" Then as they
waited, extremely on their guard now: "Neither more nor

less, if you please, than that one of your ancestors in the last century—Mr Cuthbert Frush, it would seem, by name—was hanged."

They never knew afterwards which of the two had first found composure—found even dignity—to respond. "And pray, Mr Patten, for what?"

"Ah, that's just what I don't yet get hold of. But if you don't mind my digging away"—and the vicar's bushy, jolly brows turned from one of the ladies to the other—"I think I can run it to earth. They hanged, in those days, you know," he added as if he had seen something in their faces, "for almost any trifle!"

"Oh, I hope it wasn't for a trifle!" Miss Susan strangely tittered.

"Yes, of course one would like that, while he was about it —well, it had been, as they say," Mr Patten laughed, "rather for a sheep than for a lamb!"

"Did they hang at that time for a sheep?" Miss Amy wonderingly asked.

It made their friend laugh again. "The question's whether *he* did! But we'll find out. Upon my word, you know, I quite want to myself. I'm awfully busy, but I think I can promise you that you shall hear. You *don't* mind?" he insisted.

"I think we could bear *anything*," said Miss Amy.

Miss Susan gazed at her, on this, as for reference and appeal. "And what is he, after all, at this time of day, *to* us?"

Her kinswoman, meeting the eyeglass fixedly, spoke with gravity. "Oh, an ancestor's always an ancestor."

"Well said and well felt, dear lady!" the vicar declared. "Whatever they may have done——"

"It isn't every one," Miss Amy replied, "that has them to be ashamed of."

"And we're not ashamed *yet*!" Miss Frush jerked out.

"Let me promise you then that you shan't be. Only, for I am busy," said Mr Patten, "give me time."

"Ah, but we want the truth!" they cried with high emphasis as he quitted them. They were much excited now.

He answered by pulling up and turning round as short as if his professional character had been challenged. "Isn't it just in the truth—and the truth only—that I deal?"

This they recognised as much as his love of a joke, and so they were left there together in the pleasant, if slightly overdone, void of the square, which wore at moments the air of a conscious demonstration, intended as an appeal, of the shrinkage of the population of Marr to a solitary cat. They walked on after a little, but they waited till the vicar was ever so far away before they spoke again; all the more that their doing so must bring them once more to a pause. Then they had a long look. "Hanged!" said Miss Amy—yet almost exultantly.

This was, however, because it was not she who had seen. "That's why his head——" but Miss Susan faltered.

Her companion took it in. "Oh, has such a dreadful twist?"

"It *is* dreadful!" Miss Susan at last dropped, speaking as if she had been present at twenty executions.

There would have been no saying, at any rate, what it didn't evoke from Miss Amy. "It breaks their neck," she contributed after a moment.

Miss Susan looked away. "That's why, I suppose, the head turns so fearfully awry. It's a most peculiar effect."

So peculiar, it might have seemed, that it made them silent afresh. "Well then, I hope he killed some one!" Miss Amy broke out at last.

Her companion thought. "Wouldn't it depend on whom ——?"

"No!" she returned with her characteristic briskness—a briskness that set them again into motion.

That Mr Patten was tremendously busy was evident indeed, as even by the end of the week he had nothing more to impart. The whole thing meanwhile came up again—on the

Sunday afternoon; as the younger Miss Frush had been quite confident that, from one day to the other, it must. They went inveterately to evening church, to the close of which supper was postponed; and Miss Susan, on this occasion, ready the first, patiently awaited her mate at the foot of the stairs. Miss Amy at last came down, buttoning a glove, rustling the tail of a frock and looking, as her kinswoman always thought, conspicuously young and smart. There was no one at Marr, she held, who dressed like her; and Miss Amy, it must be owned, had also settled to this view of Miss Susan, though taking it in a different spirit. Dusk had gathered, but our frugal pair were always tardy lighters, and the grey close of day, in which the elder lady, on a high-backed hall chair, sat with hands patiently folded, had for all cheer the subdued glow—always subdued—of the small fire in the drawing-room, visible through a door that stood open. Into the drawing-room Miss Amy passed in search of the prayer-book she had laid down there after morning church, and from it, after a minute, without this volume, she returned to her companion. There was something in her movement that spoke—spoke for a moment so largely that nothing more was said till, with a quick unanimity, they had got themselves straight out of the house. There, before the door, in the cold, still twilight of the winter's end, while the church bells rang and the windows of the great choir showed across the empty square faintly red, they had it out again. But it was Miss Susan herself, this time, who had to bring it.

"He's there?"

"Before the fire—with his back to it."

"Well, now you see!" Miss Susan exclaimed with elation and as if her friend had hitherto doubted her.

"Yes, I see—and what you mean." Miss Amy was deeply thoughtful.

"About his head?"

"It *is* on one side," Miss Amy went on. "It makes

him——" she considered. But she faltered as if still in his presence.

"It makes him awful!" Miss Susan murmured. "The way," she softly moaned, "he looks at you!"

Miss Amy, with a glance, met this recognition. "Yes— doesn't he?" Then her eyes attached themselves to the red windows of the church. "But it means something."

"The Lord knows what it means!" her associate gloomily sighed. Then, after an instant, "Did he move?" Miss Susan asked.

"No—and *I* didn't."

"Oh, I did!" Miss Susan declared, recalling to her more precipitous retreat.

"I mean I took my time. I waited."

"To see him fade?"

Miss Amy for a moment said nothing. "He doesn't fade. That's *it*."

"Oh, then you did move!" her relative rejoined.

Again for a little she was silent. "One *has* to. But I don't know what really happened. Of course I came back to you. What I mean is that I took him thoroughly in. He's young," she added.

"But he's *bad*!" said Miss Susan.

"He's handsome!" Miss Amy brought out after a moment. And she showed herself even prepared to continue: "Splendidly."

"'Splendidly'!—with his neck broken and with that terrible look?"

"It's just the look that makes him so. It's the wonderful eyes. They mean something," Amy Frush brooded.

She spoke with a decision of which Susan presently betrayed the effect. "And what do they mean?"

Her friend had stared again at the glimmering windows of St Thomas of Canterbury. "That it's time we should get to church."

III

THE curate that evening did duty alone; but on the morrow the vicar called and, as soon as he got into the room, let them again have it. "He was hanged for smuggling!"

They stood there before him almost cold in their surprise and diffusing an air in which, somehow, this misdemeanour sounded out as the coarsest of all. "*Smuggling?*" Miss Susan disappointedly echoed—as if it presented itself to the first chill of their apprehension that he had then only been vulgar.

"Ah, but they hanged for it freely, you know, and I was an idiot for not having taken it, in his case, for granted. If a man swung, hereabouts, it *was* mostly for that. Don't you know it's on that we stand here to-day, such as we are—on the fact of what our bold, bad forefathers were not afraid of? It's in the floors we walk on and under the roofs that cover us. They smuggled so hard that they never had time to do anything else; and if they broke a head not their own it was only in the awkwardness of landing their brandy-kegs. I mean, dear ladies," good Mr Patten wound up, "no disrespect to *your* forefathers when I tell you that—as I've rather been supposing that, like all the rest of us, you were aware—they conveniently lived by it."

Miss Susan wondered—visibly almost doubted. "Gentlefolks?"

"It was the gentlefolks who were the worst."

"They must have been the bravest!" Miss Amy interjected. She had listened to their visitor's free explanation with a rapid return of colour. "And since if they lived by it they also died for it——"

"There's nothing at all to be said against them? I quite agree with you," the vicar laughed, "for all my cloth; and

I even go so far as to say, shocking as you may think me, that
we owe them, in our shabby little shrunken present, the sense
of a bustling background, a sort of undertone of romance.
They give us"—he humorously kept it up, verging perilously
near, for his cloth, upon positive paradox—"our little handful
of legend and our small possibility of ghosts." He paused an
instant, with his lighter pulpit manner, but the ladies exchanged no look. They were in fact already, with an immense
revulsion, carried quite as far away. "Every penny in the
place, really, that hasn't been earned by subtler—not nobler—
arts in our own virtuous time, and though it's a pity there
are not more of 'em: every penny in the place was picked up,
somehow, by a clever trick, and at the risk of your neck,
when the backs of the king's officers were turned. It's shocking, you know, what I'm saying to you, and I wouldn't say
it to every one, but I think of some of the shabby old things
about us, that represent such pickings, with a sort of sneaking
kindness—as of relics of our heroic age. What are we now?
We were at any rate devils of fellows then!"

Susan Frush considered it all solemnly, struggling with the
spell of this evocation. "But must we forget that they were
wicked?"

"Never!" Mr Patten laughed. "Thank you, dear friend,
for reminding me. Only I'm worse than they!"

"But would you do it?"

"Murder a coastguard——?" The vicar scratched his head.

"I hope," said Miss Amy rather surprisingly, "you'd de-
fend yourself." And she gave Miss Susan a superior glance.
"*I* would!" she distinctly added.

Her companion anxiously took it up. "Would you defraud
the revenue?"

Miss Amy hesitated but a moment; then with a strange
laugh, which she covered, however, by turning instantly
away, "Yes!" she remarkably declared.

Their visitor, at this, amused and amusing, eagerly seized

her arm. "Then may I count on you on the stroke of midnight to help me——?"

"To help you——?"

"To land the last new Tauchnitz."

She met the proposal as one whose fancy had kindled, while her cousin watched them as if they had suddenly improvised a drawing-room charade. "A service of danger?"

"Under the cliff—when you see the lugger stand in!"

"Armed to the teeth?"

"Yes—but invisibly. Your old waterproof——!"

"Mine is new. I'll take Susan's!"

This good lady, however, had her reserves. "Mayn't one of them, all the same—here and there—have been sorry?"

Mr Patten wondered, "For the jobs he muffed?"

"For the wrong—as it *was* wrong—he did."

"'One' of them?" She had gone too far, for the vicar suddenly looked as if he divined in the question a reference.

They became, however, as promptly unanimous in meeting this danger, as to which Miss Susan in particular showed an inspired presence of mind. "Two of them!" she sweetly smiled. "May not Amy and I——?"

"Vicariously repent?" said Mr Patten. "That depends—for the true honour of Marr—on how you show it."

"Oh, we *sha'n't* show it!" Miss Amy cried.

"Ah, then," Mr Patten returned, "though atonements, to be efficient, are supposed to be public, you may do penance in secret as much as you please!"

"Well, *I* shall do it," said Susan Frush.

Again, by something in her tone, the vicar's attention appeared to be caught. "Have you then in view a particular form——?"

"Of atonement?" She coloured now, glaring rather helplessly, in spite of herself, at her companion. "Oh, if you're sincere you'll always find one."

Amy came to her assistance. "The way she often treats me

has made her—though there's after all no harm in her—familiar with remorse. Mayn't we, at any rate," the younger lady continued, "now have our letters back?" And the vicar left them with the assurance that they should receive the bundle on the morrow.

They were indeed so at one as to shrouding their mystery that no explicit agreement, no exchange of vows, needed to pass between them; they only settled down, from this moment, to an unshared possession of their secret, an economy in the use and, as may even be said, the enjoyment of it, that was part of their general instinct and habit of thrift. It had been the disposition, the practice, the necessity of each to keep, fairly indeed to clutch, everything that, as they often phrased it, came their way; and this was not the first time such an influence had determined for them an affirmation of property in objects to which ridicule, suspicion, or some other inconvenience, might attach. It was their simple philosophy that one never knew of what service an odd object might *not* be; and there were days now on which they felt themselves to have made a better bargain with their aunt's executors than was witnessed in those law-papers which they had at first timorously regarded as the record of advantages taken of them in matters of detail. They had got, in short, more than was vulgarly, more than was even shrewdly supposed—such an indescribable unearned increment as might scarce more be divulged as a dread than as a delight. They drew together, old-maidishly, in a suspicious, invidious grasp of the idea that a dread of their very own—and blissfully not, of course, that of a failure of any essential supply—might, on nearer acquaintance, positively turn to a delight.

Upon some such attempted consideration of it, at all events, they found themselves embarking after their last interview with Mr Patten, an understanding conveyed between them in no redundancy of discussion, no flippant repetitions nor profane recurrences, yet resting on a sense of added margin, of appropriated history, of liberties taken with time and space, that would leave them prepared both for the worst and for the best. The best would be that something that would turn out to their advantage might prove to be hidden about the place; the worst would be that they might find themselves growing to depend only too much on excitement. They found themselves amazingly reconciled, on Mr. Patten's information, to the particular character thus fixed on their visitor; they knew by tradition and fiction that even the highwaymen of the same picturesque age were often gallant gentlemen; therefore a smuggler, by such a measure, fairly belonged to the aristocracy of crime. When their packet of documents came back from the vicarage Miss Amy, to whom her associate continued to leave them, took them once more in hand; but with an effect, afresh, of discouragement and languor—a headachy sense of faded ink, of strange spelling and crabbed characters, of allusions she couldn't follow and parts she couldn't match. She placed the tattered papers piously together, wrapping them tenderly in a piece of old figured silken stuff; then, as solemnly as if they had been archives or statutes or title-deeds, laid them away in one of the several small cupboards lodged in the thickness of the wainscoted walls. What really most sustained our friends in all ways was their consciousness of having, after all—and so contrariwise to what appeared— a man in the house. It removed them from that category of the manless into which no lady really lapses till every issue is closed. Their visitor was an issue—at least to the imagination, and they arrived finally, under provocation, at intensities of flutter in which they felt themselves so compromised by his hoverings that they could only consider with relief the fact of nobody's knowing.

The real complication indeed at first was that for some weeks after their talks with Mr Patten the hoverings quite ceased; a circumstance that brought home to them in some degree a sense of indiscretion and indelicacy. They hadn't

mentioned him, no; but they had come perilously near it, and
they had doubtless, at any rate, too recklessly let in the light
on old buried and sheltered things, old sorrows and shames.
They roamed about the house themselves at times, fitfully and
singly, when each supposed the other out or engaged; they
paused and lingered, like soundless apparitions, in corners,
doorways, passages, and sometimes suddenly met, in these
experiments, with a suppressed start and a mute confession.
They talked of him practically never; but each knew how the
other thought—all the more that it was (oh yes, unmistakably!)
in a manner different from her own. They were together, none
the less, in feeling, while, week after week, he failed again to
show, as if they had been guilty of blowing, with an effect
of sacrilege, on old gathered silvery ashes. It frankly came out
for them that, possessed as they so strangely, yet so ridiculously were, they should be able to settle to nothing till their
consciousness was yet again confirmed. Whatever the subject
of it might have for them of fear or favour, profit or loss, he
had taken the taste from everything else. He had converted
them into wandering ghosts. At last, one day, with nothing
they could afterwards perceive to have determined it, the
change came came, as the previous splash in their stillness
had come, by the pale testimony of Miss Susan.

She waited till after breakfast to speak of it—or Miss Amy,
rather, waited to hear her; for she showed during the meal the
face of controlled commotion that her comrade already knew
and that must, with the game loyally played, serve as preface
to a disclosure. The younger of the friends really watched the
elder, over their tea and toast, as if seeing her for the first time
as possibly tortuous, suspecting in her some intention of keeping back what had happened. What had happened was that
the image of the hanged man had reappeared in the night; yet
only after they had moved together to the drawing-room did
Miss Amy learn the facts.

"I was beside the bed—in that low chair; about"—since

Miss Amy must know—"to take off my right shoe. I had noticed nothing before, and had had time partly to undress— had got into my wrapper. So, suddenly—as I happened to look—there he was. And there," said Susan Frush, "he stayed."

"But where do you mean?"

"In the high-backed chair, the old flowered chintz 'ear-chair' beside the chimney."

"All night?—and you in your wrapper?" Then as if this image almost challenged her credulity, "Why didn't you go to bed?" Miss Amy inquired.

"With a—a person in the room?" her friend wonderfully asked; adding after an instant as with positive pride: "I never broke the spell!"

"And didn't freeze to death?"

"Yes, almost. To say nothing of not having slept, I can assure you, one wink. I shut my eyes for long stretches, but whenever I opened them he was still there, and I never for a moment lost consciousness."

Miss Amy gave a groan of conscientious sympathy. "So that you're feeling now of course half dead."

Her companion turned to the chimney-glass a wan, glazed eye. "I dare say I *am* looking impossible."

Miss Amy, after an instant, found herself still conscientious. "You are." Her own eyes strayed to the glass, lingering there while she lost herself in thought. "Really," she reflected with a certain dryness, "if that's the kind of thing it's to be——!" there would seem, in a word, to be no withstanding it for either. Why, she afterwards asked herself in secret, should the restless spirit of a dead adventurer have addressed itself, in its trouble, to such a person as her queer, quaint, inefficient housemate? It was in *her*, she dumbly and somewhat sorely argued, that an unappeased soul of the old race should show a confidence. To this conviction she was the more directed by the sense that Susan had, in relation to the preference shown,

vain and foolish complacencies. She had her idea of what, in
their prodigious predicament, should be, as she called it,
"done," and that was a question that Amy from this time
began to nurse the small aggression of not so much as dis-
cussing with her. She had certainly, poor Miss Frush, a new,
an obscure reticence, and since she wouldn't speak first she
should have silence to her fill. Miss Amy, however, peopled
the silence with conjectural visions of her kinswoman's secret
communion. Miss Susan, it was true, showed nothing, on any
particular occasion, more than usual; but this was just a part
of the very felicity that had begun to harden and uplift her.
Days and nights hereupon elapsed without bringing felicity
of any order to Amy Frush. If she had no emotions it was, she
suspected, because Susan had them all; and—it would have
been preposterous had it not been pathetic—she proceeded
rapidly to hug the opinion that Susan was selfish and even
something of a sneak. Politeness, between them, still reigned,
but confidence had flown, and its place was taken by open
ceremonies and confessed precautions. Miss Susan looked
blank but resigned; which maintained again, unfortunately,
her superior air and the presumption of her duplicity. Her
manner was of not knowing where her friend's shoe pinched;
but it might have been taken by a jaundiced eye for surprise
at the challenge of her monopoly. The unexpected resistance
of her nerves was indeed a wonder: was that then the result,
even for a shaky old woman, of shocks sufficiently repeated?
Miss Amy brooded on the rich inference that, if the first of
them didn't prostrate and the rest didn't undermine, one might
keep them up as easily as—well, say an unavowed acquaintance
or a private commerce of letters. She was startled at the comparison into which she fell—but what was this but an intrigue
like another? And fancy Susan carrying one on! That history
of the long night hours of the pair in the two chairs kept
before her—for it was always present—the extraordinary
measure. Was the situation it involved only grotesque—or was

it quite grimly grand? It struck her as both; but that was the case with all their situations. Would it be in herself, at any rate, to show such a front? She put herself such questions till she was tired of them. A few good moments of her own would have cleared the air. Luckily they were to come.

IV

IT was on a Sunday morning in April, a day brimming over with the turn of the season. She had gone into the garden before church; they cherished alike, with pottering intimacies and opposed theories and a wonderful apparatus of old gloves and trowels and spuds and little botanical cards on sticks, this feature of their establishment, where they could still differ without fear and agree without diplomacy, and which now, with its vernal promise, threw beauty and gloom and light and space, a great good-natured ease, into their wavering scales. She was dressed for church; but when Susan, who had, from a window, seen her wandering, stooping, examining, touching, appeared in the doorway to signify a like readiness, she suddenly felt her intention checked. "Thank you," she said, drawing near; "I think that, though I've dressed, I won't, after all, go. Please therefore, proceed without me."

Miss Susan fixed her. "You're not well?"

"Not particularly. I shall be better—the morning's so perfect—here."

"Are you really ill?"

"Indisposed; but not enough so, thank you, for you to stay with me."

"Then it has come on but just now?"

"No—I felt not quite fit when I dressed. But it won't do."

"Yet you'll stay out here?"

Miss Amy looked about. "It will depend!"

Her friend paused long enough to have asked what it would depend on, but abruptly, after this contemplation, turned instead and, merely throwing over her shoulder an "At least take care of yourself!" went rustling, in her stiffest Sunday fashion, about her business. Miss Amy, left alone, as she clearly desired to be, lingered a while in the garden, where the sense of things was somehow made still more delicious by the sweet, vain sounds from the church tower; but by the end of ten minutes she had returned to the house. The sense of things was not delicious there, for what it had at last come to was that, as they thought of each other what they couldn't say, all their contacts were hard and false. The real wrong was in what Susan thought—as to which she was much too proud and too sore to undeceive her. Miss Amy went vaguely to the drawing-room.

They sat as usual, after church, at their early Sunday dinner, face to face; but little passed between them save that Miss Amy felt better, that the curate had preached, that nobody else had stayed away, and that everybody had asked why Amy had. Amy, hereupon, satisfied everybody by feeling well enough to go in the afternoon; on which occasion, on the other hand—and for reasons even less luminous than those that had operated with her mate in the morning—Miss Susan remained within. Her comrade came back late, having, after church, paid visits; and found her, as daylight faded, seated in the drawing-room, placid and dressed, but without so much as a Sunday book—the place contained whole shelves of such reading—in her hand. She looked so as if a visitor had just left her that Amy put the question: "Has any one called?"

"Dear, no; I've been quite alone."

This again was indirect, and it instantly determined for Miss Amy a conviction—a conviction that, on her also sitting down just as she was and in a silence that prolonged itself, promoted in its turn another determination. The April dusk gathered, and still, without further speech, the companions sat there. But at last Miss Amy said in a tone not quite her commonest: "This morning he came—while you were at church. I suppose it must have been really—though of course I couldn't know it—what I was moved to stay at home for." She spoke now—out of her contentment—as if to oblige with explanations.

But it was strange how Miss Susan met her. "You stay at home for him? *I* don't!" She fairly laughed at the triviality of the idea.

Miss Amy was naturally struck by it and after an instant even nettled. "Then why did you do so this afternoon?"

"Oh, it wasn't for *that!*" Miss Susan lightly quavered. She made her distinction. "I *really* wasn't well."

At this her cousin brought it out. "But he has been with you?"

"My dear child," said Susan, launched unexpectedly even to herself, "he's with me so often that if I put myself out for him——!" But as if at sight of something that showed, through the twilight, in her friend's face, she pulled herself up.

Amy, however, spoke with studied stillness. "You've ceased then to put yourself out? You gave me, you remember, an instance of how you once did!" And she tried, on her side, a laugh.

"Oh yes—that was at first. But I've seen such a lot of him since. Do you mean *you* hadn't?" Susan asked. Then as her companion only sat looking at her: "Has this been really the first time for you—since we last talked?"

Miss Amy for a minute said nothing. "You've actually believed me——"

"To be enjoying on your own account what *I* enjoy? How couldn't I, at the very least," Miss Susan cried—"so grand and strange as you must allow me to say you've struck me?"

Amy hesitated. "I hope I've sometimes struck you as decent!"

But it was a touch that, in her friend's almost amused preoccupation with the simple fact, happily fell short. "You've only been waiting for what didn't come?"

Miss Amy coloured in the dusk. "It came, as I tell you, to-day."

"Better late than never!" And Miss Susan got up.

Amy Frush sat looking. "It's because you thought you had ground for jealousy that *you've* been extraordinary?"

Poor Susan, at this, quite bounced about. "Jealousy?"

It was a tone—never heard from her before—that brought Amy Frush to her feet; so that for a minute, in the unlighted room where, in honour of the spring, there had been no fire and the evening chill had gathered, they stood as enemies. It lasted, fortunately, even long enough to give one of them time suddenly to find it horrible. "But why should we quarrel *now?*" Amy broke out in a different voice.

Susan was not too alienated quickly enough to meet it. "It *is* rather wretched."

"Now when we're equal," Amy went on.

"Yes—I suppose we are." Then, however, as if just to attenuate the admission, Susan had her last lapse from grace. "They say, you know, that when women do quarrel it's usually about a man."

Amy recognised it, but also with a reserve. "Well then, let there first *be* one!"

"And don't you call *him*——?"

"No!" Amy declared and turned away, while her companion showed her a vain wonder for what she could in that case have expected. Their identity of privilege was thus established, but it is not certain that the air with which she indicated that the subject had better drop didn't press down for an instant her side of the balance. She knew that she knew most about men.

The subject did drop for the time, it being agreed between them that neither should from that hour expect from the other any confession or report. They would treat all occurrences now as not worth mentioning—a course easy to pursue from the moment the suspicion of jealousy had, on each side, been so completely laid to rest. They led their life a month or two on the smooth ground of taking everything for granted; by the end of which time, however, try as they would, they had set up no question that—while they met as a pair of gentlewomen living together only must meet—could successfully pretend to take the place of that of Cuthbert Frush. The spring softened and deepened, reached out its tender arms and scattered its shy graces; the earth broke, the air stirred, with emanations that were as touches and voices of the past; our friends bent their backs in their garden and their noses over its symptoms; they opened their windows to the mildness and tracked it in the lanes and by the hedges; yet the plant of conversation between them markedly failed to renew itself with the rest. It was not indeed that the mildness was not within them as well as without; all asperity, at least, had melted away; they were more than ever pleased with their general acquisition, which, at the winter's end, seemed to give out more of its old secrets, to hum, however faintly, with more of its old echoes, to creak, here and there, with the expiring throb of old aches. The deepest sweetness of the spring at Marr was just in its being in this way an attestation of age and rest. The place never seemed to have lived and lingered so long as when kind nature, like a maiden blessing a crone, laid rosy hands on its grizzled head. Then the new season was a light held up to show all the dignity of the years, but also all the wrinkles and scars. The good ladies in whom we are interested changed, at any rate, with the happy days, and it finally came out not only that the invidious note had dropped, but that it had positively turned to music. The whole tone of the time made so for tenderness that it really seemed as if at moments they were sad for each other. They had their grounds at last: each found them in her own consciousness; but it was as if each waited, on the other hand, to be sure she could speak without offence. Fortunately, at last, the tense cord snapped.

The old churchyard at Marr is still liberal; it does its immemorial utmost to people, with names and dates and memories and eulogies, with generations fore-shortened and confounded, the high empty table at which the grand old cripple of the church looks down over the low wall. It serves as an easy thoroughfare, and the stranger finds himself pausing in it with a sense of respect and compassion for the great maimed, ivied shoulders—as the image strikes him—of stone. Miss Susan and Miss Amy were strangers enough still to have sunk down one May morning on the sun-warmed tablet of an ancient tomb and to have remained looking about them in a sort of anxious peace. Their walks were all pointless now, as if they always stopped and turned, for an uncon- fessed want of interest, before reaching their object. That object presented itself at every start as the same to each, but they had come back too often without having got near it. This morning, strangely, on the return and almost in sight of their door, they were more in presence of it than they had ever been, and they seemed fairly to touch it when Susan said at last, quite in the air and with no traceable reference: "I hope you don't mind, dearest, if I'm awfully sorry for you."

"Oh, I know it," Amy returned—"I've felt it. But what does it do for us?" she asked.

Then Susan saw, with wonder and pity, how little resent- ment for penetration or patronage she had had to fear and out of what a depth of sentiment similar to her own her companion helplessly spoke. "You're sorry for *me*?"

Amy at first only looked at her with tired eyes, putting out a hand that remained a while on her arm. "Dear old girl!

You might have told me before," she went on as she took everything in; "though, after all, haven't we each really known it?"

"Well," said Susan, "we've waited. We could only wait."

"Then if we've waited together," her friend returned, "that *has* helped us."

"Yes—to keep him in his place. Who would ever believe in him?" Miss Susan wearily wondered. "If it wasn't for you and for me——"

"Not doubting of each other?"—her companion took her up: "yes, there wouldn't be a creature. It's lucky for us," said Miss Amy, "that we *don't* doubt."

"Oh, if we did we shouldn't be sorry."

"No—except, selfishly, for ourselves. I am, I assure you, for *my* self—it has made me older. But, luckily, at any rate, we trust each other."

"We do," said Miss Susan.

"We do," Miss Amy repeated—they lingered a little on that. "But except making one feel older, what has it done for one?"

"There it is!"

"And though we've kept him in his place," Miss Amy continued, "he has also kept us in ours. We've lived with it," she declared in melancholy justice. "And we wondered at first if we could!" she ironically added. "Well, isn't just what we feel now that we can't any longer?"

"No—it must stop. And I've my idea," said Susan Frush.

"Oh, I assure you I've mine!" her cousin responded.

"Then if you want to act, don't mind me."

"Because you certainly won't *me*? No, I suppose not. Well!" Amy sighed, as if, merely from this, relief had at last come. Her comrade echoed it; they remained side by side; and nothing could have had more oddity than what was assumed alike in what they had said and in what they still kept back. There would have been this at least in their favour for a questioner of their case, that each, charged dejectedly with her own experience, took, on the part of the other, the extraordinary—the ineffable, in fact—all for granted. They never named it again—as indeed it was not easy to name; the whole matter shrouded itself in personal discriminations and privacies; the comparison of notes had become a thing impossible. What was definite was that they had lived into their queer story, passed through it as through an observed, a studied, eclipse of the usual, a period of reclusion, a financial, social or moral crisis, and only desired now to live out of it again. The questioner we have been supposing might even have fancied that each, on her side, had hoped for something from it that she finally perceived it was never to give, which would have been exactly, moreover, the core of her secret and the explanation of her reserve. They at least, as the business stood, put each other to no test, and, if they were in fact disillusioned and disappointed, came together, after their long blight, solidly on that. It fully appeared between them that they felt a great deal older. When they got up from their sun-warmed slab, however, reminding each other of luncheon, it was with a visible increase of ease and with Miss Susan's hand drawn, for the walk home, into Miss Amy's arm. Thus the "idea" of each had continued unspoken and ungrudged. It was as if each wished the other to try her own first; from which it might have been gathered that they alike presented difficulty and even entailed expense. The great questions remained. What then did he mean? what then did he want? Absolution, peace, rest, his final reprieve—merely to say that saw them no further on the way than they had already come. What were they at last to do for him? What could they give him that he would take? The ideas they respectively nursed still bore no fruit, and at the end of another month Miss Susan was frankly anxious about Miss Amy. Miss Amy as freely admitted that people must have begun to notice strange marks in them and to look for reasons. They were changed—they must change back.

V

YET it was not till one morning at midsummer, on their meeting for breakfast, that the elder lady fairly attacked the younger's last entrenchment. "Poor, poor Susan!" Miss Amy had said to herself as her cousin came into the room; and a moment later she brought out, for very pity, her appeal. "What then *is* yours?"

"My idea?" It was clearly, at last, a vague comfort to Miss Susan to be asked. Yet her answer was desolate. "Oh, it's no use!"

"But how do you know?"

"Why, I tried it—ten days ago, and I thought at first it had answered. But it hasn't."

"He's back again?"

Wan, tired, Miss Susan gave it up. "Back again."

Miss Amy, after one of the long, odd looks that had now become their most frequent form of intercourse, thought it over. "And just the same?"

"Worse."

"Dear!" said Miss Amy, clearly knowing what that meant. "Then what did you do?"

Her friend brought it roundly out. "I made my sacrifice."

Miss Amy, though still more deeply interrogative, hesitated. "But of what?"

"Why, of my little all—or almost."

The "almost" seemed to puzzle Miss Amy, who, moreover, had plainly no clue to the property or attribute so described. "Your 'little all'?"

"Twenty pounds."

"Money?" Miss Amy gasped.

Her tone produced on her companion's part a wonder as great as her own. "What then is it yours to give?"

"My idea? It's not to *give*!" cried Amy Frush.

At the finer pride that broke out in this poor Susan's blankness flushed. "What then is it to do?"

But Miss Amy's bewilderment outlasted her reproach. "Do you mean he takes money?"

"The Chancellor of the Exchequer does—for 'conscience.'"

Her friend's exploit shone larger. "Conscience-money? You sent it to Government?" Then while, as the effect of her surprise, her mate looked too much a fool, Amy melted to kindness. "Why, you secretive old thing!"

Miss Susan presently pulled herself more together. "When your ancestor has robbed the revenue and his spirit walks for remorse——"

"You pay to get rid of him? I see—and it becomes what the vicar called his atonement by deputy. But what if it isn't remorse?" Miss Amy shrewdly asked.

"But it *is*—or it seemed to me so."

"Never to me," said Miss Amy.

Again they searched each other. "Then, evidently, with you he's different."

Miss Amy looked away. "I dare say!"

"So what *is* your idea?"

Miss Amy thought. "I'll tell you only if it works."

"Then, for God's sake, try it!"

Miss Amy, still with averted eyes and now looking easily wise, continued to think. "To try it I shall have to leave you. That's why I've waited so long." Then she fully turned, and with expression: "Can you face three days alone?"

"Oh—'alone!' I wish I ever were!"

At this her friend, as for very compassion, kissed her; for it seemed really to have come out at last—and welcome!— that poor Susan was the worse beset. "I'll do it! But I must go up to town. Ask me no questions. All I can tell you now is——"

"Well?" Susan appealed while Amy impressively fixed her. "It's no more remorse than *I'm* a smuggler."

"What is it then?"

"It's bravado."

An "Oh!" more shocked and scared than any that, in the whole business, had yet dropped from her, wound up poor Susan's share in this agreement, appearing as it did to represent for her a somewhat lurid inference. Amy, clearly, had lights of her own. It was by their aid, accordingly, that she immediately prepared for the first separation they had had yet to suffer; of which the consequence, two days later, was that Miss Susan, bowed and anxious, crept singly, on the return from their parting, up the steep hill that leads from the station of Marr and passed ruefully under the ruined town-gate, one of the old defences, that arches over it.

But the full sequel was not for a month—one hot August night when, under the dim stars, they sat together in their little walled garden. Though they had by this time, in general, found again—as women only can find—the secret of easy speech, nothing, for the half-hour, had passed between them: Susan had only sat waiting for her comrade to wake up. Miss Amy had taken of late to interminable dozing—as if with forfeits and arrears to recover; she might have been a convalescent from fever repairing tissue and getting through time. Susan Frush watched her in the warm dimness, and the question between them was fortunately at last so simple that she had freedom to think her pretty in slumber and to fear that she herself, so unguarded, presented an appearance less graceful. She was impatient, for her need had at last come, but she waited, and while she waited she thought. She had already often done so, but the mystery deepened to-night in the story told, as it seemed to her, by her companion's frequent relapses. What had been, three weeks before, the effort intense enough to leave behind such a trail of fatigue? The marks, sure enough, had shown in the poor girl that morning of the termination of the arranged absence for which not three days, but ten, without word or sign, were to prove no more than sufficient. It was at an unnatural hour that Amy had turned up, dusty, dishevelled, inscrutable, confessing for the time to nothing more than a long night-journey. Miss Susan prided herself on having played the game and respected, however tormenting, the conditions. She had her conviction that her friend had been out of the country, and she marvelled, thinking of her own old wanderings and her present settled fears, at the spirit with which a person who, whatever she had previously done, had not travelled, could carry off such a flight. The hour had come at last for this person to name her remedy. What determined it was that, as Susan Frush sat there, she took home the fact that the remedy was by this time not to be questioned. It had acted as her own had not, and Amy, to all appearance, had only waited for her to admit it. Well, she was ready when Amy woke—woke immediately to meet her eyes and to show, after a moment, in doing so, a vision of what was in her mind. "What *was* it now?" Susan finally said.

"My idea? Is it possible you've not guessed?"

"Oh, you're deeper, much deeper," Susan sighed, "than I."

Amy didn't contradict that—seemed indeed, placidly enough, to take it for truth; but she presently spoke as if the difference, after all, didn't matter now. "Happily for us to-day — isn't it so?—our case is the same. I can speak, at any rate, for myself. He has left me."

"Thank God then!" Miss Susan devoutly murmured. "For he has left *me*."

"Are you sure?"

"Oh, I think so."

"But how?"

"Well," said Miss Susan after an hesitation, "how are *you*?"

Amy, for a little, matched her pause. "Ah, that's what I can't tell you. I can only answer for it that he's gone."

"Then allow me also to prefer not to explain. The sense of relief has for some reason grown strong in me during the last half-hour. That's such a comfort that it's enough, isn't it?"

"Oh, plenty!" The garden-side of their old house, a window or two dimly lighted, massed itself darkly in the summer night, and, with a common impulse, they gave it, across the little lawn, a long, fond look. Yes, they could be sure. "Plenty!" Amy repeated. "He's gone."

Susan's elder eyes hovered, in the same way, through her elegant glass, at his purified haunt. "He's gone. And how," she insisted, "*did* you do it?"

"Why, you dear goose"—Miss Amy spoke a little strangely —"I went to Paris."

"To Paris?"

"To see what I could bring back—that I mightn't, that I shouldn't. To do a stroke with!" Miss Amy brought out.

But it left her friend still vague. "A stroke——?"

"To get through the Customs—under their nose."

It was only with this that, for Miss Susan, a pale light dawned. "You wanted to smuggle? *That* was your idea?"

"It was *his*," said Miss Amy. "He wanted no 'conscience money' spent for him," she now more bravely laughed: "it was quite the other way about—he wanted some bold deed done, of the old wild kind; he wanted some big risk taken. And I took it." She sprang up, rebounding, in her triumph.

Her companion, gasping, gazed at her. "Might they have hanged you too?"

Miss Amy looked up at the dim stars. "If I had defended myself. But luckily it didn't come to that. What I brought in I brought"—she rang out, more and more lucid, now, as she talked—"triumphantly. To appease him—I braved them. I chanced it, at Dover, and they never knew."

"Then you hid it——?"

"About my person."

With the shiver of this Miss Susan got up, and they stood there duskily together. "It was so small?" the elder lady wonderingly murmured.

"It was big enough to have satisfied him," her mate replied with just a shade of sharpness. "I chose it, with much thought, from the forbidden list."

The forbidden list hung a moment in Miss Susan's eyes, suggesting to her, however, but a pale conjecture. "A Tauchnitz?"

Miss Amy communed again with the August stars. "It was the *spirit* of the deed that told."

"A Tauchnitz?" her friend insisted.

Then at last her eyes again dropped, and the Misses Frush moved together to the house. "Well, he's satisfied."

"Yes, and"—Miss Susan mused a little ruefully as they went—"you got at last your week in Paris!"

THE SPECIAL TYPE

I NOTE it as a wonderful case of its kind—the finest of all perhaps, in fact, that I have ever chanced to encounter. The kind, moreover, is the greatest kind, the roll recruited, for our high esteem and emulation, from history and fiction, legend and song. In the way of service and sacrifice for love I've really known nothing go beyond it. However, you can judge. My own sense of it happens just now to be remarkably rounded off by the sequel—more or less looked for on her part—of the legal step taken by Mrs Brivet. I hear from America that, a decent interval being held to have elapsed since her gain of her divorce, she is about to marry again—an event that will, it would seem, put an end to any question of the disclosure of the real story. It's this that's the real story, or will be, with nothing wanting, as soon as I shall have heard that her husband (who, on his side, has only been waiting for her to move first) has sanctified his union with Mrs Cavenham.

I

SHE was, of course, often in and out, Mrs Cavenham, three years ago, when I was painting her portrait; and the more so that I found her, I remember, one of those comparatively rare sitters who present themselves at odd hours, turn up without an appointment. The thing is to get most women to keep those they do make; but she used to pop in, as she called it, on the

171

chance, letting me know that if I had a moment free she was quite at my service. When I hadn't the moment free she liked to stay to chatter, and she more than once expressed to me, I recollect, her theory that an artist really, for the time, could never see too much of his model. I must have shown her rather frankly that I understood her as meaning that a model could never see too much of her artist. I understood in fact everything, and especially that she was, in Brivet's absence, so unoccupied and restless that she didn't know what to do with herself. I was conscious in short that it was he who would pay for the picture, and that gives, I think, the measure of my enlightenment. If I took such pains and bore so with her folly, it was fundamentally for Brivet.

I was often at that time, as I had often been before, occupied —for various "subjects"—with Mrs Dundene, in connection with which a certain occasion comes back to me as the first slide in the lantern. If I had invented my story I couldn't have made it begin better than with Mrs Cavenham's irruption during the presence one morning of that lady. My door, by some chance, had been unguarded, and she was upon us without a warning. This was the sort of thing my model hated—the one, I mean, who, after all, sat mainly to oblige; but I remember how well she behaved. She was not dressed for company, though indeed a dress was never strictly necessary to her best effect. I recall that I had a moment of uncertainty, but I must have dropped the name of each for the other, as it was Mrs Cavenham's line always, later on, that I had made them acquainted; and inevitably, though I wished her not to stay and got rid of her as soon as possible, the two women, of such different places in the scale, but of such almost equal beauty, were face to face for some minutes, of which I was not even at the moment unaware that they made an extraordinary use for mutual inspection. It was sufficient; they from that instant knew each other.

"Isn't she lovely?" I remember asking—and quite without

the spirit of mischief—when I came back from restoring my
visitor to her cab.

"Yes, awfully pretty. But I hate her."

"Oh," I laughed, "she's not so bad as that."

"Not so handsome as I, you mean?" And my sitter protested. "It isn't fair of you to speak as if I were one of those
who can't bear even at the worst—or the best—another
woman's looks. I should hate her even if she were ugly."

"But what have you to do with her?"

She hesitated; then with characteristic looseness: "What
have I to do with anyone?"

"Well, there's no one else I know of that you do hate."

"That shows," she replied, "how good a reason there must
be, even if I don't know it yet."

She knew it in the course of time, but I have never seen a
reason, I must say, operate so little for relief. As a history of
the hatred of Alice Dundene my anecdote becomes wondrous
indeed. Meanwhile, at any rate, I had Mrs Cavenham again
with me for her regular sitting, and quite as curious as I had
expected her to be about the person of the previous time.

"Do you mean she isn't, so to speak, a lady?" she asked
after I had, for reasons of my own, fenced a little. "Then if
she's not 'professional' either, what is she?"

"Well," I returned as I got at work, "she escapes, to my
mind, any classification save as one of the most beautiful and
good-natured of women."

"I see her beauty," Mrs Cavenham said. "It's immense.
Do you mean that her good-nature's as great?"

I had to think a little. "On the whole, yes."

"Then I understand. That represents a greater quantity
than *I*, I think, should ever have occasion for."

"Oh, the great thing's to be sure to have enough," I
growled.

But she laughed it off. "Enough, certainly, is as good as a
feast!"

It was—I forget how long, some months—after this that Frank Brivet, whom I had not seen for two years, knocked again at my door. I didn't at all object to him at my other work as I did to Mrs Cavenham, but it was not till he had been in and out several times that Alice—which is what most people still really call her—chanced to see him and received in such an extraordinary way the impression that was to be of such advantage to him. She had been obliged to leave me that day before he went—though he stayed but a few minutes later; and it was not till the next time we were alone together that I was struck with her sudden interest, which became frankly pressing. I had met her, to begin with, expansively enough.

"An American? But what *sort*—don't you know? There are so many."

I didn't mean it as an offence, but in the matter of men, and though her acquaintance with them is so large, I always simplify with her. " *The* sort. He's rich."

"And how rich?"

"Why, *as* an American. Disgustingly."

I told her on this occasion more about him, but it was on that fact, I remember, that, after a short silence, she brought out with a sigh: "Well, I'm sorry. I should have liked to love him for himself."

II

QUITE apart from having been at school with him, I'm conscious—though at times he so puts me out—that I've a taste for Frank Brivet. I'm quite aware, by the same token—and even if when a man's so rich it's difficult to tell—that he's not everyone's affinity. I was struck, at all events, from the first of the affair, with the way he clung to me and seemed inclined to haunt my studio. He's fond of art, though he has some

awful pictures, and more or less understands mine; but it
wasn't this that brought him. Accustomed as I was to notice
what his wealth everywhere does for him, I was rather struck
with his being so much thrown upon me and not giving
London—the big fish that rises so to the hook baited with
gold—more of a chance to perform to him. I very soon, however, understood. He had his reasons for wishing not to be
seen much with Mrs Cavenham, and, as he was in love with
her, felt the want of some machinery for keeping temporarily
away from her. I was his machinery, and, when once I perceived this, was willing enough to turn his wheel. His situation, moreover, became interesting from the moment I fairly
grasped it, which he soon enabled me to do. His old reserve
on the subject of Mrs Brivet went to the winds, and it's not
my fault if I let him see how little I was shocked by his confidence. His marriage had originally seemed to me to require
much more explanation than anyone could give, and indeed
in the matter of women in general, I confess, I've never seized
his point of view. His inclinations are strange, and strange,
too, perhaps, his indifferences. Still, I can enter into some of
his aversions, and I agreed with him that his wife was odious.

"She has hitherto, since we began practically to live apart,"
he said, "mortally hated the idea of doing anything so pleasant
for me as to divorce me. But I've reason to believe she has
now changed her mind. She'd like to get clear."

I waited a moment. "For a man?"

"Oh, such a jolly good one! Remson Sturch."

I wondered. "Do you call *him* good?"

"Good for *her*. If she only can be got to be—which it
oughtn't to be difficult to make her—fool enough to marry
him, he'll give her the real size of his foot, and I shall be
avenged in a manner positively ideal."

"Then will she institute proceedings?"

"She can't, as things stand. She has nothing to go upon.
I've been," said poor Brivet, "I positively have, so blameless."

I thought of Mrs Cavenham, and, though I said nothing, he went on after an instant as if he knew it. "They can't put a finger. I've been so d——d particular."

I hesitated. "And your idea is now not to be particular any more?"

"Oh, about *her*," he eagerly replied, "always!" On which I laughed out and he coloured. "But my idea is nevertheless, at present," he went on, "to pave the way; that is, I mean, if I can keep the person you're thinking of so totally out of it that not a breath in the whole business can possibly touch her."

"I see," I reflected. "She isn't willing?"

He stared. "To be compromised? Why the devil *should* she be?"

"Why shouldn't she—for *you?* Doesn't she love you?"

"Yes, and it's because she does, dearly, that I don't feel the right way to repay her is by spattering her over."

"Yet if she stands," I argued, "straight in the splash——!"

"She doesn't!" he interrupted me, with some curtness. "She stands a thousand miles out of it; she stands on a pinnacle; she stands as she stands in your charming portrait—lovely, lonely, untouched. And so she must remain."

"It's beautiful, it's doubtless inevitable," I returned after a little, "that you should feel so. Only, if your wife doesn't divorce you for a woman you love, I don't quite see how she can do it for the woman you don't."

"Nothing is more simple," he declared; on which I saw he had figured it out rather more than I thought. "It will be quite enough if she *believes* I love her."

"If the lady in question does—or Mrs Brivet?"

"Mrs Brivet—confound her! If she believes I love somebody else. I must have the appearance, and the appearance must of course be complete. All I've got to do is to take up——"

"To take up——?" I asked, as he paused.

"Well, publicly, with someone or other; someone who

could easily be squared. One would undertake, after all, to produce the impression."

"On your wife naturally, you mean?"

"On my wife, and on the person concerned."

I turned it over and did justice to his ingenuity. "But what impression would you undertake to produce on——?"

"Well?" he inquired as I just faltered.

"On the person *not* concerned. How would the lady you just accused me of having in mind be affected toward such a proceeding?"

He had to think a little, but he thought with success. "Oh, I'd answer for her."

"To the other lady?" I laughed.

He remained quite grave. "To myself. She'd leave us alone. As it would be for her good, she'd understand."

I was sorry for him, but he struck me as artless. "Understand, in that interest, the 'spattering' of another person?"

He coloured again, but he was sturdy. "It must of course be exactly the right person—a special type. Someone who, in the first place," he explained, "wouldn't mind, and of whom, in the second, she wouldn't be jealous."

I followed perfectly, but it struck me as important all round that we should be clear. "But wouldn't the danger be great that any woman who shouldn't have that effect—the effect of jealousy—upon her wouldn't have it either on your wife?"

"Ah," he acutely returned, "my wife wouldn't be warned. She wouldn't be 'in the know.' "

"I see." I quite caught up. "The two other ladies distinctly would."

But he seemed for an instant at a loss. "Wouldn't it be indispensable only as regards one?"

"Then the other would be simply sacrificed?"

"She would be," Brivet splendidly put it, "remunerated."

I was pleased even with the sense of financial power betrayed by the way he said it, and I at any rate so took the measure of his intention of generosity and his characteristically big view of the matter that this quickly suggested to me what at least might be his exposure. "But suppose that, in spite of 'remuneration,' this secondary personage should perversely like you? She would have to be indeed, as you say, a special type, but even special types may have general feelings. Suppose she should like you too much."

It had pulled him up a little. "What do you mean by 'too much'?"

"Well, more than enough to leave the case quite as simple as you'd require it."

"Oh, money always simplifies. Besides, I should make a point of being a brute." And on my laughing at this: "I should pay her enough to keep her down, to make her easy. But the thing," he went on with a drop back to the less mitigated real—"the thing, hang it! is first to find her."

"Surely," I concurred; "for she should have to lack, you see, no requirement whatever for plausibility. She must be, for instance, not only 'squareable,' but—before anything else even—awfully handsome."

"Oh, 'awfully'!" He could make light of *that*, which was what Mrs Cavenham was.

"It wouldn't do for her, at all events," I maintained, "to be a bit less attractive than——"

"Well, than who?" he broke in, not only with a comic effect of disputing my point, but also as if he knew whom I was thinking of.

Before I could answer him, however, the door opened, and we were interrupted by a visitor—a visitor who, on the spot, in a flash, primed me with a reply. But I had of course for the moment to keep it to myself. "Than Mrs Dundene!"

III

I HAD nothing more than that to do with it, but before I could turn round it was done; by which I mean that Brivet, whose previous impression of her had, for some sufficient reason, failed of sharpness, now jumped straight to the perception that here to his hand for the solution of his problem was the missing quantity and the appointed aid. They were in presence on this occasion, for the first time, half an hour, during which he sufficiently showed me that he felt himself to have found the special type. He was certainly to that extent right that nobody could—in those days in particular—without a rapid sense that she was indeed "special," spend any such time in the company of our extraordinary friend. I couldn't quarrel with his recognising so quickly what I had myself instantly recognised, yet if it did in truth appear almost at a glance that she would, through the particular facts of situation, history, aspect, tone, temper, beautifully "do," I felt from the first so affected by the business that I desired to wash my hands of it. There was something I wished to say to him before it went further, but after that I cared only to be out of it. I may as well say at once, however, that I never *was* out of it; for a man habitually ridden by the twin demons of imagination and observation is never—enough for his peace—out of anything. But I wanted to be able to apply to either, should anything happen, " 'Thou canst not say *I* did it!' " What might in particular happen was represented by what I said to Brivet the first time he gave me a chance. It was what I had wished before the affair went further, but it had then already gone so far that he had been twice—as he immediately let me know— to see her at home. He clearly desired me to keep up with him, which I was eager to declare impossible; but he came again to

see me only after he had called. Then I instantly made my
point, which was that she was really, hang it! too good for his
fell purpose.

"But, my dear man, my purpose is a sacred one. And if,
moreover, she herself doesn't think she's too good——."

"Ah," said I, "she's in love with you, and so it isn't fair."

He wondered. "Fair to *me?*"

"Oh, I don't care a button for you! What I'm thinking of
is her risk."

"And what do you mean by her risk?"

"Why, her finding, of course, before you've done with
her, that she can't do without you."

He met me as if he had quite thought of that. "Isn't it much
more *my* risk?"

"Ah, but you take it deliberately, walk into it with your
eyes open. What I want to be sure of, liking her as I do, is
that she fully understands."

He had been moving about my place with his hands in his
pockets, and at this he stopped short. "How much do you
like her?"

"Oh, ten times more than she likes me; so *that* needn't
trouble you. Does she understand that it can be only to help
somebody else?"

"Why, my dear chap, she's as sharp as a steam-whistle."

"So that she also already knows who the other person is?"

He took a turn again, then brought out, "There's no other
person for her but me. Of course, as yet, there are things one
doesn't say; I haven't set straight to work to dot all my i's, and
the beauty of her, as she's really charming—and would be
charming in *any* relation—is just exactly that I don't expect to
have to. We'll work it out all right, I think, so that what I
most wanted just to make sure of from you was what you've
been good enough to tell me. I mean that you don't object—
for yourself."

I could with philosophic mirth allay that scruple, but what I couldn't do was to let him see what really most worried me. It stuck, as they say, in my crop that a woman like—yes, when all was said and done—Alice Dundene should simply minister to the convenience of a woman like Rose Cavenham. "But there's one thing more." This was as far as I could go. "I may take from you then that she not only knows it's for your divorce and remarriage, but can fit the shoe on the very person?"

He waited a moment. "Well, you may take from me that I find her no more of a fool than, as I seem to see, many other fellows have found her."

I too was silent a little, but with a superior sense of being able to think it all out further than he. "She's magnificent!"

"Well, so am I!" said Brivet. And for months afterward there was much—in fact everything—in the whole picture to justify his claim. I remember how it struck me as a lively sign of this that Mrs Cavenham, at an early day, gave up her pretty house in Wilton Street and withdrew for a time to America. That was palpable design and diplomacy, but I'm afraid that I quite as much, and doubtless very vulgarly, read into it that she had had money from Brivet to go. I even promised myself, I confess, the entertainment of finally making out that, whether or no the marriage should come off, she would not have been the person to find the episode least lucrative.

She left the others, at all events, completely together, and so, as the plot, with this, might be said definitely to thicken, it came to me in all sorts of ways that the curtain had gone up on the drama. It came to me, I hasten to add, much less from the two actors themselves than from other quarters—the usual sources, which never fail, of chatter; for after my friends' direction was fairly taken they had the good taste on either side to handle it, in talk, with gloves, not to expose it to what I should have called the danger of definition. I even seemed to divine that, allowing for needful preliminaries, they dealt even with each other on this same unformulated plane, and that it well might be that no relation in London at that moment, between a remarkable man and a beautiful woman, had more of the general air of good manners. I saw for a long time, directly, but little of them, for they were naturally much taken up, and Mrs Dundene in particular intermitted, as she had never yet done in any complication of her chequered career, her calls at my studio. As the months went by I couldn't but feel—partly, perhaps, for this very reason—that their undertaking announced itself as likely not to fall short of its aim. I gathered from the voices of the air that nothing whatever was neglected that could make it a success, and just this vision it was that made me privately project wonders into it, caused anxiety and curiosity often again to revisit me, and led me in fine to say to myself that so rich an effect could be arrived at on either side only by a great deal of heroism. As the omens markedly developed I supposed the heroism had likewise done so, and that the march of the matter was logical I inferred from the fact that even though the ordeal, all round, was more protracted than might have been feared, Mrs Cavenham made no fresh appearance. This I took as a sign that she knew she was safe—took indeed as the feature not the least striking of the situation constituted in her interest. I held my tongue, naturally, about her interest, but I watched it from a distance with an attention that, had I been caught in the act, might have led to a mistake about the direction of my sympathy. I had to make it my proper secret that, while I lost as little as possible of what was being done for her, I felt more and more that I myself could never have begun to do it.

IV

SHE came back at last, however, and one of the first things she did on her arrival was to knock at my door and let me know

immediately, to smooth the way, that she was there on particular business. I was not to be surprised—though even if I
were she shouldn't mind—to hear that she wished to bespeak
from me, on the smallest possible delay, a portrait, full-
length for preference, of our delightful friend Mr Brivet. She
brought this out with a light perfection of assurance of which
the first effect—I couldn't help it—was to make me show
myself almost too much amused for good manners. She first
stared at my laughter, then wonderfully joined in it, looking
meanwhile extraordinarily pretty and elegant—more completely handsome in fact, as well as more completely happy,
than I had ever yet seen her. She was distinctly the better, I
quickly saw, for what was being done for her, and it was an
odd spectacle indeed that while, out of her sight and to the
exclusion of her very name, the good work went on, it put
roses in her cheeks and rings on her fingers and the sense of
success in her heart. What had made me laugh, at all events,
was the number of other ideas suddenly evoked by her
request, two of which, the next moment, had disengaged
themselves with particular brightness. She wanted, for all her
confidence, to omit no precaution, to close up every issue, and
she had acutely conceived that the possession of Brivet's
picture—full-length, above all!—would constitute for her the
strongest possible appearance of holding his supreme pledge.
If that had been her foremost thought her second then had
been that if I should paint him he would have to sit, and that
in order to sit he would have to return. He had been at this
time, as I knew, for many weeks in foreign cities—which
helped moreover to explain to me that Mrs Cavenham had
thought it compatible with her safety to reopen her London
house. Everything accordingly seemed to make for a victory,
but there *was* such a thing, her proceeding implied, as one's—
at least as *her*—susceptibility and her nerves. This question of
his return I of course immediately put to her; on which she
immediately answered that it was expressed in her very

proposal, inasmuch as this proposal was nothing but the offer that Brivet had himself made her. The thing was to be his gift; she had only, he had assured her, to choose her artist and arrange the time; and she had amiably chosen me—chosen me for the dates, as she called them, immediately before us. I doubtless—but I don't care—give the measure of my native cynicism in confessing that I didn't the least avoid showing her that I saw through her game. "Well, I'll do him," I said, "if he'll come himself and ask me."

She wanted to know, at this, of course, if I impugned her veracity. "You don't believe what I tell you? You're afraid for your money?"

I took it in high good-humour "For my money not a bit."

"For what then?"

I had to think first how much I could say, which seemed to me, naturally, as yet but little. "I know perfectly that whatever happens Brivet always pays. But let him come; then we'll talk."

"Ah, well," she returned, "you'll see if he doesn't come." And come he did in fact—though without a word from myself directly—at the end of ten days; on which we immediately got to work, an idea highly favourable to it having meanwhile shaped itself in my own breast. Meanwhile too, however, before his arrival, Mrs Cavenham had been again to see me, and this it was precisely, I think, that determined my idea. My present explanation of what afresh passed between us is that she really felt the need to build up her security a little higher by borrowing from my own vision of what had been happening. I had not, she saw, been very near to that, but I had been at least, during her time in America, nearer than she. And I had doubtless somehow "aggravated" her by appearing to disbelieve in the guarantee she had come in such pride to parade to me. It had in any case befallen that, on the occasion of her second visit, what I least expected or desired—her avowal of being "in the know"—suddenly went too far to stop. When she

did speak she spoke with elation. "Mrs Brivet has filed her
petition."

"For getting rid of him?"

"Yes, in order to marry again; which is exactly what he
wants her to do. It's wonderful—and, in a manner, I think,
quite splendid—the way he has made it easy for her. He has
met her wishes handsomely—obliged her in every particular."

As she preferred, subtly enough, to put it all as if it were for
the sole benefit of his wife, I was quite ready for this tone; but
I privately defied her to keep it up. "Well, then, he hasn't
laboured in vain."

"Oh, it *couldn't* have been in vain. What has happened has
been the sort of thing that she couldn't possibly fail to act
upon."

"Too great a scandal, eh?"

She but just paused at it. "Nothing neglected, certainly, or
omitted. He was not the man to undertake it——"

"And not put it through? No, I should say he wasn't the
man. In any case he apparently hasn't been. But he must have
found the job——"

"Rather a bore?" she asked as I had hesitated.

"Well, not so much a bore as a delicate matter."

She seemed to demur. "Delicate?"

"Why, your sex likes him so."

"But isn't just that what has made it easy?"

"Easy for *him*—yes," I after a moment admitted.

But it wasn't what she meant. "And not difficult, also, for
them."

This was the nearest approach I was to have heard her
make, since the day of the meeting of the two women at my
studio, to naming Mrs Dundene. She never, to the end of the
affair, came any closer to her in speech than by the collective
and promiscuous plural pronoun. There might have been a
dozen of them, and she took cognizance, in respect to them,
only of quantity. It was as if it had been a way of showing how

little of anything else she imputed. Quality, as distinguished from quantity, was what *she* had. "Oh, I think," I said, "that we can scarcely speak for them."

"Why not? They must certainly have had the most beautiful time. Operas, theatres, suppers, dinners, diamonds, carriages, journeys hither and yon with him, poor dear, telegrams sent by each from everywhere to everywhere and always lying about, elaborate arrivals and departures at stations for everyone to see, and, in fact, quite a crowd usually collected—as many witnesses as you like. Then," she wound up, "his brougham standing always—half the day and half the night—at their doors. He has had to keep a brougham, and the proper sort of man, just for that alone. In other words unlimited publicity."

"I see. What more can they have wanted? Yes," I pondered, "they like, for the most part, we suppose, a studied, outrageous *affichage*, and they must have thoroughly enjoyed it."

"Ah, but it was only that."

I wondered. "Only what?"

"Only *affiché*. Only outrageous. Only the *form* of—well, of what would definitely serve. He never saw them alone."

I wondered—or at least appeared to—still more. "Never?"

"Never. Never once." She had a wonderful air of answering for it. "I know."

I saw that, after all, she really believed she knew, and I had indeed, for that matter, to recognise that I myself believed her knowledge to be sound. Only there went with it a complacency, an enjoyment of having really made me see what could be done for her, so little to my taste that for a minute or two I could scarce trust myself to speak: she looked somehow, as she sat there, so lovely, and yet, in spite of her loveliness—or perhaps even just because of it—so smugly selfish; she put it to me with so small a consciousness of anything but her personal triumph that, while she had kept her skirts clear, her name unuttered and her reputation untouched, "they" had been in it even more than her success required. It was their skirts, their name and their reputation that, in the proceedings at hand, would bear the brunt. It was only after waiting a while that I could at last say: "You're perfectly sure then of Mrs Brivet's intention?"

"Oh, we've had formal notice."

"And he's himself satisfied of the sufficiency——?"

"Of the sufficiency——?"

"Of what he has done."

She rectified. "Of what he has *appeared* to do."

"That *is* then enough?"

"Enough," she laughed, "to send him to the gallows!" To which I could only reply that all was well that ended well.

V

ALL for me, however, as it proved, had not ended yet. Brivet, as I have mentioned, duly reappeared to sit for me, and Mrs Cavenham, on his arrival, as consistently went abroad. He confirmed to me that lady's news of how he had "fetched," as he called it, his wife—let me know, as decently owing to me after what had passed, on the subject, between us, that the forces set in motion had logically operated; but he made no other allusion to his late accomplice—for I now took for granted the close of the connection—than was conveyed in this intimation. He spoke—and the effect was almost droll— as if he had had, since our previous meeting, a busy and responsible year and wound up an affair (as he was accustomed to wind up affairs) involving a mass of detail; he even dropped into occasional reminiscence of what he had seen and enjoyed and disliked during a recent period of rather far-reaching adventure; but he stopped just as short as Mrs Cavenham had done—and, indeed, much shorter than she—of introducing

Mrs Dundene by name into our talk. And what was singular in this, I soon saw, was—apart from a general discretion—that he abstained not at all because his mind was troubled, but just because, on the contrary, it was so much at ease. It was perhaps even more singular still, meanwhile, that, though I had scarce been able to bear Mrs Cavenham's manner in this particular, I found I could put up perfectly with that of her friend. She had annoyed me, but he didn't—I give the inconsistency for what it is worth. The obvious state of his conscience had always been a strong point in him and one that exactly irritated some people as much as it charmed others; so that if, in general, it was positively, and in fact quite aggressively approving, this monitor, it had never held its head so high as at the juncture of which I speak. I took all this in with eagerness, for I saw how it would play into my work. Seeking as I always do, instinctively, to represent sitters in the light of the thing, whatever it may be, that facially, least wittingly or responsibly, gives the pitch of their aspect, I felt immediately that I should have the clue for making a capital thing of Brivet were I to succeed in showing him in just this freshness of his cheer. His cheer was that of his being able to say to himself that he had got all he wanted precisely *as* he wanted: without having harmed a fly. He had arrived so neatly where most men arrive besmirched, and what he seemed to cry out as he stood before my canvas—wishing everyone well all round—was: "See how clever and pleasant and practicable, how jolly and lucky and rich I've been!" I determined, at all events, that I would make some such characteristic words as these cross, at any cost, the footlights, as it were, of my frame.

Well, I can't but feel to this hour that I really hit my nail—that the man *is* fairly painted in the light and that the work remains as yet my high-water mark. He himself was delighted with it—and all the more, I think, that before it was finished he received from America the news of his liberation. He had not defended the suit—as to which judgment, therefore, had

been expeditiously rendered; and he was accordingly free as
air and with the added sweetness of every augmented appearance that his wife was herself blindly preparing to seek chas-
tisement at the hands of destiny. There being at last no
obstacle to his open association with Mrs Cavenham, he
called her directly back to London to admire my achievement,
over which, from the very first glance, she as amiably let
herself go. It was the very view of him she had desired to
possess; it was the dear man in his intimate essence for those
who knew him; and for any one who should ever be deprived
of him it would be the next best thing to the sound of his voice.
We of course by no means lingered, however, on the contingency of privation, which was promptly swept away in the
rush of Mrs Cavenham's vision of how straight also, above
and beyond, I had, as she called it, attacked. I couldn't quite
myself, I fear, tell how straight, but Mrs Cavenham perfectly
could, and did, for everybody: she had at her fingers' ends all
the reasons why the thing would be a treasure even for those
who had never seen "Frank."

I had finished the picture, but was, according to my practice, keeping it near me a little, for afterthoughts, when I
received from Mrs Dundene the first visit she had paid me
for many a month. "I've come," she immediately said, "to
ask you a favour"; and she turned her eyes, for a minute, as
if contentedly full of her thought, round the large workroom
she already knew so well and in which her beauty had really
rendered more services than could ever be repaid. There were
studies of her yet on the walls; there were others thrust away
in corners; others still had gone forth from where she stood
and carried to far-away places the reach of her lingering look.
I had greatly, almost inconveniently missed her, and I don't
know why it was that she struck me now as more beautiful
than ever. She had always, for that matter, had a way of seeming each time a little different and a little better. Dressed very
simply in black materials, feathers and lace, that gave the

impression of being light and fine, she had indeed the air of a special type, but quite as some great lady might have had it. She looked like a princess in Court mourning. Oh, she had been a case for the petitioner—was everything the other side wanted! "Mr Brivet," she went on to say, "has kindly offered me a present. I'm to ask of him whatever in the world I most desire."

I knew in an instant, on this, what was coming, but I was at first wholly taken up with the simplicity of her allusion to her late connection. Had I supposed that, like Brivet, she wouldn't allude to it at all? or had I stupidly assumed that if she did it would be with ribaldry and rancour? I hardly know; I only know that I suddenly found myself charmed to receive from her thus the key of my own freedom. There was something I wanted to say to her, and she had thus given me leave. But for the moment I only repeated as with amused interest: "Whatever in the world——?"

"Whatever in all the world."

"But that's immense, and in what way can poor *I* help——?"

"By painting him for me. I want a portrait of him."

I looked at her a moment in silence. She was lovely. "That's what—'in all the world'—you've chosen?"

"Yes—thinking it over: full-length. I want it for remembrance, and I want it as you will do it. It's the only thing I do want."

"Nothing else?"

"Oh, it's enough." I turned about—she was wonderful. I had whisked out of sight for a month the picture I had produced for Mrs Cavenham, and it was now completely covered with a large piece of stuff. I stood there a little, thinking of it, and she went on as if she feared I might be unwilling. "*Can't* you do it?"

It showed me that she had not heard from him of my having painted him, and this, further, was an indication that, his purpose effected, he had ceased to see her. "I suppose you know," I presently said, "what you've done for him?"

"Oh yes; it was what I wanted."

"It was what *he* wanted!" I laughed.

"Well, I want what he wants."

"Even to his marrying Mrs Cavenham?"

She hesitated. "As well her as anyone, from the moment he couldn't marry *me*."

"It was beautiful of you to be so sure of that," I returned.

"How could I be anything else but sure? He doesn't so much as *know* me!" said Alice Dundene.

"No," I declared, "I verily believe he doesn't. There's your picture," I added, unveiling my work.

She was amazed and delighted. "I may have *that?*"

"So far as I'm concerned—absolutely."

"Then he had himself the beautiful thought of sitting for me?"

I faltered but an instant. "Yes."

Her pleasure in what I had done was a joy to me. "Why, it's of a truth——! It's perfection."

"I think it is."

"It's the whole story. It's life."

"That's what I tried for," I said; and I added to myself: "Why the deuce *do* we?"

"It will be *him* for me," she meanwhile went on. "I shall *live* with it, keep it all to myself, and—do you know what it will do?—it will seem to make up."

"To make up?"

"I never saw him alone," said Mrs Dundene.

I am still keeping the thing to send to her, punctually, on the day he's married; but I had of course, on my understanding with her, a tremendous bout with Mrs Cavenham, who protested with indignation against my "base treachery" and made to Brivet an appeal for redress which, enlightened, face to face with the magnificent humility of his other friend's selection, he couldn't, for shame, entertain. All he was able to do was to suggest to me that I might for one or other of the ladies, at my choice, do him again; but I had no difficulty in replying that my best was my best and that what was done was done. He assented with the awkwardness of a man in dispute between women, and Mrs Cavenham remained furious. "Can't 'they'—of *all* possible things, think!—take something else?"

"Oh, they want *him!*"

"Him?" It was monstrous.

"To live with," I explained—"to make up."

"To make up for what?"

"Why, you know, they never saw him alone."

THE TONE OF TIME

I

I WAS too pleased with what it struck me that, as an old, old friend, I had done for her, not to go to her that very afternoon with the news. I knew she worked late, as in general I also did; but I sacrificed for her sake a good hour of the February daylight. She was in her studio, as I had believed she would be, where her card ("Mary J. Tredick"—not Mary Jane, but Mary Juliana) was manfully on the door; a little tired, a little old and a good deal spotted, but with her ugly spectacles taken off, as soon as I appeared, to greet me. She kept on, while she scraped her palette and wiped her brushes, the big stained apron that covered her from head to foot and that I have often enough before seen her retain in conditions giving the measure of her renunciation of her desire to dazzle. Every fresh reminder of this brought home to me that she had given up everything but her work, and that there had been in her history some reason. But I was as far from the reason as ever. She had given up too much; this was just why one wanted to lend her a hand. I told her, at any rate, that I had a lovely job for her.

"To copy something I do like?"

Her complaint, I knew, was that people only gave orders, if they gave them at all, for things she did not like. But this wasn't a case of copying—not at all, at least, in the common sense. "It's for a portrait—quite in the air."

"Ah, you do portraits yourself!"

"Yes, and you know how. My trick won't serve for this. What's wanted is a pretty picture."

"Then of whom?"

"Of nobody. That is of anybody. Anybody you like."

She naturally wondered. "Do you mean I'm myself to choose my sitter?"

"Well, the oddity is that there is to *be* no sitter."

"Whom then is the picture to represent?"

"Why, a handsome, distinguished, agreeable man, of not more than forty, clean-shaven, thoroughly well-dressed, and a perfect gentleman."

She continued to stare. "And I'm to find him myself?"

I laughed at the term she used. "Yes, as you 'find' the canvas, the colours and the frame." After which I immediately explained. "I've just had the 'rummest' visit, the effect of which was to make me think of you. A lady, unknown to me and unintroduced, turned up at my place at three o'clock. She had come straight, she let me know, without preliminaries, on account of one's high reputation—the usual thing—and of her having admired one's work. Of course I instantly saw—I mean I saw it as soon as she named her affair—that she hadn't understood my work at all. What am I good for in the world but just the impression of the given, the presented case? I can do but the face I see."

"And do you think I can do the face I don't?"

"No, but you see so many more. You see them in fancy and memory, and they come out, for you, from all the museums you've haunted and all the great things you've studied. I *know* you'll be able to see the one my visitor wants and to give it—what's the *crux* of the business—the tone of time."

She turned the question over. "What does she want it for?"

"Just *for* that—for the tone of time. And, except that it's to hang over her chimney, she didn't tell me. I've only my idea that it's to represent, to symbolise, as it were, her husband, who's not alive and who perhaps never was. This is exactly what will give you a free hand."

"With nothing to go by—no photographs or other portraits?"

"Nothing."

"She only proposes to describe him?"

"Not even; she wants the picture itself to do that. Her only
condition is that he be a *très-bel homme.*"

She had begun at last, a little thoughtfully, to remove her
apron. "Is she French?"

"I don't know. I give it up. She calls herself Mrs Bridgenorth."

Mary wondered. "*Connais pas!* I never heard of her."

"You wouldn't."

"You mean it's not her real name?"

I hesitated. "I mean that she's a very downright fact, full of
the implication that she'll pay a downright price. It's clear to
me that you can ask what you like; and it's therefore a chance
that I can't consent to your missing." My friend gave no sign
either way, and I told my story. "She's a woman of fifty,
perhaps of more, who has been pretty, and who still presents
herself, with her grey hair a good deal powdered, as I judge, to
carry it off, extraordinarily well. She was a little frightened
and a little free; the latter because of the former. But she did
uncommonly well, I thought, considering the oddity of her
wish. This oddity she quite admits; she began indeed by insisting on it so in advance that I found myself expecting I
didn't know what. She broke at moments into French, which
was perfect, but no better than her English, which isn't
vulgar; not more at least than that of everybody else. The
things people *do* say, and the way they say them, to artists!
She wanted immensely, I could see, not to fail of her errand,
not to be treated as absurd; and she was extremely grateful to
me for meeting her so far as I did. She was beautifully dressed
and she came in a brougham."

My listener took it in; then, very quietly, "Is she respectable?" she inquired.

"Ah, there you are!" I laughed; "and how you always pick the point right out, even when one has endeavoured to diffuse a specious glamour! She's extraordinary," I pursued after an instant; "and just what she wants of the picture, I think, is to make her a little less so."

"Who is she, then? What is she?" my companion simply went on.

It threw me straightway back on one of my hobbies. "Ah, my dear, what is so interesting as life? What is, above all, so stupendous as London? There's everything in it, everything in the world, and nothing too amazing not some day to pop out at you. What is a woman, faded, preserved, pretty, powdered, vague, odd, dropping on one without credentials, but with a carriage and very good lace? What is such a person but a person who *may* have had adventures, and have made them, in one way or another, pay? They're, however, none of one's business; it's scarcely on the cards that one should ask her. I should like, with Mrs Bridgenorth, to see a fellow ask! She goes in for propriety, the real thing. If I suspect her of being the creation of her own talents, she has clearly, on the other hand, seen a lot of life. Will you meet her?" I next demanded.

My hostess waited. "No."

"Then you won't try?"

"Need I meet her to try?" And the question made me guess that, so far as she had understood, she began to feel herself a little taken. "It seems strange," she none the less mused, "to attempt to please her on such a basis. To attempt," she presently added, "to please her at all. It's your idea that she's not married?" she, with this, a trifle inconsequently asked.

"Well," I replied, "I've only had an hour to think of it, but I somehow already see the scene. Not immediately, not the day after, or even perhaps the year after the thing she desires is set up there, but in due process of time and on convenient opportunity, the transfiguration will occur. 'Who is that awfully

handsome man?' 'That? Oh, that's an old sketch of my dear
dead husband.' Because I told her—insidiously sounding her
—that she would want it to look old, and that the tone of time
is exactly what you're full of."

"I believe I am," Mary sighed at last.

"Then put on your hat." I had proposed to her on my
arrival to come out to tea with me, and it was when left alone
in the studio while she went to her room that I began to feel
sure of the success of my errand. The vision that had an hour
before determined me grew deeper and brighter for her while
I moved about and looked at her things. There were more of
them there on her hands than one liked to see; but at least they
sharpened my confidence, which was pleasant for me in view
of that of my visitor, who had accepted without reserve my
plea for Miss Tredick. Four or five of her copies of famous
portraits—ornaments of great public and private collections
—were on the walls, and to see them again together was to
feel at ease about my guarantee. The mellow manner of them
was what I had had in my mind in saying, to excuse myself to
Mrs Bridgenorth, "Oh, my things, you know, look as if they
had been painted to-morrow!" It made no difference that
Mary's Vandykes and Gainsboroughs were reproductions and
replicas, for I had known her more than once to amuse herself
with doing the thing quite, as she called it, off her own bat.
She had copied so bravely so many brave things that she had
at the end of her brush an extraordinary bag of tricks. She had
always replied to me that such things were mere clever humbug, but mere clever humbug was what our client happened
to want. The thing was to let her have it—one could trust her
for the rest. And at the same time that I mused in this way I
observed to myself that there was already something more
than, as the phrase is, met the eye in such response as I felt my
friend had made. I had touched, without intention, more than
one spring; I had set in motion more than one impulse. I
found myself indeed quite certain of this after she had come

back in her hat and her jacket. She was different—her idea had flowered; and she smiled at me from under her tense veil, while she drew over her firm, narrow hands a pair of fresh gloves, with a light distinctly new. "Please tell your friend that I'm greatly obliged to both of you and that I take the order."

"Good. And to give him all his good looks?"

"It's just to do *that* that I accept. I shall make him supremely beautiful—and supremely base."

"Base?" I just demurred.

"The finest gentleman you'll ever have seen, and the worst friend."

I wondered, as I was startled; but after an instant I laughed for joy. "Ah well, so long as he's not mine! I see we *shall* have him," I said as we went, for truly I had touched a spring. In fact I had touched *the* spring.

It rang, more or less, I was presently to find, all over the place. I went, as I had promised, to report to Mrs Bridgenorth on my mission, and though she declared herself much gratified at the success of it I could see she a little resented the apparent absence of any desire on Miss Tredick's part for a preliminary conference. "I only thought she might have liked just to see me, and have imagined I might like to see *her*."

But I was full of comfort. "You'll see her when it's finished. You'll see her in time to thank her."

"And to pay her, I suppose," my hostess laughed, with an asperity that was, after all, not excessive. "Will she take very long?"

I thought. "She's so full of it that my impression would be that she'll do it off at a heat."

"She *is* full of it then?" she asked; and on hearing to what tune, though I told her but half, she broke out with admiration. "You artists are the most extraordinary people!" It was almost with a bad conscience that I confessed we indeed were, and while she said that what she meant was that we seemed to understand everything, and I rejoined that this was also what *I* meant, she took me into another room to see the place for the picture—a proceeding of which the effect was singularly to confirm the truth in question. The place for the picture— in her own room, as she called it, a boudoir at the back, over- looking the general garden of the approved modern row and, as she said, only just wanting that touch—proved exactly the place (the space of a large panel in the white woodwork over the mantel) that I had spoken of to my friend. She put it quite candidly, "Don't you see what it will do?" and looked at me, wonderfully, as for a sign that I could sympathetically take from her what she didn't literally say. She said it, poor woman, so very nearly that I had no difficulty whatever. The portrait, tastefully enshrined there, of the finest gentleman one should ever have seen, would do even more for herself than it would do for the room.

I may as well mention at once that my observation of Mrs Bridgenorth was not in the least of a nature to unseat me from the hobby I have already named. In the light of the impression she made on me life seemed quite as prodigious and London quite as amazing as I had ever contended, and nothing could have been more in the key of that experience than the manner in which everything was vivid between us and nothing ex- pressed. We remained on the surface with the tenacity of ship- wrecked persons clinging to a plank. Our plank was our con- centrated gaze at Mrs Bridgenorth's mere present. We allowed her past to exist for us only in the form of the prettiness that she had gallantly rescued from it and to which a few scraps of its identity still adhered. She was amiable, gentle, con- sistently proper. She gave me more than anything else the sense, simply, of waiting. She was like a house so freshly and successfully "done up" that you were surprised it wasn't occupied. She was waiting for something to happen—for somebody to come. She was waiting, above all, for Mary Tredick's work. She clearly counted that it would help her.

I had foreseen the fact—the picture was produced at a heat; rapidly, directly, at all events, for the sort of thing it proved to be. I left my friend alone at first, left the ferment to work, troubling her with no questions and asking her for no news; two or three weeks passed, and I never went near her. Then at last, one afternoon as the light was failing, I looked in. She immediately knew what I wanted. "Oh yes, I'm doing him."

"Well," I said, "I've respected your intensity, but I *have* felt curious."

I may not perhaps say that she was never so sad as when she laughed, but it's certain that she always laughed when she was sad. When, however, poor dear, for that matter, was she, secretly, not? Her little gasps of mirth were the mark of her worst moments. But why should she have one of these just now? "Oh, I know your curiosity!" she replied to me; and the small chill of her amusement scarcely met it. "He's coming out, but I can't show him to you yet. I must muddle it through in my own way. It has insisted on being, after all, a 'likeness,' " she added. "But nobody will ever know."

"Nobody?"

"Nobody *she* sees."

"Ah, she doesn't, poor thing," I returned, "seem to see anybody!"

"So much the better. I'll risk it." On which I felt I should have to wait, though I had suddenly grown impatient. But I still hung about, and while I did so she explained. "If what I've done is really a portrait, the conditions itself prescribed it. If I was to do the most beautiful man in the world I could do but one."

We looked at each other; then I laughed. "It can scarcely be *me!* But you're getting," I asked, "the great thing?"

"The infamy? Oh yes, please God."

It took away my breath a little, and I even for the moment scarce felt at liberty to press. But one could always be cheerful. "What I meant is the tone of time."

"Getting it, my dear man? Didn't I get it long ago? Don't I *show* it—the tone of time?" she suddenly, strangely sighed at me, with something in her face I had never yet seen. "I can't give it to him more than—for all these years—he was to have given it to *me*."

I scarce knew what smothered passion, what remembered wrong, what mixture of joy and pain my words had accidentally quickened. Such an effect of them could only become, for me, an instant pity, which, however, I brought out but indirectly. "It's the tone," I smiled, "in which you're speaking now."

This served, unfortunately, as something of a check. "I didn't mean to speak now." Then with her eyes on the picture, "I've said everything there. Come back," she added, "in three days. He'll be all right."

He was indeed when at last I saw him. She had produced an extraordinary thing—a thing wonderful, ideal, for the part it was to play. My only reserve, from the first, was that it was too fine for its part, that something much less "sincere" would equally have served Mrs Bridgenorth's purpose, and that relegation to that lady's "own room"—whatever charm it was to work there—might only mean for it cruel obscurity. The picture is before me now, so that I could describe it if description availed. It represents a man of about five-and-thirty, seen only as to the head and shoulders, but dressed, the observer gathers, in a fashion now almost antique and which was far from contemporaneous with the date of the work. His high, slightly narrow face, which would be perhaps too aquiline but for the beauty of the forehead and the sweetness of the mouth, has a charm that even, after all these years, still stirs my imagination. His type has altogether a distinction that you feel to have been firmly caught and yet not vulgarly emphasised. The eyes are just too near together, but they are, in a wondrous way, both careless and intense, while lip, cheek, and chin, smooth and clear, are admirably drawn.

Youth is still, you see, in all his presence, the joy and pride of life, the perfection of a high spirit and the expectation of a great fortune, which he takes for granted with unconscious insolence. Nothing has ever happened to humiliate or disappoint him, and if my fancy doesn't run 'away with me the whole presentation of him is a guarantee that he will die without having suffered. He is so handsome, in short, that you can scarcely say what he means, and so happy that you can scarcely guess what he feels.

It is of course, I hasten to add, an appreciably feminine rendering, light, delicate, vague, imperfectly synthetic—insistent and evasive, above all, in the wrong places; but the composition, none the less, is beautiful and the suggestion infinite. The grandest air of the thing struck me in fact, when first I saw it, as coming from the high artistic impertinence with which it offered itself as painted about 1850. It would have been a rare flower of refinement for that dark day. The "tone"—that of such a past as it pretended to—was there almost to excess, a brown bloom into which the image seemed mysteriously to retreat. The subject of it looks at me now across more years and more knowledge, but what I felt at the moment was that he managed to be at once a triumphant trick and a plausible evocation. He hushed me, I remember, with so many kinds of awe that I shouldn't have dreamt of asking who he was. All I said, after my first incoherences of wonder at my friend's practised skill, was: "And you've arrived at this truth without documents?"

"It depends on what you call documents."

"Without notes, sketches, studies?"

"I destroyed them years ago."

"Then you once had them?"

She just hung fire. "I once had everything."

It told me both more and less than I had asked; enough at all events to make my next question, as I uttered it, sound even to myself a little foolish. "So that it's all memory?"

From where she stood she looked once more at her work; after which she jerked away and, taking several steps, came back to me with something new—whatever it was I had already seen—in her air and answer. "It's all *hate!*" she threw at me, and then went out of the room. It was not till she had gone that I quite understood why. Extremely affected by the impression visibly made on me, she had burst into tears but had wished me not to see them. She left me alone for some time with her wonderful subject, and I again, in her absence, made things out. He was dead—he had been dead for years; the sole humiliation, as I have called it, that he was to know had come to him in that form. The canvas held and cherished him, in any case, as it only holds the dead. She had suffered from him, it came to me, the worst that a woman can suffer, and the wound he had dealt her, though hidden, had never effectually healed. It had bled again while she worked. Yet when she at last reappeared there was but one thing to say. "The beauty, heaven knows, I see. But I don't see what you call the infamy."

She gave him a last look—again she turned away. "Oh, he was like that."

"Well, whatever he was like," I remember replying, "I wonder you can bear to part with him. Isn't it better to let her see the picture first here?"

As to this she doubted. "I don't think I want her to come."

I wondered. "You continue to object so to meet her?"

"What good will it do? It's quite impossible I should alter him for her."

"Oh, she won't want *that!*" I laughed. "She'll adore him as he is."

"Are you quite sure of your idea?"

"That he's to figure as Mr Bridgenorth? Well, if I hadn't been from the first, my dear lady, I should be now. Fancy, with the chance, her *not* jumping at him! Yes, he'll figure as Mr Bridgenorth."

"Mr Bridgenorth!" she echoed, making the sound, with her small, cold laugh, grotesquely poor for him. He might really have been a prince, and I wondered if he hadn't been. She had, at all events, a new notion. "Do you mind my having it taken to your place and letting her come to see it there?" Which—as I immediately embraced her proposal, deferring to her reasons, whatever they were—was what was speedily arranged.

II

THE next day therefore I had the picture in charge, and on the following Mrs Bridgenorth, whom I had notified, arrived. I had placed it, framed and on an easel, well in evidence, and I have never forgotten the look and the cry that, as she became aware of it, leaped into her face and from her lips. It was an extraordinary moment, all the more that it found me quite unprepared—so extraordinary that I scarce knew at first what had happened. By the time I really perceived, moreover, more things had happened than one, so that when I pulled myself together it was to face the situation as a whole. She had recognised on the instant the subject; that came first and was irrepressibly vivid in her. Her recognition had, for the length of a flash, lighted for her the possibility that the stroke had been directed. That came second, and she flushed with it as with a blow in the face. What came third—and it was what was really most wondrous—was the quick instinct of getting both her strange recognition and her blind suspicion well in hand. She couldn't control, however, poor woman, the strong colour in her face and the quick tears in her eyes. She could only glare at the canvas, gasping, grimacing, and try to gain time. Whether in surprise or in resentment she intensely reflected, feeling more than anything else how little she might prudently show; and I was conscious even at the moment that nothing of its kind could have been finer than her effort to swallow her shock in ten seconds.

How many seconds she took I didn't measure; enough, assuredly, for me also to profit. I gained more time than she, and the greatest oddity doubtless was my own private manœuvre—the quickest calculation that, acting from a mere confused instinct, I had ever made. If she had known the great gentleman represented there and yet had determined on the spot to carry herself as ignorant, all my loyalty to Mary Tredick came to the surface in a prompt counter-move. What gave me opportunity was the red in her cheek. "Why, you've known him!"

I saw her ask herself for an instant if she mightn't successfully make her startled state pass as the mere glow of pleasure —her natural greeting to her acquisition. She was pathetically, yet at the same time almost comically, divided. Her line was so to cover her tracks that every avowal of a past connection was a danger; but it also concerned her safety to learn, in the light of our astounding coincidence, how far she already stood exposed. She meanwhile begged the question. She smiled through her tears. "He's too magnificent!"

But I gave her, as I say, all too little time. "Who is he? Who *was* he?"

It must have been my look still more than my words that determined her. She wavered but an instant longer, panted, laughed, cried again, and then, dropping into the nearest seat, gave herself up so completely that I was almost ashamed. "Do you think I'd tell you his *name?*" The burden of the backward years—all the effaced and ignored—lived again, almost like an accent unlearned but freshly breaking out at a touch, in the very sound of the words. These perceptions she, however, the next thing showed me, were a game at which two could play. She had to look at me but an instant. "Why, you really *don't* know it!"

I judged best to be frank. "I don't know it."

"Then how does *she?*"

"How do you?" I laughed. "I'm a different matter."

She sat a minute turning things round, staring at the picture. "The likeness, the likeness!" It was almost too much.

"It's so true?"

"Beyond everything."

I considered. "But a resemblance to a known individual— that wasn't what you wanted."

She sprang up at this in eager protest. "Ah, no one else would see it."

I showed again, I fear, my amusement. "No one but you and she?"

"It's her doing *him!*" She was held by her wonder. "Doesn't she, on your honour, know?"

"That his is the very head you would have liked if you had dared? Not a bit. How *should* she? She knows nothing— on my honour."

Mrs Bridgenorth continued to marvel. "She just painted him for the kind of face———?"

"That corresponds with my description of what you wished? Precisely."

"But *how*—after so long? From memory? As a friend?"

"As a reminiscence—yes. Visual memory, you see, in our uncanny race, is wonderful. As the ideal thing, simply, for your purpose. You *are* then suited?" I after an instant added.

She had again been gazing, and at this turned her eyes on me; but I saw she couldn't speak, couldn't do more at least than sound, unutterably, "Suited!" so that I was positively not surprised when suddenly—just as Mary had done, the power to produce this effect seeming a property of the model —she burst into tears. I feel no harsher in relating it, however I may appear, than I did at the moment, but it is a fact that while she just wept I literally had a fresh inspiration on behalf of Miss Tredick's interests. I knew exactly, moreover, before my companion had recovered herself, what she would next ask me; and I consciously brought this appeal on in order to have it over. I explained that I had not the least idea of the identity of our artist's sitter, to which she had given me no clue. I had nothing but my impression that she had known him—known him well; and, from whatever material she had worked, the fact of his having also been known to Mrs Bridgenorth was a coincidence pure and simple. It partook of the nature of prodigy, but such prodigies did occur. My visitor listened with avidity and credulity. She was so far reassured. Then I saw her question come. "Well, if she doesn't dream he was ever anything to me—or what he will be now—I'm going to ask you, as a very particular favour, never to tell her. She will want to know of course exactly how I've been struck. You'll naturally say that I'm delighted, but may I exact from you that you say nothing else?"

There was supplication in her face, but I had to think. "There are conditions I must put to you first, and one of them is also a question, only more frank than yours. Was this mysterious personage—frustrated by death—to have married you?"

She met it bravely. "Certainly, if he had lived."

I was only amused at an artlessness in her "certainly." "Very good. But why do you wish the coincidence——"

"Kept from her?" She knew exactly why. "Because if she suspects it she won't let me have the picture. Therefore," she added with decision, "you must let me pay for it on the spot."

"What do you mean by on the spot?"

"I'll send you a cheque as soon as I get home."

"Oh," I laughed, "let us understand. Why do you consider she won't let you have the picture?"

She made me wait a little for this, but when it came it was perfectly lucid. "Because she'll then see how much more I must want it."

"How much less—wouldn't it be rather, since the bargain was, as the more convenient thing, not for a likeness?"

"Oh," said Mrs Bridgenorth with impatience, "the likeness will take care of itself. She'll put this and that together." Then she brought out her real apprehension. "She'll be jealous."

"Oh!" I laughed. But I was startled.

"She'll hate me!"

I wondered. "But I don't think she liked him."

"Don't think?" She stared at me, with her echo, over all that might be in it, then seemed to find little enough. "I *say!*"

It was almost comically the old Mrs Bridgenorth. "But I gather from her that he was bad."

"Then what was *she?*"

I barely hesitated. "What were *you?*"

"That's my own business." And she turned again to the picture. "He was good enough for her to do *that* of him."

I took it in once more. "Artistically speaking, for the way it's done, it's one of the most curious things I've ever seen."

"It's a grand treat!" said poor Mrs Bridgenorth more simply.

It was, it *is* really; which is exactly what made the case so interesting. "Yet I feel somehow that, as I say, it wasn't done with love."

It was wonderful how she understood. "It was done with rage."

"Then what have you to fear?"

She knew again perfectly. "What happened when he made *me* jealous. So much," she declared, "that if you'll give me your word for silence——"

"Well?"

"Why, I'll double the money."

"Oh," I replied, taking a turn about in the excitement of our concurrence, "that's exactly what—to do a still better stroke for her—it had just come to *me* to propose!"

"It's understood then, on your oath as a gentleman?" She

was so eager that practically this settled it, though I moved to and fro a little while she watched me in suspense. It vibrated all round us that she had gone out to the thing in a stifled flare, that a whole close relation had in the few minutes revived. We know it of the truly amiable person that he will strain a point for another that he wouldn't strain for himself. The stroke to put in for Mary was positively prescribed. The work represented really much more than had been covenanted, and if the purchaser chose so to value it this was her own affair. I decided. "If it's understood also on *your* word."

We were so at one that we shook hands on it. "And when may I send?"

"Well, I shall see her this evening. Say early to-morrow."

"Early to-morrow." And I went with her to her brougham, into which, I remember, as she took leave, she expressed regret that she mightn't then and there have introduced the canvas for removal. I consoled her with remarking that she couldn't have got it in—which was not quite true.

I saw Mary Tredick before dinner, and though I was not quite ideally sure of my present ground with her I instantly brought out my news. "She's so delighted that I felt I must in conscience do something still better for you. She's not to have it on the original terms. I've put up the price."

Mary wondered. "But to what?"

"Well, to four hundred. If you say so I'll try even for five."

"Oh, she'll never give that."

"I beg your pardon."

"After the agreement?" She looked grave. "I don't like such leaps and bounds."

"But, my dear child, they're yours. You contracted for a decorative trifle and you've produced a breathing master-piece."

She thought. "Is that what she calls it?" Then, as having to think too, I hesitated, "What does she know?" she pursued.

"She knows she wants it."

"So much as that?"

At this I had to brace myself a little. "So much that she'll send me the cheque this afternoon, and that you'll have mine by the first post in the morning."

"Before she has even received the picture?"

"Oh, she'll send for it to-morrow." And as I was dining out and had still to dress, my time was up. Mary came with me to the door, where I repeated my assurance. "You shall receive my cheque by the first post." To which I added: "If it's little enough for a lady so much in need to pay for *any* husband, it isn't worth mentioning as the price of such a one as you've given her!"

I was in a hurry, but she held me. "Then you've felt your idea confirmed?"

"My idea?"

"That that's what I *have* given her?"

I suddenly fancied I had perhaps gone too far; but I had kept my cab and was already in it. "Well, put it," I called with excess of humour over the front, "that you've, at any rate, given *him* a wife!"

When on my return from dinner that night I let myself in, my first care, in my dusky studio, was to make light for another look at Mary's subject. I felt the impulse to bid him good night, but, to my astonishment, he was no longer there. His place was a void—he had already disappeared. I saw, however, after my first surprise, what had happened—saw it moreover, frankly, with some relief. As my servants were in bed I could ask no questions, but it was clear that Mrs Bridgenorth, whose note, containing its cheque, lay on my table, had been after all unable to wait. The note, I found, mentioned nothing but the enclosure; but it had come by hand, and it was her silence that told the tale. Her messenger had been instructed to "act"; he had come with a vehicle, he had transferred to it canvas and frame. The prize was now therefore landed and the incident closed. I didn't altogether, the next morning, know why, but I had slept the better for the sense of these things, and as soon as my attendant came in I asked for details. It was on this that his answer surprised me. "No, sir, there was no man; she came herself. She had only a four-wheeler, but I helped her, and we got it in. It was a squeeze, sir, but she *would* take it."

I wondered. "She had a four-wheeler? and not her servant?"

"No, no, sir. She came, as you may say, single-handed."

"And not even in her brougham, which would have been larger?"

My man, with his habit, weighed it. "But *have* she a brougham, sir?"

"Why, the one she was here in yesterday."

Then light broke. "Oh, *that* lady! It wasn't her, sir. It was Miss Tredick."

Light broke, but darkness a little followed it—a darkness that, after breakfast, guided my steps back to my friend. There, in its own first place, I met her creation; but I saw it would be a different thing meeting *her*. She immediately put down on a table, as if she had expected me, the cheque I had sent her overnight. "Yes, I've brought it away. And I can't take the money."

I found myself in despair. "You want to keep him?"

"I don't understand what has happened."

"You just back out?"

"I don't understand," she repeated, "what has happened." But what I had already perceived was, on the contrary, that she very nearly, that she in fact quite remarkably, did understand. It was as if in my zeal I had given away my case, and I felt that my test was coming. She had been thinking all night with intensity, and Mrs Bridgenorth's generosity, coupled with Mrs Bridgenorth's promptitude, had kept her awake. Thence, for a woman nervous and critical, imaginations, visions, questions. "Why, in writing me last night, did you take for granted it

was *she* who had swooped down? Why," asked Mary Tredick,
"should she swoop?"

Well, if I could drive a bargain for Mary I felt I could *a
fortiori* lie for her. "Because it's her way. She does swoop.
She's impatient and uncontrolled. And it's affectation for you
to pretend," I said with diplomacy, "that you see no reason
for her falling in love——"

"Falling in love?" She took me straight up.

"With that gentleman. Certainly. What woman wouldn't?
What woman didn't? I really don't see, you know, your right
to back out."

"I won't back out," she presently returned, "if you'll
answer me a question. Does she know the man represented?"
Then as I hung fire: "It has come to me that she must. It
would account for so much. For the strange way I feel," she
went on, "and for the extraordinary sum you've been able to
extract from her."

It was a pity, and I flushed with it, besides wincing at the
word she used. But Mrs Bridgenorth and I, between us, had
clearly made the figure too high. "You think that, if she *had*
guessed, I would naturally work it to 'extract' more?"

She turned away from me on this and, looking blank in her
trouble, moved vaguely about. Then she stopped. "I see him
set up there. I hear her say it. What you said she would make
him pass for."

I believe I foolishly tried—though only for an instant—to
look as if I didn't remember what I had said. "Her husband?"

"He wasn't."

The next minute I had risked it. "Was he yours?"

I don't know what I had expected, but I found myself surprised at her mere pacific head-shake. "No."

"Then why mayn't he have been——?"

"Another woman's? Because he died, to my absolute knowledge, unmarried." She spoke as quietly. "He had known
many women, and there was one in particular with whom he

became—and too long remained—ruinously intimate. She
tried to make him marry her, and he was very near it. Death,
however, saved him. But she was the reason——"

"Yes?" I feared again from her a wave of pain, and I went
on while she kept it back. "Did you know her?"

"She was one I wouldn't." Then she brought it out. "She
was the reason he failed me." Her successful detachment somehow said all, reduced me to a flat, kind "Oh!" that marked
my sense of her telling me, against my expectation, more than
I knew what to do with. But it was just while I wondered
how to turn her confidence that she repeated, in a changed
voice, her challenge of a moment before. "Does she know the
man represented?"

"I haven't the least idea." And having so acquitted myself
I added, with what strikes me now as futility: "She certainly
—yesterday—didn't name him."

"Only recognised him?"

"If she did she brilliantly concealed it."

"So that you got nothing from her?"

It was a question that offered me a certain advantage. "I
thought you accused me of getting too much."

She gave me a long look, and I now saw everything in her
face. "It's very nice—what you're doing for me, and you do it
handsomely. It's beautiful—beautiful, and I thank you with
all my heart. But I know."

"And what do you know?"

She went about now preparing her usual work. "What he
must have been to her."

"You mean she was the person?"

"Well," she said, putting on her old spectacles, "she was
one of them."

"And you accept so easily the astounding coincidence——?"

"Of my finding myself, after years, in so extraordinary a
relation with her? What do you call easily? I've passed a night
of torment."

"But what put it into your head——?"

"That I had so blindly and strangely given him back to her? *You* put it—yesterday."

"And how?"

"I can't tell you. You didn't in the least mean to—on the contrary. But you dropped the seed. The plant, after you had gone," she said with a business-like pull at her easel, "the plant began to grow. I *saw* them there—in your studio—face to face."

"You were jealous?" I laughed.

She gave me through her glasses another look, and they seemed, from this moment, in their queerness, to have placed her quite on the other side of the gulf of time. She was firm there; she was settled; I couldn't get at her now. "I see she told you I *would* be." I doubtless kept down too little my start at it, and she immediately pursued. "You say I accept the coincidence, which is of course prodigious. But such things happen. Why shouldn't I accept it if you do?"

"*Do* I?" I smiled.

She began her work in silence, but she presently exclaimed: "I'm glad I didn't meet her!"

"I don't yet see why you wouldn't."

"Neither do I. It was an instinct."

"Your instincts"—I tried to be ironic—"are miraculous."

"They *have* to be, to meet such accidents. I must ask you kindly to tell her, when you return her gift, that now I have done the picture I find I must after all keep it for myself."

"Giving no reason?"

She painted away. "She'll know the reason."

Well, by this time I knew it too; I knew so many things that I fear my resistance was weak. If our wonderful client hadn't been his wife in fact, she was not to be helped to become his wife in fiction. I knew almost more than I can say, more at any rate than I could then betray. He had been bound in common mercy to stand by my friend, and he had basely forsaken her. This indeed brought up the obscure, into which I shyly gazed. "Why, even granting your theory, should you grudge her the portrait? It was painted in bitterness."

"Yes. Without that——!"

"It wouldn't have come? Precisely. Is it in bitterness, then, you'll keep it?"

She looked up from her canvas. "In what would *you* keep it?"

It made me jump. "Do you mean I *may?*" Then I had my idea. "I'd give you her price for it!"

Her smile through her glasses was beautiful. "And afterwards make it over to her? You shall have it when I die." With which she came away from her easel, and I saw that I was staying her work and should properly go. So I put out my hand to her. "It took—whatever you will!—to paint it," she said, "but I shall keep it in joy." I could answer nothing now—had to cease to pretend; the thing was in her hands. For a moment we stood there, and I had again the sense, melancholy and final, of her being, as it were, remotely glazed and fixed into what she had done. "He's taken from me, and for all those years he's kept. Then she herself, by a prodigy——!" She lost herself again in the wonder of it.

"Unwittingly gives him back?"

She fairly, for an instant over the marvel, closed her eyes. "Gives him back."

Then it was I saw how he would be kept! But it was the end of my vision. I could only write, ruefully enough, to Mrs Bridgenorth, whom I never met again, but of whose death— preceding by a couple of years Mary Tredick's—I happened to hear. This is an old man's tale. I have inherited the picture, in the deep beauty of which, however, darkness still lurks. No one, strange to say, has ever recognised the model, but everyone asks his name. I don't even know it.

BROKEN WINGS

I

CONSCIOUS as he was of what was between them, though perhaps less conscious than ever of why there should at that time of day be anything, he would yet scarce have supposed they could be so long in a house together without some word or some look. It had been since the Saturday afternoon, and that made twenty-four hours. The party—five-and-thirty people, and some of them great—was one in which words and looks might more or less have gone astray. The effect, none the less, he judged, would have been, for her quite as for himself, that no sound and no sign from the other had been picked up by either. They had happened, both at dinner and at luncheon, to be so placed as not to have to glare—or to grin—across; and for the rest they could each, in such a crowd, as freely help the general ease to keep them apart as assist it to bring them together. One chance there was, of course, that might be beyond their control. He had been the night before half surprised at not finding her his "fate" when the long procession to the dining-room solemnly hooked itself together. He would have said in advance—recognising it as one of the sharp "notes" of Mundham—that, should the gathering contain a literary lady, the literary lady would, for congruity, be apportioned to the arm, when there was a question of arms, of the gentleman present who represented the nearest thing to literature. Poor Straith represented "art," and that, no doubt, would have been near enough had not the party offered for choice a slight excess of men. The representative of art had been of the two or three who went in alone, whereas Mrs Harvey had gone in with one of the representatives of banking.

It was certain, however, that she would not again be consigned to Lord Belgrove, and it was just possible that he himself should not be again alone. She would be, on the whole, the most probable remedy to that state, on his part, of disgrace; and this precisely was the great interest of their situation —they were the only persons present without some advantage over somebody else. They hadn't a single advantage; they could be named for nothing but their cleverness; they were at the bottom of the social ladder. The social ladder, even at Mundham, had—as they might properly have been told, as indeed practically they *were* told—to end somewhere; which is no more than to say that, as he strolled about and thought of many things, Stuart Straith had, after all, a good deal the sense of helping to hold it up. Another of the things he thought of was the special oddity—for it was nothing else— of his being there at all, and being there in particular so out of his order and his turn. He couldn't answer for Mrs Harvey's turn. It might well be that she was *in* hers; but these Saturday-to-Monday occasions had hitherto mostly struck him as great gilded cages as to which care was taken that the birds should be birds of a feather.

There had been a wonderful walk in the afternoon, within the limits of the place, to a far-away tea-house; and, in spite of the combinations and changes of this episode, he had still escaped the necessity of putting either his old friend or himself to the test. Also it had been all, he flattered himself, without the pusillanimity of his avoiding her. Life was, indeed, well understood in these great conditions; the conditions constituted in their greatness a kind of fundamental facility, provided a general exemption, bathed the hour, whatever it was, in a universal blandness, that were all a happy solvent for awkward relations. It was beautiful, for instance, that if their failure to meet amid so much meeting had been of Mrs

Harvey's own contrivance he couldn't be in the least vulgarly sure of it. There were places in which he would have had no doubt, places different enough from Mundham. He felt all the same and without anguish that these were much more *his* places—even if she didn't feel that they were much more hers. The day had been warm and splendid, and this moment of its wane—with dinner in sight, but as across a field of polished pink marble which seemed to say that wherever in such a house there was space there was also, benignantly, time—formed, of the whole procession of the hours, the one dearest to our friend, who on such occasions interposed it, whenever he could, between the set of impressions that ended and the set that began with "dressing." The great terraces and gardens were almost void; people had scattered, though not altogether even yet to dress. The air of the place, with the immense house all seated aloft in strength, robed with summer and crowned with success, was such as to contribute something of its own to the poetry of early evening. This visitor, at any rate, saw and felt it all through one of those fine hazes of August that remind you—at least, they reminded *him*—of the artful gauze stretched across the stage of a theatre when an effect of mystery or some particular pantomimic ravishment is desired.

Should he, in fact, have to pair with Mrs Harvey for dinner it would be a shame to him not to have addressed her sooner; and should she, on the contrary, be put with someone else the loss of so much of the time would have but the greater ugliness. Didn't he meanwhile make out that there were ladies in the lower garden, from which the sound of voices, faint, but, as always in the upper air of Mundham, exceedingly sweet, was just now borne to him? She might be among them, and if he should find her he would let her know he had sought her. He would treat it frankly as an occasion for declaring that what had happened between them—or rather what had *not* happened—was too absurd. What at present occurred, however, was that in his quest of her he suddenly, at the turn of an alley, perceived her, not far off, seated in a sort of bower with the Ambassador. With this he pulled up, going another way and pretending not to see them. Three times already that afternoon he had observed her in different situations with the Ambassador. He was the more struck accordingly when, upward of an hour later, again alone and with his state unremedied, he saw her placed for dinner next his Excellency. It was not at all what would have been at Mundham her right seat, so that it could only be explained by his Excellency's direct request. She *was* a success! This time Straith was well in her view and could see that in the candlelight of the wonderful room, where the lustres were, like the table, all crystal and silver, she was as handsome as anyone, taking the women of her age, and also as "smart" as the evening before, and as true as any of the others to the law of a marked difference in her smartness. If the beautiful way she held herself—for decidedly it *was* beautiful—came in a great measure from the good thing she professionally made of it all, our observer could reflect that the poor thing *he* professionally made of it probably affected his attitude in just the opposite way; but they communicated neither in the glare nor in the grin that he had dreaded. Still, their eyes did now meet, and then it seemed to him that her own were strange.

II

SHE, on her side, had her private consciousness, and quite as full a one, doubtless, as he, but with the advantage that, when the company separated for the night, she was not, like her friend, reduced to a vigil unalloyed. Lady Claude, at the top of the stairs, had said, "May I look in—in five minutes—if you don't mind?" and then had arrived in due course and in a wonderful new beribboned gown, the thing just launched for such occasions. Lady Claude was young and earnest and delightfully bewildered and bewildering, and however interesting she might, through certain elements in her situation, have seemed to a literary lady, her own admirations and curiosities were such as from the first promised to rule the hour. She had already expressed to Mrs Harvey a really informed enthusiasm. She not only delighted in her numerous books, which was a tribute the author had not infrequently met, but she even appeared to have read them— an appearance with which her interlocutress was much less acquainted. The great thing was that she also yearned to write, and that she had turned up in her fresh furbelows not only to reveal this secret and to ask for direction and comfort, but literally to make a stranger confidence, for which the mystery of midnight seemed propitious. Midnight was, indeed, as the situation developed, well over before her confidence was spent, for it had ended by gathering such a current as floated forth, with everything in Lady Claude's own life, many things more in that of her adviser. Mrs Harvey was, at all events, amused, touched, and effectually kept awake; and at the end of half an hour they had quite got what might have been called their second wind of frankness and were using it for a discussion of the people in the house. Their primary communion had been simply on the question of the pecuniary profits of literature as the producer of so many admired volumes was prepared to present them to an aspirant. Lady Claude was in financial difficulties and desired the literary issue. This was the breathless revelation she had rustled over a mile of crimson velvet corridor to make.

"Nothing?" she had three minutes later incredulously gasped. "I can make nothing at all?" But the gasp was slight compared with the stupefaction produced in her by a brief further parley, in the course of which Mrs Harvey had, after a hesitation, taken her own plunge. "*You* make so little— wonderful *you!*" And then, as the producer of the admired volumes simply sat there in her dressing-gown, with the saddest of slow head-shakes, looking suddenly too wan even to care that it was at last all out: "What, in that case, is the use of success and celebrity and genius? You *have* no success?" She had looked almost awestruck at this further confession of her friend. They were face to face in a poor human crudity, which transformed itself quickly into an effusive embrace. "You've had it and lost it? Then when it has been as great as yours one *can* lose it?"

"More easily than one can get it."

Lady Claude continued to marvel. "But you do so much— and it's so beautiful!" On which Mrs Harvey simply smiled again in her handsome despair, and after a moment found herself again in the arms of her visitor. The younger woman had remained for a little a good deal arrested and hushed, and had, at any rate, sensitive and charming, immediately dropped, in the presence of this almost august unveiling, the question of her own thin troubles. But there are short cuts at that hour of night that morning scarce knows, and it took but little more of the breath of the real to suggest to Lady Claude more questions in such a connection than she could answer for herself. "How, then, if you haven't private means, do you get on?"

"Ah! I don't get on."

Lady Claude looked about. There were objects scattered in the fine old French room. "You have lovely things."

"Two."

"Two?"

"Two frocks. I couldn't stay another day."

"Ah, what is *that?* I couldn't either," said Lady Claude soothingly. "And you have," she continued, in the same spirit, "your nice maid——"

"Who's indeed a charming woman, but my cook in disguise!" Mrs Harvey dropped.

"Ah, you *are* clever!" her friend cried, with a laugh that was as a climax of reassurance.

"Extraordinarily. But don't think," Mrs Harvey hastened to add, "that I mean that that's why I'm here."

Her companion candidly thought. "Then why are you?"

"I haven't the least idea. I've been wondering all the while, as I've wondered so often before on such occasions, and without arriving at any other reason than that London is so wild."

Lady Claude wondered. "Wild?"

"Wild!" said her friend, with some impatience. "That's the way London strikes."

"But do you call such an invitation a blow?"

"Yes—crushing. No one else, at all events, either," Mrs Harvey added, "could tell you why I'm here."

Lady Claude's power to receive—and it was perhaps her most attaching quality—was greater still, when she felt strongly, than her power to protest. "Why, how can you say that when you've only to see how everyone likes and admires you? Just look at the Ambassador," she had earnestly insisted. And this was what had precisely, as I have mentioned, carried the stream of their talk a good deal away from its source. It had therefore not much further to go before setting in motion the name of Stuart Straith, as to whom Lady Claude confessed to an interest—good-looking, distinguished, "sympathetic," as he was—that she could really almost hate him for having done nothing whatever to encourage. He had not spoken to her once.

"But, my dear, if he hasn't spoken to *me!*"

Lady Claude appeared to regret this not too much for a hint that, after all, there might be a difference. "Oh, but *could* he?"

"Without my having spoken to him first?" Mrs Harvey turned it over. "Perhaps not; but I couldn't have done that." Then, to explain, and not only because Lady Claude was naturally vague, but because what was still visibly most vivid to her was her independent right to have been "made up" to: "And yet not because we're not acquainted."

"You know him, then?"

"But too well."

"You mean you don't like him?"

"On the contrary, I like him—to distraction."

"Then what's the matter?" Lady Claude asked with some impatience.

Her friend hesitated but a moment. "Well, he wouldn't have me."

" 'Have' you?"

"Ten years ago, after Mr Harvey's death, when, if he had lifted a finger, I would have married him."

"But he didn't lift it?"

"He was too grand. I was too small—by *his* measure. He wanted to keep himself; he saw his future."

Lady Claude earnestly followed. "His present position?"

"Yes—everything that was to come to him; his steady rise in value."

"Has it been so great?"

"Surely—his situation and name. Don't you know his lovely work and what's thought of it?"

"Oh yes, I know. That's why——" But Lady Claude stopped. After which: "But if he's still keeping himself?"

"Oh, it's not for me," said Mrs Harvey.

"And evidently not for *me*. Whom then," her visitor asked, "does he think good enough?"

"Oh, these great people!" Mrs Harvey smiled.

"But *we're* great people—you and I!" And Lady Claude kissed her good night.

"You mustn't, all the same," the elder woman said, "betray the secret of *my* greatness, which I've told you, please remember, only in the deepest confidence."

Her tone had a quiet purity of bitterness that for a moment longer held her friend, after which Lady Claude had the happy inspiration of meeting it with graceful gaiety. "It's quite for the best, I'm sure, that Mr Straith wouldn't have you. You've

kept yourself too; you'll marry yet—an ambassador!" And
with another good night she reached the door. "You say you
don't get on, but you do."

"Ah!" said Mrs Harvey with vague attenuation.

"Oh yes, you do," Lady Claude insisted, while the door
emphasised it with a little clap that sounded through the still
house.

III

THE first night of *The New Girl* occurred, as everyone remembers, three years ago, and the play is running yet, a fact
that may render strange the failure to be widely conscious of
which two persons in the audience were guilty. It was not till
afterward present either to Mrs Harvey or to Stuart Straith
that *The New Girl* was one of the greatest successes of
modern times. Indeed if the question had been put to them
on the spot they might have appeared much at sea. But this,
I may as well immediately say, was the result of their having
found themselves side by side in the stalls and thereby given
most of their attention to their own predicament. Straith
showed that he felt the importance of meeting it promptly, for
he turned to his neighbour, who was already in her place, as
soon as her identity had come distinct through his own arrival
and subsidence. "I don't quite see how you can help speaking
to me now."

Her face could only show him how long she had been
aware of his approach. "The sound of your voice, coming
to me straight, makes it indeed as easy for me as I could
possibly desire."

He looked about at the serried rows, the loaded galleries
and the stuffed boxes, with recognitions and nods; and this
made between them another pause, during which, while the

music seemed perfunctory and the bustle that, in a London audience, represents concentration increased, they felt how effectually, in the thick, preoccupied medium, how extraordinarily, they were together.

"Well, that second afternoon at Mundham, just before dinner, I was very near forcing your hand. But something put me off. You're really too grand."

"Oh!" she murmured.

"Ambassadors," said Stuart Straith.

"Oh!" she again sounded. And before anything more could pass the curtain was up. It came down in due course and achieved, after various intervals, the rest of its movements without interrupting, for our friends, the sense of an evening of talk. They said when it was down almost nothing about the play, and when one of them toward the end put to the other, vaguely, "Is—a—this thing going?" the question had scarce the effect of being even relevant. What was clearest to them was that the people about were somehow enough taken up to leave them at their ease—but what taken up with they but half made out. Mrs Harvey had, none the less, mentioned early that her presence had a reason and that she ought to attend, and her companion had asked her what she thought of a certain picture made at a given moment by the stage, in the reception of which he was so interested that it was really what had brought him. These were glances, however, that quickly strayed—strayed, for instance (as this could carry them far), in its coming to one of them to say that, whatever the piece might be, the real thing, as they had seen it at Mundham, was more than a match for any piece. For it was Mundham that *was*, theatrically, the real thing; better for scenery, dresses, music, pretty women, bare shoulders, everything—even incoherent dialogue; a much bigger and braver show, and got up, as it were, infinitely more "regardless." By Mundham they were held long enough to find themselves, though with an equal surprise, quite at one as to the special oddity of their having caught each other in such a plight. Straith said that he supposed what his friend meant was that it was odd *he* should have been there; to which she returned that she had been imputing to him exactly that judgment of her own presence.

"But why shouldn't *you* be?" he asked. "Isn't that just what you *are?* Aren't you, in your way—like those people—a child of fortune and fashion?"

He got no more answer to this for some time than if he had fairly wounded her; he indeed that evening got no answer at all that was direct. But in the next interval she brought out with abruptness, taking no account of some other matter he had just touched, "Don't you really know——?"

She had paused.

"Know what?"

Again she went on without heeding. "A place like Mundham is, for me, a survival, though poor Mundham in particular won't, for me, have survived that visit—for which it's to be pitied, isn't it? It was a glittering ghost—since laid!—of my old time."

Straith at this almost gave a start. "Have *you* got a new time?"

"Do you mean that you have?"

"Well," said Straith, "mine may now be called middle-aged. It seems so long, I mean, since I set my watch to it."

"Oh, I haven't even a watch!" she returned with a laugh. "I'm beyond watches." After which she added: "We *might* have met more—or, I should say perhaps, have got more out of it when we *have* met."

"Yes, it has been too little. But I've always explained it by our living in such different worlds."

Mrs Harvey had an occasional incoherence. "Are you unhappy?"

He gave her a singular smile. "You said just now that you're beyond watches. I'm beyond unhappiness."

She turned from him and presently brought out: "I ought absolutely to take away *something* of the play."

"By all means. There's certainly something *I* shall take."

"Ah, then you must help me—give it me."

"With all my heart," said Straith, "if it *can* help you. It's my feeling of our renewal."

She had one of the sad, slow head-shakes that at Mundham had been impressive to Lady Claude. "That won't help me."

"Then you must let me put to you now what I should have tried to get near enough to you there to put if I hadn't been so afraid of the Ambassador. What has it been so long—our impossibility?"

"Well, I can only answer for my own vision of it, which is —which always was—that you were sorry for me, but felt a sort of scruple of showing me that you had nothing better than pity to give."

"May I come to see you?" Straith asked some minutes after this.

Her words, for which he had also awhile to wait, had, in truth, as little as his own the appearance of a reply. "*Are* you unhappy—really? Haven't you everything?"

"You're beautiful!" he said for all answer. "Mayn't I come?"

She hesitated.

"Where is your studio?"

"Oh, not too far to reach from it. Don't be anxious; I can walk, or even take the bus."

Mrs Harvey once more delayed. Then she answered: "Mayn't I rather come there?"

"I shall be but too delighted."

It was said with promptness, even precipitation; yet the understanding, shortly after, appeared to have left between them a certain awkwardness, and it was almost as if to change the subject and relieve them equally that she suddenly reminded him of something he had spoken earlier. "You were to tell me why in particular you had to be here."

"Oh yes. To see my dresses."

"Yours!" She wondered.

"The second act. I made them out for them—drew them."

Before she could check it her tone escaped. "You?"

"I." He looked straight before him. "For the fee. And we didn't even notice them."

"*I* didn't," she confessed. But it offered the fact as a sign of her kindness for him, and this kindness was traceably what inspired something she said in the draughty porch, after the performance, while the footman of the friend, a fat, rich, immensely pleased lady, who had given her a lift and then rejoined her from a seat in the balcony, went off to make sure of the brougham. "May I do something about your things?"

" 'Do something'?"

"When I've paid you my visit. Write something—about your pictures. I do a correspondence," said Mrs Harvey.

He wondered as she had done in the stalls. "For a paper?"

"The *Blackport Banner*. A 'London Letter.' The new books, the new plays, the new twaddle of any sort—a little music, a little gossip, a little 'art.' You'll help me—I need it awfully—with the art. I do three a month."

"*You*—wonderful you?" He spoke as Lady Claude had done, and could no more help it again than Mrs Harvey had been able to help it in the stalls.

"Oh, as you say, for the fee!" On which, as the footman signalled, her old lady began to plunge through the crowd.

IV

AT the studio, where she came to him within the week, her first movement had been to exclaim on the splendid abundance of his work. She had looked round charmed—so struck as to be, as she called it, crushed. "You've such a wonderful lot to show."

"Indeed I have!" said Stuart Straith.

"That's where you beat *us*."

"I think it may very well be," he went on, "where I beat almost everyone."

"And is much of it new?"

He looked about with her. "Some of it is pretty old. But my things have a way, I admit, of growing old extraordinarily fast. They seem to me in fact, nowadays, quite 'born old.'"

She had the manner, after a little, of coming back to something. "You *are* unhappy. You're *not* beyond it. You're just nicely, just fairly and squarely, in the middle of it."

"Well," said Straith, "if it surrounds me like a desert, so that I'm lost in it, that comes to the same thing. But I want you to tell me about yourself."

She had continued at first to move about, and had taken out a pocket-book, which she held up at him. "This time I shall insist on notes. You made my mind a blank about that play, which is the sort of thing we can't afford. If it hadn't been for my fat old lady and the next day's papers!" She kept looking, going up to things, saying, "How wonderful!" and "Oh, your *way!*" and then stopping for a general impression, something in the whole charm. The place, high, handsome, neat, with two or three pale tapestries and several rare old pieces of furniture, showed a perfection of order, an absence of loose objects, as if it had been swept and squared for the occasion and made almost too immaculate. It was polished and cold—rather cold for the season and the weather; and Stuart Straith himself, buttoned and brushed, as fine and as clean as his room, might at her arrival have reminded her of the master of a neat, bare ship on his deck awaiting a cargo. "May I see everything? May I 'use' everything?"

"Oh no; you mayn't by any means use everything. You

mayn't use half. *Did* I spoil your 'London Letter'?" he
continued after a moment.

"No one can spoil them as I spoil them myself. I can't do
them—I don't know how, and don't want to. I do them
wrong, and the people want such trash. Of course they'll
sack me."

She was in the centre, and he had the effect of going round
her, restless and vague, in large, slow circles. "Have you done
them long?"

"Two or three months—this lot. But I've done others, and
I know what happens. Oh, my dear, I've done strange
things!"

"And is it a good job?"

She hesitated, then puffed, prettily enough, an indifferent
sigh. "Three-and-ninepence. Is that good?" He had stopped
before her, looking at her up and down. "What do you get,"
she went on, "for what you do for a play?"

"A little more, it would seem, than you. Four-and-six-
pence. But I've only done, as yet, that one. Nothing else has
offered."

"I see. But something *will*, eh?"

Poor Straith took a turn again. "Did you like them—for
colour?" But again he pulled up. "Oh, I forgot; we didn't
notice them!"

For a moment they could laugh about it. "I noticed them,
I assure you, in the *Banner*. 'The costumes in the second act
are of the most marvellous beauty.' That's what I said."

"Oh, that will fetch the managers!" But before her again
he seemed to take her in from head to foot. "You speak of
'using' things. If you'd only use yourself—for my enlightenment. Tell me all."

"You look at me," said Mrs Harvey, "as with the wonder
of who designs *my* costumes. How I dress on it, how I do even
what I still do on it, is *that* what you want to know?"

"What has happened to you?" Straith asked.

"How do I keep it up?" she continued, as if she had not heard him. "But I *don't* keep it up. *You* do," she declared as she again looked round her.

Once more it set him off, but for a pause once more almost as quick. "How long have you been——?"

"Been what?" she asked as he faltered.

"Unhappy."

She smiled at him from a depth of indulgence. "As long as you've been ignorant—that what I've been *wanting* is your pity. Ah, to have to know, as I believed I did, that you supposed it would wound me, and not to have been able to make you see that it was the one thing left to me that would help me! Give me your pity now. It's all I want. I don't care for anything else. But give me that."

He had, as it happened at the moment, to do a smaller and a usual thing before he could do one so great and so strange. The youth whom he kept for service arrived with a tea-tray, in arranging a place for which, with the sequel of serving Mrs Harvey, seating her and seeing the youth again out of the room, some minutes passed.

"What pity could I dream of for you," he demanded as he at last dropped near her, "when I was myself so miserably sore?"

"Sore?" she wondered. "But you were happy—then."

"Happy not to have struck you as good enough? For I didn't, you know," he insisted. "You had your success, which was so immense. You had your high value, your future, your big possibilities; and I perfectly understood that, given those things, and given also my very much smaller situation, you should wish to keep yourself."

"Oh, oh!" She gasped as if hurt.

"I understand it; but how could it really make me 'happy'?" he asked.

She turned at him as with her hand on the old scar she could now carry. "You mean that all these years you've really not known——?"

"But not known what?"

His voice was so blank that at the sound of it, and at something that looked out from him, she only found another "Oh, oh!" which became the next instant a burst of tears.

V

SHE had appeared at first unwilling to receive him at home; but he understood it after she had left him, turning over more and more everything their meeting had shaken to the surface, and piecing together memories that at last, however darkly, made a sense. He was to call on her, it was finally agreed, but not till the end of the week, when she should have finished "moving"—she had but just changed quarters; and meanwhile, as he came and went, mainly in the cold chamber of his own past endeavour, which looked even to himself as studios look when artists are dead and the public, in the arranged place, are admitted to stare, he had plenty to think about. What had come out—he could see it now—was that each, ten years before, had miserably misunderstood and then had turned for relief from pain to a perversity of pride. But it was himself above all that he now sharply judged, since women, he felt, have to get on as they can, and for the mistake of this woman there were reasons he had, with a sore heart, to acknowledge. She had really found in the pomp of his early success, at the time they used to meet, and to care to, exactly the ground for her sense of failure with him that he had found in the vision of her gross popularity for his conviction that she judged him as comparatively small. Each had blundered, as sensitive souls of the "artistic temperament" blunder, into a conception not only of the other's attitude, but of the other's material situation at the moment, that had thrown them back on stupid secrecy, where their estrangement had

grown like an evil plant in the shade. He had positively believed her to have gone on all the while making the five
thousand a year that the first eight or ten of her so supremely
happy novels had brought her in, just as she, on her side, had
read into the felicity of his first new hits, his pictures "of the
year" at three or four Academies, the absurdest theory of the
sort of career that, thanks to big dealers and intelligent buyers,
his gains would have built up for him. It looked vulgar
enough now, but it had been grave enough then. His long,
detached delusion about her "prices," at any rate, appeared to
have been more than matched by the strange stories occasionally floated to her—and all to make her but draw more
closely in—on the subject of his own.

It was with each equally that everything had changed—
everything but the stiff consciousness in either of the need to
conceal changes from the other. If she had cherished for long
years the soreness of her not being "good" enough, so this
was what had counted most in her sustained effort to appear
at least as good as he. London, meanwhile, was big; London
was blind and benighted; and nothing had ever occurred to
undermine for him the fiction of her prosperity. Before his
eyes there, while she sat with him, she had pulled off one by
one those vain coverings of her state that she confessed she
had hitherto done her best—and so always with an eye on
himself—deceptively to draw about it. He had felt frozen, as
he listened, at such likenesses to things he knew. He recognised as she talked, and he groaned as he understood. He
understood—oh, at last, whatever he had not done before!
And yet he could well have smiled, out of their common
abyss, at such odd identities and recurrences. Truly the arts
were sisters, as was so often said; for what apparently could
be more like the experience of one than the experience of
another? And she spared him things with it all. He felt that
too, just as, even while showing her how he followed, he had
bethought himself of closing his lips for the hour, none too soon,

on his own stale story. There had been a beautiful intelligence, for that matter, in her having asked him nothing more. She had overflowed because shaken by not finding him happy, and her surrender had somehow offered itself to him as her way—the first that sprang up—of considering his trouble. She had left him, at all events, in full possession of all the phases through which in "literary circles" acclaimed states may pass on their regular march to eclipse and extinction. One had but one's hour, and if one had it soon—it was really almost a case of choice—one didn't have it late. It might, moreover, never even remotely have approached, at its best, things ridiculously rumoured. Straith felt, on the whole, how little he had known of literary circles or of any mystery but his own, indeed; on which, up to actual impending collapse, he had mounted such anxious guard.

It was when he went on the Friday to see her that he took in the latest of the phases in question, which might very well be almost the final one; there was at least that comfort in it. She had just settled in a small flat, where he recognised in the steady disposal, for the best, of various objects she had not yet parted with, her reason for having made him wait. Here they had together—these two worn and baffled workers—a wonderful hour of gladness in their lost battle and of freshness in their lost youth; for it was not till Stuart Straith had also raised the heavy mask and laid it beside her own on the table, that they began really to feel themselves recover something of that possibility of each other they had so wearily wasted. Only she couldn't get over it that he was like herself, and that what she had shrunken to in her three or four simplified rooms had its perfect image in the hollow show of his ordered studio and his accumulated work. He told her everything now, kept as little back as she had kept at their previous meeting, while she repeated over and over, "You—wonderful you?" as if the knowledge made a deeper darkness of fate, as if the pain of his having come down at all almost quenched the joy of his having come so much nearer. When she learned that he had not for three years sold a picture—"You, beautiful you?"—it seemed a new cold breath out of the dusk of her own outlook. Disappointment and despair were in such relations contagious, and there was clearly as much less again left to her as the little that was left to him. He showed her, laughing at the long queerness of it, how awfully little, as they called it, this was. He let it all come, but with more mirth than misery, and with a final abandonment of pride that was like changing at the end of a dreadful day from tight boots to slippers. There were moments when they might have resembled a couple united by some misdeed and meeting to decide on some desperate course; they gave themselves so to the great irony—the vision of the comic in contrasts—that precedes surrenders and extinctions.

They went over the whole thing, remounted the dwindling stream, reconstructed, explained, understood—recognised, in short, the particular example they gave, and how, without mutual suspicion, they had been giving it side by side. "We're simply the case," Straith familiarly put it, "of having been had enough of. No case is perhaps more common, save that, for you and for me, each in our line, it did look in the good time—didn't it?—as if nobody *could* have enough." With which they counted backward, gruesome as it was, the symptoms of satiety up to the first dawn, and lived again together the unforgettable hours—distant now—out of which it had begun to glimmer that the truth had to be faced and the right names given to the wrong facts. They laughed at their original explanations and the minor scale, even, of their early fears; compared notes on the fallibility of remedies and hopes, and, more and more united in the identity of their lesson, made out perfectly that, though there appeared to be many kinds of success, there was only one kind of failure. And yet what had been hardest had not been to have to shrink, but—the long game of bluff, as Straith called it—to have to keep up. It fairly swept them away at present, however, the hugeness of the relief of no longer keeping up as against each other. This gave them all the measure of the motive their courage, on either side, in silence and gloom, had forced into its service.

"Only what shall we do now for a motive?" Straith went on. She thought. "A motive for courage?"

"Yes—to keep up."

"And go again, for instance, do you mean, to Mundham? We shall, thank heaven, never go again to Mundham. The Mundhams are over."

> "Nous n'irons plus au bois;
> Les lauriers sont coupés,"

sang Straith. "It does cost."

"As everything costs that one does for the rich. It's not our poor relations who make us pay."

"No; one must have means to acknowledge the others. We can't afford the opulent. But it isn't only the money they take."

"It's the imagination," said Mrs Harvey. "As they have none themselves——"

"It's an article we have to supply? We have certainly to use a lot to protect ourselves," Straith agreed. "And the strange thing is that they like us."

She thought again. "That's what makes it easy to cut them. They forgive."

"Yes," her companion laughed; "once they really don't know you enough——   !"

"They treat you as old friends. But what do we want now of courage?" she went on.

He wondered. "Yes, after all, what?"

"To keep up, I mean. Why *should* we keep up?"

It seemed to strike him. "I see. After all, why? The courage *not* to keep up——"

"We have *that*, at least," she declared, "haven't we?" Standing there at her little high-perched window, which overhung grey housetops, they let the consideration of this pass between them in a deep look, as well as in a hush of which the intensity had something commensurate. "If we're beaten!" she then continued.

"Let us at least be beaten together!" He took her in his arms; she let herself go, and he held her long and close for the compact. But when they had recovered themselves enough to handle their agreement more responsibly, the words in which they confirmed it broke in sweetness as well as sadness from both together: "And now to work!"

THE TWO FACES

I

THE servant, who, in spite of his sealed, stamped look, appeared to have his reasons, stood there for instruction, in a manner not quite usual, after announcing the name. Mrs Grantham, however, took it up "Lord Gwyther?"—with a quick surprise that for an instant justified him even to the small scintilla in the glance she gave her companion, which might have had exactly the sense of the butler's hesitation. This companion, a shortish, fairish, youngish man, clean-shaven and keen-eyed, had, with a promptitude that would have struck an observer—which the butler indeed was— sprung to his feet and moved to the chimney-piece, though his hostess herself, meanwhile, managed not otherwise to stir. "Well?" she said, as for the visitor to advance; which she immediately followed with a sharper "He's not there?"

"Shall I show him up, ma'am?"

"But of course!" The point of his doubt made her at last rise for impatience, and Bates, before leaving the room, might still have caught the achieved irony of her appeal to the gentleman into whose communion with her he had broken. "Why in the world not——? What a way——!" she exclaimed, as Sutton felt beside his cheek the passage of her eyes to the glass behind him.

"He wasn't sure you'd see anyone."

"I don't see 'anyone,' but I see individuals."

"That's just it; and sometimes you don't see them."

"Do you mean ever because of *you?*" she asked as she

239

touched into place a tendril of hair. "That's just his impertinence, as to which I shall speak to him."

"Don't," said Shirley Sutton. "Never notice anything."

"That's nice advice from you," she laughed, "who notice everything!"

"Ah, but I speak of nothing."

She looked at him a moment. "You're still more impertinent than Bates. You'll please not budge," she went on.

"Really? I must sit him out?" he continued as, after a minute, she had not again spoken—only glancing about, while she changed her place, partly for another look at the glass and partly to see if she could improve her seat. What she felt was rather more than, clever and charming though she was, she could hide. "If you're wondering how you seem, I can tell you. Awfully cool and easy."

She gave him another stare. She was beautiful and conscious. "And if you're wondering how *you* seem——"

"Oh, I'm not!" he laughed from before the fire; "I always perfectly know."

"How you seem," she retorted, "is as if you didn't!"

Once more for a little he watched her. "You're looking lovely for him—extraordinarily lovely, within the marked limits of your range. But that's enough. Don't be clever."

"Then who *will* be?"

"There you are!" he sighed with amusement.

"Do you know him?" she asked as, through the door left open by Bates, they heard steps on the landing.

Sutton had to think an instant, and produced a "No" just as Lord Gwyther was again announced, which gave an unexpectedness to the greeting offered him a moment later by this personage—a young man, stout and smooth and fresh, but not at all shy, who, after the happiest rapid passage with Mrs Grantham, put out a hand with a frank, pleasant "How d'ye do?"

"Mr Shirley Sutton," Mrs Grantham explained.

"Oh yes," said her second visitor, quite as if he knew; which, as he couldn't have known, had for her first the interest of confirming a perception that his lordship would be—no, not at all, in general, embarrassed, only was now exceptionally and especially agitated. As it is, for that matter, with Sutton's total impression that we are particularly and almost exclusively concerned, it may be further mentioned that he was not less clear as to the really handsome way in which the young man kept himself together and little by little—though with all proper aid indeed—finally found his feet. All sorts of things, for the twenty minutes, occurred to Sutton, though one of them was certainly not that it would, after all, be better he should go. One of them was that their hostess was doing it in perfection—simply, easily, kindly, yet with something the least bit queer in her wonderful eyes; another was that if he had been recognised without the least ground it was through a tension of nerves on the part of his fellow-guest that produced inconsequent motions; still another was that, even had departure been indicated, he would positively have felt dissuasion in the rare promise of the scene. This was in especial after Lord Gwyther not only had announced that he was now married, but had mentioned that he wished to bring his wife to Mrs Grantham for the benefit so certain to be derived. It was the passage immediately produced by that speech that provoked in Sutton the intensity, as it were, of his arrest. He already knew of the marriage as well as Mrs Grantham herself, and as well also as he knew of some other things; and this gave him, doubtless, the better measure of what took place before him and the keener consciousness of the quick look that, at a marked moment—though it was not absolutely meant for him any more than for his companion—Mrs Grantham let him catch.

She smiled, but it had a gravity. "I think, you know, you ought to have told me before."

"Do you mean when I first got engaged? Well, it all took

place so far away, and we really told, at home, so few people."

Oh, there might have been reasons; but it had not been quite right. "You were married at Stuttgart? That wasn't too far for *my* interest, at least, to reach."

"Awfully kind of you—and of course one knew you *would* be kind. But it wasn't at Stuttgart; it was over there, but quite in the country. We should have managed it in England but that her mother naturally wished to be present, yet was not in health to come. So it was really, you see, a sort of little hole-and-corner German affair."

This didn't in the least check Mrs Grantham's claim, but it started a slight anxiety. "Will she be—a, then, German?"

Sutton knew her to know perfectly what Lady Gwyther would "be," but he had by this time, while their friend explained, his independent interest. "Oh dear, no! My father-in-law has never parted with the proud birthright of a Briton. But his wife, you see, holds an estate in Würtemberg from *her* mother, Countess Kremnitz, on which, with the awful condition of his English property, you know, they've found it for years a tremendous saving to live. So that though Valda was luckily born at home she has practically spent her life over there."

"Oh, I see." Then, after a slight pause, "Is Valda her pretty name?" Mrs Grantham asked.

"Well," said the young man, only wishing, in his candour, it was clear, to be drawn out—"well, she has, in the manner of her mother's people, about thirteen; but that's the one we generally use."

Mrs Grantham hesitated but an instant. "Then may *I* generally use it?"

"It would be too charming of you; and nothing would give her—as, I assure you, nothing would give *me*, greater pleasure." Lord Gwyther quite glowed with the thought.

"Then I think that instead of coming alone you might have brought her to see me."

"It's exactly what," he instantly replied, "I came to ask your leave to do." He explained that for the moment Lady Gwyther was not in town, having as soon as she arrived gone down to Torquay to put in a few days with one of her aunts, also her godmother, to whom she was an object of great interest. She had seen no one yet, and no one—not that *that* mattered—had seen her; she knew nothing whatever of London and was awfully frightened at facing it and at what—however little—might be expected of her. "She wants some one," he said, "some one who knows the whole thing, don't you see? and who's thoroughly kind and clever, as you would be, if I may say so, to take her by the hand." It was at this point and on these words that the eyes of Lord Gwyther's two auditors inevitably and wonderfully met. But there was nothing in the way he kept it up to show that he caught the encounter. "She wants, if I may tell you so, for the great labyrinth, a real friend; and asking myself what I could do to make things ready for her, and who would be absolutely the best woman in London——"

"You thought, naturally, of *me?*" Mrs Grantham had listened with no sign but the faint flash just noted; now, however, she gave him the full light of her expressive face—which immediately brought Shirley Sutton, looking at his watch, once more to his feet.

"She *is* the best woman in London!" He addressed himself with a laugh to the other visitor, but offered his hand in farewell to their hostess.

"You're going?"

"I must," he said without scruple.

"Then we do meet at dinner?"

"I hope so." On which, to take leave, he returned with interest to Lord Gwyther the friendly clutch he had a short time before received.

II

THEY did meet at dinner, and if they were not, as it happened, side by side, they made that up afterwards in the
happiest angle of a drawing-room that offered both shine and
shadow and that was positively much appreciated, in the
circle in which they moved, for the favourable "corners"
created by its shrewd mistress. Her face, charged with something produced in it by Lord Gwyther's visit, had been with
him so constantly for the previous hours that, when she
instantly challenged him on his "treatment" of her in the
afternoon, he was on the point of naming it as his reason for
not having remained with her. Something new had quickly
come into her beauty; he couldn't as yet have said what, nor
whether on the whole to its advantage or its loss. Till he
could make up his mind about that, at any rate, he would say
nothing; so that, with sufficient presence of mind, he found a
better excuse. If in short he had in defiance of her particular
request left her alone with Lord Gwyther, it was simply because the situation had suddenly turned so exciting that he
had fairly feared the contagion of it—the temptation of its
making him, most improperly, put in his word.

They could now talk of these things at their ease. Other
couples, ensconced and scattered, enjoyed the same privilege,
and Sutton had more and more the profit, such as it was, of
feeling that his interest in Mrs Grantham had become—what
was the luxury of so high a social code—an acknowledged and
protected relation. He knew his London well enough to know
that he was on the way to be regarded as her main source of
consolation for the trick that, several months before, Lord
Gwyther had publicly played her. Many persons had not held
that, by the high social code in question, his lordship could

have "reserved the right" to turn up in that way, from one day to another, engaged. For himself London took, with its short cuts and its cheap psychology, an immense deal for granted. To his own sense he was never—could in the nature of things never be—any man's "successor." Just what had constituted the predecessorship of other men was apparently that they had been able to make up their mind. He, worse luck, was at the mercy of her face, and more than ever at the mercy of it now, which meant, moreover, not that it made a slave of him, but that it made, disconcertingly, a sceptic. It was the absolute perfection of the handsome; but things had a way of coming into it. "I felt," he said, "that you were there together at a point at which you had a right to the ease that the absence of a listener would give. I reflected that when you made me promise to stay you hadn't guessed——"

"That he could possibly have come to me on such an extraordinary errand? No, of course I hadn't guessed. Who *would?* But didn't you see how little I was upset by it?"

Sutton demurred. Then with a smile, "I think *he* saw how little."

"You yourself didn't, then?"

He again held back, but not, after all, to answer. "He was wonderful, wasn't he?"

"I think he was," she replied after a moment. To which she added: "Why did he pretend that way he knew you?"

"He didn't pretend. He felt on the spot as if we were friends." Sutton had found this afterwards, and found truth in it. "It was an effusion of cheer and hope. He was so glad to see me there, and to find you happy."

"Happy?"

"Happy. Aren't you?"

"Because of *you?*"

"Well—according to the impression he received as he came in."

"That was sudden then," she asked, "and unexpected?"

Her companion thought. "Prepared in some degree, but confirmed by the sight of us, there together, so awfully jolly and sociable over your fire."

Mrs Grantham turned this round. "If he knew I was 'happy' then—which, by the way, is none of his business, nor of yours either—why in the world did he come?"

"Well, for good manners, and for his idea," said Sutton.

She took it in, appearing to have no hardness of rancour that could bar discussion. "Do you mean by his idea his proposal that I should grandmother his wife? And, if you do, is the proposal your reason for calling him wonderful?"

Sutton laughed. "Pray, what's yours?" As this was a question, however, that she took her time to answer or not to answer—only appearing interested for a moment in a combination that had formed itself on the other side of the room —he presently went on. "What's *his*?—that would seem to be the point. His, I mean, for having decided on the extraordinary step of throwing his little wife, bound hands and feet, into your arms. Intelligent as you are, and with these three or four hours to have thought it over, I yet don't see how that can fail still to mystify you."

She continued to watch their opposite neighbours. "'Little,' you call her. Is she so very small?"

"Tiny, tiny—she *must* be; as different as possible in every way—of necessity—from you. They always *are* the opposite pole, you know," said Shirley Sutton.

She glanced at him now. "You strike me as of an impudence——!"

"No, no. I only like to make it out with you."

She looked away again and, after a little, went on. "I'm sure she's charming, and only hope one isn't to gather that he's already tired of her."

"Not a bit! He's tremendously in love, and he'll remain so."

"So much the better. And if it's a question," said Mrs

Grantham, "of one's doing what one can for her, he has only, as I told him when you had gone, to give me the chance."

"Good! So he *is* to commit her to you?"

"You use extraordinary expressions, but it's settled that he brings her."

"And you'll really and truly help her?"

"Really and truly?" said Mrs Grantham, with her eyes again upon him. "Why not? For what do you take me?"

"Ah, isn't that just what I still have the discomfort, every day I live, of asking myself?"

She had made, as she spoke, a movement to rise, which, as if she was tired of his tone, his last words appeared to determine. But, also getting up, he held her, when they were on their feet, long enough to hear the rest of what he had to say. "If you do help her, you know, you'll show him that you've understood."

"Understood what?"

"Why, his idea—the deep, acute train of reasoning that has led him to take, as one may say, the bull by the horns; to reflect that as you might, as you probably *would*, in any case, get at her, he plays the wise game, as well as the bold one, by assuming your generosity and placing himself publicly under an obligation to you."

Mrs Grantham showed not only that she had listened, but that she had for an instant considered. "What is it you elegantly describe as my getting 'at' her?"

"He takes his risk, but puts you, you see, on your honour."

She thought a moment more. "What profundities indeed then over the simplest of matters! And if your idea is," she went on, "that if I do help her I shall show him I've understood them, so it will be that if I don't——"

"You'll show him"—Sutton took her up—"that you haven't? Precisely. But in spite of not wanting to appear to have understood *too* much——"

"I may still be depended on to do what I can? Quite

certainly. You'll see what I may still be depended on to do."
And she moved away.

III

IT was not, doubtless, that there had been anything in their
rather sharp separation at that moment to sustain or prolong
the interruption; yet it definitely befell that, circumstances
aiding, they practically failed to meet again before the great
party at Burbeck. This occasion was to gather in some thirty
persons from a certain Friday to the following Monday, and
it was on the Friday that Sutton went down. He had known
in advance that Mrs Grantham was to be there, and this
perhaps, during the interval of hindrance, had helped him a
little to be patient. He had before him the certitude of a real
full cup—two days brimming over with the sight of her. He
found, however, on his arrival that she was not yet in the
field, and presently learned that her place would be in a small
contingent that was to join the party on the morrow. This
knowledge he extracted from Miss Banker, who was always
the first to present herself at any gathering that was to enjoy
her, and whom, moreover—partly on that very account—the
wary not less than the speculative were apt to hold themselves well-advised to engage with at as early as possible a
stage of the business. She was stout, red, rich, mature, universal—a massive, much-fingered volume, alphabetical, wonderful, indexed, that opened of itself at the right place. She
opened for Sutton instinctively at G——, which happened to
be remarkably convenient. "What she's really waiting over
for is to bring down Lady Gwyther."

"Ah, the Gwythers are coming?"

"Yes; caught, through Mrs Grantham, just in time. *She'll*
be the feature—everyone wants to see her."

Speculation and wariness met and combined at this moment in Shirley Sutton. "Do you mean—a—Mrs Grantham?"

"Dear no! Poor little Lady Gwyther, who, but just arrived in England, appears now literally for the first time in her life in any society whatever, and whom (don't you know the extraordinary story? you ought to—*you!*) she, of all people, has so wonderfully taken up. It will be quite—here—as if she were 'presenting' her."

Sutton, of course, took in more things than even appeared. "I never know what I ought to know; I only know, inveterately, what I oughtn't. So what *is* the extraordinary story?"

"You really haven't heard——?"

"Really!" he replied without winking.

"It happened, indeed, but the other day," said Miss Banker, "yet everyone is already wondering. Gwyther has thrown his wife on her mercy—but I won't believe you if you pretend to me you don't know why he shouldn't."

Sutton asked himself then what he *could* pretend. "Do you mean because she's merciless?"

She hesitated. "If you don't know, perhaps I oughtn't to tell you."

He liked Miss Banker, and found just the right tone to plead. "*Do* tell me."

"Well," she sighed, "it will be your own fault——! They had been such friends that there could have been but one name for the crudity of his original *procédé*. When I was a girl we used to call it throwing over. They call it in French to *lâcher*. But I refer not so much to the act itself as to the manner of it, though you may say indeed, of course, that there is in such cases, after all, only one manner. Least said, soonest mended."

Sutton seemed to wonder. "Oh, he said too much?"

"He said nothing. That was it."

Sutton kept it up. "But was *what?*"

"Why, what she must, like any woman in her shoes, have felt to be his perfidy. He simply went and *did* it—took to himself this child, that is, without the preliminary of a scandal or a rupture—before she could turn round."

"I follow you. But it would appear from what you say that she *has* turned round now."

"Well," Miss Banker laughed, "we shall see for ourselves how far. It will be what everyone will try to see."

"Oh, then we've work cut out!" And Sutton certainly felt that he himself had—an impression that lost nothing from a further talk with Miss Banker in the course of a short stroll in the grounds with her the next day. He spoke as one who had now considered many things.

"Did I understand from you yesterday that Lady Gwyther's a 'child'?"

"Nobody knows. It's prodigious the way she has managed."

"The way Lady Gwyther has——?"

"No; the way May Grantham has kept her till this hour in her pocket."

He was quick at his watch. "Do you mean by 'this hour' that they're due now?"

"Not till tea. All the others arrive together in time for that." Miss Banker had clearly, since the previous day, filled in gaps and become, as it were, revised and enlarged. "She'll have kept a cat from seeing her, so as to produce her entirely herself."

"Well," Sutton mused, "that will have been a very noble sort of return——"

"For Gwyther's behaviour? Very. Yet I feel creepy."

"Creepy?"

"Because so much depends for the girl—in the way of the right start or the wrong start—on the signs and omens of this first appearance. It's a great house and a great occasion, and we're assembled here, it strikes me, very much as the Roman mob at the circus used to be to see the next Christian maiden brought out to the tigers."

"Oh, if she *is* a Christian maiden——!" Sutton murmured. But he stopped at what his imagination called up.

It perhaps fed that faculty a little that Miss Banker had the effect of making out that Mrs Grantham might individually be, in any case, something of a Roman matron. "She has kept her in the dark so that we may only take her from her hand. She will have formed her for us."

"In so few days?"

"Well, she will have prepared her—decked her for the sacrifice with ribbons and flowers."

"Ah, if you only mean that she will have taken her to her dressmaker——!" And it came to Sutton, at once as a new light and as a check, almost, to anxiety, that this was all poor Gwyther, mistrustful probably of a taste formed by Stuttgart, might have desired of their friend.

There were usually at Burbeck many things taking place at once; so that wherever else, on such occasions, tea might be served, it went forward with matchless pomp, weather permitting, on a shaded stretch of one of the terraces and in presence of one of the prospects. Shirley Sutton, moving, as the afternoon waned, more restlessly about and mingling in dispersed groups only to find they had nothing to keep him quiet, came upon it as he turned a corner of the house—saw it seated there in all its state. It might be said that at Burbeck it was, like everything else, made the most of. It constituted immediately, with multiplied tables and glittering plate, with rugs and cushions and ices and fruit and wonderful porcelain and beautiful women, a scene of splendour, almost an incident of grand opera. One of the beautiful women might quite have been expected to rise with a gold cup and a celebrated song.

One of them did rise, as it happened, while Sutton drew near, and he found himself a moment later seeing nothing and nobody but Mrs Grantham. They met on the terrace, just away from the others, and the movement in which he had the effect of arresting her might have been that of withdrawal. He quickly saw, however, that if she had been about to pass into the house it was only on some errand—to get something or to call someone—that would immediately have restored her to the public. It somehow struck him on the spot—and more than ever yet, though the impression was not wholly new to him—that she felt herself a figure for the forefront of the stage and indeed would have been recognised by anyone at a glance as the *prima donna assoluta*. She caused, in fact, during the few minutes he stood talking to her, an extraordinary series of waves to roll extraordinarily fast over his sense, not the least mark of the matter being that the appearance with which it ended was again the one with which it had begun. "The face—the face," as he kept dumbly repeating; that was at last, as at first, all he could clearly see. She had a perfection resplendent, but what in the world had it done, this perfection, to her beauty? It was her beauty, doubtless, that looked out at him, but it was into something else that, as their eyes met, he strangely found himself looking.

It was as if something had happened in consequence of which she had changed, and there was that in this swift perception that made him glance eagerly about for Lady Gwyther. But as he took in the recruited group—identities of the hour added to those of the previous twenty-four—he saw, among his recognitions, one of which was the husband of the person missing, that Lady Gwyther was not there. Nothing in the whole business was more singular than his consciousness that, as he came back to his interlocutress after the nods and smiles and hand-waves he had launched, she knew what had been his thought. She knew for whom he had looked without success; but why should this knowledge visibly have hardened and sharpened her, and precisely at a moment when she was unprecedentedly magnificent? The indefinable apprehension that had somewhat sunk after his second talk with Miss Banker and then had perversely risen again—this nameless anxiety now produced on him, with a sudden sharper pinch, the effect of a great suspense. The action of that, in turn, was to show him that he had not yet fully known how much he had at stake on a final view. It was revealed to him for the first time that he "really cared" whether Mrs Grantham were a safe nature. It was too ridiculous by what a thread it hung, but something was certainly in the air that would definitely tell him.

What was in the air descended the next moment to earth. He turned round as he caught the expression with which her eyes attached themselves to something that approached. A little person, very young and very much dressed, had come out of the house, and the expression in Mrs Grantham's eyes was that of the artist confronted with her work and interested, even to impatience, in the judgment of others. The little person drew nearer, and though Sutton's companion, without looking at him now, gave it a name and met it, he had jumped for himself at certitude. He saw many things—too many, and they appeared to be feathers, frills, excrescences of silk and lace—massed together and conflicting, and after a moment also saw struggling out of them a small face that struck him as either scared or sick. Then, with his eyes again returning to Mrs Grantham, he saw another.

He had no more talk with Miss Banker till late that evening —an evening during which he had felt himself too noticeably silent; but something had passed between this pair, across dinner-table and drawing-room, without speech, and when they at last found words it was in the needed ease of a quiet end of the long, lighted gallery, where she opened again at the very paragraph.

"You were right—that *was* it. She did the only thing that, at such short notice, she *could* do. She took her to her dressmaker."

Sutton, with his back to the reach of the gallery, had, as if to banish a vision, buried his eyes for a minute in his hands. "And oh, the face—the face!"

"Which?" Miss Banker asked.

"Whichever one looks at."

"But May Grantham's glorious. She has turned herself out——"

"With a splendour of taste and a sense of effect, eh? Yes." Sutton showed he saw far.

"She *has* the sense of effect. The sense of effect as exhibited in Lady Gwyther's clothes——!" was something Miss Banker failed of words to express. "Everybody's overwhelmed. Here, you know, that sort of thing's grave. The poor creature's lost."

"Lost?"

"Since on the first impression, as we said, so much depends. The first impression's made—oh, made! I defy her now ever to unmake it. Her husband, who's proud, won't like her the better for it. And I don't see," Miss Banker went on, "that her prettiness *was* enough—a mere little feverish, frightened freshness; what *did* he see in her?—to be so blasted. It has been done with an atrocity of art——"

"That supposes the dressmaker then also a devil?"

"Oh, your London women and their dressmakers!" Miss Banker laughed.

"But the face—the face!" Sutton woefully repeated.

"May's?"

"The little girl's. It's exquisite."

"Exquisite?"

"For unimaginable pathos."

"Oh!" Miss Banker dropped.

"She has at last begun to see." Sutton showed again how far *he* saw. "It glimmers upon her innocence, she makes it dimly out—what has been done with her. She's even worse this evening—the way, my eye, she looked at dinner!—than when she came. Yes"—he was confident—"it has dawned (how couldn't it, out of all of you?) and she knows."

"She ought to have known before!" Miss Banker intelligently sighed.

"No; she wouldn't in that case have been so beautiful."

"Beautiful?" cried Miss Banker; "overloaded like a monkey in a show!"

"The face, yes; which goes to the heart. It's that that makes it," said Shirley Sutton. "And it's that"—he thought it out— "that makes the other."

"I see. Conscious?"

"Horrible!"

"You take it hard," said Miss Banker.

Lord Gwyther, just before she spoke, had come in sight and now was near them. Sutton on this, appearing to wish to avoid him, reached, before answering his companion's observation, a door that opened close at hand. "So hard," he replied from that point, "that I shall be off to-morrow morning."

"And not see the rest?" she called after him.

But he had already gone, and Lord Gwyther, arriving, amiably took up her question. "The rest of what?"

Miss Banker looked him well in the eyes. "Of Mrs Grantham's clothes."

MRS MEDWIN

I

"WELL, we *are* a pair!" the poor lady's visitor broke out
to her, at the end of her explanation, in a manner disconcerting
enough. The poor lady was Miss Cutter, who lived in South
Audley Street, where she had an "upper half" so concise
that it had to pass, boldly, for convenient; and her visitor
was her half-brother, whom she had not seen for three years.
She was remarkable for a maturity of which every symptom
might have been observed to be admirably controlled, had
not a tendency to stoutness just affirmed its independence.
Her present, no doubt, insisted too much on her past, but
with the excuse, sufficiently valid, that she must certainly
once have been prettier. She was clearly not contented with
once—she wished to be prettier again. She neglected nothing
that could produce that illusion, and, being both fair and fat,
dressed almost wholly in black. When she added a little
colour it was not, at any rate, to her drapery. Her small rooms
had the peculiarity that everything they contained appeared
to testify with vividness to her position in society, quite as if
they had been furnished by the bounty of admiring friends.
They were adorned indeed almost exclusively with objects
that nobody buys, as had more than once been remarked by
spectators of her own sex, for herself, and would have been
luxurious if luxury consisted mainly in photographic portraits slashed across with signatures, in baskets of flowers
beribboned with the cards of passing compatriots, and in a
neat collection of red volumes, blue volumes, alphabetical
volumes, aids to London lucidity, of every sort, devoted to

addresses and engagements. To be in Miss Cutter's tiny drawing-room, in short, even with Miss Cutter alone— should you by any chance have found her so—was somehow to be in the world and in a crowd. It was like an agency—it bristled with particulars.

This was what the tall, lean, loose gentleman lounging there before her might have appeared to read in the suggestive scene over which, while she talked to him, his eyes moved without haste and without rest. "Oh, come, Mamie!" he occasionally threw off; and the words were evidently connected with the impression thus absorbed. His comparative youth spoke of waste even as her positive—her too positive—spoke of economy. There was only one thing, that is, to make up in him for everything he had lost, though it was distinct enough indeed that this thing might sometimes serve. It consisted in the perfection of an indifference, an indifference at the present moment directed to the plea—a plea of inability, of pure destitution—with which his sister had met him. Yet it had even now a wider embrace, took in quite sufficiently all consequences of queerness, confessed in advance to the false note that, in such a setting, he almost excruciatingly constituted. He cared as little that he looked at moments all his impudence as that he looked all his shabbiness, all his cleverness, all his history. These different things were written in him—in his premature baldness, his seamed, strained face, the lapse from bravery of his long tawny moustache; above all, in his easy, friendly, universally acquainted eye, so much too sociable for mere conversation. What possible relation with him could be natural enough to meet it? He wore a scant, rough Inverness cape and a pair of black trousers, wanting in substance and marked with the sheen of time, that had presumably once served for evening use. He spoke with the slowness helplessly permitted to Americans—as something too slow to be stopped —and he repeated that he found himself associated with Miss Cutter in a harmony worthy of wonder. She had been telling

him not only that she couldn't possibly give him ten pounds,
but that his unexpected arrival, should he insist on being much
in view, might seriously interfere with arrangements necessary
to her own maintenance; on which he had begun by replying
that he of course knew she had long ago spent her money,
but that he looked to her now exactly because she had, without
the aid of that convenience, mastered the art of life.

"I'd really go away with a fiver, my dear, if you'd only
tell me how you do it. It's no use saying only, as you've
always said, that 'people are very kind to you.' What the
devil are they kind to you *for?*"

"Well, one reason is precisely that no particular inconvenience has hitherto been supposed to attach to me. I'm just
what I am," said Mamie Cutter; "nothing less and nothing
more. It's awkward to have to explain to you, which, moreover, I really needn't in the least. I'm clever and amusing and
charming." She was uneasy and even frightened, but she kept
her temper and met him with a grace of her own. "I don't
think you ought to ask me more questions than I ask you."

"Ah, my dear," said the odd young man, "*I've* no mysteries. Why in the world, since it was what you came out for
and have devoted so much of your time to, haven't you pulled
it off? Why haven't you married?"

"Why haven't *you?*" she retorted. "Do you think that if I
had it would have been better for you?—that my husband
would for a moment have put up with you? Do you mind my
asking you if you'll kindly go *now?*" she went on after a
glance at the clock. "I'm expecting a friend, whom I must see
alone, on a matter of great importance——"

"And my being seen with you may compromise your respectability or undermine your nerve?" He sprawled imperturbably in his place, crossing again, in another sense, his
long black legs and showing, above his low shoes, an absurd
reach of parti-coloured sock. "I take your point well enough,
but mayn't you be after all quite wrong? If you can't do

anything for me couldn't you at least do something *with* me? If it comes to that, I'm clever and amusing and charming too! I've been such an ass that you don't appreciate me. But people like me—I assure you they do. They usually don't know what an ass I've been; they only see the surface, which"—and he stretched himself afresh as she looked him up and down—"you *can* imagine them, can't you, rather taken with? *I'm* 'what I am' too; nothing less and nothing more. That's true of us as a family, you see. We *are* a crew!" He delivered himself serenely. His voice was soft and flat, his pleasant eyes, his simple tones tending to the solemn, achieved at moments that effect of quaintness which is, in certain connections, socially so known and enjoyed. "English people have quite a weakness for me—more than any others. I get on with them beautifully. I've always been with them abroad. They think me," the young man explained, "diabolically American."

"You!" Such stupidity drew from her a sigh of compassion.

Her companion apparently quite understood it. "Are you homesick, Mamie?" he asked, with wondering irrelevance.

The manner of the question made her for some reason, in spite of her preoccupations, break into a laugh. A shade of indulgence, a sense of other things, came back to her. "You *are* funny, Scott!"

"Well," remarked Scott, "that's just what I claim. But *are* you so homesick?" he spaciously inquired, not as if to a practical end, but from an easy play of intelligence.

"I'm just dying of it!" said Mamie Cutter.

"Why, so am I!" Her visitor had a sweetness of concurrence.

"We're the only decent people," Miss Cutter declared. "And I know. *You* don't—you can't; and I can't explain. Come in," she continued with a return of her impatience and an increase of her decision, "at seven sharp."

She had quitted her seat some time before, and now, to get him into motion, hovered before him while, still motionless, he

looked up at her. Something intimate, in the silence, appeared
to pass between them—a community of fatigue and failure
and, after all, of intelligence. There was a final, cynical humour
in it. It determined him, at any rate, at last, and he slowly rose,
taking in again as he stood there the testimony of the room.
He might have been counting the photographs, but he looked
at the flowers with detachment. "Who's coming?"

"Mrs Medwin."

"American?"

"Dear no!"

"Then what are you doing for her?"

"I work for everyone," she promptly returned.

"For everyone who pays? So I suppose. Yet isn't it only
we who do pay?"

There was a drollery, not lost on her, in the way his queer
presence lent itself to his emphasised plural. "Do you consider that *you* do?"

At this, with his deliberation, he came back to his charming
idea. "Only try me, and see if I can't be *made* to. Work me
in." On her sharply presenting her back he stared a little at
the clock. "If I come at seven may I stay to dinner?"

It brought her round again. "Impossible. I'm dining out."

"With whom?"

She had to think. "With Lord Considine."

"Oh, my eye!" Scott exclaimed.

She looked at him gloomily. "Is *that* sort of tone what
makes you pay? I think you might understand," she went on,
"that if you're to sponge on me successfully you mustn't ruin
me. I must have *some* remote resemblance to a lady."

"Yes? But why must *I?*" Her exasperated silence was full
of answers, of which, however, his inimitable manner took no
account. "You don't understand my real strength; I doubt
if you even understand your own. You're clever, Mamie, but
you're not so clever as I supposed. However," he pursued,
"it's out of Mrs Medwin that you'll get it."

"Get what?"

"Why, the cheque that will enable you to assist me."

On this, for a moment, she met his eyes. "If you'll come back at seven sharp—not a minute before, and not a minute after, I'll give you two five-pound notes."

He thought it over. "Whom are you expecting a minute after?"

It sent her to the window with a groan almost of anguish, and she answered nothing till she had looked at the street. "If you injure me, you know, Scott, you'll be sorry."

"I wouldn't injure you for the world. What I want to do in fact is really to help you, and I promise you that I won't leave you—by which I mean won't leave London—till I've effected something really pleasant for you. I like you, Mamie, because I like pluck; I like you much more than you like me. I like you very, *very* much." He had at last with this reached the door and opened it, but he remained with his hand on the latch. "What does Mrs Medwin want of you?" he thus brought out.

She had come round to see him disappear, and in the relief of this prospect she again just indulged him. "The impossible."

He waited another minute. "And you're going to do it?"

"I'm going to do it," said Mamie Cutter.

"Well, then, that ought to be a haul. Call it *three* fivers!" he laughed. "At seven sharp." And at last he left her alone.

II

MISS CUTTER waited till she heard the house-door close; after which, in a sightless, mechanical way, she moved about the room, readjusting various objects that he had not touched. It was as if his mere voice and accent had spoiled her form.

But she was not left too long to reckon with these things, for Mrs Medwin was promptly announced. This lady was not, more than her hostess, in the first flush of her youth; her appearance—the scattered remains of beauty manipulated by taste—resembled one of the light repasts in which the fragments of yesterday's dinner figure with a conscious ease that makes up for the want of presence. She was perhaps of an effect still too immediate to be called interesting, but she was candid, gentle and surprised—not fatiguingly surprised, only just in the right degree; and her white face—it was too white —with the fixed eyes, the somewhat touzled hair and the Louis Seize hat, might at the end of the very long neck have suggested the head of a princess carried, in a revolution, on a pike. She immediately took up the business that had brought her, with the air, however, of drawing from the omens then discernible less confidence than she had hoped. The complication lay in the fact that if it was Mamie's part to present the omens, that lady yet had so to colour them as to make her own service large. She perhaps over-coloured, for her friend gave way to momentary despair.

"What you mean is then that it's simply impossible?"

"Oh no," said Mamie, with a qualified emphasis. "It's *possible*."

"But disgustingly difficult?"

"As difficult as you like."

"Then what can I do that I haven't done?"

"You can only wait a little longer."

"But that's just what I *have* done. I've done nothing else. I'm always waiting a little longer!"

Miss Cutter retained, in spite of this pathos, her grasp of the subject. "*The* thing, as I've told you, is for you first to be seen."

"But if people won't look at me?"

"They will."

"They *will?*" Mrs Medwin was eager.

"They shall," her hostess went on. "It's their only having heard—without having seen."

"But if they stare straight the other way?" Mrs Medwin continued to object. "You can't simply go up to them and twist their heads about."

"It's just what I can," said Mamie Cutter.

But her charming visitor, heedless for the moment of this attenuation, had found the way to put it. "It's the old story. You can't go into the water till you swim, and you can't swim till you go into the water. I can't be spoken to till I'm seen, but I can't be seen till I'm spoken to."

She met this lucidity, Miss Cutter, with but an instant's lapse. "You say I can't twist their heads about. But I *have* twisted them."

It had been quietly produced, but it gave her companion a jerk. "They say 'Yes'?"

She summed it up. "All but one. *She* says 'No.'"

Mrs Medwin thought; then jumped. "Lady Wantridge?"

Miss Cutter, as more delicate, only bowed admission. "I shall see her either this afternoon or late to-morrow. But she has written."

Her visitor wondered again. "May I see her letter?"

"No." She spoke with decision. "But I shall square her."

"Then how?"

"Well"—and Miss Cutter, as if looking upward for inspiration, fixed her eyes awhile on the ceiling—"well, it will come to me."

Mrs Medwin watched her—it was impressive. "And will *they* come to you—the others?" This question drew out the fact that they would—so far, at least, as they consisted of Lady Edward, Lady Bellhouse and Mrs Pouncer, who had engaged to muster, at the signal of tea, on the 14th—prepared, as it were, for the worst. There was of course always the chance that Lady Wantridge might take the field in such force as to paralyse them, though that danger, at the same time, seemed inconsistent with her being squared. It didn't perhaps all quite ideally hang together; but what it sufficiently came to was that if she was the one who could do most *for* a person in Mrs Medwin's position she was also the one who could do most against. It would therefore be distinctly what our friend familiarly spoke of as "collar-work." The effect of these mixed considerations was at any rate that Mamie eventually acquiesced in the idea, handsomely thrown out by her client, that she should have an "advance" to go on with. Miss Cutter confessed that it seemed at times as if one scarce *could* go on; but the advance was, in spite of this delicacy, still more delicately made—made in the form of a banknote, several sovereigns, some loose silver and two coppers, the whole contents of her purse, neatly disposed by Mrs Medwin on one of the tiny tables. It seemed to clear the air for deeper intimacies, the fruit of which was that Mamie, lonely, after all, in her crowd, and always more helpful than helped, eventually brought out that the way Scott had been going on was what seemed momentarily to overshadow her own power to do so.

"I've had a descent from him." But she had to explain. "My half-brother—Scott Homer. A wretch."

"What kind of a wretch?"

"Every kind. I lose sight of him at times—he disappears abroad. But he always turns up again, worse than ever."

"Violent?"

"No."

"Maudlin?"

"No."

"Only unpleasant?"

"No. Rather pleasant. Awfully clever—awfully travelled and easy."

"Then what's the matter with him?"

Mamie mused, hesitated—seemed to see a wide past. "I don't know."

"Something in the background?" Then as her friend was

silent, "Something queer about cards?" Mrs Medwin threw off.

"I don't know—and I don't want to!"

"Ah well, I'm sure *I* don't," Mrs Medwin returned with spirit. The note of sharpness was perhaps also a little in the observation she made as she gathered herself to go. "Do you mind my saying something?"

Mamie took her eyes quickly from the money on the little stand. "You may say what you like."

"I only mean that anything awkward you may have to keep out of the way does seem to make more wonderful, doesn't it, that you should have got just where you are? I allude, you know, to your position."

"I see." Miss Cutter somewhat coldly smiled. "To my power."

"So awfully remarkable in an American."

"Ah, you like us so."

Mrs Medwin candidly considered. "But we don't, dearest."

Her companion's smile brightened. "Then why do you come to me?"

"Oh, I like *you!*" Mrs Medwin made out.

"Then that's it. There are no 'Americans.' It's always 'you.' "

"Me?" Mrs Medwin looked lovely, but a little muddled.

"*Me!*" Mamie Cutter laughed. "But if you like me, you dear thing, you can judge if I like *you.*" She gave her a kiss to dismiss her. "I'll see you again when I've seen her."

"Lady Wantridge? I hope so, indeed. I'll turn up late to-morrow, if you don't catch me first. Has it come to you yet?" the visitor, now at the door, went on.

"No; but it will. There's time."

"Oh, a little less every day!"

Miss Cutter had approached the table and glanced again at the gold and silver and the note, not indeed absolutely over-looked the two coppers. "The balance," she put it, "the day after?"

"That very night, if you like."

"Then count on me."

"Oh, if I didn't——!" But the door closed on the dark idea. Yearningly then, and only when it had done so, Miss Cutter took up the money.

She went out with it ten minutes later, and, the calls on her time being many, remained out so long that at half-past six she had not come back. At that hour, on the other hand, Scott Homer knocked at her door, where her maid, who opened it with a weak pretence of holding it firm, ventured to announce to him, as a lesson well learnt, that he had not been expected till seven. No lesson, none the less, could prevail against his native art. He pleaded fatigue, her, the maid's, dreadful depressing London, and the need to curl up somewhere. If she would just leave him quiet half an hour that old sofa upstairs would do for it, of which he took quickly such effectual possession that when, five minutes later, she peeped, nervous for her broken vow, into the drawing-room, the faithless young woman found him extended at his length and peacefully asleep.

III

THE situation before Miss Cutter's return developed in other directions still, and when that event took place, at a few minutes past seven, these circumstances were, by the foot of the stair, between mistress and maid, the subject of some interrogative gasps and scared admissions. Lady Wantridge had arrived shortly after the interloper, and wishing, as she said, to wait, had gone straight up in spite of being told he was lying down.

"She distinctly understood he was there?"

"Oh yes, ma'am; I thought it right to mention."

"And what did you call him?"

"Well, ma'am, I thought it unfair to *you* to call him anything but a gentleman."

Mamie took it all in, though there might well be more of it than one could quickly embrace. "But if she has had time," she flashed, "to find out he isn't one?"

"Oh, ma'am, she had a quarter of an hour."

"Then she isn't with him still?"

"No, ma'am; she came down again at last. She rang, and I saw her here, and she said she wouldn't wait longer."

Miss Cutter darkly mused. "Yet had already waited——?"

"Quite a quarter."

"Mercy on us!" She began to mount. Before reaching the top, however, she had reflected that quite a quarter was long if Lady Wantridge had only been shocked. On the other hand, it was short if she had only been pleased. But how *could* she have been pleased? The very essence of their actual crisis was just that there was no pleasing her. Mamie had but to open the drawing-room door indeed to perceive that this was not true at least of Scott Homer, who was horribly cheerful.

Miss Cutter expressed to her brother without reserve her sense of the constitutional, the brutal selfishness that had determined his mistimed return. It had taken place, in violation of their agreement, exactly at the moment when it was most cruel to her that he should be there, and if she must now completely wash her hands of him he had only himself to thank. She had come in flushed with resentment and for a moment had been voluble; but it would have been striking that, though the way he received her might have seemed but to aggravate, it presently justified him by causing their relation really to take a stride. He had the art of confounding those who would quarrel with him by reducing them to the humiliation of an irritated curiosity.

"What *could* she have made of you?" Mamie demanded.

"My dear girl, she's not a woman who's eager to make too much of anything—anything, I mean, that will prevent her from doing as she likes, what she takes into her head. Of course," he continued to explain, "if it's something she doesn't want to do, she'll make as much as Moses."

Mamie wondered if that was the way he talked to her visitor, but felt obliged to own to his acuteness. It was an exact description of Lady Wantridge, and she was conscious of tucking it away for future use in a corner of her miscellaneous little mind. She withheld, however, all present acknowledgment, only addressing him another question. "Did you really get on with her?"

"Have you still to learn, darling—I can't help again putting it to you—that I get on with everybody? That's just what I don't seem able to drive into you. Only see how I get on with *you*."

She almost stood corrected. "What I mean is, of course, whether——"

"Whether she made love to me? Shyly, yet—or because—shamefully? She would certainly have liked awfully to stay."

"Then why didn't she?"

"Because, on account of some other matter—and I could see it was true—she hadn't time. Twenty minutes—she was here less—were all she came to give you. So don't be afraid I've frightened her away. She'll come back."

Mamie thought it over. "Yet you didn't go with her to the door?"

"She wouldn't let me, and I know when to do what I'm told—quite as much as what I'm not told. She wanted to find out about me. I mean from your little creature; a pearl of fidelity, by the way."

"But what on earth did she come up for?" Mamie again found herself appealing, and, just by that fact, showing her need of help.

"Because she always goes up." Then, as, in the presence of this rapid generalisation, to say nothing of that of such a relative altogether, Miss Cutter could only show as comparatively blank: "I mean she knows when to go up and when to come down. She has instincts; she didn't know whom you might have up here. It's a kind of compliment to you anyway. Why, Mamie," Scott pursued, "you don't know the curiosity we any of us inspire. You wouldn't believe what I've seen. The bigger bugs they are the more they're on the look-out."

Mamie still followed, but at a distance. "The look-out for what?"

"Why, for anything that will help them to live. You've been here all this time without making out then, about them, what I've had to pick out as I can? They're dead, don't you see? And *we're* alive."

"You? Oh!"—Mamie almost laughed about it.

"Well, they're a worn-out old lot, anyhow; they've used up their resources. They do look out; and I'll do them the justice to say they're not afraid—not even of me!" he continued as his sister again showed something of the same irony. "Lady Wantridge, at any rate, wasn't; that's what I mean by her having made love to me. She does what she likes. Mind it, you know." He was by this time fairly teaching her to know one of her best friends, and when, after it, he had come back to the great point of his lesson—that of her failure, through feminine inferiority, practically to grasp the truth that their being just as they were, he and she, was the real card for them to play—when he had renewed that reminder he left her absolutely in a state of dependence. Her impulse to press him on the subject of Lady Wantridge dropped; it was as if she had felt that, whatever had taken place, something would somehow come of it. She was to be, in a manner, disappointed, but the impression helped to keep her over to the next morning, when, as Scott had foretold, his new acquaintance did reappear, explaining to Miss Cutter that she had acted the day before to gain time and that she even now sought to gain it by not waiting longer. What, she promptly intimated she had

asked herself, could that friend be thinking of? She must
show where she stood before things had gone too far. If she
had brought her answer without more delay she wished to
make it sharp. Mrs Medwin? Never! "No, my dear—not I.
There I stop."

Mamie had known it would be "collar-work," but somehow now, at the beginning, she felt her heart sink. It was not
that she had expected to carry the position with a rush, but
that, as always after an interval, her visitor's defences really
loomed—and quite, as it were, to the material vision—too
large. She was always planted with them, voluminous, in the
very centre of the passage; was like a person accommodated
with a chair in some unlawful place at the theatre. She
wouldn't move and you couldn't get round. Mamie's calculation indeed had not been on getting round; she was obliged
to recognise that, too foolishly and fondly, she had dreamed
of producing a surrender. Her dream had been the fruit of
her need; but, conscious that she was even yet unequipped
for pressure, she felt, almost for the first time in her life,
superficial and crude. She was to be paid—but with what was
she, to that end, to pay? She had engaged to find an answer
to this question, but the answer had not, according to her
promise, "come." And Lady Wantridge meanwhile massed
herself, and there was no view of her that didn't show her as
verily, by some process too obscure to be traced, the hard
depository of the social law. She was no younger, no fresher,
no stronger, really, than any of them; she was only, with a
kind of haggard fineness, a sharpened taste for life, and, with
all sorts of things behind and beneath her, more abysmal and
more immoral, more secure and more impertinent. The points
she made were two in number. One was that she absolutely
declined; the other was that she quite doubted if Mamie herself
had measured the job. The thing couldn't be done. But say
it *could* be; was Mamie quite the person to do it? To this Miss
Cutter, with a sweet smile, replied that she quite understood

how little she might seem so. "I'm only one of the persons to whom it has appeared that *you* are."

"Then who are the others?"

"Well, to begin with, Lady Edward, Lady Bellhouse and Mrs Pouncer."

"Do you mean that they'll come to meet her?"

"I've seen them, and they've promised."

"To come, of course," Lady Wantridge said, "if *I* come."

Her hostess hesitated. "Oh, of course, you could prevent them. But I should take it as awfully kind of you not to. *Won't* you do this for me?" Mamie pleaded.

Her friend looked about the room very much as Scott had done. "Do they really understand what it's *for?*"

"Perfectly. So that she may call."

"And what good will that do her?"

Miss Cutter faltered, but she presently brought it out. "Of course what one hopes is that you'll ask her."

"Ask her to call?"

"Ask her to dine. Ask her, if you'd be so *truly* sweet, for a Sunday, or something of that sort, and even if only in one of your *most* mixed parties, to Catchmore."

Miss Cutter felt the less hopeful after this effort in that her companion only showed a strange good nature. And it was not the amiability of irony; yet it *was* amusement. "Take Mrs Medwin into my family?"

"Some day, when you're taking forty others."

"Ah, but what I don't see is what it does for *you*. You're already so welcome among us that you can scarcely improve your position even by forming for us the most delightful relation."

"Well, I know how dear you are," Mamie Cutter replied; "but one has, after all, more than one side, and more than one sympathy. I like her, you know." And even at this Lady Wantridge was not shocked; she showed that ease and bland-ness which were her way, unfortunately, of being most impossible. She remarked that *she* might listen to such things, because she was clever enough for them not to matter; only Mamie should take care how she went about saying them at large. When she became definite, however, in a minute, on the subject of the public facts, Miss Cutter soon found herself ready to make her own concession. Of course, she didn't dispute *them:* there they were; they were unfortunately on record, and nothing was to be done about them but to— Mamie found it, in truth, at this point, a little difficult.

"Well, what? Pretend already to have forgotten them?"

"Why not, when you've done it in so many other cases?"

"There *are* no other cases so bad. One meets them, at any rate, as they come. Some you can manage, others you can't. It's no use, you must give them up. They're past patching; there's nothing to be done with them. There's nothing, accordingly, to be done with Mrs Medwin but to put her off." And Lady Wantridge rose to her height.

"Well, you know, I *do* do things," Mamie quavered with a smile so strained that it partook of exaltation.

"You help people? Oh yes, I've known you to do wonders. But stick," said Lady Wantridge with strong and cheerful emphasis, "to your Americans!"

Miss Cutter, gazing, got up. "You don't do justice, Lady Wantridge, to your own compatriots. Some of them are really charming. Besides," said Mamie, "working for mine often strikes me, so far as the interest—the inspiration and excitement, don't you know? go, as rather too easy. You all, as I constantly have occasion to say, like us so!"

Her companion frankly weighed it. "Yes; it takes that to account for your position. I've always thought of you, nevertheless, as keeping, for their benefit, a regular working agency. They come to you, and you place them. There remains, I confess," her ladyship went on in the same free spirit, "the great wonder——"

"Of how I first placed my poor little self? Yes," Mamie

bravely conceded, "when *I* began there was no agency. I just worked my passage. I didn't even come to *you*, did I? You never noticed me till, as Mrs Short Stokes says, 'I was 'way, 'way up!' Mrs Medwin," she threw in, "can't get over it." Then, as her friend looked vague: "Over my social situation."

"Well, it's no great flattery to you to say," Lady Wantridge good-humouredly returned, "that she certainly can't hope for one resembling it." Yet it really seemed to spread there before them. "You simply *made* Mrs Short Stokes."

"In spite of her name!" Mamie smiled.

"Oh, your names——! In spite of everything."

"Ah, I'm something of an artist." With which, and a relapse marked by her wistful eyes into the gravity of the matter, she supremely fixed her friend. She felt how little she minded betraying at last the extremity of her need, and it was out of this extremity that her appeal proceeded. "Have I really had your last word? It means so much to me."

Lady Wantridge came straight to the point. "You mean you depend on it?"

"Awfully!"

"Is it all you have?"

"All. Now."

"But Mrs Short Stokes and the others—'rolling,' aren't they? Don't they pay up?"

"Ah," sighed Mamie, "if it wasn't for them——!"

Lady Wantridge perceived. "You've had so much?"

"I couldn't have gone on."

"Then what do you do with it all?"

"Oh, most of it goes back to them. There are all sorts, and it's all help. Some of them have nothing."

"Oh, if you feed the hungry," Lady Wantridge laughed, "you're indeed in a great way of business. Is Mrs Medwin" —her transition was immediate—"really rich?"

"Really. He left her everything."

"So that if I do say 'yes'——"

"It will quite set me up."

"I see—and how much more responsible it makes one! But I'd rather myself give you the money."

"Oh!" Mamie coldly murmured.

"You mean I mayn't suspect your prices? Well, I daresay I don't! But I'd rather give you ten pounds."

"Oh!" Mamie repeated in a tone that sufficiently covered her prices. The question was in every way larger. "Do you *never* forgive?" she reproachfully inquired. The door opened, however, at the moment she spoke, and Scott Homer presented himself.

IV

SCOTT HOMER wore exactly, to his sister's eyes, the aspect he had worn the day before, and it also formed, to her sense, the great feature of his impartial greeting.

"How d'ye do, Mamie? How d'ye do, Lady Wantridge?"

"How d'ye do again?" Lady Wantridge replied with an equanimity striking to her hostess. It was as if Scott's own had been contagious; it was almost indeed as if she had seen him before. *Had* she ever so seen him—before the previous day? While Miss Cutter put to herself this question her visitor, at all events, met the one she had previously uttered.

"Ever 'forgive'?" this personage echoed in a tone that made as little account as possible of the interruption. "Dear, yes! The people I *have* forgiven!" She laughed—perhaps a little nervously; and she was now looking at Scott. The way she looked at him was precisely what had already had its effect for his sister. "The people I *can*!"

"Can you forgive *me*?" asked Scott Homer.

She took it so easily. "But—what?"

Mamie interposed; she turned directly to her brother.

"Don't try her. Leave it so." She had had an inspiration; it was the most extraordinary thing in the world. "Don't try *him*"—she had turned to their companion. She looked grave, sad, strange. "Leave it so." Yes, it was a distinct inspiration, which she couldn't have explained, but which had come, prompted by something she had caught—the extent of the recognition expressed—in Lady Wantridge's face. It had come absolutely of a sudden, straight out of the opposition of the two figures before her—quite as if a concussion had struck a light. The light was helped by her quickened sense that her friend's silence on the incident of the day before showed some sort of consciousness. She looked surprised. "Do you know my brother?"

"*Do* I know you?" Lady Wantridge asked of him.

"No, Lady Wantridge," Scott pleasantly confessed, "not one little mite!"

"Well, then, if you *must* go——!" and Mamie offered her a hand. "But I'll go down with you. Not *you!*" she launched at her brother, who immediately effaced himself. His way of doing so—and he had already done so, as for Lady Wantridge, in respect to their previous encounter—struck her even at the moment as an instinctive, if slightly blind, tribute to her possession of an idea; and as such, in its celerity, made her so admire him, and their common wit, that, on the spot, she more than forgave him his queerness. He was right. He could be as queer as he liked! The queerer the better! It was at the foot of the stairs, when she had got her guest down, that what she had assured Mrs Medwin would come did indeed come. "*Did* you meet him here yesterday?"

"Dear, yes. Isn't he too funny?"

"Yes," said Mamie gloomily. "He *is* funny. But had you ever met him before?"

"Dear, no!"

"Oh!"—and Mamie's tone might have meant many things.

Lady Wantridge, however, after all, easily overlooked it.

"I only knew he was one of your odd Americans. That's why, when I heard yesterday, here, that he was up there awaiting your return, I didn't let that prevent me. I thought he might be. He certainly," her ladyship laughed, "*is*."

"Yes, he's very American," Mamie went on in the same way.

"As you say, we *are* fond of you! Good-bye," said Lady Wantridge.

But Mamie had not half done with her. She felt more and more—or she hoped at least—that she looked strange. She *was*, no doubt, if it came to that, strange. "Lady Wantridge," she almost convulsively broke out, "I don't know whether you'll understand me, but I seem to feel that I must act with you—I don't know what to call it!—responsibly. He *is* my brother."

"Surely—and why not?" Lady Wantridge stared. "He's the image of you!"

"Thank you!"—and Mamie was stranger than ever.

"Oh, he's good-looking. He's handsome, my dear. Oddly—but distinctly!" Her ladyship was for treating it much as a joke.

But Mamie, all sombre, would have none of this. She boldly gave him up. "I think he's awful."

"He is indeed—delightfully. And where *do* you get your ways of saying things? It isn't anything—and the things aren't anything. But it's so droll."

"Don't let yourself, all the same," Mamie consistently pursued, "be carried away by it. The thing can't be done—simply."

Lady Wantridge wondered. "'Done simply'?"

"Done at all."

"But what can't be?"

"Why, what you might think—from his pleasantness. What he spoke of your doing for him."

Lady Wantridge recalled. "Forgiving him?"

"He asked you if you couldn't. But you can't. It's too dreadful for me, as so near a relation, to have, loyally—loyally to *you*—to say it. But he's impossible."

It was so portentously produced that her ladyship had somehow to meet it. "What's the matter with him?"

"I don't know."

"Then what's the matter with *you?*" Lady Wantridge inquired.

"It's because I *won't* know," Mamie—not without dignity—explained.

"Then *I* won't either!"

"Precisely. Don't. It's something," Mamie pursued, with some inconsequence, "that—somewhere or other, at some time or other—he appears to have done; something that has made a difference in his life."

" 'Something'?" Lady Wantridge echoed again. "What kind of thing?"

Mamie looked up at the light above the door, through which the London sky was doubly dim. "I haven't the least idea."

"Then what kind of difference?"

Mamie's gaze was still at the light. "The difference you see."

Lady Wantridge, rather obligingly, seemed to ask herself what she saw. "But I don't see any! It seems, at least," she added, "such an amusing one! And he has such nice eyes."

"Oh, *dear* eyes!" Mamie conceded; but with too much sadness, for the moment, about the connections of the subject, to say more.

It almost forced her companion, after an instant, to proceed. "Do you mean he can't go home?"

She weighed her responsibility. "I only make out—more's the pity!—that he doesn't."

"Is it then something too terrible——?"

She thought again. "I don't know what—for men—*is* too terrible."

"Well then, as you don't know what 'is' for women either—good-bye!" her visitor laughed.

It practically wound up the interview; which, however, terminating thus on a considerable stir of the air, was to give Miss Cutter, the next few days, the sense of being much blown about. The degree to which, to begin with, she had been drawn—or perhaps rather pushed—closer to Scott was marked in the brief colloquy that, on her friend's departure, she had with him. He had immediately said it. "You'll see if she doesn't ask me down!"

"So soon?"

"Oh, I've known them at places—at Cannes, at Pau, at Shanghai—to do it sooner still. I always know when they will. You *can't* make out they don't love me!" He spoke almost plaintively, as if he wished she could.

"Then I don't see why it hasn't done you more good."

"Why, Mamie," he patiently reasoned, "what more good *could* it? As I tell you," he explained, "it has just been my life."

"Then why do you come to me for money?"

"Oh, they don't give me *that!*" Scott returned.

"So that it only means then, after all, that I, at the best, must keep you up?"

He fixed on her the nice eyes that Lady Wantridge admired. "Do you mean to tell me that already—at this very moment —I am not distinctly keeping *you?*"

She gave him back his look. "Wait till she *has* asked you, and then," Mamie added, "decline."

Scott, not too grossly, wondered. "As acting for *you?*"

Mamie's next injunction was answer enough. " But *before*— yes—call."

He took it in. "Call—but decline. Good."

"The rest," she said, "I leave to you." And she left it, in fact, with such confidence that for a couple of days she was not only conscious of no need to give Mrs Medwin another turn

of the screw, but positively evaded, in her fortitude, the reappearance of that lady. It was not till the third day that she
waited upon her, finding her, as she had expected, tense.

"Lady Wantridge *will*——?"

"Yes, though she says she won't."

"She says she won't? O—oh!" Mrs Medwin moaned.

"Sit tight all the same. I *have* her!"

"But how?"

"Through Scott—whom she wants."

"Your bad brother!" Mrs Medwin stared. "What does she
want of him?"

"To amuse them at Catchmore. Anything for that. And he
would. But he sha'n't!" Mamie declared. "He sha'n't go unless
she comes. She must meet you first—you're my condition."

"O—o—oh!" Mrs Medwin's tone was a wonder of hope
and fear. "But doesn't he want to go?"

"He wants what *I* want. She draws the line at *you*. I draw
the line at *him*."

"But *she*—doesn't she mind that he's bad?"

It was so artless that Mamie laughed. "No; it doesn't touch
her. Besides, perhaps he isn't. It isn't as for *you*—people seem
not to know. He has settled everything, at all events, by going
to see her. It's before her that he's the thing she will have to
have."

"Have to?"

"For Sundays in the country. A feature—*the* feature."

"So she has asked him?"

"Yes; and he has declined."

"For *me*?" Mrs Medwin panted.

"For me," said Mamie, on the doorstep. "But I don't leave
him for long." Her hansom had waited. "She'll come."

Lady Wantridge did come. She met in South Audley
Street, on the fourteenth, at tea, the ladies whom Mamie had
named to her, together with three or four others, and it was
rather a masterstroke for Miss Cutter that, if Mrs Medwin was

modestly present, Scott Homer was as markedly not. This occasion, however, is a medal that would take rare casting, as would also, for that matter, even the minor light and shade, the lower relief, of the pecuniary transaction that Mrs Medwin's flushed gratitude scarce awaited the dispersal of the company munificently to complete. A new understanding indeed on the spot rebounded from it, the conception of which, in Mamie's mind, had promptly bloomed. "He sha'n't go *now* unless he takes you." Then, as her fancy always moved quicker for her client than her client's own—"Down with him to Catchmore! When he goes to amuse them, *you*," she comfortably declared, "shall amuse them too." Mrs Medwin's response was again rather oddly divided, but she was sufficiently intelligible when it came to meeting the intimation that this latter would be an opportunity involving a separate fee. "Say," Mamie had suggested, "the same."

"Very well; the same."

The knowledge that it was to be the same had perhaps something to do, also, with the obliging spirit in which Scott eventually went. It was all, at the last, rather hurried—a party rapidly got together for the Grand Duke, who was in England but for the hour, who had good-naturedly proposed himself, and who liked his parties small, intimate and funny. This one was of the smallest, and it was finally judged to conform neither too little nor too much to the other conditions—after a brief whirlwind of wires and counterwires, and an iterated waiting of hansoms at various doors—to include Mrs Medwin. It was from Catchmore itself that, snatching a moment on the wondrous Sunday afternoon, this lady had the harmonious thought of sending the new cheque. She was in bliss enough, but her scribble none the less intimated that it was Scott who amused them most. He *was* the feature.

THE BELDONALD HOLBEIN

I

MRS MUNDEN had not yet been to my studio on so good a pretext as when she first put it to me that it would be quite open to me—should I only care, as she called it, to throw the handkerchief—to paint her beautiful sister-in-law. I needn't go here, more than is essential, into the question of Mrs Munden, who would really, by the way, be a story in herself. She has a manner of her own of putting things, and some of those she has put to me——! Her implication was that Lady Beldonald had not only seen and admired certain examples of my work, but had literally been prepossessed in favour of the painter's "personality." Had I been struck with this sketch I might easily have imagined that Lady Beldonald was throwing *me* the handkerchief. "She hasn't done," my visitor said, "what she ought."

"Do you mean she has done what she oughtn't?"

"Nothing horrid—oh dear, no." And something in Mrs Munden's tone, with the way she appeared to muse a moment, even suggested to me that what she "oughtn't" was perhaps what Lady Beldonald had too much neglected. "She hasn't got on."

"What's the matter with her?"

"Well, to begin with, she's American."

"But I thought that was the way of ways to get on."

"It's one of them. But it's one of the ways of being awfully out of it too. There are so many!"

"So many Americans?" I asked.

"Yes, plenty of *them*," Mrs Munden sighed. "So many ways, I mean, of being one."

"But if your sister-in-law's way is to be beautiful——?"

"Oh, there are different ways of that too."

"And she hasn't taken the right way?"

"Well," my friend returned, as if it were rather difficult to express, "she hasn't done with it——"

"I see," I laughed; "what she oughtn't!"

Mrs Munden in a manner corrected me, but it *was* difficult to express. "My brother, at all events, was certainly selfish. Till he died she was almost never in London; they wintered, year after year, for what he supposed to be his health—which it didn't help, since he was so much too soon to meet his end —in the south of France and in the dullest holes he could pick out, and when they came back to England he always kept her in the country. I must say for her that she always behaved beautifully. Since his death she has been more in London, but on a stupidly unsuccessful footing. I don't think she quite understands. She hasn't what *I* should call a life. It may be, of course, that she doesn't want one. That's just what I can't exactly find out. I can't make out how much she knows."

"I can easily make out," I returned with hilarity, "how much *you* do!"

"Well, you're very horrid. Perhaps she's too old."

"Too old for what?" I persisted.

"For anything. Of course she's no longer even a little young; only preserved—oh, but preserved, like bottled fruit, in syrup! I want to help her, if only because she gets on my nerves, and I really think the way of it would be just the right thing of yours at the Academy and on the line."

"But suppose," I threw out, "she should give on *my* nerves?"

"Oh, she will. But isn't that all in the day's work, and don't great beauties always——?"

"*You* don't," I interrupted; but I at any rate saw Lady

Beldonald later on—the day came when her kinswoman brought her, and then I understood that her life had its centre in her own idea of her appearance. Nothing else about her mattered—one knew her all when one knew that. She is indeed in one particular, I think, sole of her kind—a person whom vanity has had the odd effect of keeping positively safe and sound. This passion is supposed surely, for the most part, to be a principle of perversion and injury, leading astray those who listen to it and landing them, sooner or later, in this or that complication; but it has landed her ladyship nowhere whatever—it has kept her from the first moment of full consciousness, one feels, exactly in the same place. It has protected her from every danger, has made her absolutely proper and prim. If she is "preserved," as Mrs Munden originally described her to me, it is her vanity that has beautifully done it—putting her years ago in a plate-glass case and closing up the receptacle against every breath of air. How shouldn't she be preserved, when you might smash your knuckles on this transparency before you could crack it? And she *is*—oh, amazingly! Preservation is scarce the word for the rare condition of her surface. She looks *naturally* new, as if she took out every night her large, lovely, varnished eyes and put them in water. The thing was to paint her, I perceived, *in* the glass case—a most tempting, attaching feat; render to the full the shining, interposing plate and the general show-window effect.

It was agreed, though it was not quite arranged, that she should sit to me. If it was not quite arranged, this was because, as I was made to understand from an early stage, the conditions for our start must be such as should exclude all elements of disturbance, such, in a word, as she herself should judge absolutely favourable. And it seemed that these conditions were easily imperilled. Suddenly, for instance, at a moment when I was expecting her to meet an appointment—the first—that I had proposed, I received a hurried visit from Mrs Munden, who came on her behalf to let me know that the season happened just not to be propitious and that our friend couldn't be quite sure, to the hour, when it would again become so. Nothing, she felt, would make it so but a total absence of worry.

"Oh, a 'total absence,' " I said, "is a large order! We live in a worrying world."

"Yes; and she feels exactly that—more than you'd think. It's in fact just why she mustn't have, as she has now, a particular distress on at the very moment. She wants to look, of course, her best, and such things tell on her appearance."

I shook my head. "Nothing tells on her appearance. Nothing reaches it in any way; nothing gets *at* it. However, I can understand her anxiety. But what's her particular distress?"

"Why, the illness of Miss Dadd."

"And who in the world's Miss Dadd?"

"Her most intimate friend and constant companion—the lady who was with us here that first day."

"Oh, the little round, black woman who gurgled with admiration?"

"None other. But she was taken ill last week, and it may very well be that she'll gurgle no more. She was very bad yesterday and is no better to-day, and Nina is much upset. If anything happens to Miss Dadd she'll have to get another, and, though she has had two or three before, that won't be so easy."

"Two or three Miss Dadds? Is it possible? And still wanting another!" I recalled the poor lady completely now. "No; I shouldn't indeed think it would be easy to get another. But why is a succession of them necessary to Lady Beldonald's existence?"

"Can't you guess?" Mrs Munden looked deep, yet impatient. "They help."

"Help what? Help whom?"

"Why, every one. You and me for instance. To do what?

Why, to think Nina beautiful. She has them for that purpose;
they serve as foils, as accents serve on syllables, as terms of
comparison. They make her 'stand out.' It's an effect of contrast that must be familiar to you artists; it's what a woman
does when she puts a band of black velvet under a pearl
ornament that may require, as she thinks, a little showing off."
I wondered. "Do you mean she always has them black?"
"Dear no; I've seen them blue, green, yellow. They may
be what they like, so long as they're always one other thing."
"Hideous?"
Mrs Munden hesitated. "Hideous is too much to say; she
doesn't really require them as bad as that. But consistently,
cheerfully, loyally plain. It's really a most happy relation. She
loves them for it."
"And for what do they love *her?*"
"Why, just for the amiability that they produce in her.
Then, also, for their 'home.' It's a career for them."
"I see. But if that's the case," I asked, "why are they so
difficult to find?"
"Oh, they must be safe; it's all in that: her being able to
depend on them to keep to the terms of the bargain and never
have moments of rising—as even the ugliest woman will now
and then (say when she's in love)—superior to themselves."
I turned it over. "Then if they can't inspire passions the
poor things mayn't even at least feel them?"
"She distinctly deprecates it. That's why such a man as
you may be, after all, a complication."
I continued to muse. "You're very sure Miss Dadd's ailment isn't an affection that, being smothered, has struck in?"
My joke, however, was not well timed, for I afterwards learned
that the unfortunate lady's state had been, even while I spoke,
such as to forbid all hope. The worst symptoms had appeared;
she was not destined to recover; and a week later I heard from
Mrs Munden that she would in fact "gurgle" no more.

II

ALL this, for Lady Beldonald, had been an agitation so great that access to her apartment was denied for a time even to her sister-in-law. It was much more out of the question, of course, that she should unveil her face to a person of my special business with it; so that the question of the portrait was, by common consent, postponed to that of the installation of a successor to her late companion. Such a successor, I gathered from Mrs Munden, widowed, childless, and lonely, as well as inapt for the minor offices, she had absolutely to have; a more or less humble *alter ego* to deal with the servants, keep the accounts, make the tea and arrange the light. Nothing seemed more natural than that she should marry again, and obviously that might come; yet the predecessors of Miss Dadd had been contemporaneous with a first husband, and others formed in her image might be contemporaneous with a second. I was much occupied in those months, at any rate, so that these questions and their ramifications lost themselves for a while to my view, and I was only brought back to them by Mrs Munden's coming to me one day with the news that we were all right again—her sister-in-law was once more "suited." A certain Mrs Brash, an American relative whom she had not seen for years, but with whom she had continued to communicate, was to come out to her immediately; and this person, it appeared, could be quite trusted to meet the conditions. She was ugly—ugly enough, without abuse of it, and she was unlimitedly good. The position offered her by Lady Beldonald was, moreover, exactly what she needed; widowed also, after many troubles and reverses, with her fortune of the smallest and her various children either buried or placed about, she had never had time or means to come to England,

and would really be grateful in her declining years for the new experience and the pleasant light work involved in her cousin's hospitality. They had been much together early in life, and Lady Beldonald was immensely fond of her—would have in fact tried to get hold of her before had not Mrs Brash been always in bondage to family duties, to the variety of her tribulations. I dare say I laughed at my friend's use of the term "position"—the position, one might call it, of a candlestick or a sign-post, and I dare say I must have asked if the special service the poor lady was to render had been made clear to her. Mrs Munden left me, at all events, with the rather droll image of her faring forth, across the sea, quite consciously and resignedly to perform it.

The point of the communication had, however, been that my sitter was again looking up and would doubtless, on the arrival and due initiation of Mrs Brash, be in form really to wait on me. The situation must, further, to my knowledge, have developed happily, for I arranged with Mrs Munden that our friend, now all ready to begin, but wanting first just to see the things I had most recently done, should come once more, as a final preliminary, to my studio. A good foreign friend of mine, a French painter, Paul Outreau, was at the moment in London, and I had proposed, as he was much interested in types, to get together for his amusement a small afternoon party. Everyone came, my big room was full, there was music and a modest spread; and I have not forgotten the light of admiration in Outreau's expressive face as, at the end of half an hour, he came up to me in his enthusiasm.

"*Bonté divine, mon cher—que cette vieille est donc belle!*"

I had tried to collect all the beauty I could, and also all the youth, so that for a moment I was at a loss. I had talked to many people and provided for the music, and there were figures in the crowd that were still lost to me. "What old woman do you mean?"

"I don't know her name—she was over by the door a moment ago. I asked somebody and was told, I think, that she's American."

I looked about and saw one of my guests attach a pair of fine eyes to Outreau very much as if she knew he must be talking of her. "Oh, Lady Beldonald! Yes, she's handsome; but the great point about her is that she has been 'put up,' to keep, and that she wouldn't be flattered if she knew you spoke of her as old. A box of sardines is only 'old' after it has been opened. Lady Beldonald never has yet been—but I'm going to do it." I joked, but I was somehow disappointed. It was a type that, with his unerring sense for the *banal*, I shouldn't have expected Outreau to pick out.

"You're going to paint her? But, my dear man, she *is* painted—and as neither you nor I can do it. *Où est-elle donc?*" He had lost her, and I saw I had made a mistake. "She's the greatest of all the great Holbeins."

I was relieved. "Ah, then, not Lady Beldonald! But do I possess a Holbein, of *any* price, unawares?"

"There she is—there she is! Dear, dear, dear, what a head!" And I saw whom he meant—and what: a small old lady in a black dress and a black bonnet, both relieved with a little white, who had evidently just changed her place to reach a corner from which more of the room and of the scene was presented to her. She appeared unnoticed and unknown, and I immediately recognised that some other guest must have brought her and, for want of opportunity, had as yet to call my attention to her. But two things, simultaneously with this and with each other, struck me with force; one of them the truth of Outreau's description of her, the other the fact that the person bringing her could only have been Lady Beldonald. She *was* a Holbein—of the first water; yet she was also Mrs Brash, the imported "foil," the indispensable "accent," the successor to the dreary Miss Dadd! By the time I had put these things together—Outreau's "American" having helped me—I was in just such full possession of her face as I had found myself, on the other first occasion, of that of her patroness. Only with so different a consequence. I couldn't look at her enough, and I stared and stared till I became aware she might have fancied me challenging her as a person un-presented. "All the same," Outreau went on, equally held, "*c'est une tête à faire.* If I were only staying long enough for a crack at her! But I tell you what"—and he seized my arm—"bring her over!"

"Over?"

"To Paris. She'd have a *succès fou.*"

"Ah, thanks, my dear fellow," I was now quite in a position to say; "she's the handsomest thing in London, and"—for what I might do with her was already before me with intensity—"I propose to keep her to myself." It was before me with intensity, in the light of Mrs Brash's distant perfection of a little white old face, in which every wrinkle was the touch of a master; but something else, I suddenly felt, was not less so, for Lady Beldonald, in the other quarter, and though she couldn't have made out the subject of our notice, continued to fix us, and her eyes had the challenge of those of the woman of consequence who has missed something. A moment later I was close to her, apologising first for not having been more on the spot at her arrival, but saying in the next breath un-controllably, "Why, my dear lady, it's a Holbein!"

"A Holbein? What?"

"Why, the wonderful sharp old face—so extraordinarily, consummately drawn—in the frame of black velvet. That of Mrs Brash, I mean—isn't it her name?—your companion."

This was the beginning of a most odd matter—the essence of my anecdote; and I think the very first note of the oddity must have sounded for me in the tone in which her ladyship spoke after giving me a silent look. It seemed to come to me out of a distance immeasurably removed from Holbein. "Mrs Brash is not my 'companion' in the sense you appear to mean. She's my rather near relation and a very dear old friend. I *love* her—and you must know her."

"Know her? Rather! Why, to see her is to want, on the spot, to 'go' for her. She also must sit for me."

"*She?* Louisa Brash?" If Lady Beldonald had the theory that her beauty directly showed it when things were not well with her, this impression, which the fixed sweetness of her serenity had hitherto struck me by no means as justifying, gave me now my first glimpse of its grounds. It was as if I had never before seen her face invaded by anything I should have called an expression. This expression, moreover, was of the faintest—was like the effect produced on a surface by an agitation both deep within and as yet much confused. "Have you told her so?" she then quickly asked, as if to soften the sound of her surprise.

"Dear no, I've but just noticed her—Outreau a moment ago put me on her. But we're both so taken, and he also wants——"

"To *paint* her?" Lady Beldonald uncontrollably murmured.

"Don't be afraid we shall fight for her," I returned with a laugh for this tone. Mrs Brash was still where I could see her without appearing to stare, and she mightn't have seen I was looking at her, though her protectress, I am afraid, could scarce have failed of this perception. "We must each take our turn, and at any rate she's a wonderful thing, so that, if you'll take her to Paris, Outreau promises her there——"

"*There?*" my companion gasped.

"A career bigger still than among *us*, as he considers that we haven't half their eye. He guarantees her a *succès fou*."

She couldn't get over it. "Louisa Brash? In Paris?"

"They do see," I exclaimed, "more than we; and they live extraordinarily, don't you know, *in* that. But she'll do something here too."

"And what will she do?"

If, frankly, now, I couldn't help giving Mrs Brash a longer

look, so after it I could as little resist sounding my interlocutress. "You'll see. Only give her time."

She said nothing during the moment in which she met my
eyes; but then: "Time, it seems to me, is exactly what you
and your friend want. If you haven't talked with her——"

"We haven't seen her? Oh, we see bang off—with a click
like a steel spring. It's our trade; it's our life; and we should
be donkeys if we made mistakes. That's the way I saw you
yourself, my lady, if I may say so; that's the way, with a long
pin straight through your body, I've got you. And just so
I've got *her*."

All this, for reasons, had brought my guest to her feet; but
her eyes, while we talked, had never once followed the direction of mine. "You call her a Holbein?"

"Outreau did, and I of course immediately recognised it.
Don't *you?* She brings the old boy to life! It's just as I should
call you a Titian. You bring *him* to life."

She couldn't be said to relax, because she couldn't be said
to have hardened; but something at any rate on this took place
in her—something indeed quite disconnected from what I
would have called her. "Don't you understand that she has
always been supposed——?" It had the ring of impatience;
nevertheless, on a scruple, it stopped short.

I knew what it was, however, well enough to say it for her
if she preferred. "To be nothing whatever to look at? To be
unfortunately plain—or even if you like repulsively ugly? Oh
yes, I understand it perfectly, just as I understand—I have to
as a part of my trade—many other forms of stupidity. It's
nothing new to one that ninety-nine people out of a hundred
have no eyes, no sense, no taste. There are whole communities
impenetrably sealed. I don't say your friend is a person to
make the men turn round in Regent Street. But it adds to the
joy of the few who do see that they have it so much to themselves. Where in the world can she have lived? You must tell
me all about that—or rather, if she'll be so good, *she* must."

"You mean then to speak to her——?"

I wondered as she pulled up again. "Of her beauty?"

"Her beauty!" cried Lady Beldonald so loud that two or three persons looked round.

"Ah, with every precaution of respect!" I declared in a much lower tone. But her back was by this time turned to me, and in the movement, as it were, one of the strangest little dramas I have ever known was well launched.

III

IT was a drama of small, smothered intensely private things, and I knew of but one other person in the secret; yet that person and I found it exquisitely susceptible of notation, followed it with an interest the mutual communication of which did much for our enjoyment, and were present with emotion at its touching catastrophe. The small case—for so small a case—had made a great stride even before my little party separated, and in fact within the next ten minutes.

In that space of time two things had happened; one of which was that I made the acquaintance of Mrs Brash, and the other that Mrs Munden reached me, cleaving the crowd, with one of her usual pieces of news. What she had to impart was that, on her having just before asked Nina if the conditions of our sitting had been arranged with me, Nina had replied, with something like perversity, that she didn't propose to arrange them, that the whole affair was "off" again, and that she preferred not to be, for the present, further pressed. The question for Mrs Munden was naturally what had happened and whether I understood. Oh, I understood perfectly, and what I at first most understood was that even when I had brought in the name of Mrs Brash intelligence was not yet in Mrs M unden. She was quite as surprised as Lady Beldonald had been on hearing of the esteem in which I held Mrs Brash's appearance. She was stupefied at learning that I had just in my ardour proposed to the possessor of it to sit to me. Only she came round promptly—which Lady Beldonald really never did. Mrs Munden was in fact wonderful; for when I had given her quickly "Why, she's a Holbein, you know," she took it up, after a first fine vacancy, with an immediate abysmal "Oh, is she?" that, as a piece of social gymnastics, did her the greatest honour; and she was in fact the first in London to spread the tidings. For a face-about it was magnificent. But she was also the first, I must add, to see what would really happen—though this she put before me only a week or two later.

"It will kill her, my dear—that's what it will do!"

She meant neither more nor less than that it would kill Lady Beldonald if I were to paint Mrs Brash; for at this lurid light had we arrived in so short a space of time. It was for me to decide whether my æsthetic need of giving life to my idea was such as to justify me in destroying it in a woman after all, in most eyes, so beautiful. The situation was, after all, sufficiently queer; for it remained to be seen what I should positively gain by giving up Mrs Brash. I appeared to have in any case lost Lady Beldonald, now too "upset"—it was always Mrs Munden's word about her and, as I inferred, her own about herself—to meet me again on our previous footing. The only thing, I of course soon saw, was to temporise—to drop the whole question for the present and yet so far as possible keep each of the pair in view. I may as well say at once that this plan and this process gave their principal interest to the next several months. Mrs Brash had turned up, if I remember, early in the new year, and her little wonderful career was in our particular circle one of the features of the following season. It was at all events for myself the most attaching; it is not my fault if I am so put together as often to find more life in situations obscure and subject to interpretation than in the gross rattle of the foreground. And there were all sorts of things, things touching, amusing, mystifying— and above all such an instance as I had never yet met—in this funny little fortune of the useful American cousin. Mrs Munden was promptly at one with me as to the rarity and, to a near and human view, the beauty and interest of the position. We had neither of us ever before seen that degree and that special sort of personal success come to a woman for the first time so late in life. I found it an example of poetic, of absolutely retributive, justice; so that my desire grew great to work it, as we say, on those lines. I had seen it all from the original moment at my studio; the poor lady had never known an hour's appreciation—which, moreover, in perfect good faith, she had never missed. The very first thing I did after producing so unintentionally the resentful retreat of her protectress had been to go straight over to her and say almost without preliminaries that I should hold myself immeasurably obliged if she would give me a few sittings. What I thus came face to face with was, on the instant, her whole unenlightened past, and the full, if foreshortened, revelation of what among us all was now unfailingly in store for her. To turn the handle and start that tune came to me on the spot as a temptation. Here was a poor lady who had waited for the approach of old age to find out what she was worth. Here was a benighted being to whom it was to be disclosed in her fifty-seventh year (I was to make that out) that she had something that might pass for a face. She looked much more than her age, and was fairly frightened—as if I had been trying on her some possibly heartless London trick—when she had taken in my appeal. That showed me in what an air she had lived and —as I should have been tempted to put it had I spoken out— among what children of darkness. Later on I did them more justice; saw more that her wonderful points must have been points largely the fruit of time, and even that possibly she might never in all her life have looked so well as at this particular moment. It might have been that if her hour had struck I just happened to be present at the striking. What had occurred, all the same, was at the worst a sufficient comedy.

The famous "irony of fate" takes many forms, but I had never yet seen it take quite this one. She had been "had over" on an understanding, and she was not playing fair. She had broken the law of her ugliness and had turned beautiful on the hands of her employer. More interesting even perhaps than a view of the conscious triumph that this might prepare for her, and of which, had I doubted of my own judgment, I could still take Outreau's fine start as the full guarantee—more interesting was the question of the process by which such a history could get itself enacted. The curious thing was that, all the while, the reasons of her having passed for plain—the reasons for Lady Beldonald's fond calculation, which they quite justified—were written large in her face, so large that it was easy to understand them as the only ones she herself had ever read. What was it, then, that actually made the old stale sentence mean something so different?—into what new combinations, what extraordinary language, unknown but understood at a glance, had time and life translated it? The only thing to be said was that time and life were artists who beat us all, working with recipes and secrets that we could never find out. I really ought to have, like a lecturer or a showman, a chart or a blackboard to present properly the relation, in the wonderful old tender, battered, blanched face, between the original elements and the exquisite final "style." I could do it with chalks, but I can scarcely do it thus. However, the thing was, for any artist who respected himself, to *feel* it—which I abundantly did; and then not to conceal from *her* that I felt it—which I neglected as little. But she was really, to do her complete justice, the last to understand; and I am not sure that, to the end—for there was an end—she quite made it all out or knew where she was. When you have been brought up for fifty years on black, it must be hard to adjust your organism, at a day's notice, to gold-colour. Her whole nature had been pitched in the key of her supposed plainness. She had known how to be ugly—it was the only thing she had learnt save, if possible, how not to mind it. Being beautiful, at any rate, took a new set of muscles. It was on the prior theory, literally, that she had developed her admirable dress, instinctively felicitous, always either black or white, and a matter of rather severe squareness and studied line. She was magnificently neat; everything she showed had a way of looking both old and fresh; and there was on every occasion the same picture in her draped head—draped in low-falling black—and the fine white plaits (of a painter's white, some-how) disposed on her chest. What had happened was that these arrangements, determined by certain considerations, lent themselves in effect much better to certain others. Adopted as a kind of refuge, they had really only deepened her accent. It was singular, moreover, that, so constituted, there was nothing in her aspect of the ascetic or the nun. She was a good, hard, sixteenth-century figure, not withered with innocence, bleached rather by life in the open. She was, in short, just what we had made of her, a Holbein for a great museum; and our position, Mrs Munden's and mine, rapidly became that of persons having such a treasure to dispose of. The world—I speak of course mainly of the art-world—flocked to see it.

IV

"But has she any idea herself, poor thing?" was the way I had put it to Mrs Munden on our next meeting after the incident at my studio; with the effect, however, only of leaving my friend at first to take me as alluding to Mrs Brash's possible prevision of the chatter she might create. I had my own sense of that—this prevision had been *nil;* the question was of her consciousness of the office for which Lady Beldonald had counted on her and for which we were so promptly proceeding to spoil her altogether.

"Oh, I think she arrived with a goodish notion," Mrs Munden had replied when I had explained; "for she's clever too, you know, as well as good-looking, and I don't see how, if she ever really *knew* Nina, she could have supposed for a moment that she was not wanted for whatever she might have left to give up. Hasn't she moreover always been made to feel that she's ugly enough for anything?" It was even at this point already wonderful how my friend had mastered the case, and what lights, alike for its past and its future, she was prepared to throw on it. "If she has seen herself as ugly enough for anything, she has seen herself—and that was the only way —as ugly enough for Nina; and she has had her own manner of showing that she understands without making Nina commit herself to anything vulgar. Women are never without ways for doing such things—both for communicating and receiving knowledge—that I can't explain to you, and that you wouldn't understand if I could, as you must *be* a woman even to do that. I dare say they've expressed it all to each other simply in the language of kisses. But doesn't it, at any rate, make something rather beautiful of the relation between them as affected by our discovery?"

I had a laugh for her plural possessive. "The point is, of course, that if there was a conscious bargain, and our action on Mrs Brash is to deprive her of the sense of keeping her side of it, various things may happen that won't be good either for her or for ourselves. She may conscientiously throw up the position."

"Yes," my companion mused—"for she *is* conscientious. Or Nina, without waiting for that, may cast her forth."

I faced it all. "Then *we* should have to keep her."

"As a regular model?" Mrs Munden was ready for anything. "Oh, that would be lovely!"

But I further worked it out. "The difficulty is that she's *not* a model, hang it—that she's too good for one, that she's the very thing herself. When Outreau and I have each had our go, that will be all; there'll be nothing left for anyone else. Therefore it behoves us quite to understand that our attitude's a responsibility. If we can't do for her positively more than Nina does——"

"We must let her alone?" My companion continued to muse. "I see!"

"Yet don't," I returned, "see too much. We *can* do more."

"Than Nina?" She was again on the spot. "It wouldn't, after all, be difficult. We only want the directly opposite thing —and which is the only one the poor dear can give. Unless, indeed," she suggested, "we simply retract—we back out."

I turned it over. "It's too late for that. Whether Mrs Brash's peace is gone, I can't say. But Nina's is."

"Yes, and there's no way to bring it back that won't sacrifice her friend. We can't turn round and say Mrs Brash *is* ugly, can we? But fancy Nina's not having *seen!*" Mrs Munden exclaimed.

"She doesn't see now," I answered. "She can't, I'm certain, make out what we mean. The woman, for *her* still, is just what she always was. But she has, nevertheless, had her stroke, and her blindness, while she wavers and gropes in the dark, only adds to her discomfort. Her blow was to see the attention of the world deviate."

"All the same, I don't think, you know," my interlocutress said, "that Nina will have made her a scene, or that, whatever we do, she'll ever make her one. That isn't the way it will happen, for she's exactly as conscientious as Mrs Brash."

"Then what *is* the way?" I asked.

"It will just happen in silence."

"And what will 'it,' as you call it, be?"

"Isn't that what we want really to see?"

"Well," I replied after a turn or two about, "whether we

want it or not, it's exactly what we *shall* see; which is a reason the more for fancying, between the pair there—in the quiet, exquisite house, and full of superiorities and suppressions as they both are—the extraordinary situation. If I said just now that it's too late to do anything but accept, it's because I've taken the full measure of what happened at my studio. It took but a few moments—but she tasted of the tree."

My companion wondered. "Nina?"

"Mrs Brash." And to have to put it so ministered, while I took yet another turn, to a sort of agitation. Our attitude *was* a responsibility.

But I had suggested something else to my friend, who appeared for a moment detached. "Should you say she'll hate her worse if she *doesn't* see?"

"Lady Beldonald? Doesn't see what *we* see, you mean, than if she does? Ah, I give *that* up!" I laughed. "But what I can tell you is why I hold that, as I said just now, we can do most. We can do this: we can give to a harmless and sensitive creature hitherto practically disinherited—and give with an unexpectedness that will immensely add to its price—the pure joy of a deep draught of the very pride of life, of an acclaimed personal triumph in our superior, sophisticated world."

Mrs Munden had a glow of response for my sudden eloquence. "Oh, it will be beautiful!"

V

WELL, that is what, on the whole, and in spite of everything, it really was. It has dropped into my memory a rich little gallery of pictures, a regular panorama of those occasions that were the proof of the privilege that had made me for a moment

—in the words I have just recorded—lyrical. I see Mrs Brash on each of these occasions practically enthroned and surrounded and more or less mobbed; see the hurrying and the nudging and the pressing and the staring; see the people "making up" and introduced, and catch the word when they have had their turn; hear it above all, the great one—"Ah yes, the famous Holbein!"—passed about with that perfection of promptitude that makes the motions of the London mind so happy a mixture of those of the parrot and the sheep. Nothing would be easier, of course, than to tell the whole little tale with an eye only for that silly side of it. Great was the silliness, but great also as to this case of poor Mrs Brash, I will say for it, the good nature. Of course, furthermore, it took in particular "our set," with its positive child-terror of the *banal*, to be either so foolish or so wise; though indeed I've never quite known where our set begins and ends, and have had to content myself on this score with the indication once given me by a lady next whom I was placed at dinner: "Oh, it's bounded on the north by Ibsen and on the south by Sargent!" Mrs Brash never sat to me; she absolutely declined; and when she declared that it was quite enough for her that I had with that fine precipitation invited her, I quite took this as she meant it, for before we had gone very far our understanding, hers and mine, was complete. Her attitude was as happy as her success was prodigious. The sacrifice of the portrait was a sacrifice to the true inwardness of Lady Beldonald, and did much, for the time, I divined, toward muffling their domestic tension. All that was thus in her power to say —and I heard of a few cases of her having said it—was that she was sure I would have painted her beautifully if she hadn't prevented me. She couldn't even tell the truth, which was that I certainly would have done so if Lady Beldonald hadn't; and she never could mention the subject at all before that personage. I can only describe the affair, naturally, from the outside, and heaven forbid indeed that I should try too closely to reconstruct the possible strange intercourse of these good friends at home.

My anecdote, however, would lose half such point as it may possess were I to omit all mention of the charming turn that her ladyship appeared gradually to have found herself able to give to her deportment. She had made it impossible I should myself bring up our old, our original question, but there was real distinction in her manner of now accepting certain other possibilities. Let me do her that justice; her effort at magnanimity must have been immense. There couldn't fail, of course, to be ways in which poor Mrs Brash paid for it. How much she had to pay we were, in fact, soon enough to see; and it is my intimate conviction that, as a climax, her life at last was the price. But while she lived, at least—and it was with an intensity, for those wondrous weeks, of which she had never dreamed—Lady Beldonald herself faced the music. This is what I mean by the possibilities, by the sharp actualities indeed, that she accepted. She took our friend out, she showed her at home, never attempted to hide or to betray her, played her no trick whatever so long as the ordeal lasted. She drank deep, on *her* side too, of the cup—the cup that for her own lips could only be bitterness. There was, I think, scarce a special success of her companion's at which she was not personally present. Mrs Munden's theory of the silence in which all this would be muffled for them was, none the less, and in abundance, confirmed by our observations. The whole thing was to be the death of one or the other of them, but they never spoke of it at tea. I remember even that Nina went so far as to say to me once, looking me full in the eyes, quite sublimely, "I've made out what you mean—she *is* a picture." The beauty of this, moreover, was that, as I am persuaded, she hadn't really made it out at all—the words were the mere hypocrisy of her reflective endeavour for virtue. She couldn't possibly have made it out; her friend was as much as ever "dreadfully plain" to her; she must have wondered to the last what on earth possessed us. Wouldn't it in fact have been, after all, just this failure of vision, this supreme stupidity in short, that kept the catastrophe so long at bay? There was a certain sense of greatness for her in seeing so many of us so absurdly mistaken; and I recall that on various occasions, and in particular when she uttered the words just quoted, this high serenity, as a sign of the relief of her soreness, if not of the effort of her conscience, did something quite visible to my eyes, and also quite unprecedented, for the beauty of her face. She got a real lift from it—such a momentary discernible sublimity that I recollect coming out on the spot with a queer, crude, amused "Do you know I believe I could paint you *now?*"

She was a fool not to have closed with me then and there; for what has happened since has altered everything—what was to happen a little later was so much more than I could swallow. This was the disappearance of the famous Holbein from one day to the other—producing a consternation among us all as great as if the Venus of Milo had suddenly vanished from the Louvre. "She has simply shipped her straight back" —the explanation was given in that form by Mrs Munden, who added that any cord pulled tight enough would end at last by snapping. At the snap, in any case, we mightily jumped, for the masterpiece we had for three or four months been living with had made us feel its presence as a luminous lesson and a daily need. We recognised more than ever that it had been, for high finish, the gem of our collection—we found what a blank it left on the wall. Lady Beldonald might fill up the blank, but *we* couldn't. That she did soon fill it up —and, heaven help us, *how?*—was put before me after an interval of no great length, but during which I had not seen her. I dined on the Christmas of last year at Mrs Munden's, and Nina, with a "scratch lot," as our hostess said, was there, and, the preliminary wait being longish, approached me very sweetly. "I'll come to you to-morrow if you like," she said;

and the effect of it, after a first stare at her, was to make me look all round. I took in, in these two motions, two things; one of which was that, though now again so satisfied herself of her high state, she could give me nothing comparable to what I should have got had she taken me up at the moment of my meeting her on her distinguished concession; the other that she was "suited" afresh, and that Mrs Brash's successor was fully installed. Mrs Brash's successor was at the other side of the room, and I became conscious that Mrs Munden was waiting to see my eyes seek her. I guessed the meaning of the wait; what *was* one, this time, to say? Oh, first and foremost, assuredly, that it was immensely droll, for this time, at least, there was no mistake. The lady I looked upon, and as to whom my friend, again quite at sea, appealed to me for a formula, was as little a Holbein, or a specimen of any other school, as she was, like Lady Beldonald herself, a Titian. The formula was easy to give, for the amusement was that her prettiness—yes, literally, prodigiously, her prettiness—was distinct. Lady Beldonald had been magnificent—had been almost intelligent. Miss What's-her-name continues pretty, continues even young, and doesn't matter a straw! She matters so ideally little that Lady Beldonald is practically safer, I judge, than she has ever been. There has not been a symptom of chatter about this person, and I believe her protectress is much surprised that we are not more struck.

It was, at any rate, strictly impossible to me to make an appointment for the day as to which I have just recorded Nina's proposal; and the turn of events since then has not quickened my eagerness. Mrs Munden remained in correspondence with Mrs Brash—to the extent, that is, of three letters, each of which she showed me. They so told, to our imagination, her terrible little story that we were quite prepared—or thought we were—for her going out like a snuffed candle. She resisted, on her return to her original conditions, less than a year; the taste of the tree, as I had called it, had been fatal to her; what she had contentedly enough lived without before for half a century she couldn't now live without for a day. I know nothing of her original conditions—some minor American city—save that for her to have gone back to them was clearly to have stepped out of her frame. We performed, Mrs Munden and I, a small funeral service for her by talking it all over and making it all out. It wasn't—the minor American city—a market for Holbeins, and what had occurred was that the poor old picture, banished from its museum and refreshed by the rise of no new movement to hang it, was capable of the miracle of a silent revolution, of itself turning, in its dire dishonour, its face to the wall. So it stood, without the intervention of the ghost of a critic, till they happened to pull it round again and find it mere dead paint. Well, it had had, if that is anything, its season of fame, its name on a thousand tongues and printed in capitals in the catalogue. *We* had not been at fault. I haven't, all the same, the least note of her—not a scratch. And I did her so in intention! Mrs Munden continues to remind me, however, that this is not the sort of rendering with which, on the other side, after all, Lady Beldonald proposes to content herself. She has come back to the question of her own portrait. Let me settle it then at last. Since she *will* have the real thing—well, hang it, she shall!

THE STORY IN IT

I

THE weather had turned so much worse that the rest of the day was certainly lost. The wind had risen and the storm gathered force; they gave from time to time a thump at the firm windows and dashed even against those protected by the verandah their vicious splotches of rain. Beyond the lawn, beyond the cliff, the great wet brush of the sky dipped deep into the sea. But the lawn, already vivid with the touch of May, showed a violence of watered green; the budding shrubs and trees repeated the note as they tossed their thick masses, and the cold, troubled light, filling the pretty drawing-room, marked the spring afternoon as sufficiently young. The two ladies seated there in silence could pursue without difficulty —as well as, clearly, without interruption—their respective tasks; a confidence expressed, when the noise of the wind allowed it to be heard, by the sharp scratch of Mrs Dyott's pen at the table where she was busy with letters.

Her visitor, settled on a small sofa that, with a palm-tree, a screen, a stool, a stand, a bowl of flowers and three photographs in silver frames, had been arranged near the light wood-fire as a choice "corner"—Maud Blessingbourne, her guest, turned audibly, though at intervals neither brief nor regular, the leaves of a book covered in lemon-coloured paper and not yet despoiled of a certain fresh crispness. This effect of the volume, for the eye, would have made it, as presumably the newest French novel—and evidently, from the attitude of the reader, "good"—consort happily with the special tone of the room, a consistent air of selection and suppression, one of the finer æsthetic evolutions. If Mrs Dyott was fond of ancient French furniture, and distinctly difficult about it, her inmates could be fond—with whatever critical cocks of charming dark-braided heads over slender sloping shoulders—of modern French authors. Nothing had passed for half an hour—nothing, at least, to be exact, but that each of the companions occasionally and covertly intermitted her pursuit in such a manner as to ascertain the degree of absorption of the other without turning round. What their silence was charged with, therefore, was not only a sense of the weather, but a sense, so to speak, of its own nature. Maud Blessingbourne, when she lowered her book into her lap, closed her eyes with a conscious patience that seemed to say she waited; but it was nevertheless she who at last made the movement representing a snap of their tension. She got up and stood by the fire, into which she looked a minute; then came round and approached the window as if to see what was really going on. At this Mrs Dyott wrote with refreshed intensity. Her little pile of letters had grown, and if a look of determination was compatible with her fair and slightly faded beauty, the habit of attending to her business could always keep pace with any excursion of her thought. Yet she was the first who spoke.

"I trust your book has been interesting."

"Well enough; a little mild."

A louder throb of the tempest had blurred the sound of the words. "A little wild?"

"Dear, no—timid and tame; unless I've quite lost my sense."

"Perhaps you have," Mrs Dyott placidly suggested—"reading so many."

Her companion made a motion of feigned despair. "Ah, you take away my courage for going to my room, as I was just meaning to, for another."

"Another French one?"

"I'm afraid."

"Do you carry them by the dozen——"

"Into innocent British homes?" Maud tried to remember. "I believe I brought three—seeing them in a shop window as I passed through town. It never rains but it pours! But I've already read two."

"And are they the only ones you do read?"

"French ones?" Maud considered. "Oh, no. D'Annunzio."

"And what's that?" Mrs Dyott asked as she affixed a stamp.

"Oh, you dear thing!" Her friend was amused, yet almost showed pity. "I know you don't read," Maud went on; "but why should you? *You* live!"

"Yes—wretchedly enough," Mrs Dyott returned, getting her letters together. She left her place, holding them as a neat, achieved handful, and came over to the fire, while Mrs Blessingbourne turned once more to the window, where she was met by another flurry.

Maud spoke then as if moved only by the elements. "Do you expect him through all this?"

Mrs Dyott just waited, and it had the effect, indescribably, of making everything that had gone before seem to have led up to the question. This effect was even deepened by the way she then said, "Whom do you mean?"

"Why, I thought you mentioned at luncheon that Colonel Voyt was to walk over. Surely he can't."

"Do you care very much?" Mrs Dyott asked.

Her friend now hesitated. "It depends on what you call 'much.' If you mean should I like to see him—then certainly."

"Well, my dear, I think he understands you're here."

"So that as he evidently isn't coming," Maud laughed, "it's particularly flattering! Or rather," she added, giving up the prospect again, "it would be, I think, quite extraordinarily flattering if he did. Except that, of course," she subjoined, "he might come partly for you."

"'Partly' is charming. Thank you for 'partly.' If you *are*

going upstairs, will you kindly," Mrs Dyott pursued, "put these into the box as you pass?"

The younger woman, taking the little pile of letters, considered them with envy. "Nine! You *are* good. You're always a living reproach!"

Mrs Dyott gave a sigh. "I don't do it on purpose. The only thing, this afternoon," she went on, reverting to the other question, "would be their not having come down."

"And as to that you don't know."

"No—I don't know." But she caught even as she spoke a rat-tat-tat of the knocker, which struck her as a sign. "Ah, there!"

"Then I go." And Maud whisked out.

Mrs Dyott, left alone, moved with an air of selection to the window, and it was as so stationed, gazing out at the wild weather, that the visitor, whose delay to appear spoke of the wiping of boots and the disposal of drenched mackintosh and cap, finally found her. He was tall, lean, fine, with little in him, on the whole, to confirm the titular in the "Colonel Voyt" by which he was announced. But he had left the army, and his reputation for gallantry mainly depended now on his fighting Liberalism in the House of Commons. Even these facts, however, his aspect scantly matched; partly, no doubt, because he looked, as was usually said, un-English. His black hair, cropped close, was lightly powdered with silver, and his dense glossy beard, that of an emir or a caliph, and grown for civil reasons, repeated its handsome colour and its somewhat foreign effect. His nose had a strong and shapely arch, and the dark grey of his eyes was tinted with blue. It had been said of him—in relation to these signs—that he would have struck you as a Jew had he not, in spite of his nose, struck you so much as an Irishman. Neither responsibility could in fact have been fixed upon him, and just now, at all events, he was only a pleasant, weather-washed, wind-battered Briton, who brought in from a struggle with the elements that he appeared quite to have enjoyed a certain amount of unremoved mud and an unusual quantity of easy expression. It was exactly the silence ensuing on the retreat of the servant and the closed door that marked between him and his hostess the degree of this ease. They met, as it were, twice: the first time while the servant was there and the second as soon as he was not. The difference was great between the two encounters, though we must add in justice to the second that its marks were at first mainly negative. This communion consisted only in their having drawn each other for a minute as close as possible—as possible, that is, with no help but the full clasp of hands. Thus they were mutually held, and the closeness was at any rate such that, for a little, though it took account of dangers, it did without words. When words presently came the pair were talking by the fire, and she had rung for tea. He had by this time asked if the note he had despatched to her after breakfast had been safely delivered.

"Yes, before luncheon. But I'm always in a state when— except for some extraordinary reason—you send such things by hand. I knew, without it, that you had come. It never fails. I'm sure when you're there—I'm sure when you're not."

He wiped, before the glass, his wet moustache. "I see. But this morning I had an impulse."

"It was beautiful. But they make me as uneasy, sometimes, your impulses, as if they were calculations; make me wonder what you have in reserve."

"Because when small children are too awfully good they die? Well, I *am* a small child compared to you—but I'm not dead yet. I cling to life."

He had covered her with his smile, but she continued grave. "I'm not half so much afraid when you're nasty."

"Thank you! What then did you do," he asked, "with my note?"

"You deserve that I should have spread it out on my

dressing-table—or left it, better still, in Maud Blessingbourne's room."

He wondered while he laughed. "Oh, but what does *she* deserve?"

It was her gravity that continued to answer. "Yes—it would probably kill her."

"She believes so in you?"

"She believes so in *you*. So don't be *too* nice to her."

He was still looking, in the chimney-glass, at the state of his beard—brushing from it, with his handkerchief, the traces of wind and wet. "If she also then prefers me when I'm nasty, it seems to me I ought to satisfy her. Shall I now, at any rate, see her?"

"She's so like a pea on a pan over the possibility of it that she's pulling herself together in her room."

"Oh then, we must try and keep her together. But why, graceful, tender, pretty too—quite, or almost—as she is, doesn't she remarry?"

Mrs Dyott appeared—and as if the first time—to look for the reason. "Because she likes too many men."

It kept up his spirits. "And how many *may* a lady like——?"

"In order not to like any of them too much? Ah, that, you know, I never found out—and it's too late now. When," she presently pursued, "did you last see her?"

He really had to think. "Would it have been since last November or so?—somewhere or other where we spent three days."

"Oh, at Surredge? I know all about that. I thought you also met afterwards."

He had again to recall. "So we did! Wouldn't it have been somewhere at Christmas? But it wasn't by arrangement!" he laughed, giving with his forefinger a little pleasant nick to his hostess's chin. Then as if something in the way she received this attention put him back to his question of a moment before, "Have you kept my note?"

She held him with her pretty eyes. "Do you want it back?"

"Ah, don't speak as if I did take things——!"

She dropped her gaze to the fire. "No, you don't; not even the hard things a really generous nature often would." She quitted, however, as if to forget that, the chimney-place. "I put it *there!*"

"You've burnt it? Good!" It made him easier, but he noticed the next moment on a table the lemon-coloured volume left there by Mrs Blessingbourne, and, taking it up for a look, immediately put it down. "You might, while you were about it, have burnt that too."

"You've read it?"

"Dear, yes. And you?"

"No," said Mrs Dyott; "it wasn't for me Maud brought it."

It pulled her visitor up. "Mrs Blessingbourne brought it?"

"For such a day as this." But she wondered. "How you look! Is it so awful?"

"Oh, like his others." Something had occurred to him; his thought was already far. "Does she know?"

"Know what?"

"Why, anything."

But the door opened too soon for Mrs Dyott, who could only murmur quickly—

"Take care!"

II

IT was in fact Mrs Blessingbourne, who had under her arm the book she had gone up for—a pair of covers that this time showed a pretty, a candid blue. She was followed next minute by the servant, who brought in tea, the consumption of which, with the passage of greetings, inquiries and other light civilities between the two visitors, occupied a quarter of an hour. Mrs Dyott meanwhile, as a contribution to so much amenity, mentioned to Maud that her fellow-guest wished to scold her for the books she read—a statement met by this friend with the remark that he must first be sure about them. But as soon as he had picked up the new volume he broke out into a frank "Dear, dear!"

"Have you read that too?" Mrs Dyott inquired. "How much you'll have to talk over together! The other one," she explained to him, "Maud speaks of as terribly tame."

"Ah, I must have that out with her! You don't feel the extraordinary force of the fellow?" Voyt went on to Mrs Blessingbourne.

And so, round the hearth, they talked—talked soon, while they warmed their toes, with zest enough to make it seem as happy a chance as any of the quieter opportunities their imprisonment might have involved. Mrs Blessingbourne did feel, it then appeared, the force of the fellow, but she had her reserves and reactions, in which Voyt was much interested. Mrs Dyott rather detached herself, mainly gazing, as she leaned back, at the fire; she intervened, however, enough to relieve Maud of the sense of being listened to. That sense, with Maud, was too apt to convey that one was listened to for a fool. "Yes, when I read a novel I mostly read a French one," she had said to Voyt in answer to a question about her usual practice; "for I seem with it to get hold more of the real thing—to get more life for my money. Only I'm not so infatuated with them but that sometimes for months and months on end I don't read any fiction at all."

The two books were now together beside them. "Then when you begin again you read a mass?"

"Dear, no. I only keep up with three or four authors."

He laughed at this over the cigarette he had been allowed to light. "I like your 'keeping up,' and keeping up in particular with 'authors.'"

"One must keep up with somebody," Mrs Dyott threw off.

"I dare say I'm ridiculous," Mrs Blessingbourne conceded without heeding it; "but that's the way we express ourselves in my part of the country."

"I only alluded," said Voyt, "to the tremendous conscience of your sex. It's more than mine can keep up with. You take everything too hard. But if you can't read the novel of British and American manufacture, heaven knows I'm at one with you. It seems really to show our sense of life as the sense of puppies and kittens."

"Well," Maud more patiently returned, "I'm told all sorts of people are now doing wonderful things; but somehow I remain outside."

"Ah, it's *they*, it's our poor twangers and twaddlers who remain outside. They pick up a living in the street. And who indeed would want them in?"

Mrs Blessingbourne seemed unable to say, and yet at the same time to have her idea. The subject, in truth, she evidently found, was not so easy to handle. "People lend me things, and I try; but at the end of fifty pages——"

"There you are! Yes—heaven help us!"

"But what I mean," she went on, "isn't that I don't get wofully weary of the eternal French thing. What's *their* sense of life?"

"Ah, *voila!*" Mrs Dyott softly sounded.

"Oh, but it *is* one; you can make it out," Voyt promptly declared. "They do what they feel, and they feel more things than we. They strike so many more notes, and with so different a hand. When it comes to any account of a relation, say, between a man and a woman—I mean an intimate or a curious or a suggestive one—where are we compared to them? They don't exhaust the subject, no doubt," he admitted; "but we don't touch it, don't even skim it. It's as if we denied its existence, its possibility. You'll doubtless tell me, however," he went on, "that as all such relations *are* for us, at the most, much simpler, we can only have all round less to say about them."

She met this imputation with the quickest amusement. "I beg your pardon. I don't think I shall tell you anything of the sort. I don't know that I even agree with your premise."

"About such relations?" He looked agreeably surprised. "You think we make them larger?—or subtler?"

Mrs Blessingbourne leaned back, not looking, like Mrs Dyott, at the fire, but at the ceiling. "I don't know what I think."

"It's not that she doesn't know," Mrs Dyott remarked. "It's only that she doesn't say."

But Voyt had this time no eye for their hostess. For a moment he watched Maud. "It sticks out of you, you know, that you've yourself written something. Haven't you—and published? I've a notion I could read *you*."

"When I do publish," she said without moving, "you'll be the last one I shall tell. I *have*," she went on, "a lovely subject, but it would take an amount of treatment———!"

"Tell us then at least what it is."

At this she again met his eyes. "Oh, to tell it would be to express it, and that's just what I can't do. What I meant to say just now," she added, "was that the French, to my sense, give us only again and again, for ever and ever, the same couple. There they are once more, as one has had them to satiety, in that yellow thing, and there I shall certainly again find them in the blue."

"Then why do you keep reading about them?" Mrs Dyott demanded.

Maud hesitated. "I don't!" she sighed. "At all events, I sha'n't any more. I give it up."

"You've been looking for something, I judge," said Colonel Voyt, "that you're not likely to find. It doesn't exist."

"What is it?" Mrs Dyott inquired.

"I never look," Maud remarked, "for anything but an interest."

"Naturally. But your interest," Voyt replied, "is in something different from life."

"Ah, not a bit! I *love* life—in art, though I hate it anywhere else. It's the poverty of the life those people show, and the awful bounders, of both sexes, that they represent."

"Oh, now we have you!" her interlocutor laughed. "To me, when all's said and done, they seem to be—as near as art can come—in the truth of the truth. It can only take what life gives it, though it certainly may be a pity that that isn't better. Your complaint of their monotony is a complaint of their conditions. When you say we get always the same couple what do you mean but that we get always the same passion? Of course we do!" Voyt declared. "If what you're looking for is another, that's what you won't anywhere find."

Maud for a while said nothing, and Mrs Dyott seemed to wait. "Well, I suppose I'm looking, more than anything else, for a decent woman."

"Oh then, you mustn't look for her in pictures of passion. That's not her element nor her whereabouts."

Mrs Blessingbourne weighed the objection. "Doesn't it depend on what you mean by passion?"

"I think one can mean only one thing: the enemy to behaviour."

"Oh, I can imagine passions that are, on the contrary, friends to it."

Her interlocutor thought. "Doesn't it depend perhaps on what you mean by behaviour?"

"Dear, no. Behaviour is just behaviour—the most definite thing in the world."

"Then what do you mean by the 'interest' you just now spoke of? The picture of that definite thing?"

"Yes—call it that. Women aren't *always* vicious, even when they're——"

"When they're what?" Voyt asked.

"When they're unhappy. They can be unhappy and good."

"That one doesn't for a moment deny. But can they be 'good' and interesting?"

"That must be Maud's subject!" Mrs Dyott explained. "To show a woman who *is*. I'm afraid, my dear," she continued, "you could only show yourself."

"You'd show then the most beautiful specimen conceivable"—and Voyt addressed himself to Maud. "But doesn't it prove that life is, against your contention, more interesting than art? Life you embellish and elevate; but art would find itself able to do nothing with you, and, on such impossible terms, would ruin you."

The colour in her faint consciousness gave beauty to her stare. " 'Ruin' me?"

"He means," Mrs Dyott again indicated, "that you would ruin 'art.' "

"Without, on the other hand"—Voyt seemed to assent— "its giving at all a coherent impression of you."

"She wants her romance cheap!" said Mrs Dyott.

"Oh, no—I should be willing to pay for it. I don't see why the romance—since you give it that name—should be all, as the French inveterately make it, for the women who are bad."

"Oh, they pay for it!" said Mrs Dyott.

"*Do* they?"

"So, at least"—Mrs Dyott a little corrected herself—"one has gathered (for I don't read your books, you know!) that they're usually shown as doing."

Maud wondered, but looking at Voyt, "They're shown often, no doubt, as paying for their badness. But are they shown as paying for their romance?"

"My dear lady," said Voyt, "their romance *is* their badness. There isn't any other. It's a hard law, if you will, and a strange, but goodness has to go without that luxury. Isn't to *be* good just exactly, all round, to go without?" He put it before her kindly and clearly—regretfully too, as if he were sorry the truth should be so sad. He and she, his pleasant eyes seemed to say, would, had they had the making of it, have made it better. "One has heard it before—at least *I* have; one has heard your question put. But always, when put to a mind not merely muddled, for an inevitable answer. 'Why don't you, *cher monsieur*, give us the drama of virtue?' 'Because, *chère madame*, the high privilege of virtue is precisely to avoid drama.' The adventures of the honest lady? The honest lady hasn't—can't possibly have adventures."

Mrs Blessingbourne only met his eyes at first, smiling with a certain intensity. "Doesn't it depend a little on what you call adventures?"

"My poor Maud," said Mrs Dyott, as if in compassion for sophistry so simple, "adventures are just adventures. That's all you can make of them!"

But her friend went on, for their companion, as if without hearing. "Doesn't it depend a good deal on what you call drama?" Maud spoke as one who had already thought it out. "Doesn't it depend on what you call romance?"

Her listener gave these arguments his very best attention. "Of course you may call things anything you like—speak of them as one thing and mean quite another. But why should it depend on anything? Behind these words we use—the adventure, the novel, the drama, the romance, the situation, in short, as we most comprehensively say—behind them all stands the same sharp fact that they all, in their different ways, represent."

"Precisely!" Mrs Dyott was full of approval.

Maud, however, was full of vagueness. "What great fact?"

"The fact of a relation. The adventure's a relation; the relation's an adventure. The romance, the novel, the drama are the picture of one. The subject the novelist treats is the rise, the formation, the development, the climax, and for the most part the decline, of one. And what is the honest lady doing on that side of the town?"

Mrs Dyott was more pointed. "She doesn't so much as *form* a relation."

But Maud bore up. "Doesn't it depend, again, on what you call a relation?"

"Oh," said Mrs Dyott, "if a gentleman picks up her pocket-handkerchief——"

"Ah, even that's one," their friend laughed, "if she has thrown it to him. We can only deal with one that *is* one."

"Surely," Maud replied. "But if it's an innocent one——?"

"Doesn't it depend a good deal," Mrs Dyott asked, "on what you call innocent?"

"You mean that the adventures of innocence have so often been the material of fiction? Yes," Voyt replied; "that's exactly what the bored reader complains of. He has asked for bread and been given a stone. What is it but, with absolute directness, a question of interest, or, as people say, of the story? What's a situation undeveloped but a subject lost? If a relation stops, where's the story? If it doesn't stop, where's the innocence? It seems to me you must choose. It would be very pretty if it were otherwise, but that's how we flounder. Art is our flounderings shown."

Mrs Blessingbourne—and with an air of deference scarce supported perhaps by its sketchiness—kept her deep eyes on this definition. "But sometimes we flounder out."

It immediately touched in Colonel Voyt the spring of a genial derision. "That's just where I expected *you* would! One always sees it come."

"He has, you notice," Mrs Dyott parenthesised to Maud, "seen it come so often; and he has always waited for it and met it."

"Met it, dear lady, simply enough! It's the old story, Mrs Blessingbourne. The relation is innocent that the heroine gets out of. The book is innocent that's the story of her getting out. But what the devil—in the name of innocence—was she doing *in?*"

Mrs Dyott promptly echoed the question. "You have to
be in, you know, to *get* out. So there you are already with
your relation. It's the end of your goodness."

"And the beginning," said Voyt, "of your play!"

"Aren't they all, for that matter, even the worst," Mrs
Dyott pursued, "supposed *some* time or other to get out?
But if, meanwhile, they've been in, however briefly, long
enough to adorn a tale——"

"They've been in long enough to point a moral. That is to
point ours!" With which, and as if a sudden flush of warmer
light had moved him, Colonel Voyt got up. The veil of the
storm had parted over a great red sunset.

Mrs Dyott also was on her feet, and they stood before his
charming antagonist, who, with eyes lowered and a somewhat
fixed smile, had not moved. "We've spoiled her subject!" the
elder lady sighed.

"Well," said Voyt, "it's better to spoil an artist's subject
than to spoil his reputation. I mean," he explained to Maud
with his indulgent manner, "his appearance of knowing what
he has got hold of, for that, in the last resort, is his happiness."

She slowly rose at this, facing him with an aspect as handsomely mild as his own. "You can't spoil my happiness."

He held her hand an instant as he took leave. "I wish I
could add to it!"

III

WHEN he had quitted them and Mrs Dyott had candidly
asked if her friend had found him rude or crude, Maud replied
—though not immediately—that she had feared showing only
too much that she found him charming. But if Mrs Dyott
took this, it was to weigh the sense. "How could you show
it too much?"

"Because I always feel that that's my only way of showing anything. It's absurd, if you like," Mrs Blessingbourne pursued, "but I never know, in such intense discussions, what strange impression I may give."

Her companion looked amused. "Was it intense?"

"*I* was," Maud frankly confessed.

"Then it's a pity you were so wrong. Colonel Voyt, you know, is right." Mrs Blessingbourne at this gave one of the slow, soft, silent headshakes to which she often resorted and which, mostly accompanied by the light of cheer, had somehow, in spite of the small obstinacy that smiled in them, a special grace. With this grace, for a moment, her friend, looking her up and down, appeared impressed, yet not too much so to take, the next minute, a decision. "Oh, my dear, I'm sorry to differ from anyone so lovely—for you're awfully beautiful to-night, and your frock's the very nicest I've ever seen you wear. But he's as right as he can be."

Maud repeated her motion. "Not so right, at all events, as he thinks he is. Or perhaps I can say," she went on, after an instant, "that I'm not so wrong. I do know a little what I'm talking about."

Mrs Dyott continued to study her. "You *are* vexed. You naturally don't like it—such destruction."

"Destruction?"

"Of your illusion."

"I *have* no illusion. If I had, moreover, it wouldn't be destroyed. I have, on the whole, I think, my little decency."

Mrs Dyott stared. "Let us grant it for argument. What, then?"

"Well, I've also my little drama."

"An attachment?"

"An attachment."

"That you shouldn't have?"

"That I shouldn't have."

"A passion?"

"A passion."

"Shared?"

"Ah, thank goodness, no!"

Mrs Dyott continued to gaze. "The object's unaware——?"

"Utterly."

Mrs Dyott turned it over. "Are you sure?"

"Sure."

"That's what you call your decency? But isn't it," Mrs Dyott asked, "rather *his?*"

"Dear, no. It's only his good fortune."

Mrs Dyott laughed. "But yours, darling—your good fortune: where does *that* come in?"

"Why, in my sense of the romance of it."

"The romance of what? Of his not knowing?"

"Of my not wanting him to. If I did"—Maud had touchingly worked it out—"where would be my honesty?"

The inquiry, for an instant, held her friend; yet only, it seemed, for a stupefaction that was almost amusement. "Can you want or not want as you like? Where in the world, if you don't want, is your romance?"

Mrs Blessingbourne still wore her smile, and she now, with a light gesture that matched it, just touched the region of her heart. "There!"

Her companion admiringly marvelled. "A lovely place for it, no doubt!—but not quite a place, that I can see, to make the sentiment a relation."

"Why not? What more is required for a relation for *me?*"

"Oh, all sorts of things, I should say! And many more, added to those, to make it one for the person you mention."

"Ah, that I don't pretend it either should be or *can* be. I only speak for myself."

It was said in a manner that made Mrs Dyott, with a visible mixture of impressions, suddenly turn away. She indulged in a vague movement or two, as if to look for something, then again found herself near her friend, on whom with the same abruptness, in fact with a strange sharpness, she conferred a kiss that might have represented either her tribute to exalted consistency or her idea of a graceful close of the discussion. "You deserve that one should speak *for* you!"

Her companion looked cheerful and secure. "How *can* you, without knowing——?"

"Oh, by guessing! It's not——?"

But that was as far as Mrs Dyott could get. "It's not," said Maud, "anyone you've ever seen."

"Ah then, I give you up!"

And Mrs Dyott conformed, for the rest of Maud's stay, to the spirit of this speech. It was made on a Saturday night, and Mrs Blessingbourne remained till the Wednesday following, an interval during which, as the return of fine weather was confirmed by the Sunday, the two ladies found a wider range of action. There were drives to be taken, calls made, objects of interest seen, at a distance; with the effect of much easy talk and still more easy silence. There had been a question of Colonel Voyt's probable return on the Sunday, but the whole time passed without a sign from him, and it was merely mentioned by Mrs Dyott, in explanation, that he must have been suddenly called, as he was so liable to be, to town. That this in fact was what had happened he made clear to her on Thursday afternoon, when, walking over again late, he found her alone. The consequence of his Sunday letters had been his taking, that day, the 4.15. Mrs Voyt had gone back on Thursday, and he now, to settle on the spot the question of a piece of work begun at his place, had rushed down for a few hours in anticipation of the usual collective move for the week's end. He was to go up again by the late train, and had to count a little—a fact accepted by his hostess with the hard pliancy of practice—his present happy moments. Too few as these were, however, he found time to make of her an inquiry or two not directly bearing on their situation. The first was a recall of the question for which Mrs Blessingbourne's entrance

on the previous Saturday had arrested her answer. Did that
lady know of anything between them?

"No. I'm sure. There's one thing she does know," Mrs
Dyott went on; "but it's quite different and not so very
wonderful."

"What, then, is it?"

"Well, that she's herself in love."

Voyt showed his interest. "You mean she told you?"

"I got it out of her."

He showed his amusement. "Poor thing! And with whom?"

"With you."

His surprise, if the distinction might be made, was less
than his wonder. "You got that out of her too?"

"No—it remains in. Which is much the best way for it.
For you to know it would be to end it."

He looked rather cheerfully at sea. "Is that then why you
tell me?"

"I mean for her to know you know it. Therefore it's in
your interest not to let her."

"I see," Voyt after a moment returned. "Your real calculation is that my interest will be sacrificed to my vanity—so
that, if your other idea is just, the flame will in fact, and thanks
to her morbid conscience, expire by her taking fright at seeing
me so pleased. But I promise you," he declared, "that she
sha'n't see it. So there you are!" She kept her eyes on him and
had evidently to admit, after a little, that there she was.
Distinct as he had made the case, however, he was not yet
quite satisfied. "Why are you so sure that I'm the man?"

"From the way she denies you."

"You put it to her?"

"Straight. If you hadn't been she would, of course, have
confessed to you—to keep me in the dark about the real one."

Poor Voyt laughed out again. "Oh, you dear souls!"

"Besides," his companion pursued, "I was not in want of
that evidence."

"Then what other had you?"

"Her state before you came—which was what made me ask you how much you had seen her. And her state after it," Mrs Dyott added. "And her state," she wound up, "while you were here."

"But her state while I was here was charming."

"Charming. That's just what I say."

She said it in a tone that placed the matter in its right light —a light in which they appeared kindly, quite tenderly, to watch Maud wander away into space with her lovely head bent under a theory rather too big for it. Voyt's last word, however, was that there was just enough in it—in the theory —for them to allow that she had not shown herself, on the occasion of their talk, wholly bereft of sense. Her consciousness, if they let it alone—as they of course after this mercifully must—*was*, in the last analysis, a kind of shy romance. Not a romance like their own, a thing to make the fortune of any author up to the mark—one who should have the invention or who *could* have the courage; but a small, scared, starved, subjective satisfaction that would do her no harm and nobody else any good. Who but a duffer—he stuck to his contention —would see the shadow of a "story" in it?

FLICKERBRIDGE

I

FRANK GRANGER had arrived from Paris to paint a portrait
—an order given him, as a young compatriot with a future,
whose early work would some day have a price, by a lady
from New York, a friend of his own people and also, as it
happened, of Addie's, the young woman to whom it was
publicly both affirmed and denied that he was engaged. Other
young women in Paris—fellow-members there of the little
tight transpontine world of art-study—professed to know
that the pair had been "several times" over so closely contracted. This, however, was their own affair; the last phase
of the relation, the last time of the times, had passed into
vagueness; there was perhaps even an impression that if they
were inscrutable to their friends they were not wholly
crystalline to each other and themselves. What had occurred
for Granger, at all events, in connection with the portrait was
that Mrs Bracken, his intending model, whose return to
America was at hand, had suddenly been called to London by
her husband, occupied there with pressing business, but had
yet desired that her displacement should not interrupt her
sittings. The young man, at her request, had followed her to
England and profited by all she could give him, making shift
with a small studio lent him by a London painter whom he
had known and liked, a few years before, in the French
atelier that then cradled, and that continued to cradle, so many
of their kind.

The British capital was a strange, grey world to him, where
people walked, in more ways than one, by a dim light; but he

was happily of such a turn that the impression, just as it came, could nowhere ever fail him, and even the worst of these things was almost as much an occupation—putting it only at that—as the best. Mrs Bracken, moreover, passed him on, and while the darkness ebbed a little in the April days he found himself consolingly committed to a couple of fresh subjects. This cut him out work for more than another month, but meanwhile, as he said, he saw a lot—a lot that, with frequency and with much expression, he wrote about to Addie. She also wrote to her absent friend, but in briefer snatches, a meagreness to her reasons for which he had long since assented. She had other play for her pen, as well as, fortunately, other remuneration; a regular correspondence for a "prominent Boston paper," fitful connections with public sheets perhaps also, in cases, fitful, and a mind, above all, engrossed at times, to the exclusion of everything else, with the study of the short story. This last was what she had mainly come out to go into, two or three years after he had found himself engulfed in the mystery of Carolus. She was indeed, on her own deep sea, more engulfed than he had ever been, and he had grown to accept the sense that, for progress too, she sailed under more canvas. It had not been particularly present to him till now that he had in the least got on, but the way in which Addie had—and evidently, still more, would—was the theme, as it were, of every tongue. She had thirty short stories out and nine descriptive articles. His three or four portraits of fat American ladies—they were all fat, all ladies and all American —were a poor show compared with these triumphs; especially as Addie had begun to throw out that it was about time they should go home. It kept perpetually coming up in Paris, in the transpontine world, that, as the phrase was, America had grown more interesting since they left. Addie was attentive to the rumour, and, as full of conscience as she was of taste, of patriotism as of curiosity, had often put it to him frankly, with what he, who was of New York, recognised as her New England emphasis: "I'm not sure, you know, that we do *real* justice to our country." Granger felt he would do it on the day—if the day ever came—he should irrevocably marry her. No other country could possibly have produced her.

II

BUT meanwhile it befell, in London, that he was stricken with influenza and with subsequent sorrow. The attack was short but sharp—had it lasted Addie would certainly have come to his aid; most of a blight, really, in its secondary stage. The good ladies his sitters—the ladies with the frizzled hair, with the diamond earrings, with the chins tending to the massive— left for him, at the door of his lodgings, flowers, soup and love, so that with their assistance he pulled through; but his convalescence was slow and his weakness out of proportion to the muffled shock. He came out, but he went about lame; it tired him to paint— he felt as if he had been ill for a month. He strolled in Kensington Gardens when he should have been at work; he sat long on penny chairs and helplessly mused and mooned. Addie desired him to return to Paris, but there were chances under his hand that he felt he had just wit enough left not to relinquish. He would have gone for a week to the sea—he would have gone to Brighton; but Mrs Bracken had to be finished—Mrs Bracken was so soon to sail. He just managed to finish her in time—the day before the date fixed for his breaking ground on a greater business still, the circumvallation of Mrs Dunn. Mrs Dunn duly waited on him, and he sat down before her, feeling, however, ere he rose, that he must take a long breath before the attack. While asking himself that night, therefore, where he should best replenish his lungs, he received from Addie, who had had from Mrs Bracken a poor report of him, a communication which, besides being of sudden and startling interest, applied directly to his case.

His friend wrote to him under the lively emotion of having from one day to another become aware of a new relative, an ancient cousin, a sequestered gentlewoman, the sole survival of "the English branch of the family," still resident, at Flickerbridge, in the "old family home," and with whom, that he might immediately betake himself to so auspicious a quarter for change of air, she had already done what was proper to place him, as she said, in touch. What came of it all, to be brief, was that Granger found himself so placed almost as he read: he was in touch with Miss Wenham of Flickerbridge, to the extent of being in correspondence with her, before twenty-four hours had sped. And on the second day he was in the train, settled for a five-hours' run to the door of this amiable woman, who had so abruptly and kindly taken him on trust and of whom but yesterday he had never so much as heard. This was an oddity—the whole incident was —of which, in the corner of his compartment, as he proceeded, he had time to take the size. But the surprise, the incongruity, as he felt, could but deepen as he went. It was a sufficiently queer note, in the light, or the absence of it, of his late experience, that so complex a product as Addie should have *any* simple insular tie; but it was a queerer note still that she should have had one so long only to remain unprofitably unconscious of it. Not to have done something with it, used it, worked it, talked about it at least, and perhaps even written —these things, at the rate she moved, represented a loss of opportunity under which, as he saw her, she was peculiarly formed to wince. She was at any rate, it was clear, doing something with it now; using it, working it, certainly, already talking—and, yes, quite possibly writing—about it. She was, in short, smartly making up what she had missed, and he could take such comfort from his own action as he had been helped to by the rest of the facts, succinctly reported from Paris on the very morning of his start.

It was the singular story of a sharp split—in a good English house—that dated now from years back. A worthy Briton, of the best middling stock, had, early in the forties, as a very young man, in Dresden, whither he had been despatched to qualify in German for a stool in an uncle's counting-house, met, admired, wooed and won an American girl, of due attractions, domiciled at that period with her parents and a sister, who was also attractive, in the Saxon capital. He had married her, taken her to England, and there, after some years of harmony and happiness, lost her. The sister in question had, after her death, come to him, and to his young child, on a visit, the effect of which, between the pair, eventually defined itself as a sentiment that was not to be resisted. The bereaved husband, yielding to a new attachment and a new response, and finding a new union thus prescribed, had yet been forced to reckon with the unaccommodating law of the land. Encompassed with frowns in his own country, however, marriages of this particular type were wreathed in smiles in his sister's-in-law, so that his remedy was not forbidden. Choosing between two allegiances he had let the one go that seemed the least close, and had, in brief, transplanted his possibilities to an easier air. The knot was tied for the couple in New York, where, to protect the legitimacy of such other children as might come to them, they settled and prospered. Children came, and one of the daughters, growing up and marrying in her turn, was, if Frank rightly followed, the mother of his own Addie, who had been deprived of the knowledge of her indeed, in childhood, by death, and been brought up, though without undue tension, by a stepmother—a character thus, in the connection, repeated.

The breach produced in England by the invidious action, as it was there held, of the girl's grandfather, had not failed to widen—all the more that nothing had been done on the

American side to close it. Frigidity had settled, and hostility had only been arrested by indifference. Darkness, therefore, had fortunately supervened, and a cousinship completely divided. On either side of the impassable gulf, of the impenetrable curtain, each branch had put forth its leaves—a foliage wanting, in the American quarter, it was distinct enough to Granger, in no sign or symptom of climate and environment. The graft in New York had taken, and Addie was a vivid, an unmistakeable flower. At Flickerbridge, or wherever, on the other hand, strange to say, the parent stem had had a fortune comparatively meagre. Fortune, it was true, in the vulgarest sense, had attended neither party. Addie's immediate belongings were as poor as they were numerous, and he gathered that Miss Wenham's pretensions to wealth were not so marked as to expose the claim of kinship to the imputation of motive. To this lady's single identity, at all events, the original stock had dwindled, and our young man was properly warned that he would find her shy and solitary. What was singular was that, in these conditions, she should desire, she should endure, to receive him. But that was all another story, lucid enough when mastered. He kept Addie's letters, exceptionally copious, in his lap; he conned them at intervals; he held the threads.

He looked out between whiles at the pleasant English land, an April *aquarelle* washed in with wondrous breadth. He knew the French thing, he knew the American, but he had known nothing of this. He saw it already as the remarkable Miss Wenham's setting. The doctor's daughter at Flickerbridge, with nippers on her nose, a palette on her thumb and innocence in her heart, had been the miraculous link. She had become aware, even there, in our world of wonders, that the current fashion for young women so equipped was to enter the Parisian lists. Addie had accordingly chanced upon her, on the slopes of Montparnasse, as one of the English girls in one of the thorough-going sets. They had met in some easy collocation and had fallen upon common ground; after which

the young woman, restored to Flickerbridge for an interlude
and retailing there her adventures and impressions, had mentioned to Miss Wenham, who had known and protected her
from babyhood, that that lady's own name of Adelaide was,
as well as the surname conjoined with it, borne, to her knowledge, in Paris, by an extraordinary American specimen. She
had then recrossed the Channel with a wonderful message, a
courteous challenge, to her friend's duplicate, who had in
turn granted through her every satisfaction. The duplicate
had, in other words, bravely let Miss Wenham know exactly
who she was. Miss Wenham, in whose personal tradition the
flame of resentment appeared to have been reduced by time to
the palest ashes—for whom, indeed, the story of the great
schism was now but a legend only needing a little less dimness
to make it romantic—Miss Wenham had promptly responded
by a letter fragrant with the hope that old threads might be
taken up. It was a relationship that they must puzzle out together, and she had earnestly sounded the other party to it on
the subject of a possible visit. Addie had met her with a
definite promise; she would come soon, she would come when
free, she would come in July; but meanwhile she sent her
deputy. Frank asked himself by what name she had described,
by what character introduced him to Flickerbridge. He felt
mainly, on the whole, as if he were going there to find out if
he were engaged to her. He was at sea, really, now, as to which
of the various views Addie herself took of it. To Miss Wenham she must definitely have taken one, and perhaps Miss
Wenham would reveal it. This expectation was really his
excuse for a possible indiscretion.

III

H E was indeed to learn on arrival to what he had been committed; but that was for a while so much a part of his first

general impression that the fact took time to detach itself, the first general impression demanding verily all his faculties of response. He almost felt, for a day or two, the victim of a practical joke, a gross abuse of confidence. He had presented himself with the moderate amount of flutter involved in a sense of due preparation; but he had then found that, however primed with prefaces and prompted with hints, he had not been prepared at all. How *could* he be, he asked himself, for anything so foreign to his experience, so alien to his proper world, so little to be preconceived in the sharp north light of the newest impressionism, and yet so recognised, after all, really, in the event, so noted and tasted and assimilated? It was a case he would scarce have known how to describe—could doubtless have described best with a full, clean brush, supplemented by a play of gesture; for it was always his habit to see an occasion, of whatever kind, primarily as a picture, so that he might get it, as he was wont to say, so that he might keep it, well together. He had been treated of a sudden, in this adventure, to one of the sweetest, fairest, coolest impressions of his life—one, moreover, visibly, from the start, complete and homogeneous. Oh, it was *there*, if that was all one wanted of a thing! It was so "there" that, as had befallen him in Italy, in Spain, confronted at last, in dusky side-chapel or rich museum, with great things dreamed of or with greater ones unexpectedly presented, he had held his breath for fear of breaking the spell; had almost, from the quick impulse to respect, to prolong, lowered his voice and moved on tiptoe. Supreme beauty suddenly revealed is apt to strike us as a possible illusion, playing with our desire—instant freedom with it to strike us as a possible rashness.

This fortunately, however—and the more so as his freedom for the time quite left him—didn't prevent his hostess, the evening of his advent and while the vision was new, from being exactly as queer and rare and *impayable*, as improbable, as impossible, as delightful at dinner at eight (she appeared to keep these immense hours) as she had overwhelmingly been at tea at five. She was in the most natural way in the world one of the oddest apparitions, but that the particular means to such an end *could* be natural was an inference difficult to make. He failed in fact to make it for a couple of days; but then—though then only—he made it with confidence. By this time indeed he was sure of everything, including, luckily, himself. If we compare his impression, with slight extravagance, to some of the greatest he had ever received, this is simply because the image before him was so rounded and stamped. It expressed with pure perfection, it exhausted its character. It was so absolutely and so unconsciously what it was. He had been floated by the strangest of chances out of the rushing stream into a clear, still backwater—a deep and quiet pool in which objects were sharply mirrored. He had hitherto in life known nothing that was old except a few statues and pictures; but here everything was old, was immemorial, and nothing so much so as the very freshness itself. Vaguely to have supposed there were such nooks in the world had done little enough, he now saw, to temper the glare of their opposites. It was the fine touches that counted, and these had to be seen to be believed.

Miss Wenham, fifty-five years of age, and unappeasably timid, unaccountably strange, had, on her reduced scale, an almost Gothic grotesqueness; but the final effect of one's sense of it was an amenity that accompanied one's steps like wafted gratitude. More flurried, more spasmodic, more apologetic, more completely at a loss at one moment and more precipitately abounding at another, he had never before in all his days seen any maiden lady; yet for no maiden lady he had ever seen had he so promptly conceived a private enthusiasm. Her eyes protruded, her chin receded and her nose carried on in conversation a queer little independent motion. She wore on the top of her head an upright circular cap that made her resemble a caryatid disburdened, and on other parts of her person strange combinations of colours, stuffs, shapes, of metal, mineral and plant. The tones of her voice rose and fell, her facial convulsions, whether tending—one could scarce make out—to expression or *re*pression, succeeded each other by a law of their own; she was embarrassed at nothing and at everything, frightened at everything and at nothing, and she approached objects, subjects, the simplest questions and answers and the whole material of intercourse, either with the indirectness of terror or with the violence of despair. These things, none the less, her refinements of oddity and intensities of custom, her suggestion at once of conventions and simplicities, of ease and of agony, her roundabout, retarded suggestions and perceptions, still permitted her to strike her guest as irresistibly charming. He didn't know what to call it; she was a fruit of time. She had a queer distinction. She had been expensively produced, and there would be a good deal more of her to come.

The result of the whole quality of her welcome, at any rate, was that the first evening, in his room, before going to bed, he relieved his mind in a letter to Addie, which, if space allowed us to embody it in our text, would usefully perform the office of a "plate." It would enable us to present ourselves as profusely illustrated. But the process of reproduction, as we say, costs. He wished his friend to know how grandly their affair turned out. She had put him in the way of something absolutely special—an old house untouched, untouchable, indescribable, an old corner such as one didn't believe existed, and the holy calm of which made the chatter of studios, the smell of paint, the slang of critics, the whole sense and sound of Paris, come back as so many signs of a huge monkey-cage. He moved about, restless, while he wrote; he lighted cigarettes and, nervous and suddenly scrupulous, put them out again; the night was mild and one of the windows of his large high room, which stood over the garden, was up. He lost himself in the things about him, in the type of the room, the last century with not a chair moved, not a point stretched. He hung over the objects and ornaments, blissfully few and adorably good, perfect pieces all, and never one, for a change, French. The scene was as rare as some fine old print with the best bits down in the corners. Old books and old pictures, allusions remembered and aspects conjectured, reappeared to him; he knew now what anxious islanders had been trying for in their backward hunt for the homely. But the homely at Flickerbridge was all style, even as style at the same time was mere honesty. The larger, the smaller past—he scarce knew which to call it—was at all events so hushed to sleep round him as he wrote that he had almost a bad conscience about having come. How one might love it, but how one might spoil it! To look at it too hard was positively to make it conscious, and to make it conscious was positively to wake it up. Its only safety, of a truth, was to be left still to sleep—to sleep in its large, fair chambers, and under its high, clean canopies.

He added thus restlessly a line to his letter, maundered round the room again, noted and fingered something else, and then, dropping on the old flowered sofa, sustained by the tight cubes of its cushions, yielded afresh to the cigarette, hesitated, stared, wrote a few words more. He wanted Addie to know, that was what he most felt, unless he perhaps felt more how much she herself would want to. Yes, what he supremely saw was all that Addie would make of it. Up to his neck in it there he fairly turned cold at the sense of suppressed opportunity, of the outrage of privation, that his correspondent would retrospectively and, as he even divined with a vague shudder, almost vindictively nurse. Well, what had happened was that the acquaintance had been kept for her, like a packet enveloped and sealed for delivery, till her attention was free. He saw her there, heard her and felt her— felt how she would feel and how she would, as she usually said, "rave." Some of her young compatriots called it "yell," and in the reference itself, alas! illustrated their meaning. She would understand the place, at any rate, down to the ground; there wasn't the slightest doubt of that. Her sense of it would be exactly like his own, and he could see, in anticipation, just the terms of recognition and rapture in which she would abound. He knew just what she would call quaint, just what she would call bland, just what she would call weird, just what she would call wild. She would take it all in with an intelligence much more fitted than his own, in fact, to deal with what he supposed he must regard as its literary relations. She would have read the obsolete, long-winded memoirs and novels that both the figures and the setting ought clearly to remind one of; she would know about the past generations—the lumbering county magnates and their turbaned wives and round-eyed daughters, who, in other days, had treated the ruddy, sturdy, tradeless town, the solid square houses and wide, walled gardens, the streets to-day all grass and gossip, as the scene of a local "season." She would have warrant for the assemblies, dinners, deep potations; for the smoked sconces in the dusky parlours; for the long, muddy century of family coaches, "holsters," highwaymen. She would put a finger, in short, just as he had done, on the vital spot—the rich humility of the whole thing, the fact that neither Flicker-bridge in general nor Miss Wenham in particular, nor anything nor anyone concerned, had a suspicion of their character and their merit. Addie and he would have to come to let in light.

He let it in then, little by little, before going to bed, through the eight or ten pages he addressed to her; assured her that it was the happiest case in the world, a little picture—yet full of "style" too—absolutely composed and transmitted, with tradition, and tradition only, in every stroke, tradition still noiselessly breathing and visibly flushing, marking strange hours in the tall mahogany clocks that were never wound up and that yet audibly ticked on. All the elements, he was sure he should see, would hang together with a charm, presenting his hostess—a strange iridescent fish for the glazed exposure of an aquarium—as floating in her native medium. He left his letter open on the table, but, looking it over next morning, felt of a sudden indisposed to send it. He would keep it to add more, for there would be more to know; yet when three days had elapsed he had still not sent it. He sent instead, after delay, a much briefer report, which he was moved to make different and, for some reason, less vivid. Meanwhile he learned from Miss Wenham how Addie had introduced him. It took time to arrive with her at that point, but after the Rubicon was crossed they went far afield.

IV

"Oh yes, she said you were engaged. That was why—since I *had* broken out so—she thought I would like to see you; as I assure you I've been so delighted to. But *aren't* you?" the good lady asked as if she saw in his face some ground for doubt.

"Assuredly—if she says so. It may seem very odd to you, but I haven't known, and yet I've felt that, being nothing whatever to you directly, I need some warrant for consenting thus to be thrust on you. We *were*," the young man explained, "engaged a year ago; but since then (if you don't mind my telling you such things; I feel now as if I could tell you anything!) I haven't quite known how I stand. It hasn't seemed that we were in a position to marry. Things are better now, but I haven't quite known how she would see them. They were so bad six months ago that I understood her, I thought, as breaking off. I haven't broken; I've only accepted, for the time—because men must be easy with women—being treated as 'the best of friends.' Well, I try to be. I wouldn't have come here if I hadn't been. I thought it would be charming for her to know you—when I heard from her the extraordinary way you had dawned upon her, and charming therefore if I could help her to it. And if I'm helping you to know *her*," he went on, "isn't that charming too?"

"Oh, I so want to!" Miss Wenham murmured, in her unpractical, impersonal way. "You're so different!" she wistfully declared.

"It's *you*, if I may respectfully, ecstatically say so, who are different. That's the point of it all. I'm not sure that anything so terrible really ought to happen to you as to know us."

"Well," said Miss Wenham, "I do know you a little, by this time, don't I? And I don't find it terrible. It's a delightful change for me."

"Oh, I'm not sure you ought to have a delightful change!"

"Why not—if you do?"

"Ah, I can bear it. I'm not sure that you can. I'm too bad to spoil—I *am* spoiled. I'm nobody, in short; I'm nothing. I've no type. You're *all* type. It has taken long, delicious years of security and monotony to produce you. You fit your frame with a perfection only equalled by the perfection with which your frame fits you. So this admirable old house, all time-softened white within and time-faded red without, so everything that surrounds you here and that has, by some extraordinary mercy, escaped the inevitable fate of exploitation: so it all, I say, is the sort of thing that, if it were the least bit to fall to pieces, could never, ah, never more, be put together again. I have, dear Miss Wenham," Granger went on, happy himself in his extravagance, which was yet all sincere, and happier still in her deep, but altogether pleased, mystification—"I've found, do you know, just the thing one has ever heard of that you most resemble. You're the Sleeping Beauty in the wood."

He still had no compunction when he heard her bewilderedly sigh: "Oh, you're too delightfully droll!"

"No, I only put things just as they are, and as I've also learned a little, thank heaven, to see them—which isn't, I quite agree with you, at all what anyone does. You're in the deep doze of the spell that has held you for long years, and it would be a shame, a crime, to wake you up. Indeed I already feel, with a thousand scruples, that I'm giving you the fatal shake. I say it even though it makes me sound a little as if I thought myself the fairy prince."

She gazed at him with her queerest, kindest look, which he was getting used to, in spite of a faint fear, at the back of his head, of the strange things that sometimes occurred when lonely ladies, however mature, began to look at interesting young men from over the seas as if the young men desired to flirt. "It's so wonderful," she said, "that you should be so very odd and yet so very good-natured." Well, it all came to the same thing—it was so wonderful that *she* should be so simple and yet so little of a bore. He accepted with gratitude the theory of his languor—which moreover was real enough and partly perhaps why he was so sensitive; he let himself go as a convalescent, let her insist on the weakness that always remained after fever. It helped him to gain time, to preserve the spell even while he talked of breaking it; saw him through slow strolls and soft sessions, long gossips, fitful, hopeless questions—there was so much more to tell than, by any contortion, she *could*—and explanations addressed gallantly and patiently to her understanding, but not, by good fortune, really reaching it. They were perfectly at cross-purposes, and it was all the better, and they wandered together in the silver haze with all communication blurred.

When they sat in the sun in her formal garden he was quite aware that the tenderest consideration failed to disguise his treating her as the most exquisite of curiosities. The term of comparison most present to him was that of some obsolete musical instrument. The old-time order of her mind and her air had the stillness of a painted spinet that was duly dusted, gently rubbed, but never tuned nor played on. Her opinions were like dried roseleaves; her attitudes like British sculpture; her voice was what he imagined of the possible tone of the old gilded, silver-stringed harp in one of the corners of the drawing-room. The lonely little decencies and modest dignities of her life, the fine grain of its conservatism, the innocence of its ignorance, all its monotony of stupidity and salubrity, its cold dulness and dim brightness, were there before him. Meanwhile, within him, strange things took place. It was literally true that his impression began again, after a lull, to make him nervous and anxious, and for reasons peculiarly confused, almost grotesquely mingled, or at least comically sharp. He was distinctly an agitation and a new taste—that he could see; and he saw quite as much therefore the excitement she already drew from the vision of Addie, an image intensified by the sense of closer kinship and presented to her, clearly, with various erratic enhancements, by her friend the doctor's daughter. At the end of a few days he said to her: "Do you know she wants to come without waiting any longer? She wants to come while I'm here. I received this morning her letter proposing it, but I've been thinking it over and have waited to speak to you. The thing is, you see, that if she writes to *you* proposing it——"

"Oh, I shall be so particularly glad!"

V

THEY were, as usual, in the garden, and it had not yet been so present to him that if he were only a happy cad there would be a good way to protect her. As she wouldn't hear of his being yet beyond precautions she had gone into the house for a particular shawl that was just the thing for his knees, and, blinking in the watery sunshine, had come back with it across the fine little lawn. He was neither fatuous nor asinine, but he had almost to put it to himself as a small task to resist the sense of his absurd advantage with her. It filled him with horror and awkwardness, made him think of he didn't know what, recalled something of Maupassant's—the smitten "Miss Harriet" and her tragic fate. There was a preposterous possibility—yes, he held the strings quite in his hands—of keeping the treasure for himself. That was the art of life—what the real artist would consistently do. He would close the door on his impression, treat it as a private museum. He would see that he could lounge and linger there, live with wonderful things there, lie up there to rest and refit. For himself he was sure that after a little he should be able to paint there—do things in a key he had never thought of before. When she brought him the rug he took it from her and made her sit down on the bench and resume her knitting; then, passing behind her with a laugh, he placed it over her own shoulders; after which he moved to and fro before her, his hands in his pockets and his cigarette in his teeth. He was ashamed of the cigarette—a villainous false note; but she allowed, liked, begged him to smoke, and what he said to her on it, in one of the pleasantries she benevolently missed, was that he did so for fear of doing worse. That only showed that the end was really in sight. "I dare say it will strike you as quite awful, what I'm going to say to you, but I can't help it. I speak out of the depths of my respect for you. It will seem to you horrid disloyalty to poor Addie. Yes—there we are; there *I* am, at least, in my naked monstrosity." He stopped and looked at her till she might have been almost frightened. "Don't let her come. Tell her not to. I've tried to prevent it, but she suspects."

The poor woman wondered. "Suspects?"

"Well, I drew it, in writing to her, on reflection, as mild as I could—having been visited, in the watches of the night, by the instinct of what might happen. Something told me to keep back my first letter—in which, under the first impression, I myself rashly 'raved'; and I concocted instead of it an

insincere and guarded report. But guarded as I was I clearly
didn't keep you 'down,' as we say, enough. The wonder of
your colour—daub you over with grey as I might—must
have come through and told the tale. She scents battle from
afar—by which I mean she scents 'quaintness.' But keep her
off. It's hideous, what I'm saying—but I owe it to you. I owe
it to the world. She'll kill you."

"You mean I shan't get on with her?"

"Oh, fatally! See how *I* have. She's intelligent, remarkably
pretty, remarkably good. And she'll adore you."

"Well then?"

"Why, that will be just how she'll do for you."

"Oh, I can hold my own!" said Miss Wenham with the
headshake of a horse making his sleigh-bells rattle in frosty
air.

"Ah, but you can't hold hers! She'll rave about you. She'll
write about you. You're Niagara before the first white
traveller—and you know, or rather you can't know, what
Niagara became *after* that gentleman. Addie will have discovered Niagara. She will understand you in perfection; she
will feel you down to the ground; not a delicate shade of you
will she lose or let anyone else lose. You'll be too weird for
words, but the words will nevertheless come. You'll be too
exactly the real thing and to be left too utterly just as you are,
and all Addie's friends and all Addie's editors and contributors
and readers will cross the Atlantic and flock to Flickerbridge,
so, unanimously, universally, vociferously, to leave you.
You'll be in the magazines with illustrations; you'll be in the
papers with headings; you'll be everywhere with everything.
You don't understand—you think you do, but you don't.
Heaven forbid you *should* understand! That's just your beauty
—your 'sleeping' beauty. But you needn't. You can take me
on trust. Don't have her. Say, as a pretext, as a reason, anything in the world you like. Lie to her—scare her away. I'll
go away and give you up—I'll sacrifice everything myself."

Granger pursued his exhortation, convincing himself more
and more. "If I saw my way out, my way completely through,
I would pile up some fabric of fiction for her—I should only
want to be sure of its not tumbling down. One would have,
you see, to keep the thing up. But I would throw dust in her
eyes. I would tell her that you don't do at all—that you're
not, in fact, a desirable acquaintance. I'd tell her you're vulgar,
improper, scandalous; I'd tell her you're mercenary, design-
ing, dangerous; I'd tell her the only safe course is immediately
to let you drop. I would thus surround you with an impenetrable legend of conscientious misrepresentation, a circle
of pious fraud, and all the while privately keep you for myself."

She had listened to him as if he were a band of music and
she a small shy garden-party. "I shouldn't like you to go
away. I shouldn't in the least like you not to come again."

"Ah, there it is!" he replied. "How can I come again if
Addie ruins you?"

"But how will she ruin me—even if she does what you
say? I know I'm too old to change and really much too queer
to please in any of the extraordinary ways you speak of. If
it's a question of quizzing me I don't think my cousin, or
anyone else, will have quite the hand for it that *you* seem to
have. So that if *you* haven't ruined me——!"

"But I *have*—that's just the point!" Granger insisted.
"I've undermined you at least. I've left, after all, terribly little
for Addie to do."

She laughed in clear tones. "Well, then, we'll admit that
you've done everything but frighten me."

He looked at her with surpassing gloom. "No—that again
is one of the most dreadful features. You'll positively like it—
what's to come. You'll be caught up in a chariot of fire like
the prophet—wasn't there, was there, one?—of old. That's
exactly why—if one could but have done it—you would
have been to be kept ignorant and helpless. There's some-·
thing or other in Latin that says that it's the finest things that

change the most easily for the worse. You already enjoy your dishonour and revel in your shame. It's too late—you're lost!"

VI

ALL this was as pleasant a manner of passing the time as any other, for it didn't prevent his old-world corner from closing round him more entirely, nor stand in the way of his making out, from day to day, some new source, as well as some new effect, of its virtue. He was really scared at moments at some of the liberties he took in talk—at finding himself so familiar; for the great note of the place was just that a certain modern ease had never crossed its threshold, that quick intimacies and quick oblivions were a stranger to its air. It had known, in all its days, no rude, no loud invasion. Serenely unconscious of most contemporary things, it had been so of nothing so much as of the diffused social practice of running in and out. Granger held his breath, on occasions, to think how Addie would run. There were moments when, for some reason, more than at others, he heard her step on the staircase and her cry in the hall. If he played freely, none the less, with the idea with which we have shown him as occupied, it was not that in every measurable way he didn't sacrifice, to the utmost, to stillness. He only hovered, ever so lightly, to take up again his thread. She wouldn't hear of his leaving her, of his being in the least fit again, as she said, to travel. She spoke of the journey to London—which was in fact a matter of many hours—as an experiment fraught with lurking complications. He added then day to day, yet only hereby, as he reminded her, giving other complications a larger chance to multiply. He kept it before her, when there was nothing else to do, that she must consider; after which he had his times of fear that she perhaps really would make for him this sacrifice.

He knew that she had written again to Paris, and knew that he must himself again write—a situation abounding for each in the elements of a quandary. If he stayed so long, why then he wasn't better, and if he wasn't better Addie might take it into her head——! They must make it clear that he *was* better, so that, suspicious, alarmed at what was kept from her, she shouldn't suddenly present herself to nurse him. If he was better, however, why did he stay so long? If he stayed only for the attraction the sense of the attraction might be contagious. This was what finally grew clearest for him, so that he had for his mild disciple hours of still sharper prophecy. It consorted with his fancy to represent to her that their young friend had been by this time unsparingly warned; but nothing could be plainer than that this was ineffectual so long as he himself resisted the ordeal. To plead that he remained because he was too weak to move was only to throw themselves back on the other horn of their dilemma. If he was too weak to move Addie would bring him her strength—of which, when she got there, she would give them specimens enough. One morning he broke out at breakfast with an intimate conviction. They would see that she was actually starting—they would receive a wire by noon. They didn't receive it, but by his theory the portent was only the stronger. It had, moreover, its grave as well as its gay side, for Granger's paradox and pleasantry were only the most convenient way for him of saying what he felt. He literally heard the knell sound, and in expressing this to Miss Wenham with the conversational freedom that seemed best to pay his way he the more vividly faced the contingency. He could never return, and though he announced it with a despair that did what might be to make it pass as a joke, he saw that, whether or no she at last understood, she quite at last believed him. On this, to his knowledge, she wrote again to Addie, and the contents of her letter excited his curiosity. But that sentiment, though not assuaged, quite dropped when, the day after, in the evening, she let him know that she had had, an hour before, a telegram.

"She comes Thursday."

He showed not the least surprise. It was the deep calm of the fatalist. It *had* to be. "I must leave you then to-morrow."

She looked, on this, as he had never seen her; it would have been hard to say whether what was in her face was the last failure to follow or the first effort to meet. "And really not to come back?"

"Never, never, dear lady. Why should I come back? You can never be again what you *have* been. I shall have seen the last of you."

"Oh!" she touchingly urged.

"Yes, for I should next find you simply brought to self-consciousness. You'll be exactly what you are, I charitably admit—nothing more or less, nothing different. But you'll be it all in a different way. We live in an age of prodigious machinery, all organised to a single end. That end is publicity—a publicity as ferocious as the appetite of a cannibal. The thing therefore is not to have any illusions—fondly to flatter yourself, in a muddled moment, that the cannibal will spare you. He spares nobody. He spares nothing. It will be all right. You'll have a lovely time. You'll be only just a public character—blown about the world for all you are and proclaimed for all you are on the housetops. It will be for *that*, mind, I quite recognise—because Addie is superior—as well as for all you aren't. So good-bye."

He remained, however, till the next day, and noted at intervals the different stages of their friend's journey; the hour, this time, she would really have started, the hour she would reach Dover, the hour she would get to town, where she would alight at Mrs Dunn's. Perhaps she would bring Mrs Dunn, for Mrs Dunn would swell the chorus. At the last, on the morrow, as if in anticipation of this, stillness settled between them; he became as silent as his hostess. But before he went she brought out, shyly and anxiously, as an appeal, the question that, for hours, had clearly been giving her thought. "Do you meet her then to-night.in London?"

"Dear, no. In what position am I, alas! to do that? When can I *ever* meet her again?" He had turned it all over. "If I could meet Addie after this, you know, I could meet *you*. And if I do meet Addie," he lucidly pursued, "what will happen, by the same stroke, is that I *shall* meet you. And that's just what I've explained to you that I dread."

"You mean that she and I will be inseparable?"

He hesitated. "I mean that she'll tell me all about you. I can hear her, and her ravings, now."

She gave again—and it was infinitely sad—her little whinnying laugh. "Oh, but if what you say is true, you'll know."

"Ah, but Addie won't! Won't, I mean, know that *I* know —or at least won't believe it. Won't believe that anyone knows. Such," he added, with a strange, smothered sigh, "*is* Addie. Do you know," he wound up, "that what, after all, has most definitely happened is that you've made me see her as I've never done before?"

She blinked and gasped, she wondered and despaired. "Oh, no, it will be *you*. I've had nothing to do with it. Everything's *all* you!"

But for all it mattered now! "You'll see," he said, "that she's charming. I shall go, for to-night, to Oxford. I shall almost cross her on the way."

"Then, if she's charming, what am I to tell her from you in explanation of such strange behaviour as your flying away just as she arrives?"

"Ah, you needn't mind about that—you needn't tell her anything."

She fixed him as if as never again. "It's none of my business, of course I feel; but isn't it a little cruel if you're engaged?"

Granger gave a laugh almost as odd as one of her own.

"Oh, you've cost me that!" and he put out his hand to her.

She wondered while she took it. "Cost you——?"

"We're not engaged. Good-bye."

THE BEAST IN THE JUNGLE

I

WHAT determined the speech that startled him in the course
of their encounter scarcely matters, being probably but some
words spoken by himself quite without intention—spoken as
they lingered and slowly moved together after their renewal
of acquaintance. He had been conveyed by friends, an hour
or two before, to the house at which she was staying; the
party of visitors at the other house, of whom he was one, and
thanks to whom it was his theory, as always, that he was lost
in the crowd, had been invited over to luncheon. There had
been after luncheon much dispersal, all in the interest of the
original motive, a view of Weatherend itself and the fine
things, intrinsic features, pictures, heirlooms, treasures of all
the arts, that made the place almost famous; and the great
rooms were so numerous that guests could wander at their
will, hang back from the principal group, and, in cases where
they took such matters with the last seriousness, give themselves up to mysterious appreciations and measurements.
There were persons to be observed, singly or in couples,
bending toward objects in out-of-the-way corners with their
hands on their knees and their heads nodding quite as with
the emphasis of an excited sense of smell. When they were
two they either mingled their sounds of ecstasy or melted into
silences of even deeper import, so that there were aspects of
the occasion that gave it for Marcher much the air of the "look
round," previous to a sale highly advertised, that excites or
quenches, as may be, the dream of acquisition. The dream of
acquisition at Weatherend would have had to be wild indeed,

and John Marcher found himself, among such suggestions, disconcerted almost equally by the presence of those who knew too much and by that of those who knew nothing. The great rooms caused so much poetry and history to press upon him that he needed to wander apart to feel in a proper relation with them, though his doing so was not, as happened, like the gloating of some of his companions, to be compared to the movements of a dog sniffing a cupboard. It had an issue promptly enough in a direction that was not to have been calculated.

It led, in short, in the course of the October afternoon, to his closer meeting with May Bartram, whose face, a reminder, yet not quite a remembrance, as they sat, much separated, at a very long table, had begun merely by troubling him rather pleasantly. It affected him as the sequel of something of which he had lost the beginning. He knew it, and for the time quite welcomed it, as a continuation, but didn't know what it continued, which was an interest, or an amusement, the greater as he was also somehow aware—yet without a direct sign from her—that the young woman herself had not lost the thread. She had not lost it, but she wouldn't give it back to him, he saw, without some putting forth of his hand for it; and he not only saw that, but saw several things more, things odd enough in the light of the fact that at the moment some accident of grouping brought them face to face he was still merely fumbling with the idea that any contact between them in the past would have had no importance. If it had had no importance he scarcely knew why his actual impression of her should so seem to have so much; the answer to which, however, was that in such a life as they all appeared to be leading for the moment one could but take things as they came. He was satisfied, without in the least being able to say why, that this young lady might roughly have ranked in the house as a poor relation; satisfied also that she was not there on a brief visit, but was more or less a part of the establishment—almost a working, a remunerated part. Didn't she enjoy at periods a protection that she paid for by helping, among other services, to show the place and explain it, deal with the tiresome people, answer questions about the dates of the buildings, the styles of the furniture, the authorship of the pictures, the favourite haunts of the ghost? It wasn't that she looked as if you could have given her shillings—it was impossible to look less so. Yet when she finally drifted toward him, distinctly handsome, though ever so much older—older than when he had seen her before—it might have been as an effect of her guessing that he had, within the couple of hours, devoted more imagination to her than to all the others put together, and had thereby penetrated to a kind of truth that the others were too stupid for. She *was* there on harder terms than anyone; she was there as a consequence of things suffered, in one way and another, in the interval of years; and she remembered him very much as she was remembered—only a good deal better.

By the time they at last thus came to speech they were alone in one of the rooms—remarkable for a fine portrait over the chimney-place—out of which their friends had passed, and the charm of it was that even before they had spoken they had practically arranged with each other to stay behind for talk. The charm, happily, was in other things too; it was partly in there being scarce a spot at Weatherend without something to stay behind for. It was in the way the autumn day looked into the high windows as it waned; in the way the red light, breaking at the close from under a low, sombre sky, reached out in a long shaft and played over old wainscots, old tapestry, old gold, old colour. It was most of all perhaps in the way she came to him as if, since she had been turned on to deal with the simpler sort, he might, should he choose to keep the whole thing down, just take her mild attention for a part of her general business. As soon as he heard her voice, however, the gap was filled up and the missing link supplied; the slight irony he divined in her attitude lost its advantage. He almost jumped at it to get there before her. "I met you years and years ago in Rome. I remember all about it." She confessed to disappointment—she had been so sure he didn't; and to prove how well he did he began to pour forth the particular recollections that popped up as he called for them. Her face and her voice, all at his service now, worked the miracle— the impression operating like the torch of a lamplighter who touches into flame, one by one, a long row of gas jets. Marcher flattered himself that the illumination was brilliant, yet he was really still more pleased on her showing him, with amusement, that in his haste to make everything right he had got most things rather wrong. It hadn't been at Rome—it had been at Naples; and it hadn't been seven years before—it had been more nearly ten. She hadn't been either with her uncle and aunt, but with her mother and her brother; in addition to which it was not with the Pembles that _he_ had been, but with the Boyers, coming down in their company from Rome—a point on which she insisted, a little to his confusion, and as to which she had her evidence in hand. The Boyers she had known, but she didn't know the Pembles, though she had heard of them, and it was the people he was with who had made them acquainted. The incident of the thunderstorm that had raged round them with such violence as to drive them for refuge into an excavation—this incident had not occurred at the Palace of the Cæsars, but at Pompeii, on an occasion when they had been present there at an important find.

He accepted her amendments, he enjoyed her corrections, though the moral of them was, she pointed out, that he _really_ didn't remember the least thing about her; and he only felt it as a drawback that when all was made conformable to the truth there didn't appear much of anything left. They lingered together still, she neglecting her office—for from the moment he was so clever she had no proper right to him—and both neglecting the house, just waiting as to see if a memory or two more wouldn't again breathe upon them. It had not taken

them many minutes, after all, to put down on the table, like
the cards of a pack, those that constituted their respective
hands; only what came out was that the pack was unfortunately
not perfect—that the past, invoked, invited, encouraged, could
give them, naturally, no more than it had. It had made them
meet—her at twenty, him at twenty-five; but nothing was so
strange, they seemed to say to each other, as that, while so
occupied, it hadn't done a little more for them. They looked at
each other as with the feeling of an occasion missed; the present
one would have been so much better if the other, in the far
distance, in the foreign land, hadn't been so stupidly meagre.
There weren't, apparently, all counted, more than a dozen
little old things that had succeeded in coming to pass between
them; trivialities of youth, simplicities of freshness, stupidities
of ignorance, small possible germs, but too deeply buried—
too deeply (didn't it seem?) to sprout after so many years.
Marcher said to himself that he ought to have rendered her
some service—saved her from a capsized boat in the Bay, or
at least recovered her dressing-bag, filched from her cab, in
the streets of Naples, by a lazzarone with a stiletto. Or it
would have been nice if he could have been taken with fever,
alone, at his hotel, and she could have come to look after him,
to write to his people, to drive him out in convalescence.
Then they would be in possession of the something or other
that their actual show seemed to lack. It yet somehow presented itself, this show, as too good to be spoiled; so that they
were reduced for a few minutes more to wondering a little
helplessly why—since they seemed to know a certain number
of the same people—their reunion had been so long averted.
They didn't use that name for it, but their delay from minute
to minute to join the others was a kind of confession that they
didn't quite want it to be a failure. Their attempted supposition of reasons for their not having met but showed how little
they knew of each other. There came in fact a moment when
Marcher felt a positive pang. It was vain to pretend she was an

old friend, for all the communities were wanting, in spite of which it was as an old friend that he saw she would have suited him. He had new ones enough—was surrounded with them, for instance, at that hour at the other house; as a new one he probably wouldn't have so much as noticed her. He would have liked to invent something, get her to make-believe with him that some passage of a romantic or critical kind *had* originally occurred. He was really almost reaching out in imagination—as against time—for something that would do, and saying to himself that if it didn't come this new incident would simply and rather awkwardly close. They would separate, and now for no second or for no third chance. They would have tried and not succeeded. Then it was, just at the turn, as he afterwards made it out to himself, that, everything else failing, she herself decided to take up the case and, as it were, save the situation. He felt as soon as she spoke that she had been consciously keeping back what she said and hoping to get on without it; a scruple in her that immensely touched him when, by the end of three or four minutes more, he was able to measure it. What she brought out, at any rate, quite cleared the air and supplied the link—the link it was such a mystery he should frivolously have managed to lose.

"You know you told me something that I've never forgotten and that again and again has made me think of you since; it was that tremendously hot day when we went to Sorrento, across the bay, for the breeze. What I allude to was what you said to me, on the way back, as we sat, under the awning of the boat, enjoying the cool. Have you forgotten?"

He had forgotten, and he was even more surprised than ashamed. But the great thing was that he saw it was no vulgar reminder of any "sweet" speech. The vanity of women had long memories, but she was making no claim on him of a compliment or a mistake. With another woman, a totally different one, he might have feared the recall possibly even some imbecile "offer." So, in having to say that he had indeed forgotten, he was conscious rather of a loss than of a gain; he already saw an interest in the matter of her reference. "I try to think—but I give it up. Yet I remember the Sorrento day."

"I'm not very sure you do," May Bartram after a moment said; "and I'm not very sure I ought to want you to. It's dreadful to bring a person back, at any time, to what he was ten years before. If you've lived away from it," she smiled, "so much the better."

"Ah, if *you* haven't why should I?" he asked.

"Lived away, you mean, from what I myself was?"

"From what *I* was. I was of course an ass," Marcher went on; "but I would rather know from you just the sort of ass I was than—from the moment you have something in your mind—not know anything."

Still, however, she hesitated. "But if you've completely ceased to be that sort——?"

"Why, I can then just so all the more bear to know. Besides, perhaps I haven't."

"Perhaps. Yet if you haven't," she added, "I should suppose you would remember. Not indeed that *I* in the least connect with my impression the invidious name you use. If I had only thought you foolish," she explained, "the thing I speak of wouldn't so have remained with me. It was about yourself." She waited, as if it might come to him; but as, only meeting her eyes in wonder, he gave no sign, she burnt her ships. "Has it ever happened?"

Then it was that, while he continued to stare, a light broke for him and the blood slowly came to his face, which began to burn with recognition. "Do you mean I told you——?" But he faltered, lest what came to him shouldn't be right, lest he should only give himself away.

"It was something about yourself that it was natural one shouldn't forget—that is if one remembered you at all. That's why I ask you," she smiled, "if the thing you then spoke of has ever come to pass?"

Oh, then he saw, but he was lost in wonder and found himself embarrassed. This, he also saw, made her sorry for him, as if her allusion had been a mistake. It took him but a moment, however, to feel that it had not been, much as it had been a surprise. After the first little shock of it her knowledge on the contrary began, even if rather strangely, to taste sweet to him. She was the only other person in the world then who would have it, and she had had it all these years, while the fact of his having so breathed his secret had unaccountably faded from him. No wonder they couldn't have met as if nothing had happened. "I judge," he finally said, "that I know what you mean. Only I had strangely enough lost the consciousness of having taken you so far into my confidence."

"Is it because you've taken so many others as well?"

"I've taken nobody. Not a creature since then."

"So that I'm the only person who knows?"

"The only person in the world."

"Well," she quickly replied, "I myself have never spoken. I've never, never repeated of you what you told me." She looked at him so that he perfectly believed her. Their eyes met over it in such a way that he was without a doubt. "And I never will."

She spoke with an earnestness that, as if almost excessive, put him at ease about her possible derision. Somehow the whole question was a new luxury to him—that is, from the moment she was in possession. If she didn't take the ironic view she clearly took the sympathetic, and that was what he had had, in all the long time, from no one whomsoever. What he felt was that he couldn't at present have begun to tell her and yet could profit perhaps exquisitely by the accident of having done so of old. "Please don't then. We're just right as it is."

"Oh, I am," she laughed, "if you are!" To which she added: "Then you do still feel in the same way?"

It was impossible to him not to take to himself that she was really interested, and it all kept coming as a sort of revelation. He had thought of himself so long as abominably alone, and, lo, he wasn't alone a bit. He hadn't been, it appeared, for an hour—since those moments on the Sorrento boat. It was *she* who had been, he seemed to see as he looked at her—she who had been made so by the graceless fact of his lapse of fidelity. To tell her what he had told her—what had it been but to ask something of her? something that she had given, in her charity, without his having, by a remembrance, by a return of the spirit, failing another encounter, so much as thanked her. What he had asked of her had been simply at first not to laugh at him. She had beautifully not done so for ten years, and she was not doing so now. So he had endless gratitude to make up. Only for that he must see just how he had figured to her. "What, exactly, was the account I gave——?"

"Of the way you did feel? Well, it was very simple. You said you had had from your earliest time, as the deepest thing within you, the sense of being kept for something rare and strange, possibly prodigious and terrible, that was sooner or later to happen to you, that you had in your bones the foreboding and the conviction of, and that would perhaps overwhelm you."

"Do you call that very simple?" John Marcher asked.

She thought a moment. "It was perhaps because I seemed, as you spoke, to understand it."

"You do understand it?" he eagerly asked.

Again she kept her kind eyes on him. "You still have the belief?"

"Oh!" he exclaimed helplessly. There was too much to say.

"Whatever it is to be," she clearly made out, "it hasn't yet come."

He shook his head in complete surrender now. "It hasn't yet come. Only, you know, it isn't anything I'm to *do*, to achieve in the world, to be distinguished or admired for. I'm not such an ass as *that*. It would be much better, no doubt, if I were."

"It's to be something you're merely to suffer?"

"Well, say to wait for—to have to meet, to face, to see suddenly break out in my life; possibly destroying all further consciousness, possibly annihilating me; possibly, on the other hand, only altering everything, striking at the root of all my world and leaving me to the consequences, however they shape themselves."

She took this in, but the light in her eyes continued for him not to be that of mockery. "Isn't what you describe perhaps but the expectation—or, at any rate, the sense of danger, familiar to so many people—of falling in love?"

John Marcher thought. "Did you ask me that before?"

"No—I wasn't so free-and-easy then. But it's what strikes me now."

"Of course," he said after a moment, "it strikes you. Of course it strikes *me*. Of course what's in store for me may be no more than that. The only thing is," he went on, "that I think that if it had been that, I should by this time know."

"Do you mean because you've *been* in love?" And then as he but looked at her in silence: "You've been in love, and it hasn't meant such a cataclysm, hasn't proved the great affair?"

"Here I am, you see. It hasn't been overwhelming."

"Then it hasn't been love," said May Bartram.

"Well, I at least thought it was. I took it for that—I've taken it till now. It was agreeable, it was delightful, it was miserable," he explained. "But it wasn't strange. It wasn't what *my* affair's to be."

"You want something all to yourself—something that nobody else knows or *has* known?"

"It isn't a question of what I 'want'—God knows I don't want anything. It's only a question of the apprehension that haunts me—that I live with day by day."

He said this so lucidly and consistently that, visibly, it

further imposed itself. If she had not been interested before she would have been interested now. "Is it a sense of coming violence?"

Evidently now too, again, he liked to talk of it. "I don't think of it as—when it does come—necessarily violent. I only think of it as natural and as of course, above all, unmistakeable. I think of it simply as *the* thing. *The* thing will of itself appear natural."

"Then how will it appear strange?"

Marcher bethought himself. "It won't—to *me*."

"To whom then?"

"Well," he replied, smiling at last, "say to you."

"Oh then, I'm to be present?"

"Why, you *are* present—since you know."

"I see." She turned it over. "But I mean at the catastrophe."

At this, for a minute, their lightness gave way to their gravity; it was as if the long look they exchanged held them together. "It will only depend on yourself—if you'll watch with me."

"Are you afraid?" she asked.

"Don't leave me *now*," he went on.

"Are you afraid?" she repeated.

"Do you think me simply out of my mind?" he pursued instead of answering. "Do I merely strike you as a harmless lunatic?"

"No," said May Bartram. "I understand you. I believe you."

"You mean you feel how my obsession—poor old thing!—may correspond to some possible reality?"

"To some possible reality."

"Then you *will* watch with me?"

She hesitated, then for the third time put her question. "Are you afraid?"

"Did I tell you I was—at Naples?"

"No, you said nothing about it."

"Then I don't know. And I should *like* to know," said

John Marcher. "You'll tell me yourself whether you think so. If you'll watch with me you'll see."

"Very good then." They had been moving by this time across the room, and at the door, before passing out, they paused as if for the full wind-up of their understanding. "I'll watch with you," said May Bartram.

II

THE fact that she "knew"—knew and yet neither chaffed him nor betrayed him—had in a short time begun to constitute between them a sensible bond, which became more marked when, within the year that followed their afternoon at Weatherend, the opportunities for meeting multiplied. The event that thus promoted these occasions was the death of the ancient lady, her great-aunt, under whose wing, since losing her mother, she had to such an extent found shelter, and who, though but the widowed mother of the new successor to the property, had succeeded—thanks to a high tone and a high temper—in not forfeiting the supreme position at the great house. The deposition of this personage arrived but with her death, which, followed by many changes, made in particular a difference for the young woman in whom Marcher's expert attention had recognised from the first a dependent with a pride that might ache though it didn't bristle. Nothing for a long time had made him easier than the thought that the aching must have been much soothed by Miss Bartram's now finding herself able to set up a small home in London. She had acquired property, to an amount that made that luxury just possible, under her aunt's extremely complicated will, and when the whole matter began to be straightened out, which indeed took time, she let him know that the happy issue was at last in view. He had seen her again before that day, both because she had more than once accompanied the ancient lady to town and because he had paid another visit to the friends who so conveniently made of Weatherend one of the charms of their own hospitality. These friends had taken him back there; he had achieved there again with Miss Bartram some quiet detachment; and he had in London succeeded in persuading her to more than one brief absence from her aunt. They went together, on these latter occasions, to the National Gallery and the South Kensington Museum, where, among vivid reminders, they talked of Italy at large—not now attempting to recover, as at first, the taste of their youth and their ignorance. That recovery, the first day at Weatherend, had served its purpose well, had given them quite enough; so that they were, to Marcher's sense, no longer hovering about the head-waters of their stream, but had felt their boat pushed sharply off and down the current.

They were literally afloat together; for our gentleman this was marked, quite as marked as that the fortunate cause of it was just the buried treasure of her knowledge. He had with his own hands dug up this little hoard, brought to light—that is to within reach of the dim day constituted by their discretions and privacies—the object of value the hiding-place of which he had, after putting it into the ground himself, so strangely, so long forgotten. The exquisite luck of having again just stumbled on the spot made him indifferent to any other question; he would doubtless have devoted more time to the odd accident of his lapse of memory if he had not been moved to devote so much to the sweetness, the comfort, as he felt, for the future, that this accident itself had helped to keep fresh. It had never entered into his plan that anyone should "know," and mainly for the reason that it was not in him to tell anyone. That would have been impossible, since nothing but the amusement of a cold world would have waited on it. Since, however, a mysterious fate had opened his mouth in youth, in spite of him, he would count that a compensation and profit by it to the utmost. That the right person *should* know tempered the asperity of his secret more even than his shyness had permitted him to imagine; and May Bartram was clearly right, because—well, because there she was. Her knowledge simply settled it; he would have been sure enough by this time had she been wrong. There was that in his situation, no doubt, that disposed him too much to see her as a mere confidant, taking all her light for him from the fact—the fact only—of her interest in his predicament, from her mercy, sympathy, seriousness, her consent not to regard him as the funniest of the funny. Aware, in fine, that her price for him was just in her giving him this constant sense of his being admirably spared, he was careful to remember that she had, after all, also a life of her own, with things that might happen to *her*, things that in friendship one should likewise take account of. Something fairly remarkable came to pass with him, for that matter, in this connection—something represented by a certain passage of his consciousness, in the suddenest way, from one extreme to the other.

He had thought himself, so long as nobody knew, the most disinterested person in the world, carrying his concentrated burden, his perpetual suspense, ever so quietly, holding his tongue about it, giving others no glimpse of it nor of its effect upon his life, asking of them no allowance and only making on his side all those that were asked. He had disturbed nobody with the queerness of having to know a haunted man, though he had had moments of rather special temptation on hearing people say that they were "unsettled." If they were as unsettled as he was—he who had never been settled for an hour in his life—they would know what it meant. Yet it wasn't, all the same, for him to make them, and he listened to them civilly enough. This was why he had such good—though possibly such rather colourless—manners; this was why, above all, he could regard himself, in a greedy world, as decently—as, in fact, perhaps even a little sublimely—unselfish. Our point is accordingly that he valued this character quite sufficiently to measure his present danger of letting it lapse, against which he promised himself to be much on his guard. He was quite ready, none the less, to be selfish just a little, since, surely, no more charming occasion for it had come to him. "Just a little," in a word, was just as much as Miss Bartram, taking one day with another, would let him. He never would be in the least coercive, and he would keep well before him the lines on which consideration for her—the very highest—ought to proceed. He would thoroughly establish the heads under which her affairs, her requirements, her peculiarities—he went so far as to give them the latitude of that name—would come into their intercourse. All this naturally was a sign of how much he took the intercourse itself for granted. There was nothing more to be done about *that*. It simply existed; had sprung into being with her first penetrating question to him in the autumn light there at Weatherend. The real form it should have taken on the basis that stood out large was the form of their marrying. But the devil in this was that the very basis itself put marrying out of the question. His conviction, his apprehension, his obsession, in short, was not a condition he could invite a woman to share; and that consequence of it was precisely what was the matter with him. Something or other lay in wait for him, amid the twists and the turns of the months and the years, like a crouching beast in the jungle. It signified little whether the crouching beast were destined to slay him or to be slain. The definite point was the inevitable spring of the creature; and the definite lesson from that was that a man of feeling didn't cause himself to be accompanied by a lady on a tiger-hunt. Such was the image under which he had ended by figuring his life.

They had at first, none the less, in the scattered hours spent together, made no allusion to that view of it; which was a sign he was handsomely ready to give that he didn't expect, that he in fact didn't care always to be talking about it. Such a feature in one's outlook was really like a hump on one's back. The difference it made every minute of the day existed quite independently of discussion. One discussed, of course, *like* a hunchback, for there was always, if nothing else, the hunchback face. That remained, and she was watching him; but people watched best, as a general thing, in silence, so that such would be predominantly the manner of their vigil. Yet he didn't want, at the same time, to be solemn; solemn was what he imagined he too much tended to be with other people. The thing to be, with the one person who knew, was easy and natural—to make the reference rather than be seeming to avoid it, to avoid it rather than be seeming to make it, and to keep it, in any case, familiar, facetious even, rather than pedantic and portentous. Some such consideration as the latter was doubtless in his mind, for instance, when he wrote pleasantly to Miss Bartram that perhaps the great thing he had so long felt as in the lap of the gods was no more than this circumstance, which touched him so nearly, of her acquiring a house in London. It was the first allusion they had yet again made, needing any other hitherto so little; but when she replied, after having given him the news, that she was by no means satisfied with such a trifle, as the climax to so special a suspense, she almost set him wondering if she hadn't even a larger conception of singularity for him than he had for himself. He was at all events destined to become aware little by little, as time went by, that she was all the while looking at his life, judging it, measuring it, in the light of the thing she knew, which grew to be at last, with the consecration of the years, never mentioned between them save as "the real truth" about him. That had always been his own form of reference to it, but she adopted the form so quietly that, looking back at the end of a period, he knew there was no moment at which it was traceable that she had, as he might say, got inside his condition, or exchanged the attitude of beautifully indulging for that of still more beautifully believing him.

It was always open to him to accuse her of seeing him but as the most harmless of maniacs, and this, in the long run—since it covered so much ground—was his easiest description of their friendship. He had a screw loose for her, but she liked him in spite of it, and was practically, against the rest of the world, his kind, wise keeper, unremunerated, but fairly amused and, in the absence of other near ties, not disreputably occupied. The rest of the world of course thought him queer, but she, she only, knew how, and above all why, queer; which was precisely what enabled her to dispose the concealing veil in the right folds. She took his gaiety from him—since it had to pass with them for gaiety—as she took everything else; but she certainly so far justified by her unerring touch his finer sense of the degree to which he had ended by convincing her. *She* at least never spoke of the secret of his life except as "the real truth about you," and she had in fact a wonderful way of making it seem, as such, the secret of her own life too. That was in fine how he so constantly felt her as allowing for him; he couldn't on the whole call it anything else. He allowed for himself, but she, exactly, allowed still more; partly because, better placed for a sight of the matter, she traced his unhappy perversion through portions of its course into which he could scarce follow it. He knew how he felt, but, besides knowing that, she knew how he *looked* as well; he knew each of the things of importance he was insidiously kept from doing, but she could add up the amount they made, understand how much, with a lighter weight on his spirit, he might have done, and thereby establish how, clever as he was, he fell short. Above all she was in the secret of the difference between the forms he went through—those of his little office under Government, those of caring for his modest patrimony, for his library, for his garden in the country, for the people in London whose invitations he accepted and repaid—and the detachment that reigned beneath them and that made of all behaviour, all that could in the least be called behaviour, a long act of dissimulation. What it had come to was that he wore a mask painted with the social simper, out of the eye-holes of which there looked eyes of an expression not in the least matching the other features. This the stupid world, even after years, had never more than half discovered. It was only May Bartram who had, and she achieved, by an art indescribable, the feat of at once—or perhaps it was only alternately —meeting the eyes from in front and mingling her own vision, as from over his shoulder, with their peep through the aper-tures.

So, while they grew older together, she did watch with him, and so she let this association give shape and colour to her own existence. Beneath *her* forms as well detachment had learned to sit, and behaviour had become for her, in the social sense, a false account of herself. There was but one account of her that would have been true all the while, and that she could give, directly, to nobody, least of all to John Marcher. Her whole attitude was a virtual statement, but the perception of that only seemed destined to take its place for him as one of the many things necessarily crowded out of his consciousness. If she had, moreover, like himself, to make sacrifices to their real truth, it was to be granted that her compensation might have affected her as more prompt and more natural. They had long periods, in this London time, during which, when they were together, a stranger might have listened to them without in the least pricking up his ears; on the other hand, the real truth was equally liable at any moment to rise to the surface, and the auditor would then have wondered indeed what they were talking about. They had from an early time made up their mind that society was, luckily, unintelligent, and the margin that this gave them had fairly become one of their commonplaces. Yet there were still moments when the situa-tion turned almost fresh—usually under the effect of some expression drawn from herself. Her expressions doubtless repeated themselves, but her intervals were generous. "What saves us, you know, is that we answer so completely to so usual an appearance: that of the man and woman whose friendship has become such a daily habit, or almost, as to be at last indispensable." That, for instance, was a remark she had frequently enough had occasion to make, though she had given it at different times different developments. What we are especially concerned with is the turn it happened to take from her one afternoon when he had come to see her in honour of her birthday. This anniversary had fallen on a Sunday, at a season of thick fog and general outward gloom; but he had brought her his customary offering, having known her now long enough to have established a hundred little customs. It was one of his proofs to himself, the present he made her on her birthday, that he had not sunk into real selfishness. It was mostly nothing more than a small trinket, but it was always fine of its kind, and he was regularly careful to pay for it more than he thought he could afford. "Our habit saves you, at least, don't you see? because it makes you, after all, for the vulgar, indistinguishable from other men. What's the most inveterate mark of men in general? Why, the capacity to spend endless time with dull women—to spend it, I won't say without being bored, but without minding that they are, without being driven off at a tangent by it; which comes to the same thing. I'm your dull woman, a part of the daily bread for which you pray at church. That covers your tracks more than anything."

"And what covers yours?" asked Marcher, whom his dull woman could mostly to this extent amuse. "I see of course what you mean by your saving me, in one way and another, so far as other people are concerned—I've seen it all along. Only, what is it that saves *you?* I often think, you know, of that."

She looked as if she sometimes thought of that too, but in rather a different way. "Where other people, you mean, are concerned?"

"Well, you're really so in with me, you know—as a sort of

result of my being so in with yourself. I mean of my having such an immense regard for you, being so tremendously grateful for all you've done for me. I sometimes ask myself if it's quite fair. Fair I mean to have so involved and—since one may say it—interested you. I almost feel as if you hadn't really had time to do anything else."

"Anything else but be interested?" she asked. "Ah, what else does one ever want to be? If I've been 'watching' with you, as we long ago agreed that I was to do, watching is always in itself an absorption."

"Oh, certainly," John Marcher said, "if you hadn't had your curiosity——! Only, doesn't it sometimes come to you, as time goes on, that your curiosity is not being particularly repaid?"

May Bartram had a pause. "Do you ask that, by any chance, because you feel at all that yours isn't? I mean because you have to wait so long."

Oh, he understood what she meant. "For the thing to happen that never does happen? For the beast to jump out? No, I'm just where I was about it. It isn't a matter as to which I can *choose*, I can decide for a change. It isn't one as to which there *can* be a change. It's in the lap of the gods. One's in the hands of one's law—there one is. As to the form the law will take, the way it will operate, that's its own affair."

"Yes," Miss Bartram replied; "of course one's fate is coming, of course it *has* come, in its own form and its own way, all the while. Only, you know, the form and the way in your case were to have been—well, something so exceptional and, as one may say, so particularly *your* own."

Something in this made him look at her with suspicion. "You say 'were to *have* been,' as if in your heart you had begun to doubt."

"Oh!" she vaguely protested.

"As if you believed," he went on, "that nothing will now take place."

She shook her head slowly, but rather inscrutably. "You're far from my thought."

He continued to look at her. "What then is the matter with you?"

"Well," she said after another wait, "the matter with me is simply that I'm more sure than ever my curiosity, as you call it, will be but too well repaid."

They were frankly grave now; he had got up from his seat, had turned once more about the little drawing-room to which, year after year, he brought his inevitable topic; in which he had, as he might have said, tasted their intimate community with every sauce, where every object was as familiar to him as the things of his own house and the very carpets were worn with his fitful walk very much as the desks in old counting-houses are worn by the elbows of generations of clerks. The generations of his nervous moods had been at work there, and the place was the written history of his whole middle life. Under the impression of what his friend had just said he knew himself, for some reason, more aware of these things, which made him, after a moment, stop again before her. "Is it, possibly, that you've grown afraid?"

"Afraid?" He thought, as she repeated the word, that his question had made her, a little, change colour; so that, lest he should have touched on a truth, he explained very kindly, "You remember that that was what you asked *me* long ago—that first day at Weatherend."

"Oh yes, and you told me you didn't know—that I was to see for myself. We've said little about it since, even in so long a time."

"Precisely," Marcher interposed—"quite as if it were too delicate a matter for us to make free with. Quite as if we might find, on pressure, that I *am* afraid. For then," he said, "we shouldn't, should we? quite know what to do."

She had for the time no answer to this question. "There have been days when I thought you were. Only, of course," she added, "there have been days when we have thought almost anything."

"Everything. Oh!" Marcher softly groaned as with a gasp, half spent, at the face, more uncovered just then than it had been for a long while, of the imagination always with them. It had always had its incalculable moments of glaring out, quite as with the very eyes of the very Beast, and, used as he was to them, they could still draw from him the tribute of a sigh that rose from the depths of his being. All that they had thought, first and last, rolled over him; the past seemed to have been reduced to mere barren speculation. This in fact was what the place had just struck him as so full of—the simplification of everything but the state of suspense. That remained only by seeming to hang in the void surrounding it. Even his original fear, if fear it had been, had lost itself in the desert. "I judge, however," he continued, "that you see I'm not afraid now."

"What I see is, as I make it out, that you've achieved something almost unprecedented in the way of getting used to danger. Living with it so long and so closely, you've lost your sense of it; you know it's there, but you're indifferent, and you cease even, as of old, to have to whistle in the dark. Considering what the danger is," May Bartram wound up, "I'm bound to say that I don't think your attitude could well be surpassed."

John Marcher faintly smiled. "It's heroic?"

"Certainly—call it that."

He considered. "I *am*, then, a man of courage?"

"That's what you were to show me."

He still, however, wondered. "But doesn't the man of courage know what he's afraid of—or *not* afraid of? I don't know *that*, you see. I don't focus it. I can't name it. I only know I'm exposed."

"Yes, but exposed—how shall I say?—so directly. So intimately. That's surely enough."

"Enough to make you feel, then—as what we may call the end of our watch—that I'm not afraid?"

"You're not afraid. But it isn't," she said, "the end of our watch. That is it isn't the end of yours. You've everything still to see."

"Then why haven't you?" he asked. He had had, all along, to-day, the sense of her keeping something back, and he still had it. As this was his first impression of that, it made a kind of date. The case was the more marked as she didn't at first answer; which in turn made him go on. "You know something I don't." Then his voice, for that of a man of courage, trembled a little. "You know what's to happen." Her silence, with the face she showed, was almost a confession—it made him sure. "You know, and you're afraid to tell me. It's so bad that you're afraid I'll find out."

All this might be true, for she did look as if, unexpectedly to her, he had crossed some mystic line that she had secretly drawn round her. Yet she might, after all, not have worried; and the real upshot was that he himself, at all events, needn't. "You'll never find out."

III

It was all to have made, none the less, as I have said, a date; as came out in the fact that again and again, even after long intervals, other things that passed between them wore, in relation to this hour, but the character of recalls and results. Its immediate effect had been indeed rather to lighten insistence—almost to provoke a reaction; as if their topic had dropped by its own weight and as if moreover, for that matter, Marcher had been visited by one of his occasional warnings against egotism. He had kept up, he felt, and very decently on the whole, his consciousness of the importance of not being selfish, and it was true that he had never sinned in that direction without promptly enough trying to press the scales the other way. He often repaired his fault, the season permitting, by inviting his friend to accompany him to the opera; and it not infrequently thus happened that, to show he didn't wish her to have but one sort of food for her mind, he was the cause of her appearing there with him a dozen nights in the month. It even happened that, seeing her home at such times, he occasionally went in with her to finish, as he called it, the evening, and, the better to make his point, sat down to the frugal but always careful little supper that awaited his pleasure. His point was made, he thought, by his not eternally insisting with her on himself; made for instance, at such hours, when it befell that, her piano at hand and each of them familiar with it, they went over passages of the opera together. It chanced to be on one of these occasions, however, that he reminded her of her not having answered a certain question he had put to her during the talk that had taken place between them on her last birthday. "What is it that saves *you?*"— saved her, he meant, from that appearance of variation from the usual human type. If he had practically escaped remark, as she pretended, by doing, in the most important particular, what most men do—find the answer to life in patching up an alliance of a sort with a woman no better than himself—how had she escaped it, and how could the alliance, such as it was, since they must suppose it had been more or less noticed, have failed to make her rather positively talked about?

"I never said," May Bartram replied, "that it hadn't made me talked about."

"Ah well then, you're not 'saved.'"

"It has not been a question for me. If you've had your woman, I've had," she said, "my man."

"And you mean that makes you all right?"

She hesitated. "I don't know why it shouldn't make me— humanly, which is what we're speaking of—as right as it makes you."

"I see," Marcher returned. " 'Humanly,' no doubt, as showing that you're living for something. Not, that is, just for me and my secret."

May Bartram smiled. "I don't pretend it exactly shows that I'm not living for you. It's my intimacy with you that's in question."

He laughed as he saw what she meant. "Yes, but since, as you say, I'm only, so far as people make out, ordinary, you're—aren't you?—no more than ordinary either. You help me to pass for a man like another. So if I *am*, as I understand you, you're not compromised. Is that it?"

She had another hesitation, but she spoke clearly enough. "That's it. It's all that concerns me—to help you to pass for a man like another."

He was careful to acknowledge the remark handsomely. "How kind, how beautiful, you are to me! How shall I ever repay you?"

She had her last grave pause, as if there might be a choice of ways. But she chose. "By going on as you are."

It was into this going on as he was that they relapsed, and really for so long a time that the day inevitably came for a further sounding of their depths. It was as if these depths, constantly bridged over by a structure that was firm enough in spite of its lightness and of its occasional oscillation in the somewhat vertiginous air, invited on occasion, in the interest of their nerves, a dropping of the plummet and a measurement of the abyss. A difference had been made moreover, once for all, by the fact that she had, all the while, not appeared to feel the need of rebutting his charge of an idea within her that she didn't dare to express, uttered just before one of the fullest of their later discussions ended. It had come up for him then that she "knew" something and that what she knew was bad—too bad to tell him. When he had spoken of it as visibly so bad that she was afraid he might find it out, her reply had left the matter too equivocal to be let alone and yet, for Marcher's special sensibility, almost too formidable again to touch. He circled about it at a distance that alternately narrowed and widened and that yet was not much affected by the consciousness in him that there was nothing she could "know," after all, any better than he did. She had no source of knowledge that he hadn't equally—except of course that she might have finer nerves. That was what women had where they were interested; they made out things, where people were concerned, that the people often couldn't have made out for themselves. Their nerves, their sensibility, their imagination, were conductors and revealers, and the beauty of May Bartram was in particular that she had given herself so to his case. He felt in these days what, oddly enough, he had never felt before, the growth of a dread of losing her by some catastrophe—some catastrophe that yet wouldn't at all be *the* catastrophe: partly because she had, almost of a sudden, begun to strike him as useful to him as never yet, and partly by reason of an appearance of uncertainty in her health, coincident and equally new. It was characteristic of the inner detachment he had hitherto so successfully cultivated and to which our whole account of him is a reference, it was characteristic that his complications, such as they were, had never yet seemed so as at this crisis to thicken about him, even to the point of making him ask himself if he were, by any chance, of a truth, within sight or sound, within touch or reach, within the immediate jurisdiction of the thing that waited.

When the day came, as come it had to, that his friend confessed to him her fear of a deep disorder in her blood, he felt somehow the shadow of a change and the chill of a shock. He immediately began to imagine aggravations and disasters, and above all to think of her peril as the direct menace for himself of personal privation. This indeed gave him one of those partial recoveries of equanimity that were agreeable to him—it showed him that what was still first in his mind was the loss she herself might suffer. "What if she should have to die before knowing, before seeing——?" It would have been brutal, in the early stages of her trouble, to put that question to her; but it had immediately sounded for him to his own concern, and the possibility was what most made him sorry for her. If she did "know," moreover, in the sense of her having had some—what should he think?—mystical, irresistible light, this would make the matter not better, but worse, inasmuch as her original adoption of his own curiosity had quite become the basis of her life. She had been living to see what would *be* to be seen, and it would be cruel to her to have to give up before the accomplishment of the vision. These reflections, as I say, refreshed his generosity; yet, make them as he might, he saw himself, with the lapse of the period, more and more disconcerted. It lapsed for him with a strange, steady sweep, and the oddest oddity was that it gave him, independently of the threat of much inconvenience, almost the only positive surprise his career, if career it could be called, had yet offered him. She kept the house as she had never done; he had to go to her to see her—she could meet him nowhere now, though there was scarce a corner of their loved old London in which she had not in the past, at one time or another, done so; and he found her always seated by her fire in the deep, old-fashioned chair she was less and less able to leave. He had been struck one day, after an absence exceeding his usual measure, with her suddenly looking much older to him than he had ever thought of her being; then he recognised that the suddenness was all on his side—he had just been suddenly struck. She looked older because inevitably, after so many years, she *was* old, or almost; which was of course true in still greater measure of her companion. If she was old, or almost, John Marcher assuredly was, and yet it was her showing of the lesson, not his own, that brought the truth home to him. His surprises began here; when once they had begun they multiplied; they came rather with a rush: it was as if, in the oddest way in the world, they had all been kept back, sown in a thick cluster, for the late afternoon of life, the time at which, for people in general, the unexpected has died out.

One of them was that he should have caught himself—for he *had* so done—*really* wondering if the great accident would take form now as nothing more than his being condemned to see this charming woman, this admirable friend, pass away from him. He had never so unreservedly qualified her as while confronted in thought with such a possibility; in spite of which there was small doubt for him that as an answer to his long riddle the mere effacement of even so fine a feature of his situation would be an abject anticlimax. It would represent, as connected with his past attitude, a drop of dignity under the shadow of which his existence could only become the most grotesque of failures. He had been far from holding it a failure —long as he had waited for the appearance that was to make it a success. He had waited for a quite other thing, not for such a one as that. The breath of his good faith came short, however, as he recognised how long he had waited, or how long, at least, his companion had. That she, at all events, might be recorded as having waited in vain—this affected him sharply, and all the more because of his at first having done little more than amuse himself with the idea. It grew more grave as the gravity of her condition grew, and the state of mind it produced in him, which he ended by watching, himself, as if it had been some definite disfigurement of his outer person, may pass for another of his surprises. This conjoined itself still with another, the really stupefying consciousness of a question that he would have allowed to shape itself had he dared. What did everything mean—what, that is, did *she* mean, she and her vain waiting and her probable death and the soundless admonition of it all—unless that, at this time of day, it was simply, it was overwhelmingly too late? He had never, at any stage of his queer consciousness, admitted the whisper of such a correction; he had never, till within these last few months, been so false to his conviction as not to hold that what was to come to him had time, whether *he* struck himself as having it or not. That at last, at last, he certainly hadn't it, to speak of, or had it but in the scantiest measure—such, soon enough, as things went with him, became the inference with which his old obsession had to reckon: and this it was not helped to do by the more and more confirmed appearance that the great vagueness casting the long shadow in which he had lived had, to attest itself, almost no margin left. Since it was in Time that he was to have met his fate, so it was in Time that his fate was to have acted; and as he waked up to the sense of no longer being young, which was exactly the sense of being stale, just as that, in turn, was the sense of being weak, he waked up to another matter beside. It all hung together; they were subject, he and the great vagueness, to an equal and indivisible law. When the possibilities themselves had, accordingly, turned stale, when the secret of the gods had grown faint, had perhaps even quite evaporated, that, and that only, was failure. It wouldn't have been failure to be bankrupt, dishonoured, pilloried, hanged; it was failure not to be anything. And so, in the dark valley into which his path had taken its unlooked-for twist, he wondered not a little as he groped. He didn't care what awful crash might overtake him, with what ignominy or what monstrosity he might yet be associated—since he wasn't, after all, too utterly old to suffer—if it would only be decently proportionate to the posture he had kept, all his life, in the promised presence of it. He had but one desire left—that he shouldn't have been "sold."

IV

THEN it was that one afternoon, while the spring of the year was young and new, she met, all in her own way, his frankest betrayal of these alarms. He had gone in late to see her, but evening had not settled, and she was presented to him in that long, fresh light of waning April days which affects us often with a sadness sharper than the greyest hours of autumn. The week had been warm, the spring was supposed to have begun early, and May Bartram sat, for the first time in the year, without a fire, a fact that, to Marcher's sense, gave the scene of which she formed part a smooth and ultimate look, an air of knowing, in its immaculate order and its cold, meaningless cheer, that it would never see a fire again. Her own aspect—he could scarce have said why—intensified this note. Almost as white as wax, with the marks and signs in her face as numerous and as fine as if they had been etched by a needle, with soft white draperies relieved by a faded green scarf, the delicate tone of which had been consecrated by the years, she was the picture of a serene, exquisite, but impenetrable sphinx, whose head, or indeed all whose person, might have been powdered with silver. She was a sphinx, yet with her white petals and green fronds she might have been a lily too—only an artificial lily, wonderfully imitated and constantly kept, without dust or stain, though not exempt from a slight droop and a complexity of faint creases, under some clear glass bell. The perfection of household care, of high polish and finish, always reigned in her rooms, but they especially looked to Marcher at present as if everything had been wound up, tucked in, put away, so that she might sit with folded hands and with nothing more to do. She was "out of it," to his vision; her work was over; she communicated with him as across some gulf, or from some island of rest that she had already reached, and it made him feel strangely abandoned. Was it—or, rather, wasn't it—that if for so long she had been watching with him the answer to their question had swum into her ken and taken on its name, so that her occupation was verily gone? He had as much as charged her with this in saying to her, many months before, that she even then knew something she was keeping from him. It was a point he had never since ventured to press, vaguely fearing, as he did, that it might become a difference, perhaps a disagreement, between them. He had in short, in this later time, turned nervous, which was what, in all the other years, he had never been; and the oddity was that his nervousness should have waited till he had begun to doubt, should have held off so long as he was sure. There was something, it seemed to him, that the wrong word would bring down on his head, something that would so at least put an end to his suspense. But he wanted not to speak the wrong word; that would make everything ugly. He wanted the knowledge he lacked to drop on him, if drop it could, by its own august weight. If she was to forsake him it was surely for her to take leave. This was why he didn't ask her again, directly, what she knew; but it was also why, approaching the matter from another side, he said to her in the course of his visit: "What do you regard as the very worst that, at this time of day, *can* happen to me?"

He had asked her that in the past often enough; they had, with the odd, irregular rhythm of their intensities and avoidances, exchanged ideas about it and then had seen the ideas washed away by cool intervals, washed like figures traced in sea-sand. It had ever been the mark of their talk that the oldest allusions in it required but a little dismissal and reaction to come out again, sounding for the hour as new. She could thus at present meet his inquiry quite freshly and patiently. "Oh yes, I've repeatedly thought, only it always seemed to me of old that I couldn't quite make up my mind. I thought of dreadful things, between which it was difficult to choose; and so must you have done."

"Rather! I feel now as if I had scarce done anything else. I appear to myself to have spent my life in thinking of nothing *but* dreadful things. A great many of them I've at different times named to you, but there were others I couldn't name."

"They were too, too dreadful?"

"Too, too dreadful—some of them."

She looked at him a minute, and there came to him as he met it an inconsequent sense that her eyes, when one got their full clearness, were still as beautiful as they had been in youth, only beautiful with a strange, cold light—a light that somehow was a part of the effect, if it wasn't rather a part of the cause, of the pale, hard sweetness of the season and the hour. "And yet," she said at last, "there are horrors we have mentioned."

It deepened the strangeness to see her, as such a figure in such a picture, talk of "horrors," but she was to do, in a few minutes, something stranger yet—though even of this he was to take the full measure but afterwards—and the note of it was already in the air. It was, for the matter of that, one of the signs that her eyes were having again such a high flicker of their prime. He had to admit, however, what she said. "Oh yes, there were times when we did go far." He caught himself in the act of speaking as if it all were over. Well, he wished it were; and the consummation depended, for him, clearly, more and more on his companion.

But she had now a soft smile. "Oh, far——!"

It was oddly ironic. "Do you mean you're prepared to go further?"

She was frail and ancient and charming as she continued to look at him, yet it was rather as if she had lost the thread. "Do you consider that we went so far?"

"Why, I thought it the point you were just making—that we *had* looked most things in the face."

"Including each other?" She still smiled. "But you're quite right. We've had together great imaginations, often great fears; but some of them have been unspoken."

"Then the worst—we haven't faced that. I *could* face it, I believe, if I knew what you think it. I feel," he explained, "as if I had lost my power to conceive such things." And he wondered if he looked as blank as he sounded. "It's spent."

"Then why do you assume," she asked, "that mine isn't?"

"Because you've given me signs to the contrary. It isn't a question for you of conceiving, imagining, comparing. It isn't a question now of choosing." At last he came out with it. "You know something that I don't. You've shown me that before."

These last words affected her, he could see in a moment, remarkably, and she spoke with firmness. "I've shown you, my dear, nothing."

He shook his head. "You can't hide it."

"Oh, oh!" May Bartram murmured over what she couldn't hide. It was almost a smothered groan.

"You admitted it months ago, when I spoke of it to you as of something you were afraid I would find out. Your answer was that I couldn't, that I wouldn't, and I don't pretend I have. But you had something therefore in mind, and I see now that it must have been, that it still is, the possibility that, of all possibilities, has settled itself for you as the worst. This," he went on, "is why I appeal to you. I'm only afraid of ignorance now—I'm not afraid of knowledge." And then as for a while she said nothing: "What makes me sure is that I see in your face and feel here, in this air and amid these appearances, that you're out of it. You've done. You've had your experience. You leave me to my fate."

Well, she listened, motionless and white in her chair, as if she had in fact a decision to make, so that her whole manner was a virtual confession, though still with a small, fine, inner stiffness, an imperfect surrender. "It *would* be the worst," she finally let herself say. "I mean the thing that I've never said."

It hushed him a moment. "More monstrous than all the monstrosities we've named?"

"More monstrous. Isn't that what you sufficiently express," she asked, "in calling it the worst?"

Marcher thought. "Assuredly—if you mean, as I do, something that includes all the loss and all the shame that are thinkable."

"It would if it *should* happen," said May Bartram. "What we're speaking of, remember, is only my idea."

"It's your belief," Marcher returned. "That's enough for me. I feel your beliefs are right. Therefore if, having this one, you give me no more light on it, you abandon me."

"No, no!" she repeated. "I'm with you—don't you see?—still." And as if to make it more vivid to him she rose from her chair—a movement she seldom made in these days—and showed herself, all draped and all soft, in her fairness and slimness. "I haven't forsaken you."

It was really, in its effort against weakness, a generous assurance, and had the success of the impulse not, happily, been great, it would have touched him to pain more than to pleasure. But the cold charm in her eyes had spread, as she hovered before him, to all the rest of her person, so that it was, for the minute, almost like a recovery of youth. He couldn't pity her for that; he could only take her as she showed—as capable still of helping him. It was as if, at the same time, her light might at any instant go out; wherefore he must make the most of it. There passed before him with intensity the three or four things he wanted most to know; but the question that came of itself to his lips really covered the others. "Then tell me if I shall consciously suffer."

She promptly shook her head. "Never!"

It confirmed the authority he imputed to her, and it produced on him an extraordinary effect. "Well, what's better than that? Do you call that the worst?"

"You think nothing is better?" she asked.

She seemed to mean something so special that he again sharply wondered, though still with the dawn of a prospect of relief. "Why not, if one doesn't *know?*" After which, as their eyes, over his question, met in a silence, the dawn deepened and something to his purpose came, prodigiously, out of her very face. His own, as he took it in, suddenly flushed to the forehead, and he gasped with the force of a perception to which, on the instant, everything fitted. The sound of his gasp filled the air; then he became articulate. "I see—if I don't suffer!"

In her own look, however, was doubt. "You see what?"

"Why, what you mean—what you've always meant."

She again shook her head. "What I mean isn't what I've always meant. It's different."

"It's something new?"

She hesitated. "Something new. It's not what you think. I see what you think."

His divination drew breath then; only her correction might be wrong. "It isn't that I *am* a donkey?" he asked between faintness and grimness. "It isn't that it's all a mistake?"

"A mistake?" she pityingly echoed. *That* possibility, for her, he saw, would be monstrous; and if she guaranteed him the immunity from pain it would accordingly not be what she had in mind. "Oh, no," she declared; "it's nothing of that sort. You've been right."

Yet he couldn't help asking himself if she weren't, thus pressed, speaking but to save him. It seemed to him he should be most lost if his history should prove all a platitude. "Are you telling me the truth, so that I sha'n't have been a bigger idiot than I can bear to know? I *haven't* lived with a vain imagination, in the most besotted illusion? I haven't waited but to see the door shut in my face?"

She shook her head again. "However the case stands *that* isn't the truth. Whatever the reality, it *is* a reality. The door isn't shut. The door's open," said May Bartram.

"Then something's to come?"

She waited once again, always with her cold, sweet eyes on him. "It's never too late." She had, with her gliding step, diminished the distance between them, and she stood nearer to him, close to him, a minute, as if still full of the unspoken. Her movement might have been for some finer emphasis of what she was at once hesitating and deciding to say. He had been standing by the chimney-piece, fireless and sparely adorned, a small, perfect old French clock and two morsels of rosy Dresden constituting all its furniture; and her hand grasped the shelf while she kept him waiting, grasped it a little as for support and encouragement. She only kept him waiting, however; that is he only waited. It had become suddenly, from her movement and attitude, beautiful and vivid to him that she had something more to give him; her wasted face delicately shone with it, and it glittered, almost as with the white lustre of silver, in her expression. She was right, incontestably, for what he saw in her face was the truth, and strangely, without consequence, while their talk of it as dreadful was still in the air, she appeared to present it as inordinately soft. This, prompting bewilderment, made him but gape the more gratefully for her revelation, so that they continued for some minutes silent, her face shining at him, her contact imponderably pressing, and his stare all kind, but all expectant. The end, none the less, was that what he had expected failed to sound. Something else took place instead, which seemed to consist at first in the mere closing of her eyes. She gave way at the same instant to a slow, fine shudder, and though he remained staring—though he stared, in fact, but the harder—she turned off and regained her chair. It was the end of what she had been intending, but it left him thinking only of that.

"Well, you don't say——?"

She had touched in her passage a bell near the chimney and had sunk back, strangely pale. "I'm afraid I'm too ill."

"Too ill to tell me?" It sprang up sharp to him, and almost to his lips, the fear that she would die without giving him light. He checked himself in time from so expressing his question, but she answered as if she had heard the words.

"Don't you know—now?"

" 'Now'——?" She had spoken as if something that had made a difference had come up within the moment. But her maid, quickly obedient to her bell, was already with them. "I know nothing." And he was afterwards to say to himself that he must have spoken with odious impatience, such an impatience as to show that, supremely disconcerted, he washed his hands of the whole question.

"Oh!" said May Bartram.

"Are you in pain?" he asked, as the woman went to her.

"No," said May Bartram.

Her maid, who had put an arm round her as if to take her to her room, fixed on him eyes that appealingly contradicted her; in spite of which, however, he showed once more his mystification. "What then has happened?"

She was once more, with her companion's help, on her feet, and, feeling withdrawal imposed on him, he had found, blankly, his hat and gloves and had reached the door. Yet he waited for her answer. "What *was* to," she said.

V

HE came back the next day, but she was then unable to see him, and as it was literally the first time this had occurred in the long stretch of their acquaintance he turned away, defeated and sore, almost angry—or feeling at least that such a break in their custom was really the beginning of the end— and wandered alone with his thoughts, especially with one of them that he was unable to keep down. She was dying, and he would lose her; she was dying, and his life would end. He stopped in the park, into which he had passed, and stared before him at his recurrent doubt. Away from her the doubt pressed again; in her presence he had believed her, but as he felt his forlornness he threw himself into the explanation that, nearest at hand, had most of a miserable warmth for him and least of a cold torment. She had deceived him to save him—to put him off with something in which he should be able to rest. What could the thing that was to happen to him be, after all, but just this thing that had begun to happen? Her dying, her death, his consequent solitude—*that* was what he had figured as the beast in the jungle, that was what had been in the lap of the gods. He had had her word for it as he left her; for what else, on earth, could she have meant? It wasn't a thing of a monstrous order; not a fate rare and distinguished; not a stroke of fortune that overwhelmed and immortalised; it had only the stamp of the common doom. But poor Marcher, at this hour, judged the common doom sufficient. It would serve his turn, and even as the consummation of infinite waiting he would bend his pride to accept it. He sat down on a bench in the twilight. He hadn't been a fool. Something had *been*, as she had said, to come. Before he rose indeed it had quite struck him that the final fact really matched with the long avenue through which he had had to reach it. As sharing his suspense, and as giving herself all, giving her life, to bring it to an end, she had come with him every step of the way. He had lived by her aid, and to leave her behind would be cruelly, damnably to miss her. What could be more overwhelming than that?

Well, he was to know within the week, for though she kept him a while at bay, left him restless and wretched during a series of days on each of which he asked about her only again to have to turn away, she ended his trial by receiving him where she had always received him. Yet she had been brought out at some hazard into the presence of so many of the things that were, consciously, vainly, half their past, and there was scant service left in the gentleness of her mere desire, all too visible, to check his obsession and wind up his long trouble. That was clearly what she wanted; the one thing more, for her own peace, while she could still put out her hand. He was so affected by her state that, once seated by her chair, he was moved to let everything go; it was she herself therefore who brought him back, took up again, before she dismissed him, her last word of the other time. She showed how she wished to leave their affair in order. "I'm not sure you understood. You've nothing to wait for more. It *has* come."

Oh, how he looked at her! "Really?"

"Really."

"The thing that, as you said, *was* to?"

"The thing that we began in our youth to watch for."

Face to face with her once more he believed her; it was a claim to which he had so abjectly little to oppose. "You mean that it has come as a positive, definite occurrence, with a name and a date?"

"Positive. Definite. I don't know about the 'name,' but, oh, with a date!"

He found himself again too helplessly at sea. "But come in the night—come and passed me by?"

May Bartram had her strange, faint smile. "Oh no, it hasn't passed you by!"

"But if I haven't been aware of it, and it hasn't touched me——?"

"Ah, your not being aware of it," and she seemed to hesitate an instant to deal with this—"your not being aware of it is the strangeness *in* the strangeness. It's the wonder *of* the wonder." She spoke as with the softness almost of a sick child, yet now at last, at the end of all, with the perfect straightness of a sibyl. She visibly knew that she knew, and the effect on him was of something co-ordinate, in its high character, with the law that had ruled him. It was the true voice of the law; so on her lips would the law itself have sounded. "It *has* touched you," she went on. "It has done its office. It has made you all its own."

"So utterly without my knowing it?"

"So utterly without your knowing it." His hand, as he leaned to her, was on the arm of her chair, and, dimly smiling always now, she placed her own on it. "It's enough if *I* know it."

"Oh!" he confusedly sounded, as she herself of late so often had done.

"What I long ago said is true. You'll never know now, and I think you ought to be content. You've *had* it," said May Bartram.

"But had what?"

"Why, what was to have marked you out. The proof of your law. It has acted. I'm too glad," she then bravely added, "to have been able to see what it's *not*."

He continued to attach his eyes to her, and with the sense that it was all beyond him, and that *she* was too, he would still have sharply challenged her, had he not felt it an abuse of her weakness to do more than take devoutly what she gave him, take it as hushed as to a revelation. If he did speak, it was out of the foreknowledge of his loneliness to come. "If you're glad of what it's 'not,' it might then have been worse?"

She turned her eyes away, she looked straight before her with which, after a moment: "Well, you know our fears."

He wondered. "It's something then we never feared?"

On this, slowly, she turned to him. "Did we ever dream, with all our dreams, that we should sit and talk of it thus?"

He tried for a little to make out if they had; but it was as if their dreams, numberless enough, were in solution in some thick, cold mist, in which thought lost itself. "It might have been that we couldn't talk?"

"Well"—she did her best for him—"not from this side. This, you see," she said, "is the *other* side."

"I think," poor Marcher returned, "that all sides are the same to me." Then, however, as she softly shook her head in correction: "We mightn't, as it were, have got across——?"

"To where we are—no. We're *here*"—she made her weak emphasis.

"And much good does it do us!" was her friend's frank comment.

"It does us the good it can. It does us the good that *it* isn't here. It's past. It's behind," said May Bartram. "Before——" but her voice dropped.

He had got up, not to tire her, but it was hard to combat his yearning. She after all told him nothing but that his light had failed—which he knew well enough without her. "Before——?" he blankly echoed.

"Before, you see, it was always to *come*. That kept it present."

"Oh, I don't care what comes now! Besides," Marcher added, "it seems to me I liked it better present, as you say, than I can like it absent with *your* absence."

"Oh, mine!"—and her pale hands made light of it.

"With the absence of everything." He had a dreadful sense of standing there before her for—so far as anything but this proved, this bottomless drop was concerned—the last time of their life. It rested on him with a weight he felt he could scarce bear, and this weight it apparently was that still pressed out what remained in him of speakable protest. "I believe you; but I can't begin to pretend I understand. *Nothing*, for me, is past; nothing *will* pass until I pass myself, which I pray my stars may be as soon as possible. Say, however," he added, "that I've eaten my cake, as you contend, to the last crumb—how can the thing I've never felt at all be the thing I was marked out to feel?"

She met him, perhaps, less directly, but she met him unperturbed. "You take your 'feelings' for granted. You were to suffer your fate. That was not necessarily to know it."

"How in the world—when what is such knowledge but suffering?"

She looked up at him a while, in silence. "No—you don't understand."

"I suffer," said John Marcher.

"Don't, don't!"

"How can I help at least *that?*"

"*Don't!*" May Bartram repeated.

She spoke it in a tone so special, in spite of her weakness, that he stared an instant—stared as if some light, hitherto hidden, had shimmered across his vision. Darkness again closed over it, but the gleam had already become for him an idea. "Because I haven't the right——?"

"Don't *know*—when you needn't," she mercifully urged. "You needn't—for we shouldn't."

"Shouldn't?" If he could but know what she meant!

"No—it's too much."

"Too much?" he still asked—but with a mystification that was the next moment, of a sudden, to give way. Her words, if they meant something, affected him in this light—the light also of her wasted face—as meaning *all*, and the sense of what knowledge had been for herself came over him with a rush which broke through into a question. "Is it of that, then, you're dying?"

She but watched him, gravely at first, as if to see, with this, where he was, and she might have seen something, or feared something, that moved her sympathy. "I would live for you still—if I could." Her eyes closed for a little, as if, withdrawn into herself, she were, for a last time, trying. "But I can't!" she said as she raised them again to take leave of him.

She couldn't indeed, as but too promptly and sharply appeared, and he had no vision of her after this that was anything but darkness and doom. They had parted forever in that strange talk; access to her chamber of pain, rigidly guarded, was almost wholly forbidden him; he was feeling now moreover, in the face of doctors, nurses, the two or three relatives attracted doubtless by the presumption of what she had to "leave," how few were the rights, as they were called in such cases, that he had to put forward, and how odd it might even

seem that their intimacy shouldn't have given him more of
them. The stupidest fourth cousin had more, even though she
had been nothing in such a person's life. She had been a feature
of features in *his*, for what else was it to have been so indispensable? Strange beyond saying were the ways of existence,
baffling for him the anomaly of his lack, as he felt it to be, of
producible claim. A woman might have been, as it were,
everything to him, and it might yet present him in no connection that anyone appeared obliged to recognise. If this was
the case in these closing weeks it was the case more sharply
on the occasion of the last offices rendered, in the great grey
London cemetery, to what had been mortal, to what had been
precious, in his friend. The concourse at her grave was not
numerous, but he saw himself treated as scarce more nearly
concerned with it than if there had been a thousand others.
He was in short from this moment face to face with the fact
that he was to profit extraordinarily little by the interest May
Bartram had taken in him. He couldn't quite have said what
he expected, but he had somehow not expected this approach
to a double privation. Not only had her interest failed him,
but he seemed to feel himself unattended—and for a reason
he couldn't sound—by the distinction, the dignity, the propriety, if nothing else, of the man markedly bereaved. It was
as if, in the view of society, he had not *been* markedly bereaved, as if there still failed some sign or proof of it, and as if,
none the less, his character could never be affirmed, nor the
deficiency ever made up. There were moments, as the weeks
went by, when he would have liked, by some almost aggres-
sive act, to take his stand on the intimacy of his loss, in order
that it *might* be questioned and his retort, to the relief of his
spirit, so recorded; but the moments of an irritation more
helpless followed fast on these, the moments during which,
turning things over with a good conscience but with a bare
horizon, he found himself wondering if he oughtn't to have
begun, so to speak, further back.

He found himself wondering indeed at many things, and this last speculation had others to keep it company. What could he have done, after all, in her lifetime, without giving them both, as it were, away? He couldn't have made it known she was watching him, for that would have published the superstition of the Beast. This was what closed his mouth now —now that the Jungle had been threshed to vacancy and that the Beast had stolen away. It sounded too foolish and too flat; the difference for him in this particular, the extinction in his life of the element of suspense, was such in fact as to surprise him. He could scarce have said what the effect resembled; the abrupt cessation, the positive prohibition, of music perhaps, more than anything else, in some place all adjusted and all accustomed to sonority and to attention. If he could at any rate have conceived lifting the veil from his image at some moment of the past (what had he done, after all, if not lift it to *her?*), so to do this to-day, to talk to people at large of the jungle cleared and confide to them that he now felt it as safe, would have been not only to see them listen as to a good-wife's tale, but really to hear himself tell one. What it presently came to in truth was that poor Marcher waded through his beaten grass, where no life stirred, where no breath sounded, where no evil eye seemed to gleam from a possible lair, very much as if vaguely looking for the Beast, and still more as if missing it. He walked about in an existence that had grown strangely more spacious, and, stopping fitfully in places where the undergrowth of life struck him as closer, asked himself yearningly, wondered secretly, and sorely, if it would have lurked here or there. It would have at all events *sprung;* what was at least complete was his belief in the truth itself of the assurance given him. The change from his old sense to his new was absolute and final: what was to happen *had* so absolutely and finally happened that he was as little able to know a fear for his future as to know a hope; so absent in short was any question of anything still to come. He was to live entirely with the other question, that of his unidentified past, that of his having to see his fortune impenetrably muffled and masked.

The torment of this vision became then his occupation; he couldn't perhaps have consented to live but for the possibility of guessing. She had told him, his friend, not to guess; she had forbidden him, so far as he might, to know, and she had even in a sort denied the power in him to learn: which were so many things, precisely, to deprive him of rest. It wasn't that he wanted, he argued for fairness, that anything that had happened to him should happen over again; it was only that he shouldn't, as an anticlimax, have been taken sleeping so sound as not to be able to win back by an effort of thought the lost stuff of consciousness. He declared to himself at moments that he would either win it back or have done with consciousness for ever; he made this idea his one motive, in fine, made it so much his passion that none other, to compare with it, seemed ever to have touched him. The lost stuff of consciousness became thus for him as a strayed or stolen child to an unappeasable father; he hunted it up and down very much as if he were knocking at doors and inquiring of the police. This was the spirit in which, inevitably, he set himself to travel; he started on a journey that was to be as long as he could make it; it danced before him that, as the other side of the globe couldn't possibly have less to say to him, it might, by a possibility of suggestion, have more. Before he quitted London, however, he made a pilgrimage to May Bartram's grave, took his way to it through the endless avenues of the grim suburban necropolis, sought it out in the wilderness of tombs, and, though he had come but for the renewal of the act of farewell, found himself, when he had at last stood by it, beguiled into long intensities. He stood for an hour, powerless to turn away and yet powerless to penetrate the darkness of death; fixing with his eyes her inscribed name and date, beating his forehead against the fact of the secret they kept, drawing his breath, while he waited as if, in pity of him, some sense would rise from the stones. He kneeled on the stones, however, in vain; they kept what they concealed; and if the face of the tomb did become a face for him it was because her two names were like a pair of eyes that didn't know him. He gave them a last long look, but no palest light broke.

VI

H E stayed away, after this, for a year; he visited the depths of Asia, spending himself on scenes of romantic interest, of superlative sanctity; but what was present to him everywhere was that for a man who had known what *he* had known the world was vulgar and vain. The state of mind in which he had lived for so many years shone out to him, in reflection, as a light that coloured and refined, a light beside which the glow of the East was garish, cheap and thin. The terrible truth was that he had lost—with everything else—a distinction as well; the things he saw couldn't help being common when he had become common to look at them. He was simply now one of them himself—he was in the dust, without a peg for the sense of difference; and there were hours when, before the temples of gods and the sepulchres of kings, his spirit turned, for nobleness of association, to the barely discriminated slab in the London suburb. That had become for him, and more intensely with time and distance, his one witness of a past glory. It was all that was left to him for proof or pride, yet the past glories of Pharaohs were nothing to him as he thought of it. Small wonder then that he came back to it on the morrow of his return. He was drawn there this time as irresistibly as the other, yet with a confidence, almost, that was doubtless the effect of the many months that had elapsed. He had lived, in spite of himself, into his change of feeling, and in wandering over the earth had wandered, as might be said, from the

circumference to the centre of his desert. He had settled to his
safety and accepted perforce his extinction; figuring to himself, with some colour, in the likeness of certain little old men
he remembered to have seen, of whom, all meagre and wizened
as they might look, it was related that they had in their time
fought twenty duels or been loved by ten princesses. They
indeed had been wondrous for others, while he was but
wondrous for himself; which, however, was exactly the cause
of his haste to renew the wonder by getting back, as he might
put it, into his own presence. That had quickened his steps and
checked his delay. If his visit was prompt it was because he
had been separated so long from the part of himself that alone
he now valued.

It is accordingly not false to say that he reached his goal
with a certain elation and stood there again with a certain
assurance. The creature beneath the sod *knew* of his rare experience, so that, strangely now, the place had lost for him its
mere blankness of expression. It met him in mildness—not, as
before, in mockery; it wore for him the air of conscious greeting that we find, after absence, in things that have closely belonged to us and which seem to confess of themselves to the
connection. The plot of ground, the graven tablet, the tended
flowers affected him so as belonging to him that he quite felt
for the hour like a contented landlord reviewing a piece of
property. Whatever had happened—well, had happened. He
had not come back this time with the vanity of that question,
his former worrying, "What, *what?*" now practically so spent.
Yet he would, none the less, never again so cut himself off
from the spot; he would come back to it every month, for if
he did nothing else by its aid he at least held up his head. It
thus grew for him, in the oddest way, a positive resource;
he carried out his idea of periodical returns, which took their
place at last among the most inveterate of his habits. What it
all amounted to, oddly enough, was that, in his now so
simplified world, this garden of death gave him the few square

feet of earth on which he could still most live. It was as if, being nothing anywhere else for anyone, nothing even for himself, he were just everything here, and if not for a crowd of witnesses, or indeed for any witness but John Marcher, then by clear right of the register that he could scan like an open page. The open page was the tomb of his friend, and *there* were the facts of the past, there the truth of his life, there the backward reaches in which he could lose himself. He did this, from time to time, with such effect that he seemed to wander through the old years with his hand in the arm of a companion who was, in the most extraordinary manner, his other, his younger self; and to wander, which was more extraordinary yet, round and round a third presence—not wandering she, but stationary, still, whose eyes, turning with his revolution, never ceased to follow him, and whose seat was his point, so to speak, of orientation. Thus in short he settled to live— feeding only on the sense that he once *had* lived, and dependent on it not only for a support but for an identity.

It sufficed him, in its way, for months, and the year elapsed; it would doubtless even have carried him further but for an accident, superficially slight, which moved him, in a quite other direction, with a force beyond any of his impressions of Egypt or of India. It was a thing of the merest chance—the turn, as he afterwards felt, of a hair, though he was indeed to live to believe that if light hadn't come to him in this particular fashion it would still have come in another. He was to live to believe this, I say, though he was not to live, I may not less definitely mention, to do much else. We allow him at any rate the benefit of the conviction, struggling up for him at the end, that, whatever might have happened or not happened, he would have come round of himself to the light. The incident of an autumn day had put the match to the train laid from of old by his misery. With the light before him he knew that even of late his ache had only been smothered. It was strangely drugged, but it throbbed; at the touch it began to bleed. And the touch, in the event, was the face of a fellow-mortal. This face, one grey afternoon when the leaves were thick in the alleys, looked into Marcher's own, at the cemetery, with an expression like the cut of a blade. He felt it, that is, so deep down that he winced at the steady thrust. The person who so mutely assaulted him was a figure he had noticed, on reaching his own goal, absorbed by a grave a short distance away, a grave apparently fresh, so that the emotion of the visitor would probably match it for frankness. This fact alone forbade further attention, though during the time he stayed he remained vaguely conscious of his neighbour, a middle-aged man apparently, in mourning, whose bowed back, among the clustered monuments and mortuary yews, was constantly presented. Marcher's theory that these were elements in contact with which he himself revived, had suffered, on this occasion, it may be granted, a sensible though inscrutable check. The autumn day was dire for him as none had recently been, and he rested with a heaviness he had not yet known on the low stone table that bore May Bartram's name. He rested without power to move, as if some spring in him, some spell vouchsafed, had suddenly been broken forever. If he could have done that moment as he wanted he would simply have stretched himself on the slab that was ready to take him, treating it as a place prepared to receive his last sleep. What in all the wide world had he now to keep awake for? He stared before him with the question, and it was then that, as one of the cemetery walks passed near him, he caught the shock of the face.

His neighbour at the other grave had withdrawn, as he himself, with force in him to move, would have done by now, and was advancing along the path on his way to one of the gates. This brought him near, and his pace was slow, so that —and all the more as there was a kind of hunger in his look— the two men were for a minute directly confronted. Marcher felt him on the spot as one of the deeply stricken—a perception so sharp that nothing else in the picture lived for it, neither his dress, his age, nor his presumable character and class; nothing lived but the deep ravage of the features that he showed. He *showed* them—that was the point; he was moved, as he passed, by some impulse that was either a signal for sympathy or, more possibly, a challenge to another sorrow. He might already have been aware of our friend, might, at some previous hour, have noticed in him the smooth habit of the scene, with which the state of his own senses so scantly consorted, and might thereby have been stirred as by a kind of overt discord. What Marcher was at all events conscious of was, in the first place, that the image of scarred passion presented to him was conscious too—of something that profaned the air; and, in the second, that, roused, startled, shocked, he was yet the next moment looking after it, as it went, with envy. The most extraordinary thing that had happened to him—though he had given that name to other matters as well—took place, after his immediate vague stare, as a consequence of this impression. The stranger passed, but the raw glare of his grief remained, making our friend wonder in pity what wrong, what wound it expressed, what injury not to be healed. What had the man *had* to make him, by the loss of it, so bleed and yet live?

Something—and this reached him with a pang—that *he*, John Marcher, hadn't; the proof of which was precisely John Marcher's arid end. No passion had ever touched him, for this was what passion meant; he had survived and maundered and pined, but where had been *his* deep ravage? The extraordinary thing we speak of was the sudden rush of the result of this question. The sight that had just met his eyes named to him, as in letters of quick flame, something he had utterly, insanely missed, and what he had missed made these things a train of fire, made them mark themselves in an anguish of inward throbs. He had seen *outside* of his life, not learned it within, the way a woman was mourned when she had been loved for herself; such was the force of his conviction of the meaning of the stranger's face, which still flared for him like a smoky torch. It had not come to him, the knowledge, on the wings of experience; it had brushed him, jostled him, upset him, with the disrespect of chance, the insolence of an accident. Now that the illumination had begun, however, it blazed to the zenith, and what he presently stood there gazing at was the sounded void of his life. He gazed, he drew breath, in pain; he turned in his dismay, and, turning, he had before him in sharper incision than ever the open page of his story. The name on the table smote him as the passage of his neighbour had done, and what it said to him, full in the face, was that *she* was what he had missed. This was the awful thought, the answer to all the past, the vision at the dread clearness of which he turned as cold as the stone beneath him. Everything fell together, confessed, explained, overwhelmed; leaving him most of all stupefied at the blindness he had cherished. The fate he had been marked for he had met with a vengeance— he had emptied the cup to the lees; he had been the man of his time, *the* man, to whom nothing on earth was to have happened. That was the rare stroke—that was his visitation. So he saw it, as we say, in pale horror, while the pieces fitted and fitted. So *she* had seen it, while he didn't, and so she served at this hour to drive the truth home. It was the truth, vivid and monstrous, that all the while he had waited the wait was itself his portion. This the companion of his vigil had at a given moment perceived, and she had then offered him the chance to baffle his doom. One's doom, however, was never baffled, and on the day she had told him that his own had come down she had seen him but stupidly stare at the escape she offered him.

The escape would have been to love her; then, *then* he would have lived. *She* had lived—who could say now with what passion?—since she had loved him for himself; whereas he had never thought of her (ah, how it hugely glared at him!)

but in the chill of his egotism and the light of her use. Her spoken words came back to him, and the chain stretched and stretched. The beast had lurked indeed, and the beast, at its hour, had sprung; it had sprung in that twilight of the cold April when, pale, ill, wasted, but all beautiful, and perhaps even then recoverable, she had risen from her chair to stand before him and let him imaginably guess. It had sprung as he didn't guess; it had sprung as she hopelessly turned from him, and the mark, by the time he left her, had fallen where it *was* to fall. He had justified his fear and achieved his fate; he had failed, with the last exactitude, of all he was to fail of; and a moan now rose to his lips as he remembered she had prayed he mightn't know. This horror of waking—*this* was knowledge, knowledge under the breath of which the very tears in his eyes seemed to freeze. Through them, none the less, he tried to fix it and hold it; he kept it there before him so that he might feel the pain. That at least, belated and bitter, had something of the taste of life. But the bitterness suddenly sickened him, and it was as if, horribly, he saw, in the truth, in the cruelty of his image, what had been appointed and done. He saw the Jungle of his life and saw the lurking Beast; then, while he looked, perceived it, as by a stir of the air, rise, huge and hideous, for the leap that was to settle him. His eyes darkened—it was close; and, instinctively turning, in his hallucination, to avoid it, he flung himself, on his face, on the tomb.

THE BIRTHPLACE

I

IT seemed to them at first, the offer, too good to be true, and their friend's letter, addressed to them to feel, as he said, the ground, to sound them as to inclinations and possibilities, had almost the effect of a brave joke at their expense. Their friend, Mr Grant-Jackson, a highly preponderant, pushing person, great in discussion and arrangement, abrupt in overture, un-expected, if not perverse, in attitude, and almost equally acclaimed and objected to in the wide midland region to which he had taught, as the phrase was, the size of his foot— their friend had launched his bolt quite out of the blue and had thereby so shaken them as to make them fear almost more than hope. The place had fallen vacant by the death of one of the two ladies, mother and daughter, who had discharged its duties for fifteen years; the daughter was staying on alone, to accommodate, but had found, though extremely mature, an opportunity of marriage that involved retirement, and the question of the new incumbents was not a little pressing. The want thus determined was of a united couple of some sort, of the right sort, a pair of educated and competent sisters pos-sibly preferred, but a married pair having its advantages if other qualifications were marked. Applicants, candidates, be-siegers of the door of everyone supposed to have a voice in the matter, were already beyond counting, and Mr Grant-Jackson, who was in his way diplomatic and whose voice, though not perhaps of the loudest, possessed notes of insis-tence, had found his preference fixing itself on some person or brace of persons who had been decent and dumb. The Gedges appeared to have struck him as waiting in silence—though absolutely, as happened, no busybody had brought them, far away in the north, a hint either of bliss or of danger; and the happy spell, for the rest, had obviously been wrought in him by a remembrance which, though now scarcely fresh, had never before borne any such fruit.

Morris Gedge had for a few years, as a young man, carried on a small private school of the order known as preparatory, and had happened then to receive under his roof the small son of the great man, who was not at that time so great. The little boy, during an absence of his parents from England, had been dangerously ill, so dangerously that they had been recalled in haste, though with inevitable delays, from a far country— they had gone to America, with the whole continent and the great sea to cross again—and had got back to find the child saved, but saved, as couldn't help coming to light, by the extreme devotion and perfect judgment of Mrs Gedge. Without children of her own, she had particularly attached herself to this tiniest and tenderest of her husband's pupils, and they had both dreaded as a dire disaster the injury to their little enterprise that would be caused by their losing him. Nervous, anxious, sensitive persons, with a pride—as they were for that matter well aware—above their position, never, at the best, to be anything but dingy, they had nursed him in terror and had brought him through in exhaustion. Exhaustion, as befell, had thus overtaken them early and had for one reason and another managed to assert itself as their permanent portion. The little boy's death would, as they said, have done for them, yet his recovery hadn't saved them; with which it was doubtless also part of a shy but stiff candour in them that they didn't regard themselves as having in a more indirect manner laid up treasure. Treasure was not to be, in any form whatever, of their dreams or of their waking sense; and the years that followed had limped under their weight, had now and then rather grievously stumbled, had even barely escaped laying them in the dust. The school had not prospered, had but dwindled to a close. Gedge's health had failed, and, still more, every sign in him of a capacity to publish himself as practical. He had tried several things, he had tried many,˙ but the final appearance was of their having tried him not less. They mostly, at the time I speak of, were trying his successors, while he found himself, with an effect of dull felicity that had come in this case from the mere postponement of change, in charge of the grey town-library of Blackport-on-Dwindle, all granite, fog and female fiction. This was a situation in which his general intelligence—acknowledged as his strong point—was doubtless conceived, around him, as feeling less of a strain than that mastery of particulars in which he was recognised as weak.

It was at Blackport-on-Dwindle that the silver shaft reached and pierced him; it was as an alternative to dispensing dog's-eared volumes the very titles of which, on the lips of innumerable glib girls, were a challenge to his temper, that the wardenship of so different a temple presented itself. The stipend named differed little from the slim wage at present paid him, but even had it been less the interest and the honour would have struck him as determinant. The shrine at which he was to preside—though he had always lacked occasion to approach it—figured to him as the most sacred known to the steps of men, the early home of the supreme poet, the Mecca of the English-speaking race. The tears came into his eyes sooner still than into his wife's while he looked about with her at their actual narrow prison, so grim with enlightenment, so ugly with industry, so turned away from any dream, so intolerable to any taste. He felt as if a window had opened into a great green woodland, a woodland that had a name, glorious, immortal, that was peopled with vivid figures, each of them renowned, and that gave out a murmur, deep as the sound of the sea, which was the rustle in forest shade of all the poetry, the beauty, the colour of life. It would be pro-digious that of this transfigured world *he* should keep the key.

No—he couldn't believe it, not even when Isabel, at sight of his face, came and helpfully kissed him. He shook his head with a strange smile. "We shan't get it. Why should we? It's perfect."

"If we don't he'll simply have been cruel; which is impossible when he has waited all this time to be kind." Mrs Gedge did believe—she *would;* since the wide doors of the world of poetry had suddenly pushed back for them it was in the form of poetic justice that they were first to know it. She had her faith in their patron; it was sudden, but it was now complete. "He remembers—that's all; and that's our strength."

"And what's *his?*" Gedge asked. "He may *want* to put us through, but that's a different thing from being able. What are our special advantages?"

"Well, that we're just the thing." Her knowledge of the needs of the case was, as yet, thanks to scant information, of the vaguest, and she had never, more than her husband, stood on the sacred spot; but she saw herself waving a nicely-gloved hand over a collection of remarkable objects and saying to a compact crowd of gaping, awe-struck persons: "And now, please, *this* way." She even heard herself meeting with promptness and decision an occasional inquiry from a visitor in whom audacity had prevailed over awe. She had been once, with a cousin, years before, to a great northern castle, and that was the way the housekeeper had taken them round. And it was not moreover, either, that she thought of herself as a housekeeper: she was well above that, and the wave of her hand wouldn't fail to be such as to show it. This, and much else, she summed up as she answered her mate. "Our special advantages are that you're a gentleman."

"Oh!" said Gedge, as if he had never thought of it, and yet as if too it were scarce worth thinking of.

"I see it all," she went on; "they've *had* the vulgar—they find they don't do. We're poor and we're modest, but anyone can see what we are."

Gedge wondered. "Do you mean——?" More modest
than she, he didn't know quite what she meant.

"We're refined. We know how to speak."

"Do we?"—he still, suddenly, wondered.

But she was, from the first, surer of everything than he;
so that when a few weeks more had elapsed and the shade of
uncertainty—though it was only a shade—had grown almost
to sicken him, her triumph was to come with the news that
they were fairly named. "We're on poor pay, though we
manage"—she had on the present occasion insisted on her
point. "But we're highly cultivated, and for them to get *that*,
don't you see? without getting too much with it in the way
of pretensions and demands, must be precisely their dream.
We've no social position, but we don't *mind* that we haven't,
do we? a bit; which is because we know the difference between realities and shams. We hold to reality, and that gives
us common sense, which the vulgar have less than anything,
and which yet must be wanted there, after all, as well as
anywhere else."

Her companion followed her, but musingly, as if his
horizon had within a few moments grown so great that he
was almost lost in it and required a new orientation. The
shining spaces surrounded him; the association alone gave a
nobler arch to the sky. "Allow that we hold also a little to the
romance. It seems to me that that's the beauty. We've missed
it all our life, and now it's come. We shall be at head-quarters
for it. We shall have our fill of it."

She looked at his face, at the effect in it of these prospects,
and her own lighted as if he had suddenly grown handsome.
"Certainly—we shall live as in a fairy-tale. But what I mean is
that we shall give, in a way—and so gladly—quite as much
as we get. With all the rest of it we're, for instance, neat."
Their letter had come to them at breakfast, and she picked a
fly out of the butter-dish. "It's the way we'll *keep* the place"
—with which she removed from the sofa to the top of the

cottage-piano a tin of biscuits that had refused to squeeze into the cupboard. At Blackport they were in lodgings—of the lowest description, she had been known, with a freedom felt by Blackport to be slightly invidious, to declare. The Birthplace—and that itself, after such a life, was exaltation—wouldn't be lodgings, since a house close beside it was set apart for the warden, a house joining on to it as a sweet old parsonage is often annexed to a quaint old church. It would all together be their home, and such a home as would make a little world that they would never want to leave. She dwelt on the gain, for that matter, to their income; as, obviously, though the salary was not a change for the better, the house, given them, would make all the difference. He assented to this, but absently, and she was almost impatient at the range of his thoughts. It was as if something, for him—the very swarm of them—veiled the view; and he presently, of himself, showed what it was.

"What I can't get over is its being such a man——!" He almost, from inward emotion, broke down.

"Such a man——?"

"Him, *him*, HIM——!" It was too much.

"Grant-Jackson? Yes, it's a surprise, but one sees how he has been meaning, all the while, the right thing by us."

"I mean *Him*," Gedge returned more coldly; "our becoming familiar and intimate—for that's what it will come to. We shall just live with Him."

"Of course—it *is* the beauty." And she added quite gaily: "The more we do the more we shall love Him."

"No doubt—but it's rather awful. The more we *know* Him," Gedge reflected, "the more we shall love Him. We don't as yet, you see, know Him so very tremendously."

"We do so quite as well, I imagine, as the sort of people they've had. And that probably isn't—unless you care, as we do—so awfully necessary. For there are the facts."

"Yes—there are the facts."

"I mean the principal ones. They're all that the people—the people who come—want."

"Yes—they must be all *they* want."

"So that they're all that those who've been in charge have needed to know."

"Ah," he said as if it were a question of honour, "*we* must know everything."

She cheerfully acceded: she had the merit, he felt, of keeping the case within bounds. "Everything. But about him personally," she added, "there isn't, is there? so very, very much."

"More, I believe, than there used to be. They've made discoveries."

It was a grand thought. "Perhaps *we* shall make some!"

"Oh, I shall be content to be a little better up in what has been done." And his eyes rested on a shelf of books, half of which, little worn but much faded, were of the florid "gift" order and belonged to the house. Of those among them that were his own most were common specimens of the reference sort, not excluding an old Bradshaw and a catalogue of the town-library. "We've not even a Set of our own. Of the Works," he explained in quick repudiation of the sense, perhaps more obvious, in which she might have taken it.

As a proof of their scant range of possessions this sounded almost abject, till the painful flush with which they met on the admission melted presently into a different glow. It was just for that kind of poorness that their new situation was, by its intrinsic charm, to console them. And Mrs Gedge had a happy thought. "Wouldn't the Library more or less have them?"

"Oh no, we've nothing of that sort: for what do you take us?" This, however, was but the play of Gedge's high spirits: the form both depression and exhilaration most frequently took with him being a bitterness on the subject of the literary taste of Blackport. No one was so deeply acquainted with it. It acted with him in fact as so lurid a sign of the future that the charm of the thought of removal was sharply enhanced by the prospect of escape from it. The institution he served didn't of course deserve the particular reproach into which his irony had flowered; and indeed if the several Sets in which the Works were present were a trifle dusty, the dust was a little his own fault. To make up for that now he had the vision of immediately giving his time to the study of them; he saw himself indeed, inflamed with a new passion, earnestly commenting and collating. Mrs Gedge, who had suggested that they ought, till their move should come, to read Him regularly of an evening—certain as they were to do it still more when in closer quarters with Him—Mrs Gedge felt also, in her degree, the spell; so that the very happiest time of their anxious life was perhaps to have been the series of lamp-light hours, after supper, in which, alternately taking the book, they declaimed, they almost performed, their beneficent author. He became speedily more than their author—their personal friend, their universal light, their final authority and divinity. Where in the world, they were already asking themselves, would they have been without him? By the time their appointment arrived in form their relation to him had immensely developed. It was amusing to Morris Gedge that he had so lately blushed for his ignorance, and he made this remark to his wife during the last hour they were able to give to their study, before proceeding, across half the country, to the scene of their romantic future. It was as if, in deep, close throbs, in cool after-waves that broke of a sudden and bathed his mind, all possession and comprehension and sympathy, all the truth and the life and the story, had come to him, and come, as the newspapers said, to stay. "It's absurd," he didn't hesitate to say, "to talk of our not 'knowing.' So far as we don't it's because we're donkeys. He's *in* the thing, over His ears, and the more we get into it the more we're with Him. I seem to myself at any rate," he declared, "to *see* Him in it as if He were painted on the wall."

"Oh, *doesn't* one rather, the dear thing? And don't you feel
where it is?" Mrs Gedge finely asked. "We see Him because
we love Him—that's what we do. How can we not, the old
darling—with what He's doing for us? There's no light"—
she had a sentding turn—"like true affection."

"Yes, I suppose that's it. And yet," her husband mused,
"I see, confound me, the faults."

"That's because you're so critical. You see them, but you
don't mind them. You see them, but you forgive them. You
mustn't mention them *there*. We shan't, you know, be there
for *that*."

"Dear no!" he laughed: "we'll chuck out anyone who
hints at them."

II

IF the sweetness of the preliminary months had been great,
great too, though almost excessive as agitation, was the
wonder of fairly being housed with Him, of treading day and
night in the footsteps He had worn, of touching the objects,
or at all events the surfaces, the substances, over which His
hands had played, which his arms, his shoulders had rubbed,
of breathing the air—or something not too unlike it—in which
His voice had sounded. They had had a little at first their
bewilderments, their disconcertedness; the place was both
humbler and grander than they had exactly prefigured, more
at once of a cottage and of a museum, a little more archaically
bare and yet a little more richly official. But the sense was
strong with them that the point of view, for the inevitable ease
of the connection, patiently, indulgently awaited them; in
addition to which, from the first evening, after closing-hour,
when the last blank pilgrim had gone, the mere spell, the
mystic presence—as if they had had it quite to themselves—

were all they could have desired. They had received, by Grant-Jackson's care and in addition to a table of instructions and admonitions by the number, and in some particulars by the nature, of which they found themselves slightly depressed, various little guides, handbooks, travellers' tributes, literary memorials and other catch-penny publications, which, however, were to be for the moment swallowed up in the interesting episode of the induction or initiation appointed for them in advance at the hands of several persons whose connection with the establishment was, as superior to their own, still more official, and at those in especial of one of the ladies who had for so many years borne the brunt. About the instructions from above, about the shilling books and the well-known facts and the full-blown legend, the supervision, the subjection, the submission, the view as of a cage in which he should circulate and a groove in which he should slide, Gedge had preserved a certain play of mind; but all power of reaction appeared suddenly to desert him in the presence of his so visibly competent predecessor and as an effect of her good offices. He had not the resource, enjoyed by his wife, of seeing himself, with impatience, attired in black silk of a make characterised by just the right shade of austerity; so that this firm, smooth, expert and consummately respectable middle-aged person had him somehow, on the whole ground, completely at her mercy.

It was evidently something of a rueful moment when, as a lesson—she being for the day or two still in the field—he accepted Miss Putchin's suggestion of "going round" with her and with the successive squads of visitors she was there to deal with. He appreciated her method—he saw there had to *be* one; he admired her as succinct and definite; for there were the facts, as his wife had said at Blackport, and they were to be disposed of in the time; yet he felt like a very little boy as he dangled, more than once, with Mrs Gedge, at the tail of the human comet. The idea had been that they should, by this attendance, more fully embrace the possible accidents and incidents, as it were, of the relation to the great public in which they were to find themselves; and the poor man's excited perception of the great public rapidly became such as to resist any diversion meaner than that of the admirable manner of their guide. It wandered from his gaping companions to that of the priestess in black silk, whom he kept asking himself if either he or Isabel could hope by any possibility ever remotely to resemble; then it bounded restlessly back to the numerous persons who revealed to him, as it had never yet been revealed, the happy power of the simple to hang upon the lips of the wise. The great thing seemed to be —and quite surprisingly—that the business was easy and the strain, which as a strain they had feared, moderate; so that he might have been puzzled, had he fairly caught himself in the act, by his recognising as the last effect of the impression an odd absence of the ability to rest in it, an agitation deep within him that vaguely threatened to grow. "It isn't, you see, so very complicated," the black silk lady seemed to throw off, with everything else, in her neat, crisp, cheerful way; in spite of which he already, the very first time—that is after several parties had been in and out and up and down—went so far as to wonder if there weren't more in it than she imagined. She was, so to speak, kindness itself—was all encouragement and reassurance; but it was just her slightly coarse redolence of these very things that, on repetition, before they parted, dimmed a little, as he felt, the light of his acknowledging smile. That, again, she took for a symptom of some pleading weakness in him—he could never be as brave as she; so that she wound up with a few pleasant words from the very depth of her experience. "You'll get into it, never fear—it will *come;* and then you'll feel as if you had never done anything else." He was afterwards to know that, on the spot, at this moment, he must have begun to wince a little at such a menace; that he might come to feel as if he had never done anything but what Miss Putchin did loomed for him, in germ, as a penalty to pay. The support she offered, none the less, continued to strike him; she put the whole thing on so sound a basis when she said: "You see they're so nice about it —they take such an interest. And they never do a thing they shouldn't. That was always everything to mother and me." "They," Gedge had already noticed, referred constantly and hugely, in the good woman's talk, to the millions who shuffled through the house; the pronoun in question was forever on her lips, the hordes it represented filled her consciousness, the addition of their numbers ministered to her glory. Mrs Gedge promptly met her. "It must be indeed delightful to see the effect on so many, and to feel that one may perhaps do some-thing to make it—well, permanent." But he was kept silent by his becoming more sharply aware that this was a new view, for him, of the reference made, that he had never thought of the quality of the place as derived from Them, but from Somebody Else, and that They, in short, seemed to have got into the way of crowding out Him. He found himself even a little resenting this for Him, which perhaps had something to do with the slightly invidious cast of his next inquiry.

"And are They always, as one might say—a—stupid?"

"Stupid!" She stared, looking as if no one *could* be such a thing in such a connection. No one had ever been anything but neat and cheerful and fluent, except to be attentive and unobjectionable and, so far as was possible, American.

"What I mean is," he explained, "is there any perceptible proportion that take an interest in Him?"

His wife stepped on his toe; she deprecated irony. But his mistake fortunately was lost on their friend. "That's just why they come, that they take such an interest. I sometimes think they take more than about anything else in the world." With which Miss Putchin looked about at the place. "It *is* pretty, don't you think, the way they've got it now?" This, Gedge saw, was a different "They"; it applied to the powers that were—the people who had appointed him, the governing, visiting Body, in respect to which he was afterwards to remark to Mrs Gedge that a fellow—it was the difficulty—didn't know "where to have her." His wife, at a loss, questioned at that moment the necessity of having her anywhere, and he said, good-humouredly, "Of course; it's all right." He was in fact content enough with the last touches their friend had given the picture. "There are many who know all about it when they come, and the Americans often are tremendously up. Mother and me really enjoyed"—it was her only slip— "the interest of the Americans. We've sometimes had ninety a day, and all wanting to see and hear everything. But you'll work them off; you'll see the way—it's all experience." She came back, for his comfort, to that. She came back also to other things: she did justice to the considerable class who arrived positive and primed. "There are those who know more about it than you do. But *that* only comes from their interest."

"Who know more about what?" Gedge inquired.

"Why, about the place. I mean they have their ideas—of what everything is, and *where* it is, and what it isn't, and where it *should* be. They do ask questions," she said, yet not so much in warning as in the complacency of being seasoned and sound; "and they're down on you when they think you go wrong. As if you ever could! You know too much," she sagaciously smiled; "or you *will*."

"Oh, you mustn't know *too* much, must you?" And Gedge now smiled as well. He knew, he thought, what he meant.

"Well, you must know as much as anybody else. I claim, at any rate, that I do," Miss Putchin declared. "They never really caught me."

"I'm very sure of *that*," Mrs Gedge said with an elation almost personal.

"Certainly," he added, "I don't want to be caught." She

rejoined that, in such a case, he would have *Them* down on him, and he saw that this time she meant the powers above. It quickened his sense of all the elements that were to reckon with, yet he felt at the same time that the powers above were not what he should most fear. "I'm glad," he observed, "that they ever ask questions; but I happened to notice, you know, that no one did to-day."

"Then you missed several—and no loss. There were three or four put to me too silly to remember. But of course they mostly *are* silly."

"You mean the questions?"

She laughed with all her cheer. "Yes, sir; I don't mean the answers."

Whereupon, for a moment snubbed and silent, he felt like one of the crowd. Then it made him slightly vicious. "I didn't know but you meant the people in general—till I remembered that I'm to understand from you that *they're* wise, only occasionally breaking down."

It was not really till then, he thought, that she lost patience; and he had had, much more than he meant no doubt, a cross-questioning air. "You'll see for yourself." Of which he was sure enough. He was in fact so ready to take this that she came round to full accommodation, put it frankly that every now and then they broke out—not the silly, oh no, the intensely inquiring. "We've had quite lively discussions, don't you know, about well-known points. They want it all *their* way, and I know the sort that are going to as soon as I see them. That's one of the things you do—you get to know the sorts. And if it's what you're afraid of—their taking you up," she was further gracious enough to say, "you needn't mind a bit. What *do* they know, after all, when for us it's our life? I've never moved an inch, because, you see, I shouldn't have been here if I didn't know where I was. No more will *you* be a year hence—you know what I mean, putting it impossibly—if *you* don't. I expect you do, in spite of your fancies." And she dropped once more to bed-rock. "There are the facts. Otherwise where would any of us be? That's all you've got to go upon. A person, however cheeky, can't have them *his* way just because he takes it into his head. There can only be *one* way, and," she gaily added as she took leave of them, "I'm sure it's quite enough!"

III

GEDGE not only assented eagerly—one way *was* quite enough if it were the right one—but repeated it, after this conversation, at odd moments, several times over to his wife. "There can only be one way, one way," he continued to remark—though indeed much as if it were a joke; till she asked him how many more he supposed she wanted. He failed to answer this question, but resorted to another repetition, "There are the facts, the facts," which, perhaps, however, he kept a little more to himself, sounding it at intervals in different parts of the house. Mrs Gedge was full of comment on their clever introductress, though not restrictively save in the matter of her speech, "Me and mother," and a general tone—which certainly was not their sort of thing. "I don't know," he said, "perhaps it comes with the place, since speaking in immortal verse doesn't seem to come. It must be, one seems to see, one thing or the other. I dare say that in a few months I shall also be at it—'me and the wife.'"

"Why not me and the missus at once?" Mrs Gedge resentfully inquired. "I don't think," she observed at another time, "that I quite know what's the matter with you."

"It's only that I'm excited, awfully excited—as I don't see how one can not be. You wouldn't have a fellow drop into this berth as into an appointment at the Post Office. Here on the spot it goes to my head; how can that be helped? But we shall live into it, and perhaps," he said with an implication of the other possibility that was doubtless but part of his fine ecstasy, "we shall live through it." The place acted on his imagination—how, surely, shouldn't it? And his imagination acted on his nerves, and these things together, with the general vividness and the new and complete immersion, made rest for him almost impossible, so that he could scarce go to bed at night and even during the first week more than once rose in the small hours to move about, up and down, with his lamp, standing, sitting, listening, wondering, in the stillness, as if positively to recover some echo, to surprise some secret, of the *genius loci*. He couldn't have explained it—and didn't in fact need to explain it, at least to himself, since the impulse simply held him and shook him; but the time after closing, the time above all after the people—Them, as he felt himself on the way to think of them, predominant, insistent, all in the foreground—brought him, or ought to have brought him, he seemed to see, nearer to the enshrined Presence, enlarged the opportunity for communion and intensified the sense of it. These nightly prowls, as he called them, were disquieting to his wife, who had no disposition to share in them, speaking with decision of the whole place as just the place to be forbidding after dark. She rejoiced in the distinctness, contiguous though it was, of their own little residence, where she trimmed the lamp and stirred the fire and heard the kettle sing, repairing the while the omissions of the small domestic who slept out; she foresaw herself with some promptness, drawing rather sharply the line between her own precinct and that in which the great spirit might walk. It would be with them, the great spirit, all day—even if indeed on her making that remark, and in just that form, to her husband, he replied with a queer "But will he though?" And she vaguely imaged the development of a domestic antidote after a while, precisely, in the shape of curtains more markedly drawn and everything most modern and lively, tea, "patterns," the newspapers, the female fiction itself that they had reacted against at Blackport, quite defiantly cultivated.

These possibilities, however, were all right, as her companion said it was, all the first autumn—they had arrived at summer's end; as if he were more than content with a special set of his own that he had access to from behind, passing out of their low door for the few steps between it and the Birthplace. With his lamp ever so carefully guarded, and his nursed keys that made him free of treasures, he crossed the dusky interval so often that she began to qualify it as a habit that "grew." She spoke of it almost as if he had taken to drink, and he humoured that view of it by confessing that the cup was strong. This had been in truth, altogether, his immediate sense of it; strange and deep for him the spell of silent sessions before familiarity and, to some small extent, disappointment had set in. The exhibitional side of the establishment had struck him, even on arrival, as qualifying too much its character; he scarce knew what he might best have looked for, but the three or four rooms bristled overmuch, in the garish light of day, with busts and relics, not even ostensibly always *His*, old prints and old editions, old objects fashioned in His likeness, furniture "of the time" and autographs of celebrated worshippers. In the quiet hours and the deep dusk, none the less, under the play of the shifted lamp and that of his own emotion, these things too recovered their advantage, ministered to the mystery, or at all events to the impression, seemed consciously to offer themselves as personal to the poet. Not one of them was really or unchallengeably so, but they had somehow, through long association, got, as Gedge always phrased it, into the secret, and it was about the secret he asked them while he restlessly wandered. It was not till months had elapsed that he found how little they had to tell him, and he was quite at his ease with them when he knew they were by no means where his sensibility had first placed them. They were as out of it as he; only, to do them justice, they had made him immensely feel. And still, too, it was not they who had done that most, since his sentiment had gradually cleared itself to deep, to deeper refinements.

The Holy of Holies of the Birthplace was the low, the sublime Chamber of Birth, sublime because, as the Americans usually said—unlike the natives they mostly found words—it was so pathetic; and pathetic because it was—well, really nothing else in the world that one could name, number or measure. It was as empty as a shell of which the kernel has withered, and contained neither busts nor prints nor early copies; it contained only the Fact—*the* Fact itself—which, as he stood sentient there at midnight, our friend, holding his breath, allowed to sink into him. He *had* to take it as the place where the spirit would most walk and where he would therefore be most to be met, with possibilities of recognition and reciprocity. He hadn't, most probably—*He* hadn't—much inhabited the room, as men weren't apt, as a rule, to convert to their later use and involve in their wider fortune the scene itself of their nativity. But as there were moments when, in the conflict of theories, the sole certainty surviving for the critic threatened to be that He had not—unlike other successful men—*not* been born, so Gedge, though little of a critic, clung to the square feet of space that connected themselves, however feebly, with the positive appearance. He was little of a critic—he was nothing of one; he hadn't pretended to the character before coming, nor come to pretend to it; also, luckily for him, he was seeing day by day how little use he could possibly have for it. It would be to him, the attitude of a high expert, distinctly a stumbling-block, and that he rejoiced, as the winter waned, in his ignorance, was one of the propositions he betook himself, in his odd manner, to enunciating to his wife. She denied it, for hadn't she, in the first place, been present, wasn't she still present, at his pious, his tireless study of everything connected with the subject?—so present that she had herself learned more about it than had ever seemed

likely. Then, in the second place, he was not to proclaim on
the housetops any point at which he might be weak, for who
knew, if it should get abroad that they were ignorant, what
effect might be produced——?

"On the attraction"—he took her up—"of the Show?"

He had fallen into the harmless habit of speaking of the
place as the "Show"; but she didn't mind this so much as to
be diverted by it. "No; on the attitude of the Body. You know
they're pleased with us, and I don't see why you should want
to spoil it. We got in by a tight squeeze—you know we've
had evidence of that, and that it was about as much as our
backers could manage. But we're proving a comfort to them,
and it's absurd of you to question your suitability to people
who were content with the Putchins."

"I don't, my dear," he returned, "question anything; but
if I should do so it would be precisely because of the greater
advantage constituted for the Putchins by the simplicity of
their spirit. They were kept straight by the quality of their
ignorance—which was denser even than mine. It was a mistake
in us, from the first, to have attempted to correct or to disguise
ours. We should have waited simply to become good parrots,
to learn our lesson—all on the spot here, so little of it is
wanted—and squawk it off."

"Ah, 'squawk,' love—what a word to use about Him!"

"It isn't about Him—nothing's about Him. None of Them
care tuppence about Him. The only thing They care about is
this empty shell—or rather, for it isn't empty, the extraneous,
preposterous stuffing of it."

"Preposterous?"—he made her stare with this as he had
not yet done.

At sight of her look, however—the gleam, as it might have
been, of a queer suspicion—he bent to her kindly and tapped
her cheek. "Oh, it's all right. We *must* fall back on the Putchins. Do you remember what she said?—'They've made it
so pretty now.' They *have* made it pretty, and it's a first-rate

show. It's a first-rate show and a first-rate billet, and He was a first-rate poet, and you're a first-rate woman—to put up so sweetly, I mean, with my nonsense."

She appreciated his domestic charm and she justified that part of his tribute which concerned herself. "I don't care how much of your nonsense you talk to me, so long as you *keep* it all for me and don't treat *Them* to it."

"The pilgrims? No," he conceded—"it isn't fair to Them. They mean well."

"What complaint have we, after all, to make of Them so long as They don't break off bits—as They used, Miss Putchin told us, so awfully—to conceal about Their Persons? She broke them at least of that."

"Yes," Gedge mused again; "I wish awfully she hadn't!"

"You would like the relics destroyed, removed? That's all that's wanted!"

"There *are* no relics."

"There won't be any soon, unless you take care." But he was already laughing, and the talk was not dropped without his having patted her once more. An impression or two, however, remained with her from it, as he saw from a question she asked him on the morrow. "What did you mean yesterday about Miss Putchin's simplicity—its keeping her 'straight'? Do you mean mentally?"

Her "mentally" was rather portentous, but he practically confessed. "Well, it kept her up. I mean," he amended, laughing, "it kept her down."

It was really as if she had been a little uneasy. "You consider there's a danger of your being affected? You know what I mean. Of its going to your head. You do know," she insisted as he said nothing. "Through your caring for him so. You'd certainly be right in that case about its having been a mistake for you to plunge so deep." And then as his listening without reply, though with his look a little sad for her, might have denoted that, allowing for extravagance of statement, he

saw there was something in it: "Give up your prowls. Keep
it for daylight. Keep it for *Them*."

"Ah," he smiled, "if one could! My prowls," he added,
"are what I most enjoy. They're the only time, as I've told
you before, that I'm really with *Him*. Then I don't see the
place. He isn't the place."

"I don't care for what you 'don't' see," she replied with
vivacity; "the question is of what you do see."

Well, if it was, he waited before meeting it. "Do you know
what I sometimes do?" And then as she waited too: "In the
Birthroom there, when I look in late, I often put out my light.
That makes it better."

"Makes what——?"

"Everything."

"What is it then you see in the dark?"

"Nothing!" said Morris Gedge.

"And what's the pleasure of that?"

"Well, what the American ladies say. It's so fascinating."

IV

THE autumn was brisk, as Miss Putchin had told them it
would be, but business naturally fell off with the winter
months and the short days. There was rarely an hour indeed
without a call of some sort, and they were never allowed to
forget that they kept the shop in all the world, as they might
say, where custom was least fluctuating. The seasons told on
it, as they tell upon travel, but no other influence, consideration or convulsion to which the population of the globe is
exposed. This population, never exactly in simultaneous
hordes, but in a full, swift and steady stream, passed through
the smoothly-working mill and went, in its variety of degrees
duly impressed and edified, on its artless way. Gedge gave

himself up, with much ingenuity of spirit, to trying to keep in relation with it; having even at moments, in the early time, glimpses of the chance that the impressions gathered from so rare an opportunity for contact with the general mind might prove as interesting as anything else in the connection. Types, classes, nationalities, manners, diversities of behaviour, modes of seeing, feeling, of expression, would pass before him and become for him, after a fashion, the experience of an un-travelled man. His journeys had been short and saving, but poetic justice again seemed inclined to work for him in placing him just at the point in all Europe perhaps where the con-fluence of races was thickest. The theory, at any rate, carried him on, operating helpfully for the term of his anxious begin-nings and gilding in a manner—it was the way he characterised the case to his wife—the somewhat stodgy gingerbread of their daily routine. They had not known many people, and their visiting-list was small—which made it again poetic justice that they should be visited on such a scale. They dressed and were at home, they were under arms and received, and except for the offer of refreshment—and Gedge had his view that there would eventually be a *buffet* farmed out to a great firm—their hospitality would have made them princely if mere hospitality ever did. Thus they were launched, and it was interesting, and from having been ready to drop, origi-nally, with fatigue, they emerged even-winded and strong in the legs, as if they had had an Alpine holiday. This experience, Gedge opined, also represented, as a gain, a like seasoning of the spirit—by which he meant a certain command of im-penetrable patience.

The patience was needed for the particular feature of the ordeal that, by the time the lively season was with them again, had disengaged itself as the sharpest—the immense assump-tion of veracities and sanctities, of the general soundness of the legend with which everyone arrived. He was well pro-vided, certainly, for meeting it, and he gave all he had, yet he had sometimes the sense of a vague resentment on the part of his pilgrims at his not ladling out their fare with a bigger spoon. An irritation had begun to grumble in him during the comparatively idle months of winter when a pilgrim would turn up singly. The pious individual, entertained for the half-hour, had occasionally seemed to offer him the promise of beguilement or the semblance of a personal relation; it came back again to the few pleasant calls he had received in the course of a life almost void of social amenity. Sometimes he liked the person, the face, the speech: an educated man, a gentleman, not one of the herd; a graceful woman, vague, accidental, unconscious of him, but making him wonder, while he hovered, who she was. These chances represented for him light yearnings and faint flutters; they acted indeed, within him, in a special, an extraordinary way. He would have liked to talk with such stray companions, to talk with them *really*, to talk with them as he might have talked if he had met them where he couldn't meet them—at dinner, in the "world," on a visit at a country-house. Then he could have said—and about the shrine and the idol always—things he couldn't say now. The form in which his irritation first came to him was that of his feeling obliged to say to them—to the single visitor, even when sympathetic, quite as to the gaping group —the particular things, a dreadful dozen or so, that they expected. If he had thus arrived at characterising these things as dreadful the reason touches the very point that, for a while turning everything over, he kept dodging, not facing, trying to ignore. The point was that he was on his way to become two quite different persons, the public and the private, and yet that it would somehow have to be managed that these persons should live together. He was splitting into halves, unmistake-ably—he who, whatever else he had been, had at least always been so entire and in his way, so solid. One of the halves, or perhaps even, since the split promised to be rather unequal, one of the quarters, was the keeper, the showman, the priest of the idol; the other piece was the poor unsuccessful honest man he had always been.

There are moments when he recognised this primary character as he had never done before; when he in fact quite shook in his shoes at the idea that it perhaps had in reserve some supreme assertion of its identity. It was honest, verily, just by reason of the possibility. It was poor and unsuccessful because here it was just on the verge of quarrelling with its bread and butter. Salvation would be of course—the salvation of the showman—rigidly to *keep* it on the verge; not to let it, in other words, overpass by an inch. He might count on this, he said to himself, if there weren't any public—if there weren't thousands of people demanding of him what he was paid for. He saw the approach of the stage at which they would affect him, the thousands of people—and perhaps even more the earnest individual—as coming really to see if he were earning his wage. Wouldn't he soon begin to fancy them in league with the Body, practically deputed by it—given, no doubt, a kindled suspicion—to look in and report observations? It was the way he broke down with the lonely pilgrim that led to his first heart-searchings—broke down as to the courage required for damping an uncritical faith. What they all most wanted was to feel that everything was "just as it was"; only the shock of having to part with that vision was greater than any individual could bear unsupported. The bad moments were upstairs in the Birthroom, for here the forces pressing on the very edge assumed a dire intensity. The mere expression of eye, all-credulous, omnivorous and fairly moistening in the act, with which many persons gazed about, might eventually make it difficult for him to remain fairly civil. Often they came in pairs—sometimes one had come before—and then they explained to each other. He never in that case corrected; he listened, for the lesson of listening: after which he would remark to his wife that there was no end to what he was learning. He saw that if he should really ever break down it would be with her he would begin. He had given her hints and digs enough, but she was so inflamed with appreciation that she either didn't feel them or pretended not to understand.

This was the greater complication that, with the return of the spring and the increase of the public, her services were more required. She took the field with him, from an early hour; she was present with the party above while he kept an eye, and still more an ear, on the party below; and how could he know, he asked himself, what she might say to them and what she might suffer *Them* to say—or in other words, poor wretches, to believe while removed from his control? Some day or other, and before too long, he couldn't but think, he must have the matter out with her—the matter, namely, of the *morality* of their position. The morality of women was special—he was getting lights on that. Isabel's conception of her office was to cherish and enrich the legend. It was already, the legend, very taking, but what was she there for but to make it more so? She certainly wasn't there to chill any natural piety. If it was all in the air—all in their "eye," as the vulgar might say—that He *had* been born in the Birth-room, where was the value of the sixpences they took? where the equivalent they had engaged to supply? "Oh dear, yes— just about *here*"; and she must tap the place with her foot. "Altered? Oh dear, no—save in a few trifling particulars; you see the place—and isn't that just the charm of it?—quite as *He* saw it. Very poor and homely, no doubt; but that's just what's so wonderful." He didn't want to hear her, and yet he didn't want to give her her head; he didn't want to make difficulties or to snatch the bread from her mouth. But he must none the less give her a warning before they had gone *too* far. That was the way, one evening in June, he put it to her; the affluence, with the finest weather, having lately been of the largest, and the crowd, all day, fairly gorged with the story. "We mustn't, you know, go *too* far."

The odd thing was that she had now ceased to be even conscious of what troubled him—she was so launched in her own career. "Too far for what?"

"To save our immortal souls. We mustn't, love, tell too many lies."

She looked at him with dire reproach. "Ah now, are you going to begin again?"

"I never *have* begun; I haven't wanted to worry you. But, you know, we don't know anything about it." And then as she stared, flushing: "About His having been born up there. About anything, really. Not the least little scrap that would weigh, in any other connection, as evidence. So don't rub it in so."

"Rub it in how?"

"That He *was* born——" But at sight of her face he only sighed. "Oh dear, oh dear!"

"Don't you think," she replied cuttingly, "that He was born anywhere?"

He hesitated—it was such an edifice to shake. "Well, we don't know. There's very little *to* know. He covered His tracks as no other human being has ever done."

She was still in her public costume and had not taken off the gloves that she made a point of wearing as a part of that uniform; she remembered how the rustling housekeeper in the Border castle, on whom she had begun by modelling herself, had worn them. She seemed official and slightly distant. "To cover His tracks. He must have had to exist. Have we got to give *that* up?"

"No, I don't ask you to give it up *yet*. But there's very little to go upon."

"And is that what I'm to tell Them in return for everything?"

Gedge waited—he walked about. The place was doubly still after the bustle of the day, and the summer evening rested on it as a blessing, making it, in its small state and ancientry, mellow and sweet. It was good to be there, and it would be good to stay. At the same time there was something incalculable in the effect on one's nerves of the great gregarious density. That was an attitude that had nothing to do with degrees and shades, the attitude of wanting all or nothing. And you couldn't talk things over with it. You could only do this with friends, and then but in cases where you were sure the friends wouldn't betray you. "Couldn't you adopt," he replied at last, "a slightly more discreet method? What we can say is that things have been *said;* that's all *we* have to do with. 'And is this really'—when they jam their umbrellas into the floor—'the very *spot* where He was born?' 'So it has, from a long time back, been described as being.' Couldn't one meet Them, to be decent a little, in some such way as that?"

She looked at him very hard. "Is that the way *you* meet them?"

"No; I've kept on lying—without scruple, without shame."

"Then why do you haul me up?"

"Because it has seemed to me that we might, like true companions, work it out a little together."

This was not strong, he felt, as, pausing with his hands in his pockets, he stood before her; and he knew it as weaker still after she had looked at him a minute. "Morris Gedge, I propose to be *your* true companion, and I've come here to stay. That's all I've got to say." It was not, however, for "You had better try yourself and see," she presently added. "Give the place, give the story away, by so much as a look, and—well, I'd allow you about nine days. Then you'd see."

He feigned, to gain time, an innocence. "They'd take it so ill?" And then, as she said nothing: "They'd turn and rend me? They'd tear me to pieces?"

But she wouldn't make a joke of it. "They wouldn't *have* it, simply."

"No—they wouldn't. That's what I say. They won't."

"You had better," she went on, "begin with Grant-Jackson. But even that isn't necessary. It would get to him, it would get to the Body, like wildfire."

"I see," said poor Gedge. And indeed for the moment he did see, while his companion followed up what she believed her advantage.

"Do you consider it's *all* a fraud?"

"Well, I grant you there was somebody. But the details are naught. The links are missing. The evidence—in particular about that room upstairs, in itself our Casa Santa—is *nil*. It was so awfully long ago." Which he knew again sounded weak.

"Of course it was awfully long ago—that's just the beauty and the interest. Tell Them, *tell* Them," she continued, "that the evidence is *nil*, and I'll tell them something else." She spoke it with such meaning that his face seemed to show a question, to which she was on the spot of replying "I'll tell them that you're a——" She stopped, however, changing it. "I'll tell them exactly the opposite. And I'll find out what you say—it won't take long—to do it. If we tell different stories, *that* possibly may save us."

"I see what you mean. It would perhaps, as an oddity, have a success of curiosity. It might become a draw. Still, they but want broad masses." And he looked at her sadly. "You're no more than one of Them."

"If it's being no more than one of them to love it," she answered, "then I certainly am. And I am not ashamed of my company."

"To love *what?*" said Morris Gedge.

"To love to think He was born there."

"You think too much. It's bad for you." He turned away with his chronic moan. But it was without losing what she called after him.

"I decline to let the place down." And what was there indeed to say? They *were* there to keep it up.

V

HE kept it up through the summer, but with the queerest consciousness, at times, of the want of proportion between his secret rage and the spirit of those from whom the friction came. He said to himself—so sore as his sensibility had grown—that They were gregariously ferocious at the very time he was seeing Them as individually mild. He said to himself that They were mild only because *he* was—he flattered himself that he was divinely so, considering what he might be; and that he should, as his wife had warned him, soon enough have news of it were he to deflect by a hair's breadth from the line traced for him. *That* was the collective fatuity—that it was capable of turning, on the instant, both to a general and to a particular resentment. Since the least breath of discrimination would get him the sack without mercy, it was absurd, he reflected, to speak of his discomfort as light. He was gagged, he was goaded, as in omnivorous companies he doubtless sometimes showed by a strange silent glare. They would get him the sack for that as well, if he didn't look out; therefore wasn't it in effect ferocity when you mightn't even hold your tongue? They wouldn't let you off with silence—They insisted on your committing yourself. It was the pound of flesh —They would have it; so under his coat he bled. But a wondrous peace, by exception, dropped on him one afternoon at the end of August. The pressure had, as usual, been high, but it had diminished with the fall of day, and the place was empty before the hour for closing. Then it was that, within a few minutes of this hour, there presented themselves a pair of pilgrims to whom in the ordinary course he would have remarked that they were, to his regret, too late. He was to wonder afterwards why the course had, at sight of the visitors—a gentleman and a lady, appealing and fairly young —shown for him as other than ordinary; the consequence sprang doubtless from something rather fine and unnameable, something, for instance, in the tone of the young man, or in the light of his eye, after hearing the statement on the subject of the hour. "Yes, we know it's late; but it's just, I'm afraid, *because* of that. We've had rather a notion of escaping the crowd—as, I suppose, you mostly have one now; and it was really on the chance of finding you alone——!"

These things the young man said before being quite admitted, and they were words that any one might have spoken who had not taken the trouble to be punctual or who desired, a little ingratiatingly, to force the door. Gedge even guessed at the sense that might lurk in them, the hint of a special tip if the point were stretched. There were no tips, he had often thanked his stars, at the Birthplace; there was the charged fee and nothing more; everything else was out of order, to the relief of a palm not formed by nature for a scoop. Yet in spite of everything, in spite especially of the almost audible chink of the gentleman's sovereigns, which might in another case exactly have put him out, he presently found himself, in the Birthroom, access to which he had gracefully enough granted, almost treating the visit as personal and private. The reason— well, the reason would have been, if anywhere, in something naturally persuasive on the part of the couple, unless it had been, rather, again, in the way the young man, once he was in the place, met the caretaker's expression of face, held it a moment and seemed to wish to sound it. That they were Americans was promptly clear, and Gedge could very nearly have told what kind; he had arrived at the point of distinguishing kinds, though the difficulty might have been with him now that the case before him was rare. He saw it, in fact, suddenly, in the light of the golden midland evening, which reached them through low old windows, saw it with a rush of feeling, unexpected and smothered, that made him wish for a moment to keep it before him as a case of inordinate happiness. It made him feel old, shabby, poor, but he watched it no less intensely for its doing so. They were children of fortune, of the greatest, as it might seem to Morris Gedge, and they were of course lately married; the husband, smooth-faced and soft, but resolute and fine, several years older than the wife, and the wife vaguely, delicately, irregularly, but mercilessly pretty. Somehow, the world was theirs; they gave the person who took the sixpences at the Birthplace such a sense of the high luxury of freedom as he had never had. The thing was that the world was theirs not simply because they had money— he had seen rich people enough—but because they could in a supreme degree think and feel and say what they liked. They had a nature and a culture, a tradition, a facility of some sort— and all producing in them an effect of positive beauty—that gave a light to their liberty and an ease to their tone. These things moreover suffered nothing from the fact that they happened to be in mourning; this was probably worn for some lately-deceased opulent father, or some delicate mother who would be sure to have been a part of the source of the beauty, and it affected Gedge, in the gathered twilight and at his odd crisis, as the very uniform of their distinction.

He couldn't quite have said afterwards by what steps the point had been reached, but it had become at the end of five minutes a part of their presence in the Birthroom, a part of the young man's look, a part of the charm of the moment, and a part, above all, of a strange sense within him of "Now or never!" that Gedge had suddenly, thrillingly, let himself go. He had not been definitely conscious of drifting to it; he had been, for that, too conscious merely of thinking how different, in all their range, were such a united couple from another united couple that he knew. They were everything he and his wife were not; this was more than anything else the lesson at first of their talk. Thousands of couples of whom the same was true certainly had passed before him, but none of whom it was true with just that engaging intensity. This was *because* of their transcendent freedom; that was what, at the end of five minutes, he saw it all come back to. The husband had been there at some earlier time, and he had his impression, which he wished now to make his wife share. But he already, Gedge could see, had not concealed it from her. A pleasant irony, in fine, our friend seemed to taste in the air—he who had not yet felt free to taste his own.

"I think you weren't here four years ago"—that was what the young man had almost begun by remarking. Gedge liked his remembering it, liked his frankly speaking to him; all the more that he had given him, as it were, no opening. He had let them look about below, and then had taken them up, but without words, without the usual showman's song, of which he would have been afraid. The visitors didn't ask for it; the young man had taken the matter out of his hands by himself dropping for the benefit of the young woman a few detached remarks. What Gedge felt, oddly, was that these remarks were not inconsiderate of him; he had heard others, both of the priggish order and the crude, that might have been called so. And as the young man had not been aided to this cognition of him as new, it already began to make for them a certain common ground. The ground became immense when the visitor presently added with a smile: "There was a good lady, I recollect, who had a great deal to say."

It was the gentleman's smile that had done it; the irony *was* there. "Ah, there has been a great deal said." And Gedge's look at his interlocutor doubtless showed his sense of being sounded. It was extraordinary of course that a perfect stranger should have guessed the travail of his spirit, should have caught the gleam of his inner commentary. That probably, in spite of him, leaked out of his poor old eyes. "Much of it, in such places as this," he heard himself adding, "is of course said very irresponsibly." *Such places as this!*—he winced at the words as soon as he had uttered them.

There was no wincing, however, on the part of his pleasant
companions. "Exactly so; the whole thing becomes a sort of
stiff, smug convention, like a dressed-up sacred doll in a
Spanish church—which you're a monster if you touch."

"A monster," said Gedge, meeting his eyes.

The young man smiled, but he thought he looked at him a
little harder. "A blasphemer."

"A blasphemer."

It seemed to do his visitor good—he certainly *was* looking
at him harder. Detached as he was he was interested—he was
at least amused. "Then you don't claim, or at any rate you
don't insist   ? I mean you personally."

He had an identity for him, Gedge felt, that he couldn't
have had for a Briton, and the impulse was quick in our friend
to testify to this perception. "I don't insist to *you*."

The young man laughed. "It really—I assure you if I may
—wouldn't do any good. I'm too awfully interested."

"Do you mean," his wife lightly inquired, "in—a—pulling
it down? That is in what you've said to me."

"Has he said to you," Gedge intervened, though quaking
a little, "that he would like to pull it down?"

She met, in her free sweetness, this directness with such a
charm! "Oh, perhaps not quite the *house*——!"

"Good. You see we live on it—I mean *we* people."

The husband had laughed, but had now so completely
ceased to look about him that there seemed nothing left for
him but to talk avowedly with the caretaker. "I'm interested,"
he explained, "in what, I think, is *the* interesting thing—or at
all events the eternally tormenting one. The fact of the
abysmally little that, in proportion, we know."

"In proportion to what?" his companion asked.

"Well, to what there must have been—to what in fact
there *is*—to wonder about. That's the interest; it's immense.
He escapes us like a thief at night, carrying off—well, carrying
off everything. And people pretend to catch Him like a flown

canáry, over whom you can close your hand and put Him back. He won't *go* back; he won't *come* back. He's not"—the young man laughed—"such a fool! It makes Him the happiest of all great men."

He had begun by speaking to his wife, but had ended, with his friendly, his easy, his indescribable competence, for Gedge—poor Gedge who quite held his breath and who felt, in the most unexpected way, that he had somehow never been in such good society. The young wife, who for herself meanwhile had continued to look about, sighed out, smiled out—Gedge couldn't have told which—her little answer to these remarks. "It's rather a pity, you know, that He *isn't* here. I mean as Goethe's at Weimar. For Goethe *is* at Weimar."

"Yes, my dear; that's Goethe's bad luck. There he sticks. *This* man isn't anywhere. I defy you to catch Him."

"Why not say, beautifully," the young woman laughed, "that, like the wind, He's everywhere?"

It wasn't of course the tone of discussion, it was the tone of joking, though of better joking, Gedge seemed to feel, and more within his own appreciation, than he had ever listened to; and this was precisely why the young man could go on without the effect of irritation, answering his wife but still with eyes for their companion. "I'll be hanged if He's *here!*"

It was almost as if he were taken—that is, struck and rather held—by their companion's unruffled state, which they hadn't meant to ruffle, but which suddenly presented its interest, perhaps even projected its light. The gentleman didn't know, Gedge was afterwards to say to himself, how that hypocrite was inwardly all of a tremble, how it seemed to him that his fate was being literally pulled down on his head. He was trembling for the moment certainly too much to speak; abject he might be, but he didn't want his voice to have the absurdity of a quaver. And the young woman—charming creature!—still had another word. It was for the guardian of the spot, and she made it, in her way, delightful. They had remained in the Holy of Holies, and she had been looking for a minute, with a ruefulness just marked enough to be pretty, at the queer old floor. "Then if you say it *wasn't* in this room He was born—well, what's the use?"

"What's the use of what?" her husband asked. "The use, you mean, of our coming here? Why, the place is charming in itself. And it's also interesting," he added to Gedge, "to know how you get on."

Gedge looked at him a moment in silence, but he answered the young woman first. If poor Isabel, he was thinking, could only have been like that!—not as to youth, beauty, arrangement of hair or picturesque grace of hat—these things he didn't mind; but as to sympathy, facility, light perceptive, and yet not cheap, detachment! "I don't say it wasn't—but I don't say it *was*."

"Ah, but doesn't that," she returned, "come very much to the same thing? And don't They want also to see where He had His dinner and where He had His tea?"

"They want everything," said Morris Gedge. "They want to see where He hung up His hat and where He kept His boots and where His mother boiled her pot."

"But if you don't show them——?"

"They show *me*. It's in all their little books."

"You mean," the husband asked, "that you've only to hold your tongue?"

"I try to," said Gedge.

"Well," his visitor smiled, "I see you *can*."

Gedge hesitated. "I can't."

"Oh, well," said his friend, "what does it matter?"

"I do speak," he continued. "I can't sometimes not."

"Then how do you get on?"

Gedge looked at him more abjectly, to his own sense, than he had ever looked at anyone—even at Isabel when she frightened him. "I don't get on. I speak," he said, "since I've spoken to *you*"

"Oh, *we* shan't hurt you!" the young man reassuringly laughed.

The twilight meanwhile had sensibly thickened; the end of the visit was indicated. They turned together out of the upper room, and came down the narrow stair. The words just exchanged might have been felt as producing an awkwardness which the young woman gracefully felt the impulse to dissipate. "You must rather wonder why we've come." And it was the first note, for Gedge, of a further awkwardness—as if he had definitely heard it make the husband's hand, in a full pocket, begin to fumble.

It was even a little awkwardly that the husband still held off. "Oh, we like it as it is. There's always *something*." With which they had approached the door of egress.

"What is there, please?" asked Morris Gedge, not yet opening the door, as he would fain have kept the pair on, and conscious only for a moment after he had spoken that his question was just having, for the young man, too dreadfully wrong a sound. This personage wondered, yet feared, had evidently for some minutes been asking himself; so that, with his preoccupation, the caretaker's words had represented to him, inevitably, "What is there, please, for *me?*" Gedge already knew, with it, moreover, that he wasn't stopping him in time. He had put his question, to show he himself wasn't afraid, and he must have had in consequence, he was subsequently to reflect, a lamentable air of waiting.

The visitor's hand came out. "I hope I may take the liberty——?" What afterwards happened our friend scarcely knew, for it fell into a slight confusion, the confusion of a queer gleam of gold—a sovereign fairly thrust at him; of a quick, almost violent motion on his own part, which, to make the matter worse, might well have sent the money rolling on the floor; and then of marked blushes all round, and a sensible embarrassment; producing indeed, in turn, rather oddly, and ever so quickly, an increase of communion. It was as if the

young man had offered him money to make up to him for
having, as it were, led him on, and then, perceiving the
mistake, but liking him the better for his refusal, had wanted
to obliterate this aggravation of his original wrong. He had
done so, presently, while Gedge got the door open, by saying
the best thing he could, and by saying it frankly and gaily.
"Luckily it doesn't at all affect the *work!*"

The small town-street, quiet and empty in the summer
eventide, stretched to right and left, with a gabled and tim-
bered house or two, and fairly seemed to have cleared itself
to congruity with the historic void over which our friends,
lingering an instant to converse, looked at each other. The
young wife, rather, looked about a moment at all there wasn't
to be seen, and then, before Gedge had found a reply to her
husband's remark, uttered, evidently in the·interest of con-
ciliation, a little question of her own that she tried to make
earnest. "It's our unfortunate ignorance, you mean, that
doesn't?"

"Unfortunate or fortunate. I like it so," said the husband.
" 'The play's the thing.' Let the author alone."

Gedge, with his key on his forefinger, leaned against the
doorpost, took in the stupid little street, and was sorry to see
them go—they seemed so to abandon him. "That's just what
They won't do—not let *me* do. It's all I want—to let the
author alone. Practically"—he felt himself getting the last of
his chance—"there *is* no author; that is for us to deal with.
There are all the immortal people—*in* the work; but there's
nobody else."

"Yes," said the young man—"that's what it comes to.
There should really, to clear the matter up, be no such Person."

"As you say," Gedge returned, "it's what it comes to.
There *is* no such Person."

The evening air listened, in the warm, thick midland
stillness, while the wife's little cry rang out. "But *wasn't*
there——?"

"There was somebody," said Gedge, against the doorpost. "But They've killed Him. And, dead as He is, They keep it up, They do it over again, They kill Him every day."

He was aware of saying this so grimly—more grimly than he wished—that his companions exchanged a glance and even perhaps looked as if they felt him extravagant. That was the way, really, Isabel had warned him all the others would be looking if he should talk to Them as he talked to *her*. He liked, however, for that matter, to hear how he should sound when pronounced incapable through deterioration of the brain. "Then if there's no author, if there's nothing to be said but that there isn't anybody," the young woman smilingly asked, "why in the world should there be a house?"

"There shouldn't," said Morris Gedge.

Decidedly, yes, he affected the young man. "Oh, I don't say, mind you, that you should pull it down!"

"Then where would you *go?*" their companion sweetly inquired.

"That's what my wife asks," Gedge replied.

"Then keep it up, keep it up!" And the husband held out his hand.

"That's what my wife says," Gedge went on as he shook it.

The young woman, charming creature, emulated the other visitor; she offered their remarkable friend her handshake. "Then mind your wife."

The poor man faced her gravely. "I would if she were such a wife as you!"

VI

IT had made for him, all the same, an immense difference; it had given him an extraordinary lift, so that a certain sweet aftertaste of his freedom might, a couple of months later, have been suspected of aiding to produce for him another, and really a more considerable, adventure. It was an odd way to think of it, but he had been, to his imagination, for twenty minutes in good society—that being the term that best described for him the company of people to whom he hadn't to talk, as he further phrased it, rot. It was his title to society that he had, in his doubtless awkward way, affirmed; and the difficulty was just that, having affirmed it, he couldn't take back the affirmation. Few things had happened to him in life, that is few that were agreeable, but at least *this* had, and he wasn't so constructed that he could go on as if it hadn't. It was going on as if it had, however, that landed him, alas! in the situation unmistakeably marked by a visit from Grant-Jackson, late one afternoon toward the end of October. This had been the hour of the call of the young Americans. Every day that hour had come round something of the deep throb of it, the successful secret, woke up; but the two occasions were, of a truth, related only by being so intensely opposed. The secret had been successful in that he had said nothing of it to Isabel, who, occupied in their own quarter while the incident lasted, had neither heard the visitors arrive nor seen them depart. It was on the other hand scarcely successful in guarding itself from indirect betrayals. There were two persons in the world, at least, who felt as he did; they were persons, also, who had treated him, benignly, as feeling as *they* did, who had been ready in fact to overflow in gifts as a sign of it, and though they were now off in space they were still with him sufficiently in spirit to make him play, as it were, with the sense of their sympathy. This in turn made him, as he was perfectly aware, more than a shade or two reckless, so that, in his reaction from that gluttony of the public for false facts which had from the first tormented him, he fell into the habit of sailing, as he would have said, too near the wind, or in other words—all in presence of the people—of washing his hands of the legend. He had crossed the line—he knew it; he had struck wild—They drove him to it; he had substituted, by a succession of uncontrollable profanities, an attitude that couldn't be understood for an attitude that but too evidently *had* been.

This was of course the franker line, only he hadn't taken it, alas! for frankness—hadn't in the least, really, *taken* it, but had been simply himself caught up and disposed of by it, hurled by his fate against the bedizened walls of the temple, quite in the way of a priest possessed to excess of the god, or, more vulgarly, that of a blind bull in a china-shop—an animal to which he often compared himself. He had let himself fatally go, in fine, just for irritation, for rage, having, in his predicament, nothing at all to do with frankness—a luxury reserved for quite other situations. It had always been his sentiment that one lived to learn; he had learned something every hour of his life, though people mostly never knew what, in spite of its having generally been—hadn't it?—at somebody's expense. What he was at present continually learning was the sense of a form of words heretofore so vain—the famous "false position" that had so often helped out a phrase. One used names in that way without knowing what they were worth; then of a sudden, one fine day, their meaning was bitter in the mouth. This was a truth with the relish of which his fireside hours were occupied, and he was quite conscious that a man was exposed who looked so perpetually as if something had disagreed with him. The look to be worn at the Birthplace was properly the beatific, and when once it had fairly been missed by those who took it for granted, who, indeed, paid sixpence for it—like the table-wine in provincial France, it was *compris*—one would be sure to have news of the remark.

News accordingly was what Gedge had been expecting—and what he knew, above all, had been expected by his wife, who had a way of sitting at present as with an ear for a certain knock. She didn't watch him, didn't follow him about the house, at the public hours, to spy upon his treachery; and that could touch him even though her averted eyes went through him more than her fixed. Her mistrust was so perfectly expressed by her manner of showing she trusted that he never felt so nervous, never so tried to keep straight, as when she most let him alone. When the crowd thickened and they had of necessity to receive together he tried himself to get off by allowing her as much as possible the word. When people appealed to him he turned to her—and with more of ceremony than their relation warranted: he couldn't help *this* either, if it seemed ironic—as to the person most concerned or most competent. He flattered himself at these moments that no one would have guessed her being his wife; especially as, to do her justice, she met his manner with a wonderful grim bravado—grim, so to say, for himself, grim by its outrageous cheerfulness for the simple-minded. The lore she *did* produce for them, the associations of the sacred spot that she developed, multiplied, embroidered; the things in short she said and the stupendous way she said them! She wasn't a bit ashamed; for why need virtue be ever ashamed? It *was* virtue, for it put bread into his mouth—he meanwhile, on his side, taking it out of hers. He had seen Grant-Jackson, on the October day, in the Birthplace itself—the right setting of course for such an interview; and what occurred was that, precisely, when the scene had ended and he had come back to their own sitting-room, the question she put to him for information was: "Have you settled it that I'm to starve?"

She had for a long time said nothing to him so straight— which was but a proof of her real anxiety; the straightness of Grant-Jackson's visit, following on the very slight sinuosity of a note shortly before received from him, made tension show for what it was. By this time, really, however, his decision had been taken; the minutes elapsing between his reappearance at the domestic fireside and his having, from the other threshold, seen Grant-Jackson's broad, well-fitted back, the back of a banker and a patriot, move away, had, though few, presented themselves to him as supremely critical. They formed, as it were, the hinge of his door, that door actually ajar so as to show him a possible fate beyond it, but which, with his hand, in a spasm, thus tightening on the knob, he might either open wide or close partly and altogether. He stood, in the autumn dusk, in the little museum that constituted the vestibule of the temple, and there, as with a concentrated push at the crank of a windlass, he brought himself round. The portraits on the walls seemed vaguely to watch for it; it was in their august presence—kept dimly august, for the moment, by Grant-Jackson's impressive check of his application of a match to the vulgar gas—that the great man had uttered, as if it said all, his "You know, my dear fellow, really——!" He had managed it with the special tact of a fat man, always, when there *was* any, very fine; he had got the most out of the time, the place, the setting, all the little massed admonitions and symbols; confronted there with his victim on the spot that he took occasion to name to him afresh as, to *his* piety and patriotism, the most sacred on earth, he had given it to be understood that in the first place he was lost in amazement and that in the second he expected a single warning now to suffice. Not to insist too much moreover on the question of gratitude, he would let his remonstrance rest, if need be, solely on the question of taste. *As* a matter of taste alone——! But he was surely not to be obliged to follow that up. Poor Gedge indeed would have been sorry to oblige him, for he saw it was precisely to the atrocious taste of unthankfulness that the allusion was made. When he said he wouldn't dwell on what the fortunate occupant of the post owed him for the stout battle originally fought on his behalf, he simply meant he *would.* That was his tact—which, with everything else that had been mentioned, in the scene, to help, really had the ground to itself. The day *had* been when Gedge couldn't have thanked him enough—though he had thanked him, he considered, almost fulsomely—and nothing, nothing that he could coherently or reputably name, had happened since then. From the moment he was pulled up, in short, he had no case, and if he exhibited, instead of one, only hot tears in his eyes, the mystic gloom of the temple either prevented his friend from seeing them or rendered it possible that they stood for remorse. He had dried them, with the pads formed by the base of his bony thumbs, before he went in to Isabel. This was the more fortunate as, in spite of her inquiry, prompt and pointed, he but moved about the room looking at her hard. Then he stood before the fire a little with his hands behind him and his coat-tails divided, quite as the person in permanent possession. It was an indication his wife appeared to take in; but she put nevertheless presently another question. "You object to telling me what he said?"

"He said 'You know, my dear fellow, really——!'"

"And is that all?"

"Practically. Except that I'm a thankless beast."

"Well!" she responded, not with dissent.

"You mean that I *am?*"

"Are those the words he used?" she asked with a scruple.

Gedge continued to think. "The words he used were that I give away the Show and that, from several sources, it has come round to Them."

"As of course a baby would have known!" And then as her husband said nothing: "Were *those* the words he used?"

"Absolutely. He couldn't have used better ones."

"Did he call it," Mrs Gedge inquired, "the 'Show'?"

"Of course he did. The Biggest on Earth."

She winced, looking at him hard—she wondered, but only for a moment. "Well, it *is.*"

"Then it's something," Gedge went on, "to have given *that* away. But," he added, "I've taken it back."

"You mean you've been convinced?"

"I mean I've been scared."

"At last, at last!" she gratefully breathed.

"Oh, it was easily done. It was only two words. But here I am."

Her face was now less hard for him. "And what two words?"

" 'You know, Mr Gedge, that it simply won't do.' That was all. But it was the way such a man says them."

"I'm glad, then," Mrs Gedge frankly averred, "that he *is* such a man. How did you ever think it *could* do?"

"Well, it was my critical sense. I didn't ever know I had one—till They came and (by putting me here) waked it up in me. Then I had, somehow, don't you see? to live with it; and I seemed to feel that, somehow or other, giving it time and in the long run, it might, it *ought* to, come out on top of the heap. Now that's where, he says, it simply won't do. So I must put it—I *have* put it—at the bottom."

"A very good place, then, for a critical sense!" And Isabel, more placidly now, folded her work. "*If*, that is, you can only keep it there. If it doesn't struggle up again."

"It can't struggle." He was still before the fire, looking round at the warm, low room, peaceful in the lamplight, with the hum of the kettle for the ear, with the curtain drawn over the leaded casement, a short moreen curtain artfully chosen by Isabel for the effect of the olden time, its virtue of letting the light within show ruddy to the street. "It's dead," he went on; "I killed it just now."

He spoke, really, so that she wondered. "Just now?"

"There in the other place—I strangled it, poor thing, in the dark. If you'll go out and see, there must be blood. Which, indeed," he added, "on an altar of sacrifice, is all right. But the place is forever spattered."

"I don't want to go out and see." She rested her locked hands on the needlework folded on her knee, and he knew, with her eyes on him, that a look he had seen before was in her face. "You're off your head you know, my dear, in a way." Then, however, more cheeringly: "It's a good job it hasn't been too late."

"Too late to get it under?"

"Too late for Them to give you the second chance that I thank God you accept."

"Yes, if it *had* been——!" And he looked away as through the ruddy curtain and into the chill street. Then he faced her again. "I've scarcely got over my fright yet. I mean," he went on, "for you."

"And I mean for *you*. Suppose what you had come to announce to me now were that we had *got* the sack. How should I enjoy, do you think, seeing you turn out? Yes, out *there!*" she added as his eyes again moved from their little warm circle to the night of early winter on the other side of the pane, to the rare, quick footsteps, to the closed doors, to the curtains drawn like their own, behind which the small flat town, intrinsically dull, was sitting down to supper.

He stiffened himself as he warmed his back; he held up his head, shaking himself a little as if to shake the stoop out of his shoulders, but he had to allow she was right. "What would have become of us?"

"What indeed? We should have begged our bread—or I should be taking in washing."

He was silent a little. "I'm too old. I should have begun sooner."

"Oh, God forbid!" she cried.

"The pinch," he pursued, "is that I can do nothing else."

"Nothing whatever!" she agreed with elation.

"Whereas here—if I cultivate it—I perhaps *can* still lie. But I must cultivate it."

"Oh, you old dear!" And she got up to kiss him.

"I'll do my best," he said.

VII

"Do you remember us?" the gentleman asked and smiled—with the lady beside him smiling too; speaking so much less as an earnest pilgrim or as a tiresome tourist than as an old acquaintance. It was history repeating itself as Gedge had somehow never expected, with almost everything the same except that the evening was now a mild April-end, except that the visitors had put off mourning and showed all their bravery—besides showing, as he doubtless did himself, though so differently, for a little older; except, above all, that —oh, seeing them again suddenly affected him as not a bit the thing he would have thought it. "We're in England again, and we were near; I've a brother at Oxford with whom we've been spending a day, and we thought we'd come over." So the young man pleasantly said while our friend took in the queer fact that he must himself seem to them rather coldly to gape. They had come in the same way, at the quiet close; another August had passed, and this was the second spring; the Birthplace, given the hour, was about to suspend operations till the morrow; the last lingerer had gone, and the fancy of the visitors was, once more, for a look round by themselves. This represented surely no greater presumption than the terms on which they had last parted with him seemed to warrant; so that if he did inconsequently stare it was just in fact because he was so supremely far from having forgotten them. But the sight of the pair luckily had a double effect, and the first precipitated the second—the second being really his sudden vision that everything perhaps depended for him on his recognising no complication. He must go straight on, since it was what had for more than a year now so handsomely answered; he must brazen it out consistently, since that only was what his dignity was at last reduced to. He mustn't be afraid in one way any more than he had been in another; besides which it came over him with a force that made him flush that their visit, in its essence, must have been for himself. It was good society again, and *they* were the same. It wasn't for him therefore to behave as if he couldn't meet them.

These deep vibrations, on Gedge's part, were as quick as they were deep; they came in fact all at once, so that his response, his declaration that it was all right—"Oh, *rather;* the hour doesn't matter for *you!*"—had hung fire but an instant; and when they were within and the door closed behind them, within the twilight of the temple, where, as before, the votive offerings glimmered on the walls, he drew the long breath of one who might, by a self-betrayal, have done something too dreadful. For what had brought them back was not, indubitably, the sentiment of the shrine itself—since he knew their sentiment; but their intelligent interest in the queer case of the priest. Their call was the tribute of curiosity, of sympathy, of a compassion really, as such things went, exquisite—a tribute *to* that queerness which entitled them to the frankest welcome. They had wanted, for the generous wonder of it, to see how he was getting on, how such a man in such a place *could;* and they had doubtless more than half expected to see the door opened by somebody who had succeeded him. Well, somebody *had*—only with a strange equivocation; as they would have, poor things, to make out for themselves, an embarrassment as to which he pitied them. Nothing could have been more odd, but verily it was this troubled vision of their possible bewilderment, and this compunctious view of such a return for their amenity, that practically determined for him his tone. The lapse of the months had but made their name familiar to him; they had on the other occasion inscribed it, among the thousand names, in the current public register, and he had since then, for reasons

of his own, reasons of feeling, again and again turned back
to it. It was nothing in itself; it told him nothing—"Mr and
Mrs B. D. Hayes, New York"—one of those American
labels that were just like every other American label and that
were, precisely, the most remarkable thing about people
reduced to achieving an identity in such other ways. They
could be Mr and Mrs B. D. Hayes and yet they could be, with
all presumptions missing—well, what these callers were. It
had quickly enough indeed cleared the situation a little further
that his friends had absolutely, the other time, as it came back
to him, warned him of his original danger, their anxiety about
which had been the last note sounded between them. What
he was afraid of, with this reminiscence, was that, finding him
still safe, they would, the next thing, definitely congratulate
him and perhaps even, no less candidly, ask him how he had
managed. It was with the sense of nipping some such inquiry
in the bud that, losing no time and holding himself with a
firm grip, he began, on the spot, downstairs, to make plain
to them how he had managed. He averted the question in short
by the assurance of his answer. "Yes, yes, I'm still here; I
suppose it *is* in a manner to one's profit that one does, such
as it is, one's best." He did his best on the present occasion,
did it with the gravest face he had ever worn and a soft
serenity that was like a large damp sponge passed over their
previous meeting—over everything in it, that is, but the fact
of its pleasantness.

"We stand here, you see, in the old living-room, happily
still to be reconstructed in the mind's eye, in spite of the
havoc of time, which we have fortunately, of late years, been
able to arrest. It was of course rude and humble, but it must
have been snug and quaint, and we have at least the pleasure
of knowing that the tradition in respect to the features that
do remain is delightfully uninterrupted. Across that threshold
He habitually passed; through those low windows, in childhood, He peered out into the world that He was to make so

much happier by the gift to it of His genius; over the boards
of this floor—that is over *some* of them, for we mustn't be
carried away!—his little feet often pattered; and the beams
of this ceiling (we must really in some places take care of *our*
heads!) he endeavoured, in boyish strife, to jump up and
touch. It's not often that in the early home of genius and
renown the whole tenor of existence is laid so bare, not often
that we are able to retrace, from point to point and from step
to step, its connection with objects, with influences—to build
it round again with the little solid facts out of which it sprang.
This, therefore, I need scarcely remind you, is what makes the
small space between these walls so modest to measurement,
so insignificant of aspect—unique on all the earth. *There is
nothing like it,*" Morris Gedge went on, insisting as solemnly
and softly, for his bewildered hearers, as over a pulpit-edge;
"there is nothing at all like it anywhere in the world. There is
nothing, only reflect, for the combination of greatness, and,
as we venture to say, of intimacy. You may find elsewhere
perhaps absolutely fewer changes, but where shall you find a
presence equally diffused, uncontested and undisturbed? Where
in particular shall you find, on the part of the abiding spirit,
an equally towering eminence? You may find elsewhere eminence of a considerable order, but where shall you find *with*
it, don't you see, changes, after all, so few, and the contemporary element caught so, as it were, in the very fact?"
His visitors, at first confounded, but gradually spellbound,
were still gaping with the universal gape—wondering, he
judged, into what strange pleasantry he had been suddenly
moved to break out, and yet beginning to see in him an intention beyond a joke, so that they started, at this point, almost
jumped, when, by as rapid a transition, he made, toward the
old fireplace, a dash that seemed to illustrate, precisely, the act
of eager catching. "It is in this old chimney corner, the quaint
inglenook of our ancestors—just there in the far angle, where
His little stool was placed, and where, I dare say, if we could

look close enough, we should find the hearthstone scraped with His little feet—that we see the inconceivable child gazing into the blaze of the old oaken logs and making out there pictures and stories, see Him conning, with curly bent head, His well-worn hornbook, or poring over some scrap of an ancient ballad, some page of some such rudely bound volume of chronicles as lay, we may be sure, in His father's window-seat."

It was, he even himself felt at this moment, wonderfully done; no auditors, for all his thousands, had ever yet so inspired him. The odd, slightly alarmed shyness in the two faces, as if in a drawing-room, in their "good society," exactly, some act incongruous, something grazing the indecent, had abruptly been perpetrated, the painful reality of which faltered before coming home—the visible effect on his friends, in fine, wound him up as to the sense that *they* were worth the trick. It came of itself now—he had got it so by heart; but perhaps really it had never come so well, with the staleness so disguised, the interest so renewed and the clerical unction, demanded by the priestly character, so successfully distilled. Mr Hayes of New York had more than once looked at his wife, and Mrs Hayes of New York had more than once looked at her husband—only, up to now, with a stolen glance, with eyes it had not been easy to detach from the remarkable countenance by the aid of which their entertainer held them. At present, however, after an exchange less furtive, they ventured on a sign that they had not been appealed to in vain. "Charming, charming, Mr Gedge!" Mr Hayes broke out; "we feel that we've caught you in the mood."

His wife hastened to assent—it eased the tension. "It *would* be quite the way; except," she smiled, "that you'd be too dangerous. You've really a genius!"

Gedge looked at her hard, but yielding no inch, even though she touched him there at a point of consciousness that quivered. This was the prodigy for him, and had been, the

year through—that he did it all, he found, easily, did it better
than he had done anything else in his life; with so high and
broad an effect, in truth, an inspiration so rich and free, that
his poor wife now, literally, had been moved more than once
to fresh fear. She had had her bad moments, he knew, after
taking the measure of his new direction—moments of re-
adjusted suspicion in which she wondered if he had not
simply embraced another, a different perversity. There would
be more than one fashion of giving away the show, and
wasn't *this* perhaps a question of giving it away by excess?
He could dish them by too much romance as well as by too
little; she had not hitherto fairly apprehended that there
might *be* too much. It was a way like another, at any rate, of
reducing the place to the absurd; which reduction, if he didn't
look out, would reduce *them* again to the prospect of the
streets, and this time surely without an appeal. It all depended,
indeed—he knew she knew that—on how much Grant-
Jackson and the others, how much the Body, in a word,
would take. He knew she knew what he himself held it would
take—that he considered no limit could be drawn to the
quantity. They simply wanted it piled up, and so did everybody else; wherefore, if no one reported him, as before, why
were They to be uneasy? It was in consequence of idiots
brought to reason that he had been dealt with before; but as
there was now no form of idiocy that he didn't systematically
flatter, goading it on really to its *own* private doom, who was
ever to pull the string of the guillotine? The axe was in the
air—yes; but in a world gorged to satiety there were no
revolutions. And it had been vain for Isabel to ask if the other
thunder-growl also hadn't come out of the blue. There was
actually proof positive that the winds were now at rest. How
could they be more so?—he appealed to the receipts. These
were golden days—the show had never so flourished. So he
had argued, so he was arguing still—and, it had to be owned,
with every appearance in his favour. Yet if he inwardly

winced at the tribute to his plausibility rendered by his flushed friends, this was because he felt in it the real ground of his optimism. The charming woman before him acknowledged his "genius" as he himself had had to do. He had been surprised at his facility until he had grown used to it. Whether or no he had, as a fresh menace to his future, found a new perversity, he had found a vocation much older, evidently, than he had at first been prepared to recognise. He had done himself injustice. He liked to be brave because it came so easy; he could measure it off by the yard. It was in the Birthroom, above all, that he continued to do this, having ushered up his companions without, as he was still more elated to feel, the turn of a hair. She might take it as she liked, but he had had the lucidity—all, that is, for his own safety—to meet without the grace of an answer the homage of her beautiful smile. She took it apparently, and her husband took it, but as a part of his odd humour, and they followed him aloft with faces now a little more responsive to the manner in which, on *that* spot, he would naturally come out. He came out, according to the word of his assured private receipt, "strong." He missed a little, in truth, the usual round-eyed question from them—the inveterate artless cue with which, from moment to moment, clustered troops had, for a year, obliged him. Mr and Mrs Hayes were from New York, but it was a little like singing, as he had heard one of his Americans once say about something, to a Boston audience. He did none the less what he could, and it was ever his practice to stop still at a certain spot in the room and, after having secured attention by look and gesture, suddenly shoot off: "Here!"

They always understood, the good people—he could fairly love them now for it; they always said, breathlessly and unanimously, "There?" and stared down at the designated point quite as if some trace of the grand event were still to be made out. This movement produced, he again looked round. "Consider it well: *the* spot of earth——!" "Oh, but

it isn't *earth!*" the boldest spirit—there was always a boldest
—would generally pipe out. Then the guardian of the Birthplace would be truly superior—as if the unfortunate had
figured the Immortal coming up, like a potato, through the
soil. "I'm not suggesting that He was born on the bare
ground. He was born *here!*"—with an uncompromising dig
of his heel. "There ought to be a brass, with an inscription,
let in." "Into the floor?"—it always came. "Birth and burial:
seedtime, summer, autumn!"—that always, with its special,
right cadence, thanks to his unfailing spring, came too. "Why
not as well as into the pavement of the church?—you've
seen our grand old church?" The former of which questions
nobody ever answered—abounding, on the other hand, to
make up, in relation to the latter. Mr and Mrs Hayes even
were at first left dumb by it—not indeed, to do them justice,
having uttered the word that produced it. They had uttered
no word while he kept the game up, and (though that made
it a little more difficult) he could yet stand triumphant before
them after he had finished with his flourish. Then it was only
that Mr Hayes of New York broke silence.

"Well, if we wanted to see, I think I may say we're quite
satisfied. As my wife says, it *would* seem to be your line." He
spoke now, visibly, with more ease, as if a light had come:
though he made no joke of it, for a reason that presently appeared. They were coming down the little stair, and it was on
the descent that his companion added her word.

"Do you know what we half *did* think——?" And then to
her husband: "Is it dreadful to tell him?" They were in the
room below, and the young woman, also relieved, expressed
the feeling with gaiety. She smiled, as before, at Morris Gedge,
treating him as a person with whom relations were possible,
yet remaining just uncertain enough to invoke Mr Hayes's
opinion. "We *have* awfully wanted—from what we had
heard." But she met her husband's graver face; he was not
quite out of the wood. At this she was slightly flurried—but

she cut it short. "You must know—don't you?—that, with the crowds who listen to you, we'd have heard."

He looked from one to the other, and once more again, with force, something came over him. They had kept him in mind, they were neither ashamed nor afraid to show it, and it was positively an interest, on the part of this charming creature and this keen, cautious gentleman, an interest resisting oblivion and surviving separation, that had governed their return. Their other visit had been the brightest thing that had ever happened to him, but this was the gravest; so that at the end of a minute something broke in him and his mask, of itself, fell off. He chucked, as he would have said, consistency; which, in its extinction, left the tears in his eyes. His smile was therefore queer. "Heard how I'm going it?"

The young man, though still looking at him hard, felt sure, with this, of his own ground. "Of course, you're tremendously talked about. You've gone round the world."

"You've heard of me in America?"

"Why, almost of nothing else!"

"That was what made us feel——!" Mrs Hayes contributed.

"That you must see for yourselves?" Again he compared, poor Gedge, their faces. "Do you mean I excite—a—scandal?"

"Dear no! Admiration. You renew so," the young man observed, "the interest."

"Ah, there it is!" said Gedge with eyes of adventure that seemed to rest beyond the Atlantic.

"They listen, month after month, when they're out here, as you must have seen; and they go home and talk. But they sing your praise."

Our friend could scarce take it in. "Over *there?*"

"Over there. I think you must be even in the papers."

"Without abuse?"

"Oh, we don't abuse everyone."

Mrs Hayes, in her beauty, it was clear, stretched the point. "They rave about you."

"Then they *don't* know?"

"Nobody knows," the young man declared; "it wasn't anyone's knowledge, at any rate, that made us uneasy."

"It was your own? I mean your own sense?"

"Well, call it that. We remembered, and we wondered what had happened. So," Mr Hayes now frankly laughed, "we came to see."

Gedge stared through his film of tears. "Came from America to see *me?*"

"Oh, a part of the way. But we wouldn't, in England, not have seen you."

"And now we *have!*" the young woman soothingly added.

Gedge still could only gape at the candour of the tribute. But he tried to meet them—it was what was least poor for him—in their own key. "Well, how do you like it?"

Mrs Hayes, he thought—if their answer were important—laughed a little nervously. "Oh, you see."

Once more he looked from one to the other. "It's too beastly easy, you know."

Her husband raised his eyebrows. "You conceal your art. The emotion—yes; that must be easy; the general tone must flow. But about your facts—you've so many: how do you get *them* through?"

Gedge wondered. "You think I get too many——?"

At this they were amused together. "That's just what we came to see!"

"Well, you know, I've felt my way; I've gone step by step; you wouldn't believe how I've tried it on. *This*—where you see me—is where I've come out." After which, as they said nothing: "You hadn't thought I *could* come out?"

Again they just waited, but the husband spoke: "Are you so awfully sure you *are* out?"

Gedge drew himself up in the manner of his moments of

emotion, almost conscious even that, with his sloping shoulders, his long lean neck and his nose so prominent in proportion to other matters, he looked the more like a giraffe. It was now at last that he really caught on. "I *may* be in danger again—and the danger is what has moved you? Oh!" the poor man fairly moaned. His appreciation of it quite weakened him, yet he pulled himself together. "You've your view of my danger?"

It was wondrous how, with that note definitely sounded, the air was cleared. Lucid Mr Hayes, at the end of a minute, had put the thing in a nutshell. "I don't know what you'll think of us—for being so beastly curious."

"I think," poor Gedge grimaced, "you're only too beastly kind."

"It's all your own fault," his friend returned, "for presenting us (who are not idiots, say) with so striking a picture of a crisis. At our other visit, you remember," he smiled, "you created an anxiety for the opposite reason. Therefore if *this* should again be a crisis for you, you'd really give us the case with an ideal completeness."

"You make me wish," said Morris Gedge, "that it might be one."

"Well, don't try—for our amusement—to bring one on. I don't see, you know, how you can have much margin. Take care—take care."

Gedge took it pensively in. "Yes, that was what you said a year ago. You did me the honour to be uneasy as my wife was."

Which determined on the young woman's part an immediate question. "May I ask, then, if Mrs Gedge is now at rest?"

"No; since you do ask. *She* fears, at least, that I go too far; *she* doesn't believe in my margin. You see, we *had* our scare after your visit. They came down."

His friends were all interest. "Ah! They came down?"

"Heavy. They brought *me* down. That's *why*——"

"Why you are down?" Mrs Hayes sweetly demanded.

"Ah, but my dear man," her husband interposed, "you're not down; you're *up!* You're only up a different tree, but you're up at the tip-top."

"You mean I take it too high?"

"That's exactly the question," the young man answered; "and the possibility, as matching your first danger, is just what we felt we couldn't, if you didn't mind, miss the measure of."

Gedge looked at him. "I feel that I know what you at bottom *hoped.*"

"We at bottom 'hope,' surely, that you're all right."

"In spite of the fool it makes of everyone?"

Mr Hayes of New York smiled. "Say *because* of that. We only ask to believe that everyone *is* a fool!"

"Only you haven't been, without reassurance, able to imagine fools of the size that my case demands?" And Gedge had a pause, while, as if on the chance of some proof, his companion waited. "Well, I won't pretend to you that your anxiety hasn't made me, doesn't threaten to make me, a bit nervous; though I don't quite understand it if, as you say, people but rave about me."

"Oh, *that* report was from the other side; people in our country so very easily rave. You've seen small children laugh to shrieks when tickled in a new place. So there are amiable millions with us who are but small children. They perpetually present new places for the tickler. What we've seen in further lights," Mr Hayes good-humouredly pursued, "is your people *here*—the Committee, the Board, or whatever the powers to whom you're responsible."

"Call them my friend Grant-Jackson then—my original backer, though I admit, for that reason, perhaps my most formidable critic. It's with him, practically, I deal; or rather it's by him I'm dealt with—*was* dealt with before. I stand or fall by him. But he has given me my head."

"Mayn't he then want you," Mrs Hayes inquired," just to show as flagrantly running away."

"Of course—I see what you mean. I'm riding, blindly, for a fall, and They're watching (to be tender of me!) for the smash that may come of itself. It's Machiavellic—but everything's possible. And what did you just now mean," Gedge asked—"especially if you've only heard of my prosperity— by your 'further lights'?"

His friends for an instant looked embarrassed, but Mr Hayes came to the point. "We've heard of your prosperity, but we've also, remember, within a few minutes, heard *you*."

"I was determined you *should*," said Gedge. "I'm good then—but I overdo?" His strained grin was still sceptical.

Thus challenged, at any rate, his visitor pronounced. "Well, if you don't; if at the end of six months more it's clear that you haven't overdone; then, *then*——"

"Then what?"

"Then it's great."

"But it *is* great—greater than anything of the sort ever was. I overdo, thank goodness, yes; or I would if it were a thing you *could*."

"Oh, well, if there's *proof* that you can't——!" With which, and an expressive gesture, Mr Hayes threw up his fears.

His wife, however, for a moment, seemed unable to let them go. "Don't They want then *any* truth?—none even for the mere look of it?"

"The look of it," said Morris Gedge, "is what I give!"

It made them, the others, exchange a look of their own. Then she smiled. "Oh, well, if they think so——!"

"You at least don't? You're like my wife—which indeed, I remember," Gedge added, "is a similarity I expressed a year ago the wish for! At any rate I frighten *her*."

The young husband, with an "Ah, wives are terrible!" smoothed it over, and their visit would have failed of further excuse had not, at this instant, a movement at the other end of the room suddenly engaged them. The evening had so nearly closed in, though Gedge, in the course of their talk, had lighted the lamp nearest them, that they had not distinguished, in connection with the opening of the door of communication to the warden's lodge, the appearance of another person, an eager woman, who, in her impatience, had barely paused before advancing. Mrs Gedge—her identity took but a few seconds to become vivid—was upon them, and she had not been too late for Mr Hayes's last remark. Gedge saw at once that she had come with news; no need even, for that certitude, of her quick retort to the words in the air—"You may say as well, sir, that they're often, poor wives, terrified!" She knew nothing of the friends whom, at so unnatural an hour, he was showing about; but there was no livelier sign for him that this didn't matter than the possibility with which she intensely charged her "Grant-Jackson, to see you at once!" —letting it, so to speak, fly in his face.

"He has been with you?"

"Only a minute—he's there. But it's you he wants to see."

He looked at the others. "And what does he want, dear?"

"God knows! There it is. It's his horrid hour—it *was* that other time."

She had nervously turned to the others, overflowing to them, in her dismay, for all their strangeness—quite, as he said to himself, like a woman of the people. She was the bare-headed goodwife talking in the street about the row in the house, and it was in this character that he instantly introduced her: "My dear doubting wife, who will do her best to entertain you while I wait upon our friend." And he explained to her as he could his now protesting companions—"Mr and Mrs Hayes of New York, who have been here before." He knew, without knowing why, that her announcement chilled him; he failed at least to see why it should chill him so much. His good friends had themselves been visibly affected by it, and heaven knew that the depths of brooding fancy in him were easily stirred by contact. If they had wanted a crisis they accordingly had found one, albeit they had already asked leave to retire before it. This he wouldn't have. "Ah no, you must really see!"

"But we shan't be able to bear it, you know," said the young woman, "if it *is* to turn you out."

Her crudity attested her sincerity, and it was the latter, doubtless, that instantly held Mrs Gedge. "It *is* to turn us out."

"Has he told you that, madam?" Mr Hayes inquired of her—it being wondrous how the breath of doom had drawn them together.

"No, not told me; but there's something in him there—I mean in his awful manner—that matches too well with other things. We've seen," said the poor pale lady, "other things enough."

The young woman almost clutched her. "Is his manner very awful?"

"It's simply the manner," Gedge interposed, "of a very great man."

"Well, very great men," said his wife, "are very awful things."

"It's exactly," he laughed, "what we're finding out! But I mustn't keep him waiting. Our friends here," he went on, "are directly interested. You mustn't, mind you, let them go until we know."

Mr Hayes, however, held him; he found himself stayed. "We're so directly interested that I want you to understand this. If anything happens——"

"Yes?" said Gedge, all gentle as he faltered.

"Well, *we* must set you up."

Mrs Hayes quickly abounded. "Oh, *do* come to us!"

Again he could but look at them. They were really wonderful folk. And but Mr and Mrs Hayes! It affected even Isabel, through her alarm; though the balm, in a manner, seemed to foretell the wound. He had reached the threshold of his own quarters; he stood there as at the door of the chamber of judgment. But he laughed; at least he could be gallant in going up for sentence. "Very good then—I'll come to you!"

This was very well, but it didn't prevent his heart, a minute later, at the end of the passage, from thumping with beats he could count. He had paused again before going in; on the other side of this second door his poor future was to be let loose at him. It was broken, at best, and spiritless, but wasn't Grant-Jackson there, like a beast-tamer in a cage, all tights and spangles and circus attitudes, to give it a cut with the smart official whip and make it spring at him? It was during this moment that he fully measured the effect for his nerves of the impression made on his so oddly earnest friends—whose earnestness he in fact, in the spasm of this last effort, came within an ace of resenting. They had upset him by contact; he was afraid, literally, of meeting his doom on his knees; it wouldn't have taken much more, he absolutely felt, to make him approach with his forehead in the dust the great man whose wrath was to be averted. Mr and Mrs Hayes of New York had brought tears to his eyes; but was it to be reserved for Grant-Jackson to make him cry like a baby? He wished, yes, while he palpitated, that Mr and Mrs Hayes of New York hadn't had such an eccentricity of interest, for it seemed somehow to come from *them* that he was going so fast to pieces. Before he turned the knob of the door, however, he had another queer instant; making out that it had been, strictly, his case that was interesting, his funny power, however accidental, to show as in a picture the attitude of others—not his poor, dingy personality. It was this latter quantity, none the less, that was marching to execution. It is to our friend's credit that he *believed*, as he prepared to turn the knob, that he was going to be hanged; and it is certainly not less to his credit that his wife, on the chance, had his supreme thought. Here it was that—possibly with his last articulate breath—he thanked his stars, such as they were, for Mr and Mrs Hayes of New York. At least they would take care of her.

They were doing that certainly with some success when, ten minutes later, he returned to them. She sat between them in the beautified Birthplace, and he couldn't have been sure afterwards that each wasn't holding her hand. The three together, at any rate, had the effect of recalling to him—it was too whimsical—some picture, a sentimental print, seen and admired in his youth, a "Waiting for the Verdict," a "Counting the Hours," or something of that sort; humble respectability in suspense about humble innocence. He didn't know how he himself looked, and he didn't care; the great thing was that he wasn't crying—though he might have been; the glitter in his eyes was assuredly dry, though that there *was* a glitter, or something slightly to bewilder, the faces of the others, as they rose to meet him, sufficiently proved. His wife's eyes pierced his own, but it was Mrs Hayes of New York who spoke. "*Was* it then for that——?"

He only looked at them at first—he felt he might now enjoy it. "Yes, it was for 'that.' I mean it was about the way I've been going on. He came to speak of it."

"And he's gone?" Mr Hayes permitted himself to inquire.

"He's gone."

"It's over?" Isabel hoarsely asked.

"It's over."

"Then we go?"

This it was that he enjoyed. "No, my dear; we stay."

There was fairly a triple gasp; relief took time to operate. "Then why did he come?"

"In the fulness of his kind heart and of *Their* discussed and decreed satisfaction. To express Their sense——!"

Mr Hayes broke into a laugh, but his wife wanted to know. "Of the grand work you're doing?"

"Of the way I polish it off. They're most handsome about it. The receipts, it appears, speak——"

He was nursing his effect; Isabel intently watched him, and the others hung on his lips. "Yes, speak——?"

"Well, volumes. They tell the truth."

At this Mr Hayes laughed again. "Oh, *they* at least do?"

Near him thus, once more, Gedge knew their intelligence as one—which was so good a consciousness to get back that his tension now relaxed as by the snap of a spring and he felt his old face at ease. "So you can't say," he continued, "that we don't want it."

"I bow to it," the young man smiled. "It's what I said then. It's *great*."

"It's great," said Morris Gedge. "It couldn't be greater."

His wife still watched him; her irony hung behind. "Then we're just as we were?"

"No, not as we were."

She jumped at it. "Better?"

"Better. They give us a rise."

"Of income?"

"Of our sweet little stipend—by a vote of the Committee. That's what, as Chairman, he came to announce."

The very echoes of the Birthplace were themselves, for the instant, hushed; the warden's three companions showed, in the conscious air, a struggle for their own breath. But Isabel, with almost a shriek, was the first to recover hers. "They double us?"

"Well—call it that. 'In recognition.' There you are." Isabel uttered another sound—but this time inarticulate; partly because Mrs Hayes of New York had already jumped at her to kiss her. Mr Hayes meanwhile, as with too much to say, but put out his hand, which our friend took in silence. So Gedge had the last word. "And there *you* are!"

A NOTE ON THE TEXT

In preparing these tales for publication, the editor had to choose between James's original magazine texts, those published in book form soon afterwards and those revised and rewritten for the New York Edition. The obvious choice, it seemed to him, was the original book fo m of the story where there was one. In that form it had the benefit of revision from magazine to volume; and in that form it was best known to James's generation. It seemed to the editor that in a chronological edition of James's shorter fictions, the New York Edition texts had no relevance. They belong exclusively to the edition for which they were designed; particularly since the revisions were often made several decades after the original publication.

The original magazine publications of the tales in this volume were as follows:

"The Great Good Place," *Scribner's Magazine*, January 1900.

"Maud-Evelyn," *Atlantic Monthly*, April 1900.

"Miss Gunton of Poughkeepsie," *Cornhill Magazine*, May 1900, and *Truth* (New York), May–June 1900.

"The Special Type," *Collier's Weekly*, 16 June 1900.

"The Tone of Time," *Scribner's Magazine*, November 1900.

"Broken Wings," *Century Magazine*, December 1900.

"The Two Faces," *Harper's Bazar*, 15 December 1900 (entitled "The Faces").

"Mrs Medwin," *Punch*, 28 August–18 September 1901.

"The Beldonald Holbein," *Harper's New Monthly Magazine*, October 1901.

"The Story in It," *Anglo-American Magazine*, January 1902.

"Flickerbridge," *Scribner's Magazine*, February 1902.

No magazine publication of "The Tree of Knowledge," "The Abasement of the Northmores" and "The Third Person" has been recorded before their appearance in *The Soft Side* (London, 1900), where "The Great Good Place," "Maud-Evelyn" and "Miss Gunton of Poughkeepsie" also made their first book appearance. "The Beast in the Jungle" and "The Birthplace" first appeared, without prior magazine publication, in *The Better Sort* (London, 1903), where the remaining tales in this volume were also reprinted for the first time. The text of these first book publications has been used here.

For the complete bibliography of the tales the reader is referred to *A Bibliography of the Writings of Henry James* by Leon Edel and Dan H. Laurence (second edition, revised, London, 1961) in the Soho Bibliographies published by Rupert Hart-Davis.